A former au pair, bookseller, marketing manager and seafront trader, **Jessica Gilmore** now works for an environmental charity in York, England. Married with one daughter, one fluffy dog and two dog-loathing cats, she spends her time avoiding housework and can usually be found with her nose in a book. Jessica writes emotional romance with a hint of humour, a splash of sunshine and a great deal of delicious food—and equally delicious heroes!

**Rebecca Winters** lives in Salt Lake City, Utah. With canyons and high alpine meadows full of wildflowers, she never runs out of places to explore. They, plus her favourite vacation spots in Europe, often end up as backgrounds for her romance novels—because writing is her passion, along with her family and her church. Rebecca loves to hear from readers. If you wish to email her, please visit her website at rebeccawinters.net.

# INDONESIAN DATE WITH THE SINGLE DAD

## JESSICA GILMORE

# RECLAIMING THE PRINCE'S HEART

## REBECCA WINTERS

**MILLS & BOON**

First Published in Great Britain 2021
by Mills & Boon, an imprint of HarperCollins*Publishers* Ltd,
1 London Bridge Street, London, SE1 9GF

www.harpercollins.co.uk

HarperCollins*Publishers*
1st Floor, Watermarque Building,
Ringsend Road, Dublin 4, Ireland

Indonesian Date with the Single Dad © 2021 Harlequin Books S.A.

Special thanks and acknowledgement are given to Jessica Gilmore
for her contribution to the Billion-Dollar Matches miniseries.

Reclaiming the Prince's Heart © 2021 Rebecca Winters

ISBN: 978-0-263-29992-2

09/21

MIX
Paper from
responsible sources
FSC® C007454

# INDONESIAN DATE WITH THE SINGLE DAD

JESSICA GILMORE

**MILLS & BOON**

For Gracie and Amy.

Thank you for our virtual weekly lunch date.

It's been vitamin D for the soul. xxx

# CHAPTER ONE

It HAD BEEN a long day, but Luke Taylor sprinted up the steps to his sister's front door, skidding to a halt as Ella opened the door, one warning finger on her lips.

'She's asleep,' she half whispered.

Luke swallowed back his disappointment. It *was* late—too late to be collecting his daughter on a school night. 'Thanks for picking her up from school,' he said instead. 'I had to finish this contract tonight and when Hannah phoned in sick—'

'I love having Isla,' his sister interrupted. 'I was glad of the opportunity to play hooky and have some girl time. Honestly, Luke, I know I say this every time but she's such a sweetheart. A real credit to you.' She held the door open and Luke walked into the hallway, bracing himself as his sister's large black Labrador, Barnacle, hurled himself enthusiastically at him. 'Down, Barnacle! Leave poor Luke alone. Do you want anything? A beer, some dinner?'

'I'm good, thanks. I ate at the office. I better just get Isla home.' Luke continued down the hallway, expertly dodging the usual jumble of trainers and discarded bags, footballs and surfboards. His three nephews aged between eight and twelve were, according to their long-suffering mother, the messiest boys in Sydney. But, messy or not, Isla adored her cousins and their comfortable suburban home. His sister's house was, he thought, not for the first time, a marked contrast to the gleaming penthouse he and Isla shared, with its views of Sydney Harbour. Although their apartment undoubtedly had the wow factor, his sister's home always felt welcoming. 'Where is she?'

'In the den. I would have put her to bed when the boys went but she said she wanted to wait up for you. She was so sleepy I knew she'd fall asleep if I tucked her in on the couch, so I let her stay down here. I hope that's okay.'

'Of course, thank you.' Luke headed into the large family room to find the lights dimmed and the six-year-old who ruled his heart and his life fast asleep on the sofa covered with a blanket. Her favourite toy cat was clasped in her arms, her red hair, her one legacy from her mother, spilling onto the cushion. Luke paused to look at her, his chest constricting with the old familiar damped-down anger and pain. How could Alyssa want nothing to do with their daughter? How could she have just walked away? He inhaled long and deep, concentrating on letting the anger drain away, turning the emotion into focus and purpose, the way he had learned many years before.

'See, fast asleep,' Ella said. 'I have her bag right here. She's done her homework and there's a letter about a school trip.'

'Thanks.' Luke turned to take the bag and as he did so he caught a glimpse of the TV screen, frozen on the image of a young girl's face in close-up, tears filling luminous hazel eyes. Recognition tugged at him. 'What was she watching?'

Ella smiled. '*Matchmaking Mischief*—it's an old Madison Morgan film. You know the one; Madison plays twins who try and set their dad up with their teacher?'

'Never heard of it. Not that I ever watched any Madison Morgan films willingly; she wasn't really my style. Whatever happened to her anyway?'

'No idea. She just disappeared, didn't she?'

Luke looked from the heartfelt expression on screen to his sleeping daughter. 'I hope that film hasn't given Isla any ideas. Her teacher is nice enough but she terrifies me. I would feel like I always had to sit up straight and ask for permission before I spoke if Isla set us up.' He grinned at his sister but she didn't smile back.

'Luke,' she said, and his heart sank at her all too familiar tone. The *Let's have a serious talk* tone. And there was only one subject which made his sister get this serious with him: his bachelor status.

'Not now, Ella.'

But she clearly wasn't to be deterred. 'Then when? You haven't dated in six years, Luke. I know several women who would be perfect for you. Just let me make some introductions. A party, or dinner…'

It was an old, old conversation. 'Like an episode of *The Bachelor*? I'm a single dad, Ella, I'm not much of a prize.'

'You're my handsome and—much as it pains me to admit it—successful, rich younger brother who is a wonderful father. You are prime real estate in the dating world, believe me.'

'I can't date. It's not fair on Isla. She can't have women waltzing in and out of her life. Not after Alyssa...' He stopped and compressed his lips. 'Look, I know you mean well, but when I meet someone—when *we* meet someone—it has to be someone who knows that Isla and I are a two-for-one deal. Someone who wants to be a mother, who will put Isla first. I can't let Isla get attached and it not work out. And I don't do casual dating. You know that.'

After all, the last time he'd entered into a casual relationship, he'd been surprised nine months later with a baby. A baby whose mother had deposited the little girl with him and walked away, never to return.

'But how will you find this perfect woman if you don't date?' Ella demanded and Luke shrugged.

'I don't know. But I'm in no hurry, Ella. I have Isla, Mum and Dad, you, Ned and the boys. That's a family, that's enough for me.'

'And we all adore you both. But Luke, is it enough for Isla?'

'Of course. She knows she's loved and that she's safe. That's all that matters.' He pushed back the doubt. They were fine just as they were; introducing another person into their lives could go so drastically wrong and Isla had lost enough already. What did it matter if he got a little lonely in the evenings when she was asleep? There was always work.

Somehow Luke managed to carry Isla to the car without waking her and she didn't stir until he pulled into their underground car park. She insisted on walking to the lift which took them up to the corner penthouse he'd occupied since he won his first Grand Slam title. He kept meaning to move to something more child-friendly, but the apartment was close to his office which meant no commute—and that meant more time for Isla.

'Did you have a good time with Aunty Ella, honey?' he asked as his daughter leaned against him, her thumb in her mouth.

She nodded. 'I played catch with Barnacle. I wish *we* had a dog.' This was a familiar refrain and he didn't respond. She nestled in closer. 'And while the boys were at karate we watched a really good film. The little girls knew their daddy was sad because he didn't have a wife so they found him one. You don't have a wife, Daddy; are you sad?'

Luke inwardly cursed his sister's taste in films. 'Not when I have you.'

'If you had a wife then we could have a house like Aunty Ella's and a dog like Barnacle.'

'We have a nice place of our own. And the beach house for weekends.'

Isla considered this. 'But Aunty Ella lives in her house all the time. I like the garden. Dogs need a garden.' She yawned and he scooped her up, her head heavy on his shoulder as she succumbed once more to sleep.

The lift opened straight into the foyer and Luke

hung Isla's bag on the peg by the call button, slipping her shoes off and dropping them onto the rack below before carrying his daughter through the reception room. It hadn't changed much from when he'd bought the apartment, designed to be a formal showpiece with its floor-to-ceiling windows leading onto the wrap-around terrace and spectacular views of the iconic Sydney skyline. The room beyond had the same views but a very different feel—this was their family room, cosy and relaxed with squashy sofas and colourful rugs, Isla's doll's house in the corner and bookshelves filled with picture books, crayons and boxes of toys.

A second hallway led from it to the bedrooms and he carried her into her pretty ocean-themed room, carefully laying her in her bed, thankful his sister had changed Isla into pyjamas and, knowing Ella, taken care of tooth-brushing and face-washing. He stopped for a moment, watching the small girl sleep and mentally going over the evening chores: empty her bag and make sure it was packed for tomorrow, retrieve her worn clothes and put them in the laundry and lay out her uniform for the next day. He had this; they were fine, just the two of them. Although he usually also had Hannah to help take care of Isla and his housekeeper did the laundry.

He took a cautious step back and Isla stirred, her eyes fluttering open. 'Go back to sleep, honey,' he said quietly and she smiled, the gap in her teeth reminding him how quickly she was growing.

'I think we should find you a wife like the girls in the film, Daddy. Find you a wife and then I can have a mummy.' Her eyes closed again and then she was fast asleep. Luke waited a long, cautious moment then tiptoed out.

*I can have a mummy.* Where had *that* come from? She didn't mean it, he told himself. Really, she wanted a dog and thought the two came together as the people she knew who had dogs mostly lived in nuclear families. It was just a phase; look at last month—they'd watched a film about a boy who befriended a dolphin and she'd asked for a pet dolphin for days afterwards. Next week it would be something else.

But, try as Luke might, he couldn't dismiss her sleepy words as he mechanically sorted out her bag for the next day before opening a cold beer and heading out to the terrace, staring out at the city lights reflecting on the water.

There were people—his mother—who thought the penthouse terrace unsafe for a child, although the thick glass barrier was unclimbable and Isla knew not to go outside without him, but as Luke sank onto a chair and took a sip of the cold light beer his conscience stirred, Isla's comments about a garden repeating in his head. He hadn't planned to raise a child here; he'd been in his twenties and a carefree bachelor when he'd bought it. Then, when Alyssa had literally handed him a baby and walked away, he'd been too shell-shocked to do much more than take fatherhood day by day. Not that it had been hard—one look into Isla's blue eyes and he'd fallen harder than he'd ever thought possible. And somehow they'd made it work; her school was close by and they had the beach house up the coast for weekends. She was healthy and happy; that was all that mattered.

Sure, she asked about Alyssa sometimes, about why her mummy never visited or sent her presents. But she'd never actually said she wanted a mother before.

This was ridiculous; he was going round in so many circles he was making himself dizzy. Pulling out his phone, Luke tried to concentrate on his emails but for once his mind couldn't focus and he switched to browsing, checking out some of his competitors and looking at the tennis scores from the day before; just because he no longer competed didn't mean he wasn't still fascinated by the game. As he skimmed the headlines, his conversation with his sister came back to him and idly he searched for Madison Morgan, adding after a moment, *Where is she now?*

Slowly the small screen filled with links, including a picture of a slim woman, dark hair pulled back from her high cheek-boned face, her hazel eyes keen and intelligent. The accompanying caption read:

There's nothing mischievous about Madison's Matchmaking!

Curious, Luke clicked through.

Most child actors remain in the only profession they know but Madison Morgan, one of Hollywood's most bankable stars in the nineties and early noughties, took a different path, inspired by one of her most loved movies—*Matchmaking Mischief.*

Madison, who studied business at Yale, now runs an extremely upmarket dating agency, which is rumoured to have some of the world's most eligible singles on its list, including some of her film star friends, tech tycoons and even royalty. But, unless you have a cool one hundred thousand to spare, don't think you'll be able to sign up for a date with your favourite heart-throb.

Her prices are high and her list is exclusive. But I hear her happy-ever-after rate makes her worth every penny...

A dating agency? That was unexpected. Luke quickly copied the link and sent it to his sister. Less than five seconds later his phone pinged.

OMG! You should totally sign up.

??????

I'm serious! You can afford it. You could marry a princess!

Oh, well, in that case...

Really?

No.

Luke! Seriously. Look, it says you can pick a VIP option where you spend a week away with your handpicked match to see if you're compatible. How romantic!

Not if you can't stand the sight of the person you're matched with.

When did you last have a proper holiday? Luke? All I'm saying is you should consider it. Don't ignore me!

Luke grinned as he sent a series of kisses to his sister and put his phone down. A dating agency? Things weren't that desperate, were they? He took a long sip of his beer, his smile fading as he considered the brief exchange.

Maybe Ella had a point, not that he would ever admit it to her. How was he ever going to meet anyone if he didn't try? The truth was his personal life was something Luke spent a lot of time deliberately not thinking about. The first two years of Isla's existence he'd been far too knackered to even consider romance, and then, as it became increasingly clear that Alyssa had no intention of ever being involved with their daughter, Luke had purposefully put away his own needs and wants to provide the stability that Isla needed. On some level he'd kind of hoped he might just click with someone one day and bypass the dating part, heading straight into happy families. But how often did that happen in the real world? Maybe he *did* need a helping hand after all. A professional helping hand.

Looking around furtively, as if his sister might somehow be spying on him, Luke clicked on the link that took him to Madison Morgan's M dating agency. The website was surprisingly tasteful, with none of the pink and hearts Luke had been dreading—friendly but businesslike with a feeling of discretion and exclusivity. One page was dedicated to mostly anonymised case studies of successful relationships and marriages set up by the former child star and Luke couldn't help but notice the statistics—M claimed an eighty per cent success rate in finding its clients long-term relationships, over half of those with their very first match. Maybe that click and move on Luke hoped for wasn't so unrealistic after all. His finger hovered over the application form. What did he have to lose? He didn't have to go ahead. But maybe a discreet enquiry wouldn't hurt. For Isla's sake.

Madison smiled at her image in the video on her laptop screen, quickly checking for lipstick on her teeth or a hair out of place. She, of all people, knew the importance of image, and if she was going to persuade someone that she was worth both one hundred thousand pounds and their romantic hopes then she needed to look professional and extremely competent.

She straightened her cream silk blouse and as she did so a message flashed up, informing her that Luke Taylor was in the online waiting room. Exactly on time. Impressive. She pulled the printout of the extensive questionnaire he'd filled out when he'd applied to join M.

*Age: Thirty-six*
*Home: Sydney*
*Family: One daughter aged six*
*Looking for: Marriage and commitment*

*Requirements: A woman willing and wanting to
be a mother*

*Interesting...*

She clicked on the message and her screen filled
with a familiar head and shoulders. Luke Taylor might
be nearly two decades older than the talented tennis
tearaway who had enthralled crowds and horrified um-
pires but his tousled blond hair still fell unrepentantly
over his forehead and he had the same surfer-style good
looks that had seen his photo pinned onto thousands
of teenagers' walls.

'Luke Taylor. It's a pleasure to meet you. I saw you
play once,' she added almost involuntarily as her heart-
beat began to speed up. What was wrong with her?
She'd interviewed princes and rock stars without as
much as a quiver of nerves—or desire—but with one
glance her own crush on the Aussie Terror, as he'd been
known, resurfaced with a resounding crash.

'Thank you for meeting with me. I hope I won,' he
added with the same half shy, half knowing sideways
smile that had captured so many hearts. Her own sped
up even more.

'You did; it was your first quarter finals at Wimbledon.'

'Lost the semis though.' His smile turned rueful. At
eighteen Luke had crashed out of the semi-finals of the
venerable tournament with a display of temper that had
made headlines all over the world and nearly seen him
banned from the sport. He'd walked away from tennis for two long years, only to resurface a little older,

clearly a lot wiser and channelling all that passion and fire into his game, only to semi retire again nine years later with a recurring injury.

Not that Madison knew his tennis career off by heart or anything. 'Do you still play?'

'When I can. I coach a little too, although I mostly take a more hands-off approach nowadays.'

Madison checked her notes; she always did her own research on prospective clients. 'The Luke Taylor Foundation? Providing sporting opportunities for inner city kids?'

'That's right. I set it up when I was still on the tour.'

'And you fund it from your company, LTF?'

'Luke Taylor Fitness, yes. Not that original, I know.' He grinned again as he sat back, completely at ease.

'You're talking to someone who called her agency M,' Madison pointed out and felt a flash of pride as he laughed. 'So, thank you for filling out the questionnaire so comprehensively. It gives me a good starting point when I assess possible matches, but at M I also like to meet each of my clients personally. Compatibility isn't just shared interests or goals or an algorithm. Sometimes real, lasting attraction can spark between people who on paper would never match. And that's what sets M apart. Not just the clientele but my ability to see beyond what you *think* you want to what you really need.'

Luke raised an eyebrow. 'Forgive me for being sceptical, but how can a few questions and a couple of video chats make you certain you know what—who—we will fall in love with?'

'I'm not infallible, but my success rate speaks for itself. I grew up surrounded by adults and I learned very quickly to see that what people left *unsaid* was as important as what they said, to read body language and to see how people interact. I use that knowledge in my work. So, tell me, Mr Taylor...'

He held up a hand. 'Luke, please.'

'Luke.' She relished the feeling of his name on her tongue. 'What's important to you?'

'My daughter, Isla,' he said promptly.

'And her mother isn't around?'

His mouth set in firm, uncompromising lines. 'No. Entirely her choice. And that's why I am only interested in women who love children, who are ready and willing to be part of a family and who will understand that Isla will always come first. My family and life are in Sydney, so she would need to be willing to live here.'

Madison held up the printout of his application. 'I have all that here, Luke. Don't worry, I won't match you with anyone who doesn't fit that criteria. However, when something as important as location is non-negotiable, it can take a while to find a suitable match, so you may need to be patient. Tell me about your favourite places.'

His forehead creased. 'My favourite places?'

'Where you feel at home. Don't think, just tell me as many as you can think of.'

'Erm. My beach house, sitting looking out at the ocean with Isla. A tennis court with the sun beating down, feeling the racquet connect on the perfect sweet spot. On a surfboard, hearing the rush of the wave. My sister's garden, helping her husband man the barbecue while the kids play. Late at night, tucking Isla in and hearing her breathe.' He stopped suddenly. 'Crikey. I don't know where that all came from.'

'You did perfectly,' Madison reassured him, moving onto the next question, doing her best to hide her reaction at the image of a close-knit family his answers had conjured up and that old traitorous yearning for people of her own that stole through her defences.

The interview continued for nearly an hour, Luke relaxing into it, open and honest and unexpectedly funny. Madison couldn't remember when she'd last laughed so much or felt so at ease and noticed the time with a pang of regret.

'If you decide to go ahead then the cost is one hundred thousand pounds,' she said as she began to wrap things up. 'This is to ensure that the exclusivity I promise clients is maintained and to weed out any time-wasters. I keep a fee of just under a third and the rest is donated anonymously to a charity of the client's choice. You also, of course, pay for your dates. I can organise those for you, though many clients do prefer me to book at least the first date for them. I see you have indicated that you are interested in the week away package?'

'It seems an efficient option,' Luke said.

'Oh, it is,' Madison agreed. 'It's perfect for those who are really serious about fast tracking a relationship. A week away, just the two of you, somewhere impossibly romantic. No interruptions, no worries, a chance to really discover whether you are compatible.

It's very popular, especially amongst those who, like you, live very busy lives.'

'Great.' Luke paused then said quickly, as if nervous to hear the answer, 'Do you think you have someone suitable? Someone perfect for Isla and me?'

Interesting that he put his daughter first. That same old painful jolt hit her chest as Madison fought to remain composed. 'I'm sure we have. Just leave it to me.'

She did her best for all of her clients; her reputation and professionalism demanded it. But as she said goodbye and ended the call Madison vowed she would go all-out for Luke Taylor. Only the perfect match would do.

# CHAPTER TWO

MADISON RUBBED HER eyes as she checked all the details for Luke Taylor's week away for the last time. The yacht was ready and waiting, the crew briefed, the itinerary perfect for the couple's adrenaline-fuelled personalities, combining activity with plenty of opportunities to get to know each other.

She'd promised herself only the best for Luke and she was confident that she'd delivered—a week cruising around the gorgeous Indonesian coastline, visiting some of the thousands of small, nature-rich islands, with kayaking, snorkelling and diving high on the agenda. More importantly, after a lot of work, she'd found the perfect match for him. At least, she hoped she had.

Although many of her clients said they wanted children, not all of them wanted to be stepparents, and Luke's insistence on staying in Sydney had shrunk the potential match pool even more. But a couple of months ago Madison had accepted an application from an Italian Olympic skier and heiress who, now she had retired, was looking to settle down. Active, bubbly and easy-going, she was flexible on location and adored children. Madison hadn't got the sixth sense about the match she sometimes got, but the signs were promising and she'd made the call.

There was every chance they would work out. Maybe then she would be able to fall asleep and not spend half the night dreaming about blue eyes and a sideways smile! She reached forward to switch off her screen when her personal phone rang. She glanced at the screen and saw Jen, her assistant's name, flash up.

'What are you doing calling me when you're on holiday?' Madison scolded as she answered. Her employee worked almost as hard as Madison herself and she deserved the two-week break in Tuscany she was currently supposed to be indulging in.

'It's Isabella. Isabella Fontini.'

'Isabella? She's currently on her way to Singapore.' Madison stilled, her stomach dipping in alarm at the panic in Jen's voice. 'In less than twenty-four hours she'll be getting on a yacht and falling in love.'

'She's pre-empted you.'

'She's *what*?'

'Isabella is currently on a boat in Sardinia with a Russian hockey player. I've just seen the front page of a gossip magazine and checked. They look besotted. I don't think she'll be looking for romance with anyone else any time soon.'

'Dammit.' Madison thought furiously. The hefty payment she asked for was supposed to guard against this kind of eventuality, but for some of her clients one hundred thousand pounds was a mere trifle. 'What am

I going to say to Luke Taylor?' She'd spoken to him several times since the first video call and he had rapidly become one of her favourite clients, not just because of that old teenage crush, but thanks to his sense of humour and easy-to-chat-to personality. It wasn't often Madison clicked easily with someone on a personal level—a childhood spent mostly alone had seen to that—and she looked forward to their interactions more than she liked to admit. But not this time.

'Shall I come back?' Jen asked.

'No. Absolutely not. Stay there and relax; that's an order. I'll just have to reschedule his date. There are other matches. I just hope he doesn't think we're unprofessional, cancelling so late. Luckily our insurance should cover the cruise; he'll need a full refund of course. Thanks, Jen. Now go and have an amazing holiday and let me do the worrying.'

'Will do,' Jen said. 'And one day you'll have to let me return the favour.'

'One day,' Madison agreed and heard Jen laugh. She'd been trying to get Madison to take a proper holiday for years, without success. Madison didn't want to relax, didn't need time away. Her business was everything—and without it, what did she have? She'd worked every day since she was a baby; the sector might have changed but working was still all she knew, all she was.

Hanging up, Madison took a deep breath, steadying her nerves before swapping to her second phone where all of her clients' details were stored under fake names—she'd been the target of tabloid journalists several times already, desperate to get a look at her client list—and scrolled quickly to Luke, pressing the call symbol before she could chicken out. But instead of a ringtone it went straight to voicemail.

Hold on… With clumsy fingers Madison pulled up the schedule. Of course, Luke was already en route to Singapore, where the cruise would depart from. He was planning a day of business and meetings in the city before starting his holiday.

Madison sat back. She could email him, but this kind of news really needed the personal touch. She could wait to call him in a few hours' time, but he'd have just spent several hours flying and would no doubt be angry about the wasted trip. She drummed her fingers on her desk and thought furiously. She prided herself on her attention to detail, her customer service, so wouldn't it be better if she told him in person? She quickly pulled up some flight details. There was a flight leaving in three hours with a seat still available in First Class. She could meet Luke on the yacht, explain in person and suggest he took the vacation on them as recompense.

Yes. That made perfect sense.

Madison refused to allow herself to think about her impulsive decision as she asked a clearly startled Lea, her PA, to book the flight and a hotel, before heading upstairs to the maisonette she occupied on the top two floors of the Hampstead terrace which served as both her home and office. She packed an overnight bag quickly, throwing in underwear, a couple of dresses, a wrap and her sunglasses, suppressing the doubts circling through her mind: flying thirteen hours to deliver a message was just good customer service; it had nothing to do with wanting to meet Luke Taylor in person. *That* would be unprofessional and Madison was always, always professional.

When Madison alighted at Singapore Airport, she felt strangely refreshed. She usually found it hard to sleep, her mind always whirling, and it didn't help that her clients were based all over the world; she never knew when an email would require an urgent answer or she might need to debrief an anxious client after a date. But, in the time-pressured rush to pack and jump into the taxi Lea had ordered, her bag containing her laptop and work phone had been left behind and so, for once, Madison had allowed herself to relax and enjoy the lie-flat bed with its comfortable mattress and cool bed linen, drifting off into the blissful deep sleep that so often eluded her.

She usually found airports frustrating, with far too much waiting around, yet not only was the processing handled quickly and seamlessly but also the architecture was so unique Madison was almost sorry when she made her way out of the arrival terminal to meet the car she had booked back in London. Replying to the driver's friendly welcome, she sank into its cushioned, air conditioned interior, pulling out her personal phone which, thankfully, had been in her handbag along with her passport and credit cards. Switching it back on, noting the low battery as she did so, it sprang into action, lighting up with notifications, including several messages from Jen, escalating in exclamation marks and emojis as they went.

You are going to Singapore? In person? Isn't it about ten different time zones and several oceans away???

He'll understand. These things happen!!

Unless you just want an excuse to go and see him...

Madison slipped her phone back into her bag—resolving to log into her work emails when she reached the hotel and had a chance to charge her phone—half amused and half embarrassed by Jen's gentle teasing. Sure, she might have admitted some details to Jen about her youthful crush on Luke Taylor, and she might have talked just a little bit about how much she admired the way his daughter evidently came first in his life and how driven he was to find a mother for her, but it didn't mean she was more invested in this one client than any other. It might seem a little impetuous to jump on a plane and travel thousands of miles just to tell him that his date wasn't coming, but that was the kind of detail people expected from M. The kind of service she prided herself on. She looked out of the window, scowling at her reflection, almost instantly losing her defensiveness as she took in the view.

Madison had never been to Singapore before, and for a moment she forgot why she was there as she was driven through the busy streets, tall futuristic buildings rising on every side of her. She'd heard enough about the famous city to recognise the botanical gardens when her driver pointed them out to her and decided to return to the fabled markets, where some of the best seafood in the world could be found, later that day. According to the schedule Lea had sent through, her flight back wasn't for two days and she had reserved Madison a room at the famous Raffles hotel. In fact, this impulsive trip might work out for the best—she could check in with her clients who lived in this part of the world and as she had successfully set up a couple of matches in the city this might be an opportunity to catch up with them and see how they were getting on.

But first she had to fulfil the duty that had brought her here. Checking her watch, Madison realised that the yacht was scheduled to depart within the half hour. She had cut the meeting very fine indeed. She just hoped that Luke wouldn't be too disappointed. She would reimburse him for his flights of course, offer a hefty discount on his fee. And if he decided against continuing with the cruise then she could even offer to take him out to dinner tonight. Strictly business, of course. It might make matching him with the perfect woman easier if she spent some time one-on-one with him...

The car slowed as they entered a marina, the ocean spread out before her, filled with boats of all sizes. The driver pulled to a stop near the curving harbour edge and Madison stepped out, adjusting her sunglasses against the piercingly bright sun and intensely blue sea. The brightness took her back to her childhood and rare days out in Malibu when she hadn't been working. How she'd envied the other children with their freedom to surf and play and be free as she'd tried to blend in despite being accompanied by her minder, the press never more than a few steps away.

Madison pushed the memory away, focusing fiercely on the here and now, walking along the marina wall peering at the extravagant boats, each one more luxurious than the rest until she saw *Siren's Call* emblazoned on the side of a particularly gorgeous yacht. Stopping, she took in the boat with a wistfulness she couldn't quite suppress. She'd spent her childhood in lavish suites and private jets, and now she met her clients in mansions and on private islands, but it was all for work, never for play and certainly not for romance. For one bitter moment she felt an almost overwhelming envy of people who allowed themselves the time to enjoy a week on a vessel such as this—people who felt they were *worth* a week's leisure on a vessel such as this. People who had the confidence and belief that they deserved love and were willing to look for it, to make themselves vulnerable.

But being vulnerable came with a price. She'd paid it once, never again. Much better, much safer to be self-contained, to maintain a shield around her feelings, her heart, her hope and live through others. She was safe, emotionally and materially; that was all that mattered. It had taken her a long time to get here, and so preserving that safety had to be her priority. Next time she might not survive.

There could be no next time. She'd made sure of that.

Adjusting her sunglasses again, Madison shifted her

overnight bag and took in a deep steadying breath. She might not be an actress any more, but she knew exactly how to act a part and right now her role demanded she be empathic, sympathetic and reassuringly business-like. Persona in place, she marched towards the gang-plank where a smartly dressed young crewmember waited at the bottom. Madison stopped and smiled. 'Hello, I am Madison Morgan. Is Mr Taylor aboard?'

'Mr Taylor? Yes, he arrived a few minutes ago. Come, let me show you.' The young man saluted smartly and gestured for Madison to precede him onto the deck. She climbed aboard and looked around her assessingly. Everything was just as it had been on the website: gleaming wood, chrome and white. Stairs led up to the middle deck where she could see chairs placed around a tablecloth-covered table, champagne chill-ing in a bucket, two glasses frosted and waiting. She frowned. What a shame it was all going to go to waste.

'Mr Taylor is this way,' the young man said and he ushered Madison up the stairs where, on the other side of the boat, she saw an instantly recognisable figure leaning over the railings, his posture stiff and wary. Sympathy rushed through her. Of course, this must be very strange for him, away from his family and his daughter and about to spend a week with a complete stranger. Maybe he'd even be secretly relieved it would be cancelled.

Madison's heels echoed on the wooden deck and Luke turned as she neared, a welcoming smile pre-pared, only for it to waver and disappear in some confusion as she removed her sunglasses and recognition lit up his blue eyes.

'Mr Taylor.' She held out her hand. 'Madison Morgan—we've spoken several times.'

'Yes, of course.' He took her hand and a tingle shot up her arm at his firm, cool touch. 'It's very kind of you to come and see us off; I wasn't expecting such personal service. M clearly takes its business seriously.' Luke moved over to the table and picked up the bottle of champagne. 'Let me pour you a glass,' he said. 'I'm sure my mystery date won't mind.'

'No, thank you.' Although Madison couldn't help thinking champagne might make the awkward next part of her conversation easier.

'Is this part of the service? An in-person introduction to help break the ice and make sure neither of us is planning to bolt?' His brows drew together. 'I thought I'd read the briefing notes clearly, but I don't recall this part.'

'Mr Taylor…'

'I thought we'd moved past the *Call-me-Luke* phase,' he said with the same devastating smile she remembered from the video chat. 'Mr Taylor makes me think I'm talking to my daughter's headteacher and I never leave her office without feeling I have just been very thoroughly told off.'

'Luke. I'm afraid there's been a slight hiccup.'

His eyebrows shot up and the confusion in his expression faded into a humorous glint. 'Hiccup?'

'Hiccup,' she confirmed, wishing desperately she could think of a new word. 'Luke, I matched you with a very promising candidate.' Madison was aware that she was sounding pompous and the humorous expression in Luke's eyes deepened as she spoke. 'Sporty, high-achieving, loves children and willing to relocate for the right man. I can assure you I was very thorough. But unfortunately this week was scheduled too late.'

'Too late?'

'She entered into a new relationship just last week, which means she won't be coming. By the time I found out, you were on your way here so I really felt I had to tell you in person. It was the least I could do. I just want to assure you that this is a highly unusual occurrence; our success rate attests to that.'

'I've been stood up?' Was that a hint of relief she saw in his eyes?

'I wouldn't put it quite that way, but your date won't be coming.'

'In my book that counts as stood up all right. In that case I could definitely do with a glass of this extremely serious-looking champagne. Please don't turn me down when I offer you a glass this time; I don't think my ego will take two rejections in a row.'

Madison opened her mouth with every intention of a polite refusal, but she closed it again. She had no idea what time it was, if it was too early or too late or just about right, but accepting was clearly the politic thing to do. 'Thank you. That would be lovely,' she said as he expertly released the cork and poured the chilled amber liquid into the two waiting glasses. 'We should make a toast, to a promise that I will do better next time.'

She took the proffered glass and sipped and Luke copied her, his intent gaze fastened on hers. 'Next time?'

'I do hope you give M a second chance. You must admit that, apart from the tiny detail of a missing date, this is all pretty spectacular.' Madison took another sip and as she moved to put her glass down staggered slightly, righting herself hurriedly, cheeks heating at her clumsiness. She really should have eaten something before having champagne. In fact, the world felt awfully bumpy. The boat lurched again and she put out a hand to steady herself, then looked around with dawning horror.

Where were the buildings, the dock? *Where was Singapore?* 'Hang on a second,' she said. 'We seem to be at sea!'

Luke watched in some amusement as Madison looked around her wildly. 'Oh, no,' she said, clapping one perfectly manicured hand over her mouth. 'The crew had instructions to cast off as soon as you were both aboard. They must have thought that I was Isabella. How didn't we hear or notice?' She stopped and bit her lip. 'What a mess.'

Pulling out one of the heavy wooden chairs, Luke gestured to Madison to take a seat and she sank into it with a grateful smile as he took the opposite one and sat back. 'It's hardly a disaster though, is it? We'll just tell them to turn around, explain there's been a mistake.' He held up the champagne. 'In the meantime we might as well enjoy this while our unexpected mini cruise continues.'

But Madison didn't relax, her back ramrod-straight and her knuckles white as she gripped the table. 'It's not quite that simple.'

'Oh?' Luke refilled the already empty glasses as he waited for her to explain.

'You see, the itinerary is set from my office and so the only changes that can be made have to be authorised by us.'

Luke couldn't see the problem 'That's easy enough; you're right here.'

'But *they* don't know that,' Madison said. 'They only take instructions from the London telephone number or M's email address. Of course, email!' She pulled her phone out of her bag, only for her triumphant expression to fall. 'Damn, how is it out of battery? My charger must be in here somewhere.' She started to root in her bag, pulling out a charger, her face falling as she looked at it. 'No, that's the wrong one. Don't say I didn't bring it. Unless it's in the bag with my laptop and other phone? Oh, no, I couldn't have mixed them up, could I?'

Luke ignored her clearly rhetorical question as he tried to make sense of Madison's words. 'Let me get this straight,' he said slowly. 'Once I was on this boat, the only person who could cut the week short or alter our direction in any way was you?' He remembered reading something about no changes to the set itinerary without authorisation from the London office, but he hadn't taken in exactly what that meant.

Madison nodded, dropping the bag to the deck in defeat. 'It's to stop any mishaps happening.'

Luke raised an eyebrow. 'Mishaps? Like setting sail with the wrong person aboard?' He tried for humour but the words sliced out like his once lethal backhand, as he realised how little control the current situation gave him.

Madison winced. 'This is unprecedented, I promise you. These dates are very carefully arranged in every single way, from itinerary to location to staff. Everyone on this boat has medical training, for instance, and some of the deckhands are also security trained. That way, if anything goes wrong they are able to step in straight away. Of course, I filter out anyone problematic long before we get to this stage but so many of my clients are used to bodyguards it's a reassurance.' She stopped and took a deep breath.

*If anything goes wrong?* Luke replayed the words, taking in a deep breath as the old, familiar heat began to rise, Madison's words a sharp reminder that he was Isla's only family and yet here he was, putting himself in the hands of a crew who answered to someone else. What was he doing drinking champagne on a boat several hours away from his daughter?

'Why can't I simply request the boat turns around?' He knew his tone was curt, authoritative as Madison looked at him with mingled apology and surprise, but for once he could feel his iron-clad control slipping. 'What if Isla falls ill? What if she's hurt and I can't get back to her?'

He stood up and strode over to the railing in agitation, needing to keep moving. 'I would never have left her if I hadn't thought that my family could contact me at any time.'

'Luke, don't worry.' Madison jumped up, joining him to lay a reassuring hand on his arm. 'The emergency details I sent you to give to your family includes a line straight through to the captain. If anything happens, they will be able to get straight in touch, I promise.'

'I still don't understand why any changes have to come from your office.' Relief that his family could contact him at any time replaced the quickly fading anger as he turned to face Madison.

'To ensure our couples give each other a real chance and don't turn tail and run after the first conversation,' she replied, leaning on the rail beside him, her hands clasped in front of her. 'Sometimes it takes a while for compatibility to show itself. That's what this week's about, giving people that space, and that's why there's no easy get-out clause just because you get off on the wrong foot or get cold feet. But it doesn't mean you're trapped here. The crew know to call us with any issues and we will sort everything—flights home if that's what's needed, alternative venue, anything.'

'So we just have to ask the captain to call the office and we're rescued?' Why hadn't she said so in the first instance?

'Yes.' Her cheeks reddened. 'Only I'm here and Jen, my assistant, is on holiday for another couple of days. Lea, my PA, will be back in the office on Monday but she isn't contactable twenty-four-seven like I am. So we're stuck for the next forty-eight hours.' She looked over at him hopefully. 'Unless you have a charger I can use?'

'Sorry, different make.' Now he'd been reassured Luke couldn't help seeing the humour of the situation and found himself grinning at Madison's distraught expression. 'So we're prisoners? You're basically some kind of pirate queen but in kidnapping me you have also managed to kidnap yourself.' He shook his head. 'I've got to admit, this date is turning out to be a lot more entertaining than I expected.'

'Technically,' she pointed out, 'this isn't a date.'

Luke had grown up on a tennis court, where instinct was everything. He had to know his shots, understand his game and his opponent's play but in the end he had to trust his intuition—overthinking was the surest way to defeat. He'd used that same instinct and intuition to guide him when injury derailed his career and he'd turned his passion for health and fitness into first a small business, then an app and then a global brand. When asked the secret to his success he'd replied *gut*. Gut and grit and channelling his famous temper rather than letting it rule him. It was as simple as that.

Even six years ago, when Alyssa thrust a tiny baby into his arms and walked away, never to return, Luke had managed to control his anger at Alyssa's heartlessness, taking all that negative emotion and using it as fuel as he threw himself into the exhausting, exhilarating business of raising his daughter the best way he could—trusting his heart to guide him. Up until now his instinct had served him well, as long as he listened to it and controlled it; his teenage experiences had demonstrated what happened when he allowed his temper free rein. He didn't ever want to be that person again, to set that kind of example for Isla.

Luke had signed up to M and agreed to his sister's insistence that the week away was his best bet because objectively he knew it made sense, but the decision had gone against all of his carefully honed instincts. Maybe it was the loss of control, being matched by a stranger to a stranger, his destiny in someone else's hands. The only part that had felt right were his communications with Madison, when he'd found himself opening up in ways he hadn't known possible, discussing his hopes, his dreams, his fears.

And now here she was, stuck on a boat with him, and every fibre in his body was telling him not to waste the opportunity.

Luke leaned forward. 'Well, now. You promised me a week away with my ideal companion and here we are. I'd call that a date. Wouldn't you?'

# CHAPTER THREE

MADISON STARED. HAD Luke just said what she thought he had? *Ideal companion? Date?* Not entirely unwelcome warmth flooded her body at the thought.

'But I'm not, we're not, I didn't…' She stopped, stung by the laughter in his blue, blue eyes. 'Of course. You're teasing me.' She didn't know whether she should be more annoyed or relieved. Of course he wasn't serious. Why would he be? Madison had seen enough captioned photos of herself to know that she was considered beautiful, but she had never been a woman that anybody really, truly wanted. She had learned that the hard way. She certainly wasn't anyone's ideal match.

Luke sauntered back to his chair and she couldn't help noticing the strength in his hand as he picked up his wineglass, his fingers circling it as he looked thoughtfully at her. 'Joking? I suppose I am. But at the same time here we are. The way I see it, we have two choices. Either we go and chat up the capable crew you've organised, let them know what has happened and hope they believe us, turn around, moor back up, go home and pretend this never happened. Or we stay put for forty-eight hours and then ask them to contact your PA, and until then we do our best to enjoy the unusual situation we've been put into. After all, you came all this way, you might as well enjoy yourself while you're here.'

Madison looked out at the blue sea tipped by white spray as the boat cut swiftly through it. Clearly the sensible thing—the *only* thing—to do was agree to Luke's first suggestion, ask to see the captain and explain the situation calmly and clearly.

But Luke had also suggested that they see the next forty-eight hours out. Enjoy themselves. It was such a foreign concept, for enjoyment to mean leisure time, self-indulgence, rather than the simple satisfaction of a job well done, but Madison couldn't deny that she was uncharacteristically tempted. She could tell herself that it was because she owed Luke part of the experience he had paid for, or even that it would be good for her to test a retreat to see it from the client side. And both of those reasons would be true. But neither were why the word 'Yes' was quivering on the edge of her tongue. No, deep inside, she knew that teenage Madison would have given anything and everything for the opportunity to spend time alone with Luke Taylor and that thirty-something her desperately wanted to agree. But thirty-something her knew better.

Madison opened her mouth, ready to tell Luke firmly that she would go and find the captain, but that if he wanted to continue the cruise once she'd been returned to Singapore he was welcome to, but stopped, transfixed by the challenge in his eyes.

The challenge and something else. Something warm and appreciative that made her whole body tingle as if she were really truly feeling for the first time in longer than she could remember.

She swallowed, desire mingling with fear, trying to get her mind back on track: see the captain. Be sensible. Be professional. Be safe.

But standing here, the sun beating down, the sea breeze caressing her cheeks—and Luke Taylor looking at her so intently—it was hard to remember why safety mattered so very much.

What would it be like to *not* do the sensible thing? She had flown here. That wasn't particularly sensible—and look where that decision had got her. At sea with a man whose smile and eyes haunted her dreams. What would be the harm in just seeing this situation out? It was just forty-eight hours after all.

Before she could talk herself out of it, Madison tilted her chin and met Luke's challenging gaze. 'If you'd really like to continue the cruise for the next couple of days, then of course I can accommodate you. Although I must make it clear that M will reimburse you for the trip, no matter how long you spend onboard.'

The gleam of humour in Luke's eyes intensified. 'Thank you for agreeing. I hope it's not too much of a chore.'

Madison took a look around her, the first real look since she'd realised they'd set sail. The sea stretched out all around, calm and so blue it defined the colour, matched only by the cloudless sky, lit by a sun so bright she couldn't look at it directly. The reality of her situation hit her. She was on an enforced vacation, no access to emails, no phone calls or messages to punctuate her every minute, nothing to do but relax and spend time with a man—a customer, she hastily corrected herself—who by anyone's standards was charming and attractive. A man whose poster she used to have pinned to her wall. 'We aim to please.'

Luke threw back his head and laughed. 'In that case—' he raised his glass '—let's toast to a successful voyage.'

'To a successful voyage,' she echoed and as she sipped their eyes met and held. Madison was trapped; she couldn't have looked away if she'd tried. The humorous gleam in Luke's eyes faded, leaving just the appreciation. Madison shifted, remembering her unwashed hair, her hastily reapplied make-up, her travel-creased linen dress. 'If I am going to stay then maybe I better freshen up.'

She put her glass down with unsteady hands and stood up, automatically adjusting to the smooth movement of the boat. 'I won't be long.'

'Take your time.' Luke sat back, long muscled legs sprawling out in front of him. 'I'm not going anywhere.'

'No. Thank you.'

She managed not to pull a frustrated face at her barely coherent response, grabbing her bag and making a hasty exit.

Desperate as she was to make herself a little more respectable, Madison couldn't resist exploring the yacht. She was quite used to over-the-top luxury, both as a child and now when interviewing clients, but didn't usually get the opportunity to relax and enjoy it. This get-away-from-it-all decadence felt very different now she was the one doing the getting away, her jaded eyes seeing the yacht as if she had never experienced this kind of indulgence before, and she took her time, taking in every detail as if all this was new to her. And in some ways—the important ways—it was. This wasn't a backdrop for work; it was a playground. Now she just had to learn how to play.

The yacht had three decks. The swimming pool took up the majority of the top deck, flanked by two inviting-looking canopied double sun loungers, and a hot tub bubbling away at the very edge of the deck so the occupants could look out at the sea beyond. The middle deck held the outdoor seating and dining area and the bottom deck included a covered exercise space complete with weights, yoga balls and mats and a treadmill, with the long main deck offering plenty more seating areas and a diving board to enable guests to directly access the sea.

The spacious communal quarters were accessed from the bottom deck. Floor-to-ceiling windows ran along both sides and the large room housed a long dining table, a cinema-sized TV and a large curved sofa. A panelled hallway led from the living-dining room, wooden doors hiding a fully equipped indoor gym and tiled steam room on one side and a booklined study with leather armchairs and a slightly incongruous-looking fireplace on the other.

A curved staircase led up to the middle deck and one of the two guest suites, the staircase continuing up to the top deck and the second suite. Walking up it, Madison peeked into the middle apartment and saw Luke's bags had been placed in the hallway and so she continued up to the top deck and the rooms she would be occupying.

The door led straight into a sizeable bedroom. The bed was invitingly made up with the crispest whitest linen imaginable, topped with azure-blue silk cushions and bedspread, the same blue picked out in the sweeping curtains and the large Persian rug that covered the polished wooden floor. Two comfortable love seats clustered around a breakfast table in one corner and a little desk and chair were placed in the other. Curved floor-to-ceiling windows led onto a balcony so she could step straight out of bed and into the sea breeze unseen by anyone.

Sliding open one of the doors, Madison stepped out into the afternoon sun, leaning over the balcony and watching the spray below, and gradually the tightness that seemed to permanently live in her chest began to ease, just a little, as she took a deep breath of the fresh air. She stayed there for a while, feeling her body and mind start to unwind with every moment she breathed in the restorative air, gazed out at the sea. She never stopped, partly because she thrived on the demands of her business, thrived on being needed, being necessary, and partly because, even with a healthy turnover and clear success, she remembered all too clearly how it had felt to have had nothing and no one.

But maybe she should allow herself to stop just occasionally.

Madison had no idea how long she stood there before remembering her decision to change. Reluctantly she pulled herself away from the balcony and headed back into the bedroom, checking the en suite bathroom and the dressing room as she did so. The suite was luxurious to the point of decadence, as unlike her neat, functional maisonette as any space could be. Madison liked the neutral greys and whites she had chosen, the lack of clutter, the way she could slip out of the maisonette leaving no sign she had been there. She had learned not to put any store in possessions, not to care about things, found the simplicity soothing, but she had to admit there was something alluring about such complete opulence.

But when she emptied out her bag—still no charger, she noted ruefully—she came plummeting back to earth with a painful thump. The sensible linen wrap dresses in neutral tones she had packed were creased and seemed frumpy against the vivid blues and sharp whites that surrounded her. It was a good thing she planned for every eventuality, including lost luggage.

Heading back into the dressing room, Madison slid back one of the wardrobe doors and an array of brightly coloured summer clothing greeted her. Likewise, the dressing table was furnished with brushes and combs, and exclusive cosmetics in several different tones and style. She'd sent Isabella's measurements and colouring to the styling service who had supplied the boat, and luckily she was of a height with the Italian, their colouring not too dissimilar.

It didn't take long to shower, shampooing her hair and washing away all the travel grime, before she slipped on the most demure swimsuit she could find, in a deep coral with a gold trim, matching it with a maxi dress in a similar colour and slipping her feet into gold flipflops. Madison automatically reached for the hairdryer and then set it down decisively. She was at sea; the wind would ruffle her hair, the salt coat it. Instead, she ran some serum through her shoulder-length strands, allowing her hair to dry naturally in the soft waves she usually ruthlessly straightened and tamed.

Right, ready to go. Unless… Pulling out the top tray, Madison examined the vast array of gorgeously packaged make-up. Her common sense tried to intervene, telling her that any make-up would soon be flayed away by the wind and the water, but vanity compelled her to add a little tinted moisturiser, some waterproof mascara and a soft raspberry lipstick.

Okay then. Madison took a deep breath as she got to her feet, the reality of her situation hitting her. Was she really going to spend two days on a boat with a man she didn't know? Worse, a man she hadn't been able to get out of her mind or her dreams for the last couple of months. The man her lonely teenage heart had weaved romantic fantasies around, convinced she could tame and reform him…

Madison straightened. That girl had been a fool, unable to see what was going on under her nose, blinded by her daydreams and the false world in which she lived. She was a lot older, a lot wiser and although she dealt with romance every day she was no longer oblivious to reality. Luke Taylor was a client and she was here to make sure he had an enjoyable few days. Nothing more.

Luke leaned over the railings and stared out at the seemingly endless sea. What on earth was he doing? It had seemed like such a good idea in the moment to suggest that he and Madison continue the cruise for a couple of days at least. Maybe the jet lag, the sunshine and the glass of champagne had combined to go to his head. Awkward as it would have been to have spent a week on this admittedly large and extraordinarily comfortable yacht with a stranger, surely it would be the height of awkward to spend it with a woman who wasn't looking for a long-term relationship, and to whom he'd found himself confiding all kinds of secrets during the video chats she'd arranged when she'd screened him.

But there was something about Madison Morgan. It wasn't just that hers had once been one of the most famous faces on the planet; child actresses had held little interest for Luke when he was growing up and his walls had instead been covered with pictures of the tennis players he longed to emulate. Nor was it the way she'd just faded from stardom, no crash and burn or stratospheric rise into adult stardom, just a neat step back into civilian life. No, it was the flash of humour he occasionally glimpsed in her usually serious hazel eyes, the quick half smile that lit up her face before she quickly corrected herself that intrigued him. The way he found himself wanting to impress her. And that wasn't like him at all.

But Madison Morgan lived in London, and she wasn't here to find love. He needed to remember those pertinent details. Remember why he was here: to find a mother for Isla, not to play games.

The sound of footsteps alerted him to Madison's return and Luke turned around, the suggestion that maybe they head back to Singapore after all hovering on his lips. But as she appeared the words disappeared as if they'd never been. Gone was the neat, business-like woman with perfectly coiled hair, professional and forgettable clothes and brisk demeanour. Instead a sea goddess strolled out of the cabin doors, still damp hair falling in perfect waves around her face, her almost transparent dress hinting at lush curves, a shy smile in her long-lashed eyes.

'You found your suite all right?' Luke kicked himself. Clearly Madison had found her suite; she hadn't taken a quick dip in the sea and changed right here on deck. His pulse began to speed at the thought of just that, at the image of her long limbs diving off the side, water caressing every curve, her hair slicked back. What was wrong with him? He was like a teen-ager, unable to look at Madison without carnal images flooding his mind.

In a way it was natural; she was a desirable woman and he had been practically celibate for six years. Plus he'd come away without his daughter to find romance; clearly sex at some point during the week had been a strong possibility. But if sex had been on the agenda it would have been with a potential life partner, not his accidental weekend companion.

'Of course you did. This is a big boat, but not that big.' Nope, that was no better. A double fault on the casual conversation.

Madison walked towards him with slow languorous steps, coming to a stop beside him and placing her hands on the rail. Her hair rippled in the breeze and she tilted her face back, eyes half closed. 'I don't think I have ever felt as relaxed as I felt just then,' she said. 'I could have spent the next forty-eight hours just going from one balcony to the other quite happily.'

'Then I'm honoured you managed to leave them to come and spend some time with me.'

'Have you had the chance to explore yet?'

He shook his head. 'They took my bags off me when I arrived, and I've yet to leave this deck.' He paused. 'Care to show me around?'

It was Madison's turn to pause, clear calculation flickering through her eyes and then she smiled. 'Okay, come on.'

The tour was the perfect icebreaker, cutting through the potential awkwardness as they realised they were actually going to do this, spend the next forty-eight hours together on a trip designed for romance. Luke couldn't help laughing at some of the more indulgent touches, like the study with its vintage leather chairs, booklined shelves and actual fireplace and the huge steam room with its menu of different steams from sweet floral fragrances to bracing mints and menthols.

'They've certainly thought of every detail; I've seen less well-equipped gyms in hotels,' he said as they emerged onto the top deck, where the swimming pool was lit by soft lights as dusk drew in. 'But what I can't get over is the sheer number of seats for just two of us. How tired do they think we get? I can't take a step without coming across another sofa or chair or hammock or lounger. In fact I am going to challenge myself to sit on each of them over the next forty-eight hours. It will probably take me forty-eight hours just to track them all down, let alone sit on each one.'

'I'm all for a challenge,' Madison said. 'But I can think of better ways to spend my time while I'm here.'

'So can I,' Luke said with a slow smile, holding Madison in his gaze as he spoke. She flushed and looked away, clearly uncomfortable. Luke cursed silently. He hadn't meant to load the phrase with any particular meaning. Somehow the pent-up frustration from following Madison around the boat, noticing the way her dress swirled around her body, revealing even as it veiled, had clearly taken its toll on him. The silence stretched out uncomfortably and Luke searched for a change of subject.

'This boat is quite something. I've chartered yachts before, friends of mine have some pretty sweet boats, but I've never been on anything like this. I guess my missing date had no idea what she was turning down.'

'It wasn't anything personal, Luke,' Madison said quickly. 'She had no idea who you were. You know these dates are anonymous right until the actual meeting to stop people googling and turning up with pre-

conceptions. She just found love on her own, that's all.'
She grinned. 'It's as much a blow to my professional
pride as it must be to your ego, believe me.'

'What's she like?' Luke had barely spared a thought
for his missing date since he'd looked up to see Madison Morgan walking towards him, but obviously
thoughts of the mystery woman who might be the
answer to Isla's prayers—and his own enforced celibacy—had consumed him over the last few weeks,
ever since Madison had contacted him to say she had
a match. 'Why did you pick her? Why did you think
we were suited?'

Madison wandered over to the sun loungers and sat
down, swinging her long legs up and hugging them into
her. 'Sometimes I just know. I know it sounds ridiculous; my friends in college used to call it witchcraft.'
She laughed a little self-consciously. 'It can make no
sense at all on paper, but after I speak to both people
I just know they'll hit it off. But other times I have to
rely on good old-fashioned detective work and that's
what happened here. You are both athletic, competitive, at the top of your game. Sometimes that works,
sometimes it's a recipe for disaster, but you both seem
to have big hearts, room for someone else's dreams in
your lives. And she genuinely loves children, which in
your case was my top priority. Lots of people say they
want them and many claim to have room in their hearts
for stepchildren, but the reality can be much harder
than their romantic daydreams. Not everyone has the
compassion to put a child first in the heady first days

of a relationship.' Her expression saddened, her eyes suddenly shadowed. 'Some people never manage it.'

Madison gazed sightlessly out for a moment, clearly lost in thought before giving herself a little shake and resuming. 'But I was confident that this woman had the maturity and confidence to understand that Isla was part of the package. She had grown up with lots of siblings, has lots of nieces and nephews and really genuinely seemed excited at the thought of a ready-made family. But honestly? I didn't get that absolute surety that you and she were a perfect match, although I knew she had all the qualities you are looking for and I thought you'd hit it off. Sometimes that works just as well as my second sense.'

'So I haven't missed out on the love of my life?' Luke was only half teasing. He didn't believe in love at first sight or 'The One', didn't think that there was just one person out there who was his other half. He didn't believe in Madison's sixth sense; compatibility on paper made a lot more sense to him. But he was still relieved that his missing date hadn't been one hundred per cent perfect for him.

'No.' Madison shook her head, taking his teasing seriously. 'Not at all. She was a good match, but to be honest I picked her for Isla as much as for you.'

'Good. I'm happy to compromise in many ways, Madison. I don't need a big love affair or perfection; I need someone who will love my daughter. That's why I'm here.' At least that was what he'd told himself, his reason for signing up with M in the first place. But he couldn't deny that since he'd first sent in his application he'd been looking forward to the next stage. Not the wooing and getting to know each other stage, but the family stage. Someone to sit with on his terrace, to share his thoughts and frustrations with, the mundane day-to-day niggles and joys. If he could fast-track to that part he'd be perfectly content.

At least he'd thought he would be. Clearly his body had other ideas, the way it was fixated on Madison's every movement.

She shifted again, pushing her hair out of her eyes. 'I said to you when you joined up that finding someone who was genuinely ready to take Isla and love her as her own was a challenge, but not an undoable one. Finding someone who was willing to move to Sydney if she wasn't already there is also a challenge, but again not undoable. It wasn't to be this time, but that doesn't mean it won't work out next time. You just need some faith and patience and to let me do the worrying.'

Luke moved to sit on the lounger next to Madison. 'Can I ask you something?' he said.

'I guess.'

He noted the wariness in her eyes. 'When you came to see me play, were you cheering for me or the other guy?'

Surprise replaced the wariness and this time her smile was unfettered, glorious and full, like sunshine. 'Always you.'

'A woman of good taste.' Luke wasn't prepared for the heat that filled him at the thought of a younger Madison in the crowd, watching his every move. Quickly he jumped to his feet and pulled off his T-shirt, slipping off his shoes and shorts, diving straight into the unheated pool, glad of the cold against his suddenly sensitive skin. He could hear Madison laugh as he struck out with strong strokes. Exercise and cold water were the answer. Otherwise he was in big trouble.

## CHAPTER FOUR

IF NOTHING ELSE this whole experience was a very useful learning tool, Madison reflected. For instance, the itinerary she put together for these weeks often included a formal dinner on the first evening. The purpose was for the couple to spend some quality time together over delicious food and drinks, getting to know each other in a classic date scenario. The reality, however, was seriously intimidating. Another thing: why had she thought a boat a good idea? There was nowhere to hide and right now she would give anything for a bolt-hole where she could sit and examine just why Luke Taylor had got under her skin.

But a formal dinner on a boat it was and there was no escaping it, so the least she could do was present a good front. After a much-needed swim Madison had escaped back to her suite and changed into a floaty sea-green dress, grateful for the good taste of the stylist who had picked out the clothes in the suite, and attempted to smooth her hair which, freed from the usual torture of straightening irons and taming products, had gone from soft waves to out-of-control curls. Finally she had upped her make-up from barely-there to confidence-boosting full-face. But, even with the armour of good clothes and hair, walking down to meet Luke on the middle deck for an evening of intimate *tête-à-tête* took all the confidence she could muster.

This wasn't a real date, she reminded herself. It was just food and talk. She could do this. So what if he was jaw-droppingly attractive and teenage Madison had wanted to run away with him? She was nearly two decades older and centuries wiser than that lonely girl.

Luke was already on the deck, relaxing on one of the sofas reading one of the magazines provided for them. He put it down and stood up as she descended the steps. 'You look lovely,' he said.

'Thank you; so do you.' Luke had changed into a short-sleeved white linen shirt teamed with lightweight grey trousers and slicked his blond hair back but hadn't shaved, the stubble making him look younger and surfer boy appealing, all too reminiscent of the tennis player she'd once fantasised about. Madison swallowed, unexpected lust fizzing through her entire body. 'In fact, all of this looks lovely,' she said quickly, looking at the table now set for two complete with crisp white tablecloths and napkins, heavy-looking silverware and sparkling crystal glasses. Olives, tiny bread rolls and a selection of Indonesian delicacies were already laid out on a platter and one of the crewmen had changed into bartender black tie and stood by the bar area, ready to mix any drink they desired. Luke pulled out a chair and gestured for her to sit. Still feeling uncharacteristically shy, Madison crossed over the deck and sat down, every sense hyperaware of his proximity. He took the chair opposite, sprawling seemingly at his ease and raised his water glass to her.

'To a happy ever after,' he said half mockingly and she raised hers back.

'It'll happen for you, Luke, I guarantee it.' She meant it. Professional pride and her own reaction to this man compelled her.

Despite her nerves the next hour or so passed easily. Madison, who'd spent her teens having her every mouthful watched, her appearance scrutinised and enduring regular weigh-ins, didn't usually have much of an appetite. Food had become purely functional to her during those years and she'd never quite shaken that off. But, whether it was the sea air or the delicious food, she managed to eat more than her fair share of the appetisers and finish her starter of delicately spiced fish while still having room for the aromatic salad served as their main. Though, admittedly, salad seemed too healthy a name for the indulgent coconut milk dressing and deep fried tofu prepared so perfectly it melted on the tongue.

Conversation also flowed, the food and view an easy talking point, and when they ran out of food chat Madison encouraged Luke to tell her about his daughter. It wasn't until the plates had been cleared and she'd suggested a break before dessert that Luke sat back in his chair and looked at her speculatively.

'We seem to have talked an awful lot about me,' he said.

Madison's stomach tightened painfully. After spending her first twenty years in the media spotlight, she much preferred being in the background, even when she was with just one other person. 'That's because I'm interested,' she said quickly. 'After all, I need to make up for the disaster of this date. The more I know about you, the better for future success.'

'I don't know; it doesn't feel too much of a disaster from where I'm sitting.' Luke's eyes gleamed dark navy in the candlelight and her stomach tightened even more. 'Beautiful food, beautiful setting and a beautiful companion. I guess I don't have too much to complain about. So, this ever happened before? Have you ever ended up having to date one of your clients or are you already happily settled down?'

*Date.* For one moment Madison allowed herself to imagine that she really was here for pleasure not work, that this back and forth was the delicious starter before an evening of passion. What would it be like to look across at the tall, broad man opposite and know that glint in his eyes was all for you, that the teasing smile was yours alone, that the athletic body was waiting for you to unwrap it?

With an effort she dampened down the outrageous thoughts, locking them away as firmly as she could. Madison saw successful relationships every day. She attended countless weddings, had a wall covered with engagement photos, wedding photos, baby photos from happy clients. She was personally responsible for plenty of matches, but where she was concerned she knew there was no happy ever after. She had made her peace with that fact long ago. She might specialise in courtship, but only for others.

A real relationship meant opening up, letting someone in, exposing secrets. Madison didn't want anyone knowing her secrets, nor did she want to risk allowing herself to really feel, to love, to trust, not when she knew how painful it was when those feelings were rejected, when love was one-sided, trust trampled on.

'Oh, no, I didn't open M to look for a partner for me; that would be really unethical. Nothing like this has ever happened before. It's a highly unusual situation; please don't think it's not.' She paused, but if she was quizzing Luke about his relationship history she guessed he had a right to expect honesty from her. 'And no, I'm not in a relationship, at least not traditionally. I guess you could say that I'm married to my work. I know it's a cliché but I don't have time for a personal relationship.'

Although it seemed easier to be happy with her solitude at home in London, in the building she had bought with her own hard-earned money, her laptop always open, managing her business, than here on a yacht with a handsome man gazing at her with an interest that she wasn't prepared for.

'It's a good thing that's not your tagline; if all your clients were too busy for a personal relationship then your business wouldn't last more than a couple of days.'

'Most of my clients *are* too busy and that's why they come to me,' Madison pointed out and Luke laughed.

'Fair point. But what made you start a dating agency in the first place? It's a long way from what you used to do. I guess I thought child stars either ended up as adult actors or has-beens chasing reality fame.'

Madison took a cautious sip of her wine while she considered her answer, how much to reveal. The food and wine, the stars and sea breeze had gone to her head a little, made it hard to trot out the usual rehearsed lines. She wanted to be honest with someone for once in her lonely life. Not totally honest, obviously. There were some secrets she could never tell. Especially not to a man who looked at her as if she was someone.

'I grew up in a very adult world,' she said at last. 'A very artificial world. A world where everyone worked very hard to present a false persona, to pretend they were straight because that's what their fans wanted to believe and the box office demanded, that they were a committed environmentalist although they had a private jet just for their dogs, that they were a committed family person although they were sleeping with a different person every night. A world where, despite never eating carbs and a lot of surgery, they still felt ugly, despite their success they still worried about money. I learnt quickly to see through what adults said to what they meant.'

Although she had never learned to see where it mattered. Had never seen through her own parents' façade. Had they been more convincing than most, or had she just been too blinded by her own pathetic need and love for them to see through their deception?

'I can't imagine what it must have been like growing up in the spotlight, always working.' Luke pushed his chair back from the table so he could sit back at his ease, long muscled legs stretching out in front. He looked so comfortable in his skin, every inch the successful alpha male he was. How did he do that? 'I lived a pretty abnormal life myself in some ways, but I didn't start to travel, to be known till I was sixteen. Until then I was at home with my family, training a lot, going to tournaments but still with other kids most of the time, at school. Wasn't it lonely?'

'I didn't know any different,' Madison prevaricated. Of course she had been lonely, almost unbearably so at times. 'I was cast in a commercial as a toddler and from there I did some modelling and got a recurring role in a soap. By five I was starring in a well-known sitcom and I shot my first movie at seven. I didn't ever attend school or hang out at the mall. Even my first boyfriends were other teen actors, mostly set up by my managers with an eye on the teen magazine headlines. But that life was my normal.'

'But not so normal you're still in that world?'

'No. When I hit twenty I got tired of playing teen roles, but I was only offered those or the young ingenue—three lines and lots of doe eyes and revealing clothes to help move the hero's story along, often with an actor twice my age as the love interest. I was used to being the star, not a supporting character, to having an arc even if it was a cliché. And I realised I just didn't want to fight for the few good young female character roles. I wanted to start again, do something different. So I went to college and studied business.'

'Impressive.'

Necessary. After seeing the state of her bank balance and realising that all the money she had earned had been squandered to pay for her parents' lavish life-style, that the people who were supposed to love her unconditionally only cared about her earning power, Madison had vowed never to be that vulnerable again. Business had been a practical choice, a shield against life. She shrugged. 'I like spreadsheets and budgets; what can I say?'

'My kind of woman. Beautiful, creative and prac-tical.'

His tone was teasing but there was a warm appre-ciation in Luke's eyes that made her quiver. Madison couldn't hold his gaze, jumping to her feet and walk-ing over to the side of the deck to hang over the railing and look at the moon's reflection on the sea, her voice unnaturally bright. 'I thought I would go with what I knew. Maybe start a managerial agency for child per-formers.' Put the kind of protection in place she had never been granted. 'But I got a reputation at college for being a bit of a matchmaker, thanks to that ability to see through people's words to their meanings, and someone suggested I start an agency. But although this was over a decade ago and people weren't so used to swiping left for a partner, there were a lot of websites out there catering for almost every kind of need or want so I knew I needed a real USP. Luckily I had dinner with an old friend from my Hollywood days who was saying how hard it was to meet men who were inter-ested in her, not her name and reputation, and it was a real Eureka moment. An exclusive agency for people who found it hard to meet possible matches naturally.

People who were well known, very rich or well connected, but just wanted to be loved for themselves. And so M was born. I pulled in some favours from old contacts who spread the word and signed up if they were single and the rest is history.'

'But you wouldn't have lasted for over a decade on favours and contacts. What's your success rate again?'

'Over eighty per cent.' She couldn't suppress the pride in her voice.

Luke whistled. 'That is impressive. Sorry to have brought your rate down.'

'You won't,' Madison said confidently, turning to grin at him. 'You're a challenge now. One I am determined to conquer.'

'If you're the prize then for once I am happy to lose.'

The air stilled and Madison froze, the grin fading from her face as if it had never been, her gaze shuttering. Luke swore under his breath. What had persuaded him to say something so blatant? He wasn't in a club flirting with a fan, hadn't been that man for a long time. Not since Isla, in fact.

It was the sea air, the champagne, the intimacy. It was her floaty dress and tousled curls and just-got-out-of-bed sun-kissed vibe. It was the attraction that had sizzled low but intensely between them since that first glass of champagne—no, since that first video call. Because the truth was that when Luke had thought about this week, when he had allowed himself to imagine the relaxing, the conversation, the flirting and yes, the seduction, it had been Madison he had imagined sharing that time with, not some mystery other woman. Madison with her olive skin, pale from living in London, her long-lashed hazel eyes, sometimes dark brown, sometimes green, occasionally golden, with her long neck and sad eyes and sudden, rare glorious smile. It made no sense. She wasn't his usual type—and nor was she looking for a relationship. But the attraction was real, it was strong—and, watching the colour flush her cheeks and the rise and fall of her chest, he was sure it was mutual.

But she wasn't here to date him or be seduced. She was all business, no matter how delectable she looked, and he needed to remember that—and respect it.

He searched for the words for an apology but she spoke before he had gathered more than an 'I'm sorry' into his brain.

'I'm not a prize,' Madison said, her voice low and husky.

'I know. I…'

But she carried on as if he hadn't spoken. 'A prize is such a passive idea. That a woman only exists to be claimed.'

'I didn't mean…'

'I own my own business and I make my own choices.' She was looking at him directly now, their gazes locked. Luke was lost in the green gold of her eyes, in the myriad of expressions passing through their depths: indignation, amusement, hope, the ever-present sadness—and need.

'What is it you choose?' His voice was as husky as hers. How had this happened? Just a few hours ago they had been strangers, half an hour ago dinner companions sharing life stories. And now? Now they were circling each other in the age-old dance and he remembered every step.

This wasn't supposed to happen. Luke knew better than to let his emotions rule his head, a lesson well learned in the dark reflective time after his racquet-throwing teenage tearaway days. Even Alyssa had been a calculated risk—more risk than calculation in the end—and he'd gone into that particular fling with his eyes wide open. She'd been after his fame and his money, he'd been after something fun and no-strings, telling himself that he worked hard enough, he deserved to play hard. This week was not about play. It was about his future. About a mother for Isla. He'd promised himself never to bring a woman into his daughter's life unless she planned to stay there.

But Isla wasn't here. He had a week to himself—well, forty-eight hours to himself—and he should make that time count.

'What do you choose, Madison?' he repeated.

But she didn't answer directly, her focus softening. 'You're a client,' she murmured, more to herself.

'Not for the next forty-eight hours.' Luke kept his tone low and soothing. One wrong move would scare her off. Maybe that would be for the best, but he couldn't resist seeing where this unexpected moment led.

'I never do anything reckless.'

His heart was hammering so hard he could hardly hear the music that had been playing all evening, his blood rushing around and around his veins as if his whole body was in a race. 'Never? Not anything like flying halfway around the world to deliver a message which could easily have been done by phone?'

'You want a wife…'

'Right now,' he said deliberately, 'I only want you.'

So they had fast-tracked from polite introduction to heat-filled seduction in a matter of hours? They only had hours. Two nights, in fact, before Madison contacted her office and got them to turn the boat around. It was nothing. Wasting a second would be the sin, not acting on flames surely enveloping them both.

'Make a choice, Madison,' he said for the third time. 'It's yours. Tell me to back off and I will order some dessert and tell you stories about my time on tour and sleep alone with no hard feelings. Scout's honour.'

Her lush mouth tilted at the corners. 'You were a Scout?'

'Well, no. But I'll make the promise and mean it. If you turn away now then I won't say another word about it.'

'It?'

'About how much I want you.'

'Oh.' She breathed the word, the soft sound enveloping him, and he fought to stay still, relaxed on his chair, to give her the space she needed to come to him entirely of her own volition. 'And what if I don't tell you to back off?' Her face was alight with mischief now, transforming her fragile beauty into something potent in its animation.

'Then I come over to you and kiss you until you ask me to stop.'

'In that case,' she said, 'what are you waiting for?'

# CHAPTER FIVE

*WHAT ARE YOU waiting for?* The words echoed around the deck before disappearing off on the sea breeze as Madison stood brave and defiant by the railings. She didn't recognise herself, didn't recognise the yearning that had engulfed her whole body, clouded her mind. Was she playing a role, the bold and confident seducer? Or was she actually shedding a role, being herself for the first time she could remember, living out those teenage fantasies, that dream that Luke Taylor, the bad boy of tennis and America's teenage sweetheart, would take one look at her and fall for her?

Because he was looking at her in exactly the way she'd fantasised about. As if she were all he could see. As if she were rare and precious and covetable. As if she was desire personified. And, as much as she tried to pretend otherwise, Madison was only human. She had wants and she had needs and she was so goddam lonely. Besides, what did it matter? In two days she'd be heading back to London to find Luke the perfect wife. Couldn't she just have this time? Have him? Just this once?

Despite the balmy heat of the evening Madison shivered, her skin goose bumping under Luke's assessing gaze, barely able to stay still as he slowly, all too slowly, got to his feet and sauntered towards her. She made herself stay still, leaning against the rails, letting him come to her, those blue, blue eyes fixed hungrily on her. He halted in front of her, so close she could feel his body heat permeating every pore of her, and she forced herself to look up to meet his eyes, to tell herself she was unafraid. That she had asked for this. That she wanted this.

Neither moved, neither spoke for long, long moments, breathing in time, gazes fused as if waiting for a sign, for permission. And then, suddenly, Madison wasn't afraid. She wanted Luke like she had never wanted anything before and, like a miracle, he seemed to want her too and she wasn't going to squander this opportunity.

'I thought,' she said, 'that you were going to kiss me.'

His answering smile was slow and sweet and wicked and her knees weakened at the deliberateness of it. 'Oh, I am,' he said, his voice a low drawl. 'But anticipation just adds to the moment, don't you think?'

Was this her body? This collection of quivering, aching, needing pulse points, all leaning in towards Luke as if he were the moon and she the sea? Her breasts felt fuller, her stomach a twist of desire, her legs barely able to support her. 'Anticipation can be overrated,' she managed and his smile widened.

'Is that so? In that case I better not keep you waiting any longer.' And then his mouth captured hers and all thoughts dissolved under pure sensation. The feel of him, the taste, the smell: Madison had never realised how arousing scent could be before, but with every sense heightened she could pick out the orange and bergamot of his shower gel overlaid with the salt tang of the sea and a warm, primal muskiness that was all Luke, the headiness of the mix almost overwhelming.

His kiss was gentle, at first. A teasing enquiry, as if he were checking to make sure she was all in, slowly increasing in intensity with every moment. Madison stood almost passively at first, taking in every detail, every sensation almost forensically, gradually relaxing into the kiss, into Luke, until, impatient, she entwined her arms around his neck, bringing him even closer. She felt amusement rumble through him for a second—just a second—before Luke turned up the dial, increasing the intensity all the way up to incendiary. Madison gasped against his mouth as the kiss heated, one of Luke's hands slipping down her hip to cup her bottom and pulling her so close she could feel the evidence of his arousal hard against her. His other hand was splayed on her ribs, brushing the underside of her breast, and she wriggled, needing, wanting more, unable to articulate just what more was, but knowing this wasn't enough.

'You're so beautiful,' Luke breathed against her mouth, his own breathing ragged but impatient as she kissed him again.

Time stopped. She was all fluid desire and sensation, the sound of the ocean lapping against the boat, Luke's breathing, her own gasps and moans mingling with the classical tracks still playing in the background creating a soundtrack to the first love scene she truly felt part of. Restraint fled, Luke caressing and touching and kissing, her dress falling off her shoulders, the material rubbing her fevered skin as she unbuttoned and pulled at his clothes, her hands splaying over taut toned flesh, her mouth seeking the hollows and contours of his salt-slick body. At some point they left the side of the boat, entwined as they backed towards one of the many sofas, falling in a tangled, laughing heap onto the cushions.

'I'm never going to mock the number of seats on this boat again.' Luke shifted, taking Madison with him so she was nestled next to him, his body partially covering hers. 'Is this okay or would you prefer to head in?' He ran a finger along her swollen lips and every nerve tingled. 'The staff here are discreet but...'

Madison blinked, suddenly aware of the warm breeze on her bare shoulder, how her dress had hiked up her thighs, her undone bra and flushed. 'Maybe in would be a good idea.' She paused. Did he mean that they should go in separately or...? There was a world of difference between making out and spending the night together. But they only had two nights. Only had this time. And she was an adult woman in her thirties not a teenager after all.

'My room, yours or shall we say goodnight here?' It was Luke's turn to pause, his gaze dark navy as he looked at her. 'Your choice, Madison. Always.'

Power skidded through her veins. Choice. Not something she'd ever had much of until she'd reached twenty-one. And even then she'd been constrained by the past, by the secrets and lies, by the burden of knowing she herself wasn't enough. But this man wanted her. For tonight at least. And oh, how she wanted him.

Confident in her skin, in her own sensuality, Madison slid off the sofa and extended a hand to Luke. 'My room,' she said. 'Coming?'

The morning sun slid through the blinds and played on the sheets, tracing a line along Madison's back. She murmured and moved, trying to escape the heat, only to collide with something large and solid and equally warm. Luke.

Luke Taylor was in her bed. Naked. She lay still and luxuriated in that knowledge for a blissful moment. Luke. Taylor. Teenage Madison would have squealed with excitement. Adult Madison was tempted. She was going to own this, she vowed. No embarrassment, no regrets. If Luke showed signs of wanting to extend their fling for the rest of the trip then fine—actually, really fine. If not then she wouldn't take it personally, not assume it was a rejection but remember why he was here in the first place and just enjoy the night for what it had been.

And it had been so much. Luke was passionate; that wasn't a surprise. But he was also tender, skilled, considerate, inventive. He was careful—after all, he was a single father. It made sense he would ensure contraception was high on any sensual agenda. He'd made her feel whole for the first time in a long, long time. Made her remember that there was more to life than work. That she was entitled to some human comfort too.

It was a long time since she'd allowed anyone to get that close physically. She had dated, on and off, since college, but none had made it further than six months before fizzling out. It was hard to maintain any kind of relationship if you were always waiting for it to end, always waiting to be discovered to be someone not worth investing in, unlovable. If you needed to keep your barriers up at all times, even in bed. Especially in bed.

Madison had come to the conclusion that if she were to date successfully then she needed an archetypal stiff-upper-lipped Victorian who had no interest in talking about his feelings and even less in understanding hers. Instead she seemed to attract twenty-first century men who took her inability to let them in personally. After a while it seemed easier to pour all of her emotions into her business, into other people's love lives rather than thinking about her own.

But there had been no barriers last night. Maybe short-term flings were the answer. Although she had a feeling Luke Taylor was going to have ruined her for other men for quite some time.

She rolled onto her side and allowed herself to drink in every inch of muscled perfection. Luke might no longer be a professional athlete but he took good care of himself. Toned and tanned, with his tousled blond hair and stubble, he looked the very stereotype of an Aussie surfer dude, but there were depths to him she was only just beginning to understand. Depths she was better off staying away from if she wanted to walk away from this fling unscathed.

'Like what you see?'

Madison jumped as Luke opened his eyes. She wouldn't have ogled quite so blatantly if she'd known he was awake. 'Not too bad,' she said as nonchalantly as she could and her heart stuttered at his slow, lazy, knowing smile.

'That's not what you said last night—or was it this morning?'

Well, he hadn't rolled immediately out of bed with an excuse. That was reassuring. Emboldened, she reached out and ran a hand down his back, allowing herself to luxuriate in every moment, enjoying seeing the way his eyes narrowed at her touch, the catch in his breath. 'I have a bad memory,' she said as lightly as she could.

'Oh? Want me to remind you?'

Madison ached in places she had never ached before, was groggy with lack of sleep, would have said she was utterly sated. But this was an offer no woman in her right mind would ever turn down. 'Yes please.'

Her stomach quivered at his low, knowing laugh and then he rolled on top of her, his mouth on her throat, his hands exploring her body, and all thought left her for a long, long time.

It was late morning by the time they finally tumbled out of bed. Luke could have stayed there all day, learning the lines of Madison's long, lithe body, exploring her contours, learning exactly what made her gasp and moan and beg him to never stop. But hunger had set in for something more substantial than lovemaking, and reluctantly he agreed to her suggestion that they shower and dress before heading back up onto the deck for breakfast.

The boat had moored up at some point during the night and, fresh from his shower, clad only in a pair of swim shorts, a short-sleeved unbuttoned shirt and sunglasses, Luke emerged from his suite to the site of last night's seduction to find the glasses cleared away, the sofas restored to their plumped-up state and the table freshly laid. He also found the sun gleaming, bright, and the yacht moored up by an idyllic-looking cove where white sand framed a curve of sea so turquoise it dazzled.

Luke stood stock-still for a moment, the intense sun and the scenery almost paralysing him with their bright perfection. He knew sun and sea and sand, but he had never seen anything quite like this. Walking over to the railings, he leaned over, drinking in the island paradise before him. There was no sign of habitation, no sign of life; it was like their own idyllic desert island. He couldn't imagine anything more perfect. Nor anyone that at this moment in time he'd rather be there with.

'Oh, my goodness,' Madison breathed as she came to stand beside him, as sun-ready casual as he in a pink bikini top paired with khaki shorts. 'I saw pictures, of course, but I never imagined anything so beautiful in real life.'

'It's quite something,' Luke agreed, reaching out and slipping one hand around her waist. Madison paused for one infinitesimal second before relaxing into the caress. 'But not quite as beautiful as you.'

She laughed, swatting him gently. 'I don't need your compliments, Luke Taylor. You already had your wicked way with me, remember?'

'I may need my memory refreshing,' Luke murmured, moving to stand behind her, kissing the back of her neck, primal satisfaction filling him as she shivered at his touch.

'I thought you wanted breakfast,' Madison said, leaning back into him.

'Maybe everything I want is right here,' he drawled, and she turned to smile up at him, cupping his cheek with one long, slender hand.

'Are you sure there's no Irish in your family history? Because you could teach that Blarney Stone a thing or two. But less of the sweet talking. I for one am hungry, even if you aren't.'

Luke laughed, but didn't protest as she grabbed his hand and towed him towards the table, which by some miracle seemed to have been set at exactly at the right time for their appearance. The bread rolls were still warm, the fruit freshly sliced, the juice so chilled the tall glasses were still frosted. He took a seat and Madison slipped into the chair opposite him and instantly, as if by magic, a stewardess appeared and offered them strong, fragrant coffee. They both accepted and then proceeded to fill their plates with delicious fresh fruit, sweet rolls and delicately spiced seafood.

Neither spoke over the next few minutes, too busy eating and sipping their delicious coffee, the silence between them as comfortable as any he'd known. That was something Luke was beginning to really appreciate about Madison; she didn't mind quiet, had no need to fill it with chatter. Stretching, he looked over at her and raised an eyebrow.

'So, what's next?'

'Next?' She flushed slightly and he couldn't help grinning at the flicker of heat in her eyes. He knew full well that she thought he was implying that they go back to bed. And it wasn't a bad call, but they were here, at this private island, and it seemed a shame to waste it.

If it was as deserted as it looked then there were plenty of things they could do out of bed after all.

'You put together the itinerary. What's in store?'

'Oh, the itinerary. Yes, of course. So, there were plenty of cruises I could have chosen from. But, fascinating as many of them are, I wasn't sure the Komodo dragons were quite the romantic feel I wanted to go for.'

'What? You mean venomous dragons that poison their victims and eat them alive whilst they lie there paralysed aren't the right backdrop for a perfect first date? To be honest, they sound less terrifying than some dates I've been on.'

'If I'd known I could have incorporated a visit there, but sadly it's too late. And, to be honest, lethal wildlife isn't quite the romantic vibe M prides itself on. I wanted to make sure that you enjoyed a week somewhere off the beaten track, getting the opportunity to spend time truly alone. This archipelago isn't far from Singapore, but it's a million miles away in ambience. Many of the islands are uninhabited, and you'll see some of the most beautiful scenery imaginable, all completely unspoiled. It's perfect for snorkelling or scuba diving and I knew both you and your intended date enjoy both of those things. The boat is also equipped with paddleboards and kayaks and there's a small boat you can take out to explore some of the small islands and bays at your leisure.' She looked across at him then, her brows drawn together in worried query. 'That sounds okay? Not too unstructured?'

'It sounds perfect,' Luke said. And it did. Would it have felt so perfect being this isolated and free with his unknown match? Structure might have been preferable with someone who he hadn't instantly felt so at home with. But the idea of a few lazy days sailing around idyllic islands like this, scuba diving and snorkelling, paddleboarding and sailing off to find their own beaches where they could be entirely alone? That didn't sound too bad at all.

In fact it sounded perfect. Too perfect to just sail away from. 'Madison?'

'Hmm?'

'Let's stay,' he said quickly, before he had time to think of all the reasons that this was a bad idea, before he remembered that Madison wasn't looking for a partner, lived on the other side of the world and hadn't mentioned wanting children once. Before he remembered that she had flown over here as a business courtesy, nothing more. Instead he focused on her long legs, showcased to perfection by the cut-off shorts, the curve of her breasts in her bikini top, her damp, waving hair, the promise of freckles on her nose. 'Let's do the whole week. You, me, some deserted islands and this glorious sea. Let's spend the week together. No worries about what comes after. Just the here and now. What do you say?'

Madison froze, her cup half held up to her mouth. 'Stay?' she squeaked after a long moment. 'You and me?'

'Why not? The boat is booked for a week, I took the time off and my flight home is booked for early next Saturday morning. A week of snorkelling and exploring deserted islands sounds exactly what I need.' And it did. He loved his daughter body and soul, didn't ever mind spending every evening at home alone working, his Saturdays ferrying her between ballet and football, the endless stream of birthday parties and playdates. Isla had a very competent nanny but Luke was determined to do all he could himself. But he had put his own needs second for six years, not allowing himself a single night off parenting. Now he was here he realised how much he needed to kick back and relax, refresh his batteries in order to give Isla all the time and attention she deserved. 'We're getting on okay, don't you think?'

'But this week is supposed to be about finding you the perfect partner,' she protested.

'I doubt you're going to rustle me up the perfect wife in the next week.' In fact, he wasn't sure he wanted Madison to matchmake him at all. Now they had slept together he couldn't help but find the idea of her choosing a partner for him a little sordid. But he didn't want to make any decisions yet, not before he'd had a chance to think it over. After all, there was still his duty to Isla. 'When did you last take a holiday?'

'I…' She tilted her chin defiantly. 'I don't really take holidays, okay. Satisfied? Is that what you wanted me to say?'

'Not wanted, expected. We all need to kick back some time, Madison. Come on, kick back with me. Let's have some fun.'

'You're a client…'

'I think we already crossed that line. Look, Madison, I'm not going to beg or coax or persuade. But I think you want to say yes because all you've done is find excuses. You haven't actually said no. So what will it be? One day here and then head back? Or some no-strings fun of the kind we really deserve?'

She stared at him for one long moment, eyes narrowed, mouth set. Luke sat as nonchalantly as he could. This wasn't a big deal in the grand scheme of things. She said yes? Then great. No? Then tomorrow the boat would get turned around and they'd be back in Singapore by nightfall. He would see Isla the next day.

So why was his chest tight as he waited for Madison to decide?

'Okay,' she said at last on an exhale. 'Let's do this.'

Relief whooshed through him. 'You sure?'

'Yes.' Slowly the pinched concentration faded away and light filled her eyes. 'Yes. I'm sure.'

'In that case,' Luke stood up slowly and held out a hand to Madison, 'I think we should celebrate. I'm sure the snorkelling can wait for an hour or two…'

# CHAPTER SIX

'WHAT DO YOU mean you can't scuba dive? Or snorkel? You can swim, can't you?'

Madison put her hands on her hips and glared at him. 'Not everyone was raised on Bondi Beach. And yes, I can swim.'

'But you were raised in Malibu. I thought that was on the ocean. Maybe I should have paid better attention in geography.'

'It is on the ocean, smartass. But I didn't get to spend much time in it. I was working,' she added, and the incredulity drained from his face to be replaced by something horribly like pity.

'Not all the time.'

'Most of the time. It was fine,' she said hurriedly, wanting to wipe the pity off his face. 'It wasn't much fun at the beach anyway, people staring or wanting photos, the paparazzi never far away. It doesn't make learning something new easy if you're being watched all the time.'

'But you surf, right? My mate had this poster...' He trailed off as she shook her head.

'Body double did the actual surfing. And now I live

in London there's not much scope for water sport, at least not for me. After growing up in California, British summers always feel a little lukewarm, apart from the two weeks when it's too humid to move and I'm no cold-water swimmer.'

'This needs remedying,' Luke said. 'By the end of this week you will be able to paddleboard and snorkel. Didn't you say two of the crew are licensed scuba diving instructors? We'll add a couple of lessons to the itinerary then.'

'Itinerary? What happened to kick back and relax?' she protested but her heart wasn't in it. There was something gratifying about Luke's determination. Determination that she have a good time. Warmth filled her; she couldn't remember the last time her welfare had been anyone's concern but hers. And usually that was the way she liked it, but there was a lot to be said for letting her guard down occasionally.

Besides, this was just a week's holiday from normality. How much harm could a week do? She'd return to London refreshed and ready to resume her life, all the more resilient for this break.

At least that was the theory...

'We'll have time for both, don't you worry.' Luke winked as he turned to speak to the captain, who was awaiting their plans for the afternoon, and Madison found herself smiling so widely her cheeks hurt. She couldn't remember the last time she'd had so much fun. The last time she'd been so happy.

Happy. It was usually a foreign concept but Luke Taylor made it all too easy. Could she hold onto this feeling when this week was over? When she was prim Madison Morgan again, ex child star and single matchmaker?

Madison's first attempts at snorkelling were not a success. It seemed completely counterintuitive to her to breathe through a small plastic bit in her mouth, to cede control to the flimsy equipment. Every practice seemed to go okay until the moment she actually put her head in the water and attempted to breathe normally, at which point every nerve screamed out in panic and she'd end up inhaling sea water and spluttering back onto her feet.

'I'm so sorry,' she said after the fifteenth try—not that she was counting—embarrassment twisting her stomach into knots. She could barely look at Luke, not wanting to see the impatience and contempt for her ineptitude he must surely be feeling. She'd known since toddlerhood that getting things wrong simply wasn't an option for her. Every take, every mistake cost money. 'I'm ruining all your fun. Why don't you go out and snorkel properly and I'll go and laze on the beach? It'll be a lot more fun for both of us.' She finally managed to look up at Luke, her gaze travelling slowly over his wet, bare chest, each muscle clearly defined, desire igniting her nerves even through her mortification, until she reached his face. To her surprised relief he didn't look impatient or frustrated; instead there was warm understanding in his clear blue eyes.

'I know it feels like you'll never get the hang of it now, but you will. You've only been trying for fifteen minutes; give yourself time,' he protested. 'Try to relax. The more stressed you get, the harder it's going to be. It's no big deal, Madison; you don't have to work it all out today. Just relax and feel your way into it. I've got you; you're not going to drown. Are you?'

'I guess not,' she said doubtfully and he gave her hand a reassuring squeeze.

'The sea only just comes to your waist and this bay has a beautiful gradual incline. You'll have to go some way to be out of your depth. Even if, for some reason, I wasn't close by and you suddenly found yourself in deeper water, there's a whole crew keeping a tactful eye on us, all dedicated to keeping you safe. And don't worry about me; with the whole week stretching ahead of us, I can get all the snorkelling and scuba diving my seafaring heart could desire. Unless...' He looked at her apologetically. 'Unless you're hating this? Am I bullying you into carrying on? My sister says I have a terrible tendency to coerce people into doing things they don't want to do, so if you'd really rather sunbathe on the beach then of course that's where you should be.'

'No,' Madison said slowly, trying to figure out how she was feeling. 'I'm not hating it, exactly. I'm frustrated, a little embarrassed at being so bad at it, but I would like to go see the fish and coral clearly, and...' she added grimly, 'I hate giving up.'

'That's the attitude,' Luke said encouragingly. 'Okay, let's try again. You don't need to take a deep breath, you don't need to fill your lungs with air; you just need to breathe normally through your mouth. Just trust in your equipment and trust me to be here.'

'Okay.' Madison set her shoulders in determination, slipped the mouthpiece back between her lips and adjusted her mask. Luke gave her an encouraging thumbs-up as she pushed forward into a relaxed floating position and put her face into the water, just as Luke had told her. For a couple of moments all seemed to be going perfectly, but then realisation hit her that she wasn't breathing normally and once again she found herself trying to take a deep breath and surfaced, spluttering.

'It's okay, I've got you.' Luke was there immediately, one arm around her waist, rubbing her back as she coughed. He waited until she had recovered and then gently removed her mask, pushing her hair off her face, cupping her face in his large, capable hands. 'You're overthinking it; just trust in the process. Not one to trust easily, are you?'

It was a light comment, but the truth of it cut straight through to Madison's heart. No, she didn't trust a piece of plastic or any equipment with her life, she didn't trust people to have her back—she didn't trust anything. And that was the best way to stay safe. It was the only way she knew. For a moment she contemplated wading out of the sea, telling Luke that she'd had enough. She glanced over at the beach, where sunbeds had been set up, a shady umbrella sheltering them from the heat of the sun, cool drinks waiting along with snacks and a stack of magazines. She could easily keep herself occupied while Luke snorkelled. Nobody would blame her for giving up; she'd tried and it wasn't for her.

But then she'd miss out, wouldn't she? She'd miss out on seeing the gorgeously coloured fish in their natural habitat, miss out on swimming amongst them, being close to them, seeing the beautiful coral reefs. She'd miss out, just like she'd missed out on so much of life's colour while keeping herself safe. Determination filled her. She wasn't going to miss out this time.

'Right,' she said, lowering her mask again and sounding as confident as she could. 'Let's try this again.'

'That's my girl.' Luke dropped a kiss on the top of her head, the casual, sweet gesture more intimate than the morning's lovemaking. 'You've got this.'

A new attitude wasn't quite enough to turn her into an expert snorkeller but relaxing certainly helped, and by the end of the afternoon Madison had just about got the hang of it. It was hard not to exclaim in delight as she slowly and carefully swam across the bay to the coral reefs, peering down at the colourful shoals of fish all around them, heart beating fast at the site of a black-tipped grey fin in the distance. The captain had reassured them that the only sharks likely to be seen around here were blacktip reef sharks, who were too small to be much danger and rarely took an interest in humans. But, even so, Madison was glad that the shark didn't come any closer and was a little relieved when Luke decided the lesson was at an end, guiding her back to shore and the luxuriously cushioned sunbeds.

'We'll have you scuba diving in no time,' Luke said as Madison took a grateful sip of cool fruit juice before she stretched out and let the sun dry her sea-damp body.

'That I *will* let you do alone,' she said decidedly. 'There are several crew who can buddy you; I think I'll take lessons properly rather than try and rush it. No, I'm quite happy to have learnt to snorkel, and tomorrow I am determined to give paddleboarding a go. Who knows? Maybe I'll find myself one of those hardy souls swimming in the Hampstead Heath ponds on a miserable February day.'

'Maybe.' Luke propped himself up on an elbow and looked at her curiously. 'How come you ended up in London? It's a long way from Hollywood.'

*That,* of course, had been the attraction.

'I wanted some time out, a chance to figure out who I was when I wasn't a child star or an actress. College helped, but I think a lot of people still expected me to return to Hollywood afterwards, armed with a degree to show I had grown up. Moving away gave me the space I needed.'

'I know a little about trying to figure out who you are and what you stand for,' Luke said wryly and she glanced at him. There had been a lot of speculation about what he'd done in the years between his famous temper tantrum and his return to the tennis circuit a more mature, considered figure. 'You found the answer in London?'

'I was never quite as famous over there as I was in the US.' Madison took another sip of her juice, unwanted memories of camera flashes and journalists trailing her every move replaying in her mind. 'I would travel to the major cities for premieres and press junkets, my movies were in the cinemas, but the tabloids were never quite as interested in me or in which teen idol I was dating as the US press were. The European tabloids can be pretty fierce, but they didn't chase me down when I was at college or try and interview my friends, unlike some of the US magazines and websites.' She winced. 'I still find myself looking for the flash of a camera when I'm out with no make-up or buying a coffee. It was bad enough when I was small, but as a teen it was relentless. I felt hunted; occasionally I still do. Everything I wore, everyone I spoke to, everything I said reported as if a teen's fashion mistake was detrimental to world peace. How anyone chooses that life I don't know. I still do interviews to promote M—my word-of-mouth is healthy but no business can do without any publicity—but I'm very picky about who I speak to. It has to fit with my clientele so upmarket titles only, but even they use the obvious hook. Every time I see the inevitable "former child star" in the headline I feel sick.'

'Can I take your "former child star" and raise you "Aussie Terror"?' Luke said. 'Two years of my life, two years when I was barely an adult, has set the tone for every piece on me. I hate knowing that one day Isla will google me and the first thing she'll see won't be the Foundation or the titles but a temper tantrum nearly two decades ago. But, like you, I have to remember that the press are a necessary evil to get the right publicity for the company and the Foundation. Yet I know that every positive interview means dredging up my past and speculation about Isla and my role as a single dad, and that I can't stand.' She heard the low rumble of anger in his voice. 'I have a zero-tolerance approach to her being photographed and mentioned.'

Madison closed her eyes. A zero-tolerance approach? So different from her own childhood, where every family occasion took place in front of a camera—from decorating the Christmas tree to her first date. A childhood packaged and commoditised. She thrust the thought away, turning to Luke, eager to move away from the memories of being hunted by the press.

'I did have visions of a little garret in Paris.' She grinned, remembering idealistic dreams of waitressing anonymously in a little café before being swept off her feet by a tall, dark, handsome Frenchman. 'But I don't speak the language and London seemed a little easier. I went over to do a postgraduate course in Business Psychology and met up with a couple of people I knew from my Hollywood days. I'd already been thinking about starting M and they were enthusiastic and offered to sign up—so the agency was born there and I never left.'

'What about your family? What did they think about you settling on the other side of the world?'

And there it was. 'I…' she started. This was where she normally said that her family were happy for her to forge her own path, the distance didn't mean anything nowadays, not when families across the globe could connect at the touch of a button. But somehow the lies wouldn't come. 'We're not that close.' It was the understatement of the century. 'But they know where I am if they need me.' She hoped he didn't hear the hope and despair in her voice. Tugging her sunglasses quickly over her eyes, she grabbed a magazine to signify the discussion was over.

It had been a day full of surprises, from waking up with Madison nestled next to him, to their laughing, easy and surprisingly tender morning lovemaking to the afternoon spent teaching her to snorkel. Luke knew he wasn't famed for his patience where sport was concerned; he liked it competitive and high octane. Usually he would want to be out on the reef, pushing the distance and speed as far as he could, doing as much as he could. But this time he'd been content to stay in the shallows with Madison, coaxing and cheering her on as she conquered her fears and managed a credible few hours of snorkelling, the payback and satisfaction as high as if he'd conquered the seas himself.

It was funny to think he'd only actually known her for just over twenty-four hours as their easy camaraderie felt born of a much older relationship. But there were times when he realised just what a stranger she was—such as the moment she'd clammed up about her family back on the beach. Had her parents been pushy stage school types? Was that why she didn't want to speak about them, was happy to live on a different continent? Somehow, for all of their easy intimacy, he hadn't been able to ask, sensing her barriers.

Oh, well, it was none of his business, not really. Because, for all that it felt as if he and Madison were having the *getting-to-know-you-with-the-intention-*

*of-potentially-being-life-partners* date this week was supposed to be, the truth was very different. Her life was in London, and she wasn't looking for marriage. He needed a mother for Isla, not a blazing passionate love affair. Mutual goals, respect and liking had to be his priorities.

Luke tugged on a clean shirt before heading up onto the deck to see what delicious dinner was in store for them tonight. Once again he was ready before Madison and he headed over to the deck railing to look out at the beginnings of what promised to be a spectacular sunset. The sun was low, burnished gold, the very few clouds lilac in the slowly darkening sky, the first stars already peeping through. Isla would love it here; it looked just like the island from her favourite Disney film. Of course, if she was here she'd be insisting he sang along to all the songs and re-enacted her favourite scenes. His heart tightened. He was having an amazing time, he couldn't deny it, and getting to know Madison was an unexpected pleasure. But he missed his daughter; he'd never spent this long away from her before.

He sensed Madison's approach before he heard her and she slipped her arms around his waist as she came to join him. They were already so easy with each other physically; it was hard to walk by her without touching her, even if it was just a brush of his hand along her arm. It was a thrill just seeing her pupils darken and hearing her breath shorten with every touch, every response the promise of another evening together.

'What are you thinking about?' she asked.

'Isla,' he said. 'She'd love it here.'

'It's an island paradise. What girl wouldn't?' Madison said. Then, in a curiously hesitant voice, 'You really love her, don't you?'

For a shocked moment Luke thought he had misheard her. 'I really *what*?'

Madison paused for a long, long moment. And then, in a voice so low he could barely make out the words, she repeated her earlier words. 'Isla. You really love her.' This time it wasn't a question. It was a statement.

He barked out an incredulous half laugh. 'Of course I do; she's my daughter. She is the most important thing in my world.'

Madison flinched, such a slight movement it was almost imperceptible. 'Lucky Isla,' she murmured as if the words were being torn from her, and Luke turned to look at her in surprise. The ease of a few moments ago had disappeared. Madison was rigid, unreadable and unreachable. What on earth was going on?

With a jolt Luke realised how little he actually knew Madison, despite all of their intimacy. They had shared a fun day today, had spent an intoxicating night together, but that was all. In many ways they were strangers. Surely she wasn't jealous of Isla and the close relationship he shared with his daughter? The old anger started to rise within him and he had to breathe deeply, push it back down, to manage his emotions. This was exactly the situation he had wanted to avoid, the reason he had come to a matchmaking service in the first place. Isla came first. Period.

'Not that lucky,' he said as levelly as he could. 'She

doesn't have a mother. I'm all she has, and that's why she has to come first.'

For another long moment Madison stayed frozen. Then she shifted and turned to look at him, seemingly her usual self again. Her eyes were warm with interest and sympathy, her body language softened as she laid a hand on his arm. 'What happened, Luke?'

But he wasn't going to be drawn into that conversation, not just yet. The trust that had so rapidly sprung between them had cracked. 'Why did you sound so surprised? As if Isla being the most important thing in my life is so hard to comprehend?'

Madison's gaze dropped as she swivelled round to look out at the sunset. 'I'm sorry, that whole question came out completely wrong. I know your life revolves around her, that you're here because of her. And that's amazing. But I also know that you were still competing when you became a father and you stopped in order to take care of her. Some people might harbour a little regret over that kind of career-ending incident, even while loving the cause. I should have known better, should have known you weren't capable of that kind of negativity. I am so sorry.'

'I see.' He might not like it but Madison wasn't the only person who had thought that he might resent the changes Isla had brought into his carefree playboy existence. He'd just thought she would see beyond, see him.

And this was why a match of shared goals and not one based on pheromones was the sensible approach.

'What happened to her mother?' Madison asked softly, turning back to him. 'Is she still involved? I know you said you were a sole parent when I interviewed you and she was out of the picture, but is she around at all? Don't feel you have to tell me,' she added hastily. 'I don't mean to pry. I'll understand if you want to drop the whole topic.'

Luke closed his eyes, memories seven years old flooding him. 'Honestly, you aren't alone in thinking that I felt hard done by back then,' he conceded. 'Isla wasn't planned, and being a single father was certainly not part of my life plan. But, truthfully, every day I thank fate for giving her to me. There is no one I'd rather be with than her, no one I'd rather be than her father. Titles were all very well, my career was brilliant while it lasted, but I have a different purpose now, a purpose I could never have imagined back then, and I don't regret a moment spent with her.'

As he spoke he had guided Madison back towards the table and a stewardess materialised as if out of nowhere to offer them a choice of champagne or cocktails. But after the last few minutes the mood between them was less rosy, less romantic, and Luke realised he didn't want champagne, but something more prosaic. 'A beer, please,' he said.

Madison nodded. 'One for me as well, thank you.'

Luke glanced at her. 'Beer?'

'I live in London,' she pointed out and he laughed, relieved at the easing of the tension that had suddenly sprung between them.

'Of course you do. It's just hard to imagine a Hollywood star downing a pint in a local pub on a Friday night.'

'It doesn't happen often,' she conceded. 'But I've become a local in some ways. And I've not been a Hollywood star for a long time.'

'A successful entrepreneur then. A cold glass of Sauvignon Blanc seems more matchmaker appropriate.'

'On the right occasion it is. And I also drink copious amounts of tea. I told you I've become a local.'

Luke waited until their food had been served before responding to Madison's earlier enquiry. While they waited he made small talk about the fish they'd seen that day and discussing plans for the next day, but at the back of his mind he'd been wondering about what to say, how much to confide in Madison. To his surprise, despite his earlier misgivings, he realised that he wanted to tell her everything.

'Injury had pretty much finished my career by the time Isla was born,' he started, taking a long swig of his beer. 'I'd started the Foundation by then, my fitness business was taking off and the app had been developed. I was starting to make serious money through non tennis activities but I wasn't ready to concede totally. I still trained and occasionally I competed. I had some dreams to fulfil and wasn't quite ready to let them go. Besides, life on tour can be fun if you're looking for that kind of entertainment. There are players who, despite the training and physical demands, like to party and many like the adulation that comes with success. I'd never really been one of them; at first I was too young and then when I came back from my hiatus I had a new focus. I might not throw my racquet and shout any more but I wanted to win just as hard and nothing was getting in my way. It wasn't worth risking a title for a party. But as I began to slow down and my knee made making finals less and less likely, I relaxed a little. I didn't turn down every invitation to party. And I didn't turn down the invitations I got at those parties.'

Luke winced as he took another sip; he wasn't particularly proud of that time in his life.

Madison nodded understandingly. 'I see.'

'Isla's mother was a model,' he continued. 'She'd gone out with a couple of the guys on tour; she was often around. She was attractive and she was entertaining and she set her sights on me. I had nothing to lose. We looked good together and she made me laugh. Looking back, for a while I thought we might actually be a couple. But when the US season came to an end she moved onto the next guy. There were no hard feelings; my pride was maybe a little bit wounded, my heart was certainly not. I didn't give her another thought for nine whole months. And then she turned up and she wasn't alone.'

'Oh...' Madison breathed in comprehension and he nodded.

'I was competing a little bit more at that point, had stopped the partying again. My knee was behaving and so, even though the business needed my focus, I couldn't stop hoping that maybe I had one more title in me. And then Alyssa showed up, Isla in her arms. She handed her to me and she walked away. I've not seen her since.'

There was an appalled silence. 'But she sees her, right? Has some presence in her life?'

Luke shook his head grimly. 'No. She doesn't want to be involved. Her choice entirely. She is Isla's mother; the door is always, always open. I've reached out, I've invited her, I've even begged her. But she isn't interested. So it's just me and Isla.'

'Poor Isla.' Madison looked at him then, eyes blazing gold in the sunset. 'Thank goodness she has you.'

'From the moment I held her I knew she was the most important thing I would ever have, could ever do. So I stopped competing, moved to Sydney full-time, put all my competitive energies into the business and concentrated on raising her as best I could. I don't regret it, not a little bit. She's my world.'

Madison's eyes shone. Although whether with tears or some other emotion he couldn't quite tell. 'Then I take it back. She's not poor; she's the luckiest girl in the world.'

Luke looked over at Madison, at the genuine emotion in her face, the almost palpable yearning in her voice, although he had no idea what it was she yearned for—she was successful and beautiful; surely the world was at her feet. Drawn by desire and the need to comfort her, to connect with her, he rose slowly to his feet and walked around the small table, taking her hand and drawing her upright. Cupping her face in his hands, he looked searchingly into her eyes. There was no trace of the envy he had suspected earlier, nothing but understanding, a warm approbation, mixed with need and want and a desire that took his breath away. She swayed towards him, eyes half closed, and Luke could wait no longer, capturing her mouth with his in a kiss that bore no relation to the sweet, teasing kisses they had shared last night but a kiss that claimed, that demanded, that possessed. Madison gasped against his mouth, opening up to him, returning the kiss with an ardour that nearly undid him.

'I'm not really hungry any more,' he murmured, reluctantly breaking the kiss, his hands tracing her curves, reminding himself of every contour, every dip and swell. 'Want to make it an early night?'

Madison didn't reply straight away, leaning back into him, nibbling his jawline, tracing his mouth with hers, her hands splayed on his back, every touch a sweet torture. 'I vote for an early night and a late morning,' she said softly at long last.

Luke needed no further encouragement, taking her hand and towing her back inside the boat. He didn't know if it was the years of near celibacy, the exotic, sensuous setting or Madison herself but he'd never been so hungry for a woman, as impatient as a teenager. They only had six nights left. He was determined to make the most of every single minute.

## CHAPTER SEVEN

'RIGHT, WHAT TREATS does today have in store for us?' Luke asked, bounding onto the deck, where Madison was finishing her breakfast.

She looked up, drinking him in, every nerve waking up as if she'd downed a triple espresso. Freshly showered, hair slicked back, all tan and stubble in denim shorts and another of those short-sleeved white linen shirts that made him look almost piratical, he was the poster boy for outdoor living.

'I'm not sure. Why are you asking me?'

'Because you organised this week. This whole itinerary is down to you.'

'That's fair.' She should know what was planned for today. She'd pored over every detail, wanting this week to be perfect, her gift to Luke. However, it felt very different living the cruise compared to planning it. She wasn't even sure what day it was, drunk on the sun, the leisure, the lovemaking. She wasn't even sure who she was right now, breakfasting on the deck of a yacht in nothing but a bikini and one of Luke's shirts, her hair in loose plaits, no make-up on, body and soul still tingling from the night before. 'I guess I'm responsible for it all.'

Luke laughed. 'You don't sound that happy about it.'

Madison couldn't help smiling back at him. Just as she couldn't help responding to his every move. After three days so physically attuned to him, she swore she could sense where he was with her eyes closed. 'I am happy; how could I not be? It's just I designed this whole week for you—for you and Isabella. It was all carefully thought out; you're both athletes, elite professional athletes, so that means competitive. Both your profiles said how much you enjoy adrenaline sports, especially scuba-diving and jet-skiing, and so I took that into consideration. Which means this is quite an activity-focused week. A week in paradise but heavy on the sports.'

'And you're not so heavy on the sport?'

'I like keeping fit, but I'm more of a gentle hike and yoga girl,' she admitted.

'So if this was the other way round, if you were the client, then what would have been the perfect week for you?'

Madison sat back and considered, sipping the delectable coffee as she did so. Her perfect week—a week where she would be at ease, get to know and be known? No one had ever asked her that before. Her wants had never been taken into account as a child, and once an adult she hadn't had the money for holidays for a long time, and then not the time. She had never really considered what kind of week she would choose if she only had to please herself.

'I don't know. Maybe a cabin high on an Alpine plain, near a frozen lake and surrounded by snow?'

'Skiing? Maybe you've got more in common with my missing date than you realised.'

Madison's heart squeezed at the teasing tone in Luke's voice as he hooked a chair round and sat next to her, reaching over to steal a piece of uneaten croissant from her plate.

She slapped his hand away. 'Oi, I thought you'd finished your breakfast.'

He smiled unrepentantly. 'There's always space for a second breakfast, Madison. You must know that.'

'Then help yourself to one of the untouched fresh pastries in that basket there…' She gestured towards the middle of the table and Luke caught her hand, sliding his fingers through hers.

'But yours tastes better. So, you're a ski bunny? I didn't see that coming.'

'Not in the slightest. I'm not really one for adrenaline sports,' she said. 'I just like the idea of the whole après-ski thing. You know, log fires and hot chocolate and winter wonderlands. But probably I'd really choose some kind of cultural break, some fine dining, art galleries and ruins. I love ruins. I think it's because I was brought up in LA, where everything is so new and shiny and a building is considered historic if it's older than ten years. That's partly what drew me to Europe—the age and the antiquities. The first time I went to Paris I was just blown away, all that history in one place. As for Rome…' Her voice trailed away, but she couldn't help laughing at the appalled look on Luke's face.

'Museums and ruins? May I just say, on behalf of myself and my absent date, I'm glad you didn't organise any of that for me.'

'Noted. No ruins.' But as she pretended to make a note she couldn't help but repress a sigh. The light-hearted conversation just went to show that, despite all the fun they were having and how easily they'd gelled with each other both physically and mentally, this was just a week's fling. They made good lovers but as partners they were completely unsuited. He got off on adrenaline-fuelled activities; she liked culture. But, even though the end was clearly in sight, Madison couldn't bring herself to regret the circumstances that had brought her here, not when her whole body was sated with lovemaking, her soul singing with the sunshine and the views—and honestly she hadn't minded the snorkelling that much in the end. She still drew the line at scuba-diving, however, and had no intention of getting onto the jet-ski, although she was tempted to do a little bit of gentle kayaking later.

'Okay.' Luke held up a piece of paper triumphantly. 'Today's itinerary. Today is…drumroll, please?'

Dutifully Madison rapped on the table.

'Today is a desert island day and night. Night? Excellent, I may not have been a Scout, but I know something about hiking and survival techniques. How about you? I guess film sets weren't big on building fires from driftwood and creating bivouacs?'

'I was castaway twice, though any bivouac was already built for me by the stage crew and the desert island was on a film lot. But I can look wistfully in the distance and say, "Is that a ship?" in different levels of hope and excitement if needed.'

'Very useful skills. Let me guess. In the first film you were an adorable urchin who got into trouble and had to be rescued? And in the second you were a teenager who got lost with a boy you couldn't stand but by the end you were madly in love?'

'You seem to have watched all my movies,' Madison said sweetly and with some satisfaction watched his cheeks tinge pink.

'My sister was a fan.'

'That's what they all say.'

'I'm definitely a fan now. So a castaway day? Excellent, sounds like a back-to-nature experience. Hope there's a penknife I can borrow.'

Madison finished her coffee, standing up and stretching, feeling Luke's gaze travel up her body as she did so. 'This is an M experience, so no bivouacking or building your own fires for warmth required. It's a private cove rather than a deserted island and all mod cons are provided to a luxurious degree. Personally, I can't wait to see it. When I planned this holiday, this day was the one I really liked the look of.'

'And now you get to experience it. No regrets?'

'Not a one,' she said, bending down to kiss him, almost unable to believe she had the right, the confidence to just casually touch him, kiss him. 'Right, this is an overnight expedition so I am off to pack. See you back here in fifteen?'

It didn't take Madison long to get ready and return to the deck. She and Luke could choose whether to sail themselves over to the small jetty or get dropped off at the beach. Either way, once there, they would be completely alone at the get-away-from-it-all resort which catered for one couple at a time exclusively. The resort was centred on a breathtakingly beautiful beach—of course, that was pretty much something to take for granted in this part of the world, ditto the beautiful safe swimming water—but the beach housed a luxurious cabin, built out over the sea, with its own pool and direct access into the sea from the deck. The retreat was supplied with everything they could possibly need for a twenty-four-hour private sojourn.

Madison had planned this particular excursion as a way of ensuring Isabella and Luke spent some real quality time together. The boat was big enough for them to spend time apart if they wished, with its many seating areas, their separate suites, the opportunity to do a variety of activities all day and into the evening. But on this particular day it would be just the two of them. She'd organised it for the fourth day of the holiday, which meant they had already had an opportunity to get to know each other and so the overnight trip shouldn't feel too much like forced intimacy. The cabin had two bedrooms and although they would be completely alone there was both a telephone and a panic button installed in case of any kind of emergency. She had also instructed the captain to miss out that part of the tour if either guest seemed uncomfortable with the other. Clearly, he hadn't thought that was a problem for her and Luke.

Humming to herself, she picked up a small bag she'd packed with a couple of bikinis, a beach towel, nightdress plus a dress and wrap for the evening and a few toiletries, and adjusted her sunhat and sunglasses. The humming turned into singing as she walked down to the bottom deck, where Luke was waiting for her. True to form, he had indignantly protested at the thought of being taken over to the island, more than happy to sail them there himself.

'Strewth, it's hardly any distance at all and the sea is as flat as a pancake,' he said indignantly when they were asked what they preferred. 'My entire family would disown me if I wasn't capable of taking a small dinghy that distance in these conditions.'

'Are you ready for an adventure?' he asked as he took her bag and then stopped. 'I've not heard you sing before. You should do it more; you have a beautiful voice.'

'Thank you.' Madison felt herself flush. She didn't sing much any more; it was too close to her acting days, making her conspicuous. But she had always enjoyed singing, enjoyed music and dancing. She'd even released a couple of singles at the height of her teen fame, although she wasn't particularly proud of either the tunes or the cheesy videos that had accompanied them.

In no time at all they were in paradise. The beach was everything she'd been promised, a perfect curve of golden sand, so fine it felt like velvet between her toes.

The beach hut itself was the ultimate in luxury, with its extensive outdoor seating area complete with sunken plunge pool and hot tub, gossamer white curtains enclosing an outdoor double sunbed. There were two bedrooms with en suite bathrooms, both looking out onto the sea and with private terraces, and the kitchen was stocked with every delicacy imaginable. As Madison explored the array of toiletries in the bathroom she heard Luke shout out happily from the kitchen, 'There's enough here to feed an army.'

'We'd better work up an appetite then,' Madison said as she joined him in the gleaming teak and steel room, noting the fancy coffee machine, the wine fridge and the array of pre-prepared meals.

'Good plan. Any ideas?' Luke's voice was suggestive as he wandered over to slip his hands around her waist and capture her mouth with his.

'Maybe a few,' she managed, but his gaze had been snagged by something behind her and, twisting, she saw a couple of spades.

'Are you thinking what I'm thinking?' he asked, and she raised her eyebrows in query.

'Enlighten me.'

'How about a sandcastle competition?'

Madison laughed. 'You're so competitive. Who would judge—and what's the prize?'

'We'll have to reach a consensus, and the winner...' His voice trailed off as he kissed her neck. 'Mmm, I love the way you smell in this particular spot. Like spring.'

Madison leaned back into the caress, tilting her head

to give him better access and closing her eyes as she did so. 'The winner?'

'The winner gets to pick dinner and the loser makes it?'

'I thought you might come up with something more imaginative,' she murmured and moaned as he kissed her again, his mouth moving up to the spot behind her ear that always made her knees weaken.

'In that case we'll both be winners.' And any retort she thought to make disappeared as his kiss intensified, his clever hands sliding up her waist to cup her breasts and her whole body liquified with need as she lost herself in the sensations only he provoked, falling onto the sofa, bodies entwined, returning his kisses, his caresses, touch for touch, moan for moan. Competitions could wait. They had all day and all night in this beautiful, secluded place. Why not start as they meant to go on?

Luke brandished his spade at Madison. 'Are you ready to be annihilated?'

Madison rocked back on her heels and stared at him. 'Have you ever had therapy for your competitive issues?'

'I'm an athlete.' He grinned at her. 'Winning is in my blood.' Luke paced around the area he'd chosen to start creating and began to mark out the design. 'Besides, you grew up by the beach; that must give you an advantage.'

'Ah, but we've already established I didn't actually get to enjoy the beach. I spent most of my time on set.

That's where I was educated as well as worked, and most trips to the beach were merely orchestrated photo opportunities. So consider me a beginner—whereas you have a small daughter so you must have some up-to-date sandcastle-building experience.'

'A little,' he admitted. 'She is very particular about what she wants. She designs and I labour. Usually she likes me to build her cars or boats; I don't get much opportunity to design my own. I'm looking forward to this.'

'Just don't take that win for granted.' Madison was bent over, her expression one of extreme concentration. She'd twisted her hair up into a knot and pulled a pair of shorts over her blue bikini, her face make-up-free, slightly shiny with suntan lotion. She looked wild and free and utterly beautiful. It was all Luke could do not to tumble her into the sand and kiss her. Later, he promised himself. Victor's spoils. 'I may not have experience but I have ambition. I may just win this yet.'

They worked in companionable silence for a bit, broken only by Madison first humming and then beginning to sing again in a low, husky voice which wound its way around Luke's senses. He didn't know the tune but he could have listened to her sing all day.

'Do you belong to a choir or do you prefer to rule the karaoke machine?' he asked when she stopped and Madison looked up at him in some surprise. Her hands were covered in sand and she had a smudge on her nose. Luke leaned over and wiped it off, his finger lingering to trace a line down her cheek. 'That voice is too lovely to hide away.'

'Thank you.' She leaned into his caress briefly before resuming digging. 'I do love singing. But I'm strictly a kitchen and radio singer, no karaoke for me.'

'Then what do you do to kick back? So far I know that you enjoy the odd pint…'

'Very occasionally! I don't make a habit of propping up the bar.'

'That you sing in the kitchen and drink tea. What else goes on in the life of Madison Morgan?' Luke really wanted to know, he realised. To be able to picture her life in London, imagine her day, her week.

Her gaze dropped and she began digging again. 'Well, my business keeps me very busy. I have clients all over the world, in every time zone, so it's not a nine-to-five thing.'

'I get that; I'm often checking emails last thing or over my breakfast too. But when you're not working? Obviously I have Isla and her ludicrous social life. Six-year-olds seem to have a party every weekend and an activity schedule more complicated than training to be an astronaut. But around that I still play tennis a couple of times a week, coach, sit on the board of my foundation, surf, hang out with my sister and her family and most weekends on a Saturday afternoon Isla and I head up to the beach house for the rest of the weekend.'

'I bought a house in Hampstead ten years ago and converted the ground floor into the office and the top two floors into a maisonette so it's hard to get away from work, even if I wanted to. I like to walk on Hampstead Heath and I've thought about getting a dog but I don't know if it's fair; a cat might make more sense.'

She shrugged a little helplessly. 'I'm a workaholic, I suppose. I didn't do hobbies as a kid. If I had riding lessons it was for a part; singing and dancing were just to enhance my career. I do a weekly yoga class, but that's it. I'm not sure I really know how to relax.'

'Then you need to learn. What have you always wanted to do but never had the chance?' Luke tried to remember his sister's myriad hobbies; she always had a project on the go. 'Crocheting? Watercolour painting? Gin distilling? Rowing?'

'Actually,' Madison said a little shyly, 'I did always want to learn to play tennis. It's the only sport I follow.'

'Why haven't you?'

'I guess I thought it was the kind of thing you should learn young.'

'That helps, but you're never too old. I'll give you some lessons if you promise to sing for me—deal?'

'I'd like that.' She looked up and smiled, and Luke wished that he could make his careless promise a reality. But it was hard to coach someone with at least two oceans between you.

And he'd really like to hear her sing again. Properly, into a microphone with a band behind her. It seemed a shame to hide that voice in the kitchen. It would be like him only playing tennis against his parents' garage door. A denial of all he had been.

For her, maybe that was the point.

'It seems insane to me, when you talk about your childhood,' he said after a while. 'I just can't imagine it. Working all the time. Not having hobbies or going to school. I suspect that if I asked Isla if she wanted to be a child star she'd jump at it, but she'd be desperate to get back to her friends and classroom after a couple of months. You must have been an incredibly focused kid.'

Madison got up and stretched, staring at her work critically. She'd gone for a walled city with a castle in the middle, decorated with a mix of the myriad shells on the beach. Shells, she'd assured him, she would replace where she'd found them because this beach was too perfect to spoil in any way, their sand creations destined to disappear with the tide. 'It's all I knew—how can you miss what you have never experienced? Besides, you must have been a pretty focused kid too. You were playing on the adult tour by sixteen; that kind of success doesn't happen after just a few lessons.'

'True,' he confessed. 'My life was pretty tennis heavy in my teens. But I stayed in school until sixteen. And before I hit my teens I was an all-rounder: football, cricket, surfing; if it was competitive and outdoors and active, I did it.'

'What changed? What made you decide on tennis?'

'A new coach started at my club and he told me that I was in with a chance of being something pretty special, but I'd have to specialise. It took me a while to figure out if I really did want to do it but, once I decided I did, I was all in.' He sat back and looked at his own efforts. He'd gone for one huge structure, all sharp lines and closely packed sand, like some Gothic castle from a fantasy film. 'My poor mum and dad. It was hard to see it back then, but I've since realised how many sacrifices they made for me. Not that I gave them much choice. I was extremely bull-headed and determined.

I'll never be able to pay them back for their unwavering support. But, although it got me where I needed to be, I wouldn't want that kind of life for Isla and, although I'm sure being a child star was very glamorous, my fervent hope is that Isla just wants to go to school like a normal kid.' He grimaced. 'Of course it would serve me right if she decided to go all in for something. She is my kid, after all.'

Madison cast a knowing look at his sandcastle, as he carefully shaved another sliver off it to make sure the sides were symmetrical. 'Have you always been so competitive?'

Luke flopped back and looked up at the sun, shading his eyes from its fierce glare. 'My mum and dad would say I was competitive from the day I was born,' he confessed. 'There's just two years between me and my sister, and there was nothing she did that I didn't want to be better at. I was a right little brat, just ask her.' He chuckled, remembering his childish attempts to keep up with the sister who seemed to succeed at everything so effortlessly. 'She was the one who started with tennis, and she was pretty good, competing in tournaments and winning a fair few as well. Of course that meant that I wanted to play too, and if she was going to win then of course I was going to win.' He shook his head. 'I'm lucky she didn't drown me when I was a toddler.'

'She doesn't play now?'

'No, she stopped when she was in her teens. Decided she wanted a more normal existence. She studied hard, got into a good university, got a good degree and now heads up a department at a charity where she is always winning awards whilst raising three sons. She is as competitive as me in many ways, but she also likes balance in her life. That's something I struggled with; in some ways I still do, I suppose. That's why it's been good for me to get away for a week.'

Madison took another walk around her carefully constructed city walls. The houses were simple mounds, each topped with a shell roof, not as architecturally ambitious as Luke's but it looked striking viewed as a whole. 'What did she and your parents think when the incident happened? At Wimbledon?'

Luke squeezed his eyes closed for a moment. His almost career-ending meltdown wasn't something he ever really talked about, although it was mentioned in every profile, asked about in every interview, those ubiquitous photos of him throwing his racquet and swearing at the umpire before forfeiting the game by storming off court reproduced, no matter the article's actual content. 'They were really disappointed in me,' he confessed. 'They always said it was great to be competitive, to want to win, but that to have grace and humility was just as important. That if I couldn't control myself then maybe I needed to rethink my choices, my career.'

'And you did. For a while.'

He nodded. 'I told myself they were right, that I was going to walk away from tennis, that I hated it and who I was when I played it, that I was never going to humiliate myself like that again. I came back to Sydney, went back to school, swallowed my pride, which was pretty damn painful let me tell you, because, as you can imagine, people were very interested in what I was doing. Every newspaper had called me a national disgrace, the epitome of what was wrong with every kid in the country; every comedian in the country had a joke about me in their routine at some point. But I kept my head down, got myself a place at uni as well. Then, after about six months, I was at home and picked up a racquet, just hitting balls against the wall, and realised how much I loved it. A couple of weeks later I called my coach.

'He said he'd been waiting to hear from me. That wanting to win was no bad thing, it was necessary if I wanted a career, but I needed to channel that urge properly—then, he said, I might be unstoppable. So that's what I did. I went back to basics, learned meditation, to focus, to take all that aggression and competitiveness and to push it into my play, not into my temper. It wasn't easy; it still isn't. I still have to work every day to think before I act. At times I felt like I'd never get back on tour, but I was determined not to return until I knew that I was match ready physically *and* mentally.'

'And it worked. Three grand slam titles, isn't it?'

'You *were* quite the fan back then,' Luke teased, laughing at her blushing indignation.

'Don't take it personally. I told you, tennis is the one sport I watch.'

'Wouldn't it be funny if we'd met back then. You should have got your people to call mine. We could have gone out for dinner.'

But Madison shook her head, enticing tendrils of

dark curls tickling her neck as she did so. 'You wouldn't have looked at me twice. My image was all wholesome teen queen; I was far too clean-cut for you. And far too boring; all I did was work. Still do, I suppose.' For a moment she looked so forlorn that all Luke wanted to do was comfort her. He reached out to grab her hand, pulling her down beside him.

'Yes, far too hardworking. Just look at how dedicated you are to your job. You look after your clients so well, offering a personal service, travelling across the globe to make sure we're happy.'

She twisted to face him, cupping his face with her other hand. 'I aim to please.'

'And you succeed...' he murmured against her mouth, rolling her on top of him.

'Careful, you'll ruin your sandcastle,' she warned him and he rolled her again, this time imprisoning her beneath him.

'I don't care. Maybe some things are more important than winning after all,' he told her before capturing her lush mouth with his, feeling the way her whole body responded, welcomed him, opened up for him.

Just as he had opened up to her, been more honest about his past than he had been with anyone outside his family. She understood, this girl who had had no childhood, who had grown up in an artificial world. She got him. And although there was a lot about Madison that she kept locked away, a lot she only revealed in small snippets, in throwaway comments, he thought that maybe he got her too.

Luke had vowed never to risk his future on a fling

again. He'd come here looking for the perfect match, not to fall in love.

But this didn't feel like a fling. Nor was Madison his perfect match. They liked different things, lived on opposite sides of the globe and she hadn't mentioned wanting a family once.

But if she wasn't a fling, nor his sensible perfect match, then what was happening here?

Luke wasn't sure but as their kiss intensified he knew that right now he couldn't walk away if he tried. He was beginning to fall, heading out of the shallows into the depths. He just didn't know if Madison was there with him or if he was swimming alone—or what, if anything, came next. But he did know that a week wasn't enough. He needed more, wanted more.

He just had to figure out how.

# CHAPTER EIGHT

It HAD BEEN a week of unforgettable experiences, from learning to snorkel and paddleboard across the coral reef filled with colourful fish, to kayaking out with Luke across to their own tiny isle where they picnicked and made love in the sand. From visiting tiny picture-perfect resorts, where just a handful of tourists enjoyed the beach bar by the sapphire-blue rock lagoon, to watching turtles on a powder-soft beach.

And now today, their last real day, they were at the beautiful Tucan Bay, the whole curved cove like a huge, private reef-filled swimming pool just for them. After a morning's swim in the clear blue water they'd enjoyed a long lunch and siesta, and now Luke was back out, snorkelling the reefs. The man never stopped—in more ways than one.

But dinner tonight would be eaten whilst at sea, and by this time tomorrow they'd be docking in Singapore before going their separate ways. Madison had sent an email to the office on the third day at sea, letting her assistant know she was well and safe and asking for her hotel reservations and flight home to be rebooked. She'd spend tomorrow night alone in a hotel and then she'd fly back to London to pick up her normal life, this week nothing but a dream-like interlude.

*Normal life.* Madison tried not to sigh as reality slowly seeped into her brain. Back to London, to the pretty house in Hampstead where she lived and worked, a house she'd bought three years after founding M, with the money she had made herself.

She'd made the money her parents had squandered too; the difference was that this time she'd chosen her path and her success was hers alone.

But that fact didn't give her the reassurance it usually did, not even when she let her mind wander through the tastefully decorated rooms of her upstairs maisonette, walls painted in expensive neutral shades named Cold Grave and Winter's Creep, down the curved stairs to the spacious ground floor offices, suitable for greeting any clients who preferred to come to her. For once the first thought in her mind when she thought of London wasn't security. It was loneliness.

Maybe it was time she got that dog she kept promising herself. She'd been in London for over a decade; she wasn't going to move home any time soon.

Wherever home might be.

Enough of this self-pity, she scolded herself. She was in a beautiful place watching a beautiful man glide through the water like some kind of Greek sea god, knowing that tonight he'd make love to her in a suitably god-like way. Of course a week like this couldn't last for ever. It wasn't designed to. She'd conceived these weeks to be a way of getting to know each other intimately and in one way that had happened—she was certainly intimately acquainted with every centimetre of Luke's toned, tanned torso. But she'd also intended these weeks not to be about sex but instead to be a meeting of minds, a chance to talk, really talk, to let each other in.

And that had happened too, more than she had realised, more than she had intended. Now she realised how dangerous it was to open the very heart and soul of you to another person, to risk them seeing all that you were and for that to not be enough. In some ways Madison knew she was a fighter, but where love was concerned she was a coward.

She had good reason. After all, there was only so much rejection a person could take. And Madison was lucky; she knew exactly who she was. She was a useful person. That was why matchmaking worked so well. Done right, it was a one-time service. Her clients left glowing and filled with gratitude. And she, idiot that she was, basked in that gratitude, in the reflected warmth of their newfound love.

Knowing it was the closest thing she'd ever get to love herself.

'Hey you. That's a serious face.'

Madison jumped; she hadn't seen Luke board the boat. She forced a smile onto her face. She liked the Madison she was with him, game for an adventure, quick to laugh, confident to tease and be teased. She knew that in some ways she was playing a part—but in others she was the Madison she'd always hoped to be deep down, the Madison she might have been in a different life.

'I was just thinking that this is the last real day we've got. It's gone so fast.'

'Then we better make it count.'

Madison leaned back in her deckchair and looked at him, wet hair slicked back, water still drying on his broad chest, damp trunks clinging lovingly to every muscle, and raised an eyebrow. 'Oh? Any ideas how we might do that?'

Was this really her, this temptress with the bold look and parted mouth, running her gaze provocatively over his long, lean body, lingering on his pecs, on the hair that snaked down his flat stomach to the bulge in his trunks? How could her body fire up so quickly, so willingly, still not sated despite long, heat filled nights and sweet lazy siestas?

'A few...' His own gaze explored her as she lay supine in the deckchair, and she could almost feel him lingering on the curve of her breasts, the little strings holding her bikini together and every pulse beat in painfully sweet unison. She shifted subtly, an invitation, but although his mouth curved in appreciation he didn't saunter over, take her by the hand and pull her from her seat to lead her into the cabin. Instead, Luke leant back against the railings of the boat, his eyes narrowed in concentration as he dragged his gaze back to meet hers. 'You're not looking forward to going home?'

Madison attempted a quick laugh. 'London has its charm, but it's a little bit lacking in the sand and sea situation.' She waved an arm, including the island and horizon in the all-encompassing gesture to illustrate her point. 'I love my job, and I'm looking forward to seeing how my couples have been getting on in my absence, but I'm also going to miss these lazy mornings and lazy afternoons and this view. I mean, I guess all this hedonism might pall after a time, but I'm not quite at that stage yet.' She shaded her eyes with her hand as she squinted up at him. 'But of course it's different for you. You must be longing to get back, to see your daughter.'

Because *of course* it was different for Luke. He had a life, people he loved and who loved him. This trip was a pleasant interlude for them both, but somehow, over the last few days, it felt more important to Madison than just a pleasant time out from normal life. Spending this week with Luke had made her realise all the things that she was missing out on: laughter, relaxation, company, good, no—fantastic—sex. She couldn't deny how much fun *that* particular part of the week had been. But mostly spending time with someone who seemed to care about her, about how she felt, what she thought, what she wanted. It had been intoxicating.

She hadn't allowed herself to realise just how lonely she was before, living vicariously through other people's happy ever afters.

Luke was still leaning against the railing, framed by the sun as it began to make its way to the horizon, every lowered centimetre a reminder that they were nearly out of time. 'Of course I can't wait to see Isla. But this week's made me realise something important and I have you to thank for that. I've put all my focus, all my energy into Isla and the business until there is nothing left for me. I thought that was the right balance, but I feel so refreshed from this time out, ready and raring to go again, to be the best dad, the best CEO I can be. This week has been a reminder that it's okay for me to take a break sometimes. He laughed then. 'Okay, this wasn't maybe the break I was expecting to have—'

'I'm still so sorry about that,' Madison broke in, mortified. She'd been so busy mourning the ending of the trip, she'd allowed herself to forget the beginning, that she should never have been here at all. 'I promise that when I get back to the office, finding you the absolutely perfect partner will be my number one priority.' Her heart squeezed painfully at the thought of finding someone for Luke to spend his whole life with, some lucky woman who would get to wake up nestled in to him every single morning, who would get to learn every inch of his torso, to discover the way he liked to touch, be touched, to kiss and be kissed. How long before she discovered that tender spot behind his ear or realised that he was only ticklish in his left rib?

She couldn't do it.

But she had to.

This was her job; she was a professional. Her own personal feelings didn't come into this situation at all. She had borrowed Luke and now it was time to return him to the dating pool where he belonged.

'You can rely on me,' she said, grateful for every single one of her acting lessons as she managed to smile, hopefully not just with her mouth, but with her eyes as well. 'I've done my research well.'

Luke didn't smile back, his body tense, jaw set. 'You're still going to try and set me up with someone?'

'Why, have you changed your mind?' Relief warred with professional pride. Occasionally clients did walk away before she'd matched them; sometimes, like Isabella, they found love on their own, more occasionally they decided that matchmaking just wasn't for them. But her hit rate was good, better than good. 'Look, I know this week hasn't worked out the way you hoped, but I promise...'

Luke shook his head disbelievingly, eyes cold. 'After everything we've shared, you're just prepared to look through your files and send me off to my happy ever after? You don't mind at all?'

Madison could only stare at him open-mouthed. 'But that's what we agreed.' *Wasn't it?* 'We decided to take advantage of the situation we found ourselves in. But only for a few days. No regrets.'

'But that was then.' He stopped, raking one hand through his hair, other hand clenched tight. 'You just want to forget that this week ever happened?'

'Oh, no. Of course not.' She would never forget it—how could she forget the best week of her life? But she couldn't tell Luke that; it would reveal far too much. How could she tell him that the last few days were the one bright spot in what had been days and weeks and months and years? She couldn't, wouldn't sound so pathetic. 'But you came to me because you want to find a wife, not a vacation buddy. That hasn't changed, has it?'

Luke strode across the deck and back again. 'Dammit, Madison. I don't know. Sure, I came here expecting one thing but then we happened, this happened.

Now you want me to just…what, forget about it and send me off on some dates? What, you want to be best woman at the wedding as well?'

'I don't understand. We agreed…'

Luke let out an exasperated sound, rounding on her, eyes no longer cold but filled with fire. 'Damn, I'm a fool. I thought we'd shared something pretty special this week, Madison. That it might be going somewhere. And I thought you might feel the same way. What an idiot I've been.'

Madison could only stare up at him, her heart hammering in her chest, shaking with adrenaline. 'You thought we were going somewhere?'

'I mean, that's what these weeks away are meant to achieve, aren't they?' Luke huffed out a sharp, bitter laugh. 'A fast track to a relationship. But only for paying clients, I guess.'

Madison stilled, her heart still beating faster than she thought it might have ever beaten before, hope and desolation warring in her soul. Because of course it wasn't her that Luke wanted. Not the real Madison. Not the conscientious, hesitant, lonely girl. Not the Madison whose only use to her parents had been as a cash machine, cast aside the second her earning power finished. Luke didn't want, didn't know that Madison. He wanted the woman she'd been pretending to be all this time, the easy-going, laughing, sensuous character she'd been playing. He wanted the part, not the actress. She couldn't blame him, because she wanted to be that Madison too.

But she wasn't. And, sooner rather than later, Luke

would find that out. Better he walk away now. Better this time stay an idyllic week out of time than allow herself to hope for more. Because when she flew home alone her heart would be bruised, she knew that, but if she gave him more time and he rejected her...? Then she would break. Again. Last time she had pulled herself and her life back together. She wasn't sure she could do it again.

She couldn't, wouldn't risk it.

'I'm sorry, Luke, but you've got it wrong. I'm not looking for anything serious; I thought I made it clear. I'm not the right match for you.'

Madison sat there utterly still, her face unreadable. Luke stopped pacing, taking a long deep breath, willing the passion and fire to subside, using the emotion positively to home in on the situation, to analyse and act not react, just as he had learned all those years ago. How had he got this situation so wrong? Everything about the last few days had indicated that Madison seemed pretty into him, just as with every second he'd found himself getting more into her. But they weren't falling for each other. It was just a holiday romance—temporary, just as his time with Alyssa had been. No more, no less.

At least this time there was no baby to be abandoned on his doorstep. If he became a father again, this time he wanted any child of his to have a mother to raise them with him. A mother who would gladly welcome Isla into her heart as well.

Did he see Madison in that role? There were moments when he felt the rightness between them so acutely it was a physical sensation. It was as much about the things they *didn't* do as much as the things they did. It was the easy silences, the way they could just relax, completely at ease with each other. It was the trust that had sprung up so completely between them. Trusting with their bodies, Madison trusting him with her fears and her safety as she'd allowed him to guide her through the coral reefs. He'd thought that maybe they were somewhere on their way to trusting each other with their hearts too.

But he'd forgotten the most important truth of all: they'd come here with completely different agendas. He'd embarked on this week ready to find somebody who might be the right partner for him and Isla. Madison had come here to deliver some bad news. It was a very different situation—and he'd misread it, misread her. He needed to put things right. Get their last evening back on track, in line with their agreement.

But before he could speak Madison looked up at him. 'You were very clear; you needed somebody who was prepared to move to Sydney. I live in London.'

Was that the issue? Because if location was all that stood between them then it could be worked out. Eventually he'd want any future partner to be in the same country, the same city, but they could work their way there slowly.

Besides, it wasn't as if Madison had family in London; she worked for herself. Surely her business could be run from anywhere?

Luke strode over to the deckchair next to hers and

sat down, taking her hand between his. It fitted so easily into his, as if it were made for him to hold. 'I know, but you've already lived on two continents. Would spending some time on a third be so bad?'

'And you want a mother for Isla. That's the whole, the only reason you're here?' Her expression was so inscrutable he couldn't read her at all. Was that what made her hold back? She didn't want to share her partner, to be a stepmother? In that case not only had he got Madison completely wrong, but she clearly wasn't the woman for him.

'That's why I came here,' he agreed. 'I have never hidden that, especially not from you. Is that a problem for you? You don't want kids?'

Or worse, she did but only her own.

She half shrugged. 'I've never thought about it.'

Luke raised a disbelieving eyebrow. Surely everybody thought about whether or not they wanted kids at some point, even if it was just a fleeting moment to decide they didn't? 'You've never thought about it?' He must have let his disbelief seep into his voice because she flinched.

'Only for long enough to confirm that not only do I not want kids but it's better for me to keep thinking that way. One thing I know is that this particular gene pool should die with me. Besides, I know nothing about parenting, how to be a good parent. It's too important a job to get wrong. No kid should be a guinea pig; the consequences are too high. I am better off alone, believe me.'

Luke could only stare at Madison in shock as she

pulled her hand from his, getting to her feet in agitation. Her eyes were hard, glittering either with rage
or tears or maybe both, her mouth set, red spots high-
lighting her cheekbones. She was ice and fire, stone
and storm-tossed sea, no longer the warm, amusing
companion of the last few days. He didn't know this
woman at all. Maybe she was right; she wasn't for him.
Maybe he'd been falling in love with a woman who
didn't even exist.

'What do you mean?'

Madison didn't answer for a long, long time, standing stock-still, emotion radiating from her like a venge-
ful goddess. And then it all seemed to bleed away as
she stared down at her hands, her shoulders slumped,
as if she was bearing the weight of the world on her
back until, with a deep breath that seemed to come
from the very soul of her, she straightened and looked
over at him.

'I've never told what I am going to tell you to a single soul,' she said quietly. 'I need you to promise never
to repeat it. Ever. If the tabloids ever found out, I…'
Her voice faded away and she gulped. 'I couldn't live
with everyone knowing.'

'I promise.' Luke deliberately kept his voice low and
calm, sensing that one wrong movement would stop
her speaking, ensure she wrapped her secrets around
her like an invisibility cloak, possibly never to trust
anyone again. Standing up, he walked over to her, taking her hand again in a reassuring grip. 'I promise,'
he repeated.

He walked with her, her hand still in his as she

moved over to the rail, standing beside her as she leaned against it, turning her face up to the low, heavy sun.

'My parents met in Hollywood,' she said at last, her voice small. 'They were both working at a swanky restaurant, waiting tables by night, auditioning by day and hoping for their big break. My mom was only nineteen, my dad just twenty-one.'

Luke didn't answer, not wanting to break the delicate thread of her speech.

'They were the classic Hollywood wannabes. They'd been celebrities in their own small towns, the homecoming and prom kings and queens, the ones everyone wanted to know, to be, to date. They headed to LA expecting to be instantly snapped up, to be stars, to become rich and famous, only to find themselves working in a restaurant.' Her voice was expressionless, and she relayed the story as if it was about somebody else. Somebody she barely knew.

'Very common, I guess,' Luke said, as conversationally as he could.

Madison nodded. 'It's the classic Hollywood story. It works out for the rare few; most either take different paths or go home a little older, a lot wiser. But then Mom got pregnant and that was definitely not in the script. Fast forward two years and they're still living in a one-room apartment, my dad still waiting tables in the restaurant, Mom at home with me, just twenty-one, still eager for the break she felt was her due. From the start I was a problem, a barrier to them living the lives they thought they deserved.'

She looked down at their conjoined hands and Luke

gave her a reassuring squeeze. After a moment she returned the pressure, faint but there. 'Then one day Mom had an audition and couldn't get anyone to watch me, so took me along. She didn't get the job but the casting director commented on how photogenic I was and asked if I had an agent, had Mom considered child modelling. I had an agent twenty-four hours later, my first role a week later and that month my wages paid the rent.'

'So they got you another job?'

'And another and another. And as the jobs came in and the money came in I guess they changed their focus. Growing up, they told interviewers that they put their ambitions aside to support me, but that wasn't true. They put all of their ambitions *into* me and this time it paid off. By the time I was five I was earning enough to keep us in some style in Malibu. Fast forward ten years and they had everything they had always wanted: the cars, the drivers, the big house, the designer wardrobes, the fancy vacations. People knew who they were; they got invited to the industry parties, were feted and networked with. Just as long as I kept starring in hits, they lived their dream life. And the money kept on coming; I put my name and image to clothing lines and make-up ranges, to dolls and any kind of merchandise you could imagine. There were Madison Morgan surfboards and a furniture range, notebooks and pens, CD players. All in that shade of pink they dressed me in.'

'That lifestyle was supported by you? They didn't work?'

'They managed me and drew a salary; that's what

they told me and it seemed fair enough. They told me they'd given up their dreams for me so how could I begrudge them a percentage of my earnings and a generous salary? How could I begrudge our living costs when I needed to be housed somewhere appropriate? Begrudge the drivers and the vacations they took without me? After all they had devoted their lives to me.' The scorn and heartbreak in her voice nearly undid him.

This wasn't the end of the story, not by a long way. 'What happened?'

'At eighteen I'd had enough. I didn't want to wear pink and pretend to date guys to get my films publicity, to be leered over on chat shows and fashion shamed in the press any more. I wanted to be normal, whatever that looked like. But when I said I wanted to go to college, my parents said it was impossible, my money was tied up in a trust fund until I was twenty-one and they couldn't afford for me to stop working. They had sacrificed everything for me and I was just going to cut them loose? You have no idea how they could lay on the guilt, make me question my decisions. So I carried on for a bit, hating every role, every camera until I turned twenty-one. I went to see my accountant to see how much there was in my trust fund so I could quit, go to college. I meant to sign the house over to them, set up an annuity as a thank you. But that's when I found out…'

'What did you find out?' But Luke already knew. The ending to this particular Hollywood tale had been clear from the beginning.

'There was nothing left. They'd spent it all, or hidden it. I've never been entirely sure which. It was...it was devastating. But I got myself to college on a scholarship, worked in a bookshop for living costs and had to listen to people sniping about how I was taking a job and a scholarship that should have gone to somebody who really needed it. As soon as I graduated I fled to Europe. I just needed to get away.'

'So what is your relationship like with them now? Where are they?'

Madison looked up at him then, and this time the shine in her eyes was clearly from unshed tears. 'I don't know.'

'You've cut them off. Understandable.' She should have sent them to jail, dragged their names through the courts. But Luke understood why she hadn't. Shame. He'd felt its bitter taste when he was eighteen, when he'd humiliated himself not by losing a match but by his reaction. Even now, when he saw it referenced, the shame hit him anew. Maybe it always would, no matter the titles he'd won, the success of his business. He could see why Madison didn't want this humiliation following her, even though she was an innocent in her downfall.

But she shook her head vehemently. 'No—no, you don't understand. I was upset, of course I was, confused. But I would have given them anything, everything. All I wanted was their love, their time, their attention. For them to be proud of me. But as soon as they realised I knew what had happened they cut me off.'

'They *what*?' Had he misheard?

'I got home about a week later and they had gone. I don't know where they are now, but that's why I still do some interviews, why I want people to know that this former child star is successful in her chosen field. To know that my business is exclusive and expensive and elite. Because one day they might pick up a magazine and see me there. They might send me an email, they might want to see me. I don't need them to apologise. I just want them to say that they are proud of me. To love me...' Her voice faded to a whisper. 'But it's been over a decade, Luke. Over a decade and I haven't heard from them once.'

Rage flooded him, hot and heavy, and this time he allowed it, resolving to track them down and drag them back to kneel in front of Madison and beg her forgiveness.

'What kind of parents can do that to their child?'

'Maybe they didn't have a choice. I'm difficult to love; that's what they said and it must be true. My mom said any other mother in her situation would have given me up and I was lucky she kept me. I did my best to make it up to her, to show her that she made the right choice, but I was never enough.'

'None of that is on you, Madison. You were a child. A baby.'

But she wasn't listening, turning away, lost to him. 'I'm an actress, Luke, I was trained to be who people want me to be. But when I'm not acting there's nothing there. If there was then they would have stayed, wanted me for me, not for my money. I'm nothing. And you're better off without me.'

'You're not nothing. I've seen your films, Madison, you're a good actress but you're not that good. You haven't faked this week. You haven't faked how you are when we're together, the woman who doesn't back down from a challenge, the woman who is quick to laugh, the woman who comes apart in my arms and makes me fall apart with a touch. Come to Sydney with me, Madison.'

Where had *that* come from? But as the words left his mouth Luke knew that he meant them, that he wanted Madison to come back to Australia, to meet his family, to try his life out for size. It had only been a week but they worked.

Madison turned to look up at him, her eyes filled with tears, a tremulous smile on her mouth as she reached up to kiss his cheek, a long lingering caress that felt like a farewell. 'I can't,' she said. 'Isla... I'm not the right person to be a mother for her, a partner for you. And you said yourself, you don't want a string of women in her life. It wouldn't be fair, not to her and not to me.'

Luke used all the focus and calm he had spent such long difficult years as a teenager learning, gathering his thoughts, channelling his emotions. If he didn't get this right it would be game over and this time he doubted he would get a second chance.

'You're right,' he said after a while. 'Isla does come first and, no, I don't want her to get too attached to anyone, only for them to leave. But you could visit as a friend, stay at my beach house, get to know her casually.' He smiled down at her. 'I was never planning to come back and present her with a stepmother even if I'd fallen head over heels for the Italian skier.'

Her answering smile was tremulous but its presence felt like a victory. 'I guess not.'

'You could work from Sydney. You've said a couple of times you'd like more clients in Australia. Here's your chance to scope out the competition and set up meetings with potential clients. And we hang out. Casually.'

Madison bit her lip, clearly still unsure. 'If I go home now then this was perfect, you were perfect. But if I come to Sydney, when it doesn't work out…'

'When? Jeez, your parents really did a number on you, didn't they? There are no guarantees, Madison, you know that; even you only have an eighty per cent success rate. We could have something good here, but we won't know unless we try. You, Madison Morgan, are no quitter. So don't quit now.'

She didn't answer and he tried again, his voice low and coaxing. 'If you walk away from a chance of happiness then your parents win. Don't let them win. You didn't let them when you got that scholarship, when you started your own business, so don't let them this time either. What do you say? I did promise you some tennis lessons after all, and it's hard to correct a serve online.'

Again Madison didn't respond, although he could see a myriad emotions pass across her face: fear, hope, worry until at last she let out a sigh, the breath whooshing out of her and with it the tension, her whole body relaxing. 'I suppose I have been intending to promote M more in Sydney and Melbourne, look up some old contacts and spread the word.'

'This is the perfect opportunity. You're just a short plane ride away after all.'

'And we keep things casual. Friendly.'

'Absolutely.'

'And…' her eyes were huge as she looked at him '…you'll let me down gently.'

'If you promise to do the same.'

'Then okay.'

'Okay?'

She nodded. 'A couple of weeks.'

'And we'll see how it goes.' Carefully, almost tentatively, Luke drew Madison to him and, when she didn't demur, kissed her, at first slowly and then with more heat. She responded as if she hadn't just agreed to come back with him, as if this was goodbye, as if she were learning him by heart.

As the kiss intensified Luke couldn't help wondering what exactly it was about Madison Morgan that had made him throw caution to the wind despite his vows. No flings he had said, only the perfect mother for Isla, and here he was, bringing home a woman who had not just tempted him into a week-long affair but who was scared of motherhood, of commitment.

He didn't know why he wanted to keep Madison close or where they would end up, but he had at least two more weeks to find out. He just hoped they had some answers by the end of it, for both their sakes.

# CHAPTER NINE

'OH, MY GOODNESS,' Madison breathed as the car sped across a narrow peninsula, ocean flashing blue on either side before the road wound between two wooded hills, each boasting a selection of spectacular-looking apartments and houses.

'Welcome to Palmy,' Luke said. 'Palm Beach. Sydney's playground—well, one of them, some would say the most exclusive of them all.'

'I can believe it.' Madison looked over at a gated mansion and then across to a glass building housing some very luxurious-looking apartments. 'I bet these don't come cheap.'

'No, but Palm Beach isn't all glitz and glamour. There is a plane back to Sydney for those in a rush, but you can also catch a bus, there's plenty of small boats in the yacht club alongside the fancier ones, and the waves and hiking are both free for everyone. But there's plenty of money here too.'

'The perfect place to find clients,' Madison said although she was finding it hard to keep her mind on work. She still couldn't believe she was here, being driven in Luke's convertible to stay in his weekend oceanside home. She'd been to Sydney a couple of times before on press junkets, to pose at the Opera House and on the bridge, to cuddle a koala and do interviews, but she'd never actually explored the city before. Not that she was staying in the city as Luke's beach house was around forty-five miles outside of the city and, she was beginning to realise, if the real estate they were driving past was anything to go by, definitely more mansion than casual beach house.

'Okay, we're here.' Luke turned into a gate and drove straight into an underground garage. There was a smaller car already there and he nodded at it as he killed the engine. 'That's yours to use while you're here. There's a bike too. You will be okay, won't you? I invited you to stay and now I'm abandoning you.'

'I'll try and cope.' But in some ways Madison was glad of the enforced time alone. She could have stayed in a hotel of course, seen Luke every day, kickstarted her relationship with Isla, but the distance gave her time to think, to breathe. To build up her protection against the inevitable heartache.

Inevitable because being whisked off your feet by a heart-throb tennis champion billionaire real-life fantasy didn't happen to people like Madison, not even in her dreams. She needed to enjoy it while it lasted and keep her heart safe. Somehow. Her very presence here showed how much she had succumbed to Luke's charm already. No, it was more than that—she'd succumbed to his kindness. It wasn't the first word most people thought of when they thought of Luke Taylor: competitive, passionate, successful maybe, not kind.

But Madison had seen that side of him and it had undone her. Kindness was very underrated in a man, but
for Madison it was the most seductive quality of all.

'I'll be fine,' she said again, more for herself than
for him.

They'd arrived back in Sydney early Saturday afternoon and she knew Luke was desperate to get back to
the city and pick up Isla, who he hadn't seen for over
a week. But first he insisted on showing her around
what was indeed more of a luxurious beachside mansion than a simple holiday home with its four bedrooms
with en suite bathrooms, huge family room and more
formal living space, outdoor plunge pool with hot tub
and the inevitable tennis court.

'That's where I'll give you your first lesson,' he said
with a wicked grin and Madison's heart tumbled in
spite of herself. Private lessons with Luke Taylor was
every single one of her teenage fantasies come true.

'I'd better get in some practice while you're gone,'
she said, eyeing the court with a mixture of excitement and trepidation. There was a practice wall at one
end and she vowed to spend at least half an hour a day
there so that she didn't look like a complete novice if
and when the promised lesson happened.

Finally he led her to a key coded door in the back
wall that led straight onto the beach. He ushered Madison through and she stopped still, taking in the view
and cosmopolitan yet laid-back vibe. The beach was
different to the cosy, idyllic Indonesian coves and bays
they'd enjoyed over the last week. It was busy for one
thing. Houses backed onto it; she could see a beach

bar not far away, serving coffees to an eager queue of surfers and sun-worshippers, and there were groups of people as far as the eye could see, surfing or just hanging out. The air was warm although Sydney was just heading into spring.

Madison walked down to the shoreline to stand with her feet in the shallows, staring out at the horizon. With a start she realised how relaxed she felt. More than relaxed—happy.

'I do need to get back,' Luke said, coming to stand next to her. 'Isla will be finishing football soon, and I need to be there to pick her up. Do you know the code to get back in? It's the same as the front gate.'

'Got it.' Madison repeated it back to him. 'See? I always was good at remembering my lines.'

'And you'll be okay? I can be here every day and work from the beach house. Hannah, Isla's nanny, usually does the school run so as long as I'm back to collect her from her ballet or playdates or whatever social activity she has planned I'm good.'

Madison laid a hand on his arm. 'I'll be fine. You don't need to babysit me. There's plenty of food in the house, you left me a car and now I have a charger for my phone and a laptop. I have all the tools I need. Come when you can, but I've got a lot of work to catch up on, as have you. I'll see you soon.'

Swiftly glancing around, as if checking to make sure nobody could see them, Luke pulled her into his arms and pressed a lingering kiss on her mouth. Madison leaned in for one blissful moment and then pulled away, not wanting to prolong the kiss for too long, afraid that if she did she might not let him go. Because although she did need to work, although she was well aware that Luke did need to get back to his daughter, although she was very sure that a little bit of separation and the chance to clear their heads would be the best thing for the pair of them, she was also afraid. Afraid that once he turned and walked away, drove back to his life, she'd fade to nothing but a memory. That she was too insubstantial to exist in his mind if she wasn't there anchoring herself to him.

She swallowed back her fears and put on her very best smile. 'Go on, get off with you.'

'You're very bossy when you want to be,' Luke complained. 'What with Isla, my sister and you, I'll never get a minute's peace.' But he was laughing as he spoke. 'Are you coming back to the house?'

'No, I think I'm going to explore, if that's all right with you.' It seemed important that Luke didn't see her waving him off, putting on a brave face, but that she showed him she was independent.

'Yes, of course. Enjoy Palm Beach. Call me. Any time. You don't need a reason.' And then he was gone, and she was alone on this vast beach, surrounded by strangers. In a strange country once again.

For a moment panic almost overwhelmed her and she thought longingly of her flat, the days spent looking at the grey walls, looking out at the grey of her London suburb, alone but safe. Her life might be dull, but it was hers and it was sensible and she'd made it exactly what she needed: private and quiet and controlled. What was she doing here in this vibrant city, the sun shining down, with the promise of happiness in the air?

She stared out at the horizon and gave herself a little shake. No, she had made a decision to come, had promised herself, promised Luke, to give this trip a fair try and she was going to live up to that promise. She would allow herself these two more weeks with Luke and she would enjoy every moment. Because when this ended she didn't want to have any regrets, not this time. She wasn't going to hang on too long. She wasn't going to see the light in Luke's eyes dim, his smile weaken, wait for his kisses to get less affectionate and demanding. She'd enjoy the situation for what it was and walk away while the going was still good, with memories to warm her on the long grey nights. She would give herself long enough to know that for once in her life she'd really been wanted, liked, maybe even needed. And then she'd leave before he realised his mistake.

After a short walk, Madison returned to the beach house and had a look around. She was exploring, she told herself, not being nosy, but she knew she wasn't being entirely honest with herself. Of course she was curious to peek inside Luke's life. How could she help but examine the photographs on the walls and bookshelves, investigate Luke's taste in books and music, try to get a glimpse of his day-to-day life?

One thing that struck her was how homely the house was despite its size and sought-after location. The photos displayed throughout clearly showed a happy family, and although Madison knew better than most how easily a picture could lie, she got the sense that these photos weren't for show. There were pictures of Isla everywhere, showing her growing up from a tiny baby to a bright-eyed, redheaded girl who so closely resembled her father in every way other than hair colour, she was like his mini me. There were photos of her dancing in a little tutu, horse riding, clutching a surfboard, laughing in all of them. Madison's heart squeezed. It was the kind of childhood she had sometimes portrayed, not the kind she'd ever known. How could she not love Luke even more when he provided so much happiness for his daughter?

Hang on a second! She *what?* She couldn't *love* him; she barely *knew* him. They were having a holiday romance, and that was no real base for love. Madison put the photo she was holding down and stared unseeingly out of the window. It was true that her success rate was almost one hundred per cent for those who spent a week together but that was because she worked hard to pair them perfectly, using psychology and common interests and goals. She and Luke might have all the chemistry in the world but on paper they were no match.

No, this wasn't love; it was a crush. An old teenage crush, resurrected by proximity and the kind of week that belonged in films, not in real life. But if she had been in the market for falling in love, then he would make it, oh, so easy because part of her, the small part who never quite gave up hope that some day someone would see through to her soul, very much wanted to belong in this kind of life. Wanted to hold hands with a small child who gazed up at her the way that Isla gazed up at Luke in the photo she had just put down, to be part of a big family like the group shot on the wall behind her. Luke's parents she recognised from interviews back during his tour days, and she guessed the woman with the warm smile must be his sister, the man with his arm around her his brother-in-law. They stood flanked by three grinning boys. What must it be like to have family who had your back, not to be always alone?

Right, this was getting her nowhere. It was time to do some work; she'd holidayed for long enough. Resolutely Madison returned to the pretty guestroom she'd been allocated, complete with its own bathroom and seating area where her new laptop was charging and ready for her. She'd gone through some emails at the airport but she needed to talk to Jen and prioritise what she should do whilst here.

But for once work failed to absorb her and instead Madison sat back in her chair and looked out of the window over the ocean beyond, moments from the week just gone playing over and over in her mind like scenes from a movie. A movie in which she was once again the star.

The beep of her phone interrupted her daydreams and a stab of happiness pierced her at the sight of Luke's name.

'Hi.'

'Hi, yourself. I'm not disturbing you, am I?'

'Of course not. Is everything okay? I didn't expect to hear from you so soon.' Momentary panic seized her. Maybe he'd realised that her being here was not a good idea after all. Maybe picking up his daughter and returning home had made him come to his senses sooner than she had anticipated.

'Everything's great. It's just… I know you said that you needed some time to get on with work, but Isla really wants to come down to the beach for the rest of the weekend. I told her I had a friend staying there, but she pointed out how rude I was to leave you alone on your first trip to Palm Beach and I can't say that she's wrong. Would it be terribly inconvenient if we came over? I'll take you out for dinner tonight; there's a great restaurant within walking distance you'll love. It's Isla's favourite.'

Madison squeezed her eyes closed. Although Luke had casually mentioned that it would be good for her to meet Isla at some point during this fortnight, she hadn't really thought it would happen. After all, Isla lived in the city itself and was at school all week. Luke had planned to come down to Palm Beach in the day and so part of her had assumed that their paths might never cross at all, and that had been a secret relief. Getting to know Isla meant becoming even more entangled in Luke's life and surely that would make it even harder for her to walk away. But Isla knew she was here so she couldn't even opt to go to a hotel without making things difficult.

Madison injected as much enthusiasm as she could into her voice. 'It's your home, Luke. Of course you should come.'

'Are you sure?'

Madison took a deep breath. She didn't need to lie to him. If she told Luke she thought it a bad idea, that it was too soon, then he would understand. Although he wouldn't hold it against her, she would have failed a test he probably didn't realise he was setting. But, on the other hand, Isla held such a huge part of her father's heart, what if she didn't like Madison? What if she saw through to the nothingness within?

If Isla rejected her then she would have to leave straight away.

'Yes,' she lied. 'Completely. I'll see you soon.'

'I want Madison to sit next to me,' Isla commanded, patting the seat by her side.

'But you haven't seen your dad for over a week,' Madison protested. 'He'll never forgive me if I take his place.'

Luke shook his head, laughing. 'I know when I'm beat,' he said, sliding into the seat opposite and picking up his menu, watching his daughter and Madison compare their menus as he did so.

It was a welcome surprise how quickly Madison and Isla seemed to have taken to each other. He hadn't doubted Madison; after all, not only did she have a Master's in Business Psychology but she also interviewed people every day, talking to them about their biggest secrets and deepest hopes. Putting people at their ease was her livelihood. But for all Isla's excitement when she'd found out that he had a friend staying at the beach house, in reality she wasn't always that forthcoming with strangers. And of course he'd never introduced a single female friend to her in such an intimate way before: a weekend stay, dinner out.

He certainly hadn't told Isla that he and Madison were dating and neither of them had given the child any indication that they were more than casual friends. They had greeted each other with just a smile and been careful not to touch or kiss. Thank goodness he had had the foresight to give Madison the guest bedroom. But, even so, it was an unusual situation for he and Isla to go out with a female companion who wasn't his mother or his sister. He'd wondered if his daughter might be a little jealous, especially as he'd been away for a week already.

He needn't have worried. In fact, he reflected, if anyone was going to be jealous it should be him. Isla had taken immediately to Madison and insisted on doing everything with her, asking Madison to help her with her spellings, to help choose her outfit, and now to sit next to her and help her decide what to eat.

Maybe it was too much too soon for Madison. After all, she had no family, probably didn't know many children; was this onslaught of adoration too much for her? But Madison didn't look overwhelmed. In fact she seemed luminescent, eyes sparkling as she chatted easily to Isla, listening with unfeigned interest to Isla's anecdotes about her friends at school, recaps of her favourite TV programmes, none of which Madison had seen, and discussing books they both liked.

The restaurant overlooked the beach and they had secured a coveted corner table on the terrace, Luke's favourite spot. Madison had agreed to Luke's recommendation that they share a bottle of a renowned local Sauvignon Blanc and together they decided to share a series of small plates of seafood served with salads, triple fried chips and a charcuterie platter, followed by tiramisu for the adults and a decadent chocolate mousse for Isla. Even when they had finally finished nobody was ready to leave, and readily agreed to coffee and babyccinos.

'It sounds to me like your school is a lot of fun,' Madison said as Isla finished telling her another involved story about some classroom crisis where she, of course, was the protagonist.

'It's not too bad as schools go.'

Luke hid a grin at Isla's blasé tone. She enjoyed school, where she was an undisputed queen bee, never happier than when she was surrounded by friends. But his amusement turned to concern when she innocently asked Madison, 'Did you like school?' He knew how much Madison disliked talking about her past.

For the first time Madison's smile faltered and she bent her head to examine the drawing Isla was working on in the colouring book Luke had brought for her, letting her hair fall over her face, hiding her expression. 'I didn't go to school. I had tutors instead.'

Isla's eyes widened. 'You didn't go to school?'

'Not everyone does,' Luke quickly interjected. 'You know that. Didn't you learn about kids out on the ranches who learn over the internet or even over the radio?'

'Did you live on a ranch? Wasn't it lonely? Did you miss having friends?'

'Isla,' Luke said sternly, 'that's too many questions. Poor Madison didn't visit us to be interrogated.'

But as Isla's face fell, Madison looked up and over at him with a reassuring smile he was beginning to rec-ognise as one she used when uncomfortable. 'No, it's fine. Isla is just interested, and it's good to be curious. I worked, Isla. I was a child actress and so I got taught on set. And yes, it was lonely and yes, I did miss having friends. I think you have a much better time than I did.'

'You are an *actress*?' Isla couldn't have sounded more awestruck if Madison had announced that she was a princess.

'Not for a long time. Now I have my own business.'

'Like Daddy? He helps people be fit and healthy but he has a lot of long meetings. Blah-blah-blah on the computer. I like his office, though.'

'It's good to know what you think about my work,' Luke said mock indignantly. 'There's a little more than blah-blah-blah I'll have you know.'

Madison laughed softly. 'I do a lot of talking too. My business is a little like your daddy's, I suppose, because it helps people, only I don't use an app and it's done by me.'

'You help people get healthy too?'

'I help people meet other people, when they want to get married but they're too busy or well known to do it themselves.'

'Like the girls in the film? They found their daddy a lady and then they had a mummy.'

Luke's eyes met Madison's and there was a charge in the air, the sense of things shifting. 'Yes,' she said. 'Like that.' She didn't, Luke noted, tell Isla that she had been the girls in the film.

'Could you find my daddy a lady? So I can have a mummy—and a dog.'

'I don't know about the dog; that's a little beyond my scope. Oh, I like the colour you've used here. I think the silver would look great there.' Madison pointed to Isla's colouring book as she deftly changed the subject.

Watching Madison help Isla colour in a picture, Luke's chest constricted with a sweet aching pain of love and regret. Was this how it would have been if Alyssa had been a different kind of woman with different needs? If somehow he'd recovered from his shock and surprise and managed to persuade her to stay for a night, a week, a lifetime? If she'd got in touch sooner and they'd used her pregnancy as a reason to try and give their relationship a real go? But no, there was no point wondering what-if because even if Alyssa had stayed around who was to say it would have lasted? Who was to say she wouldn't have got bored eventually and still ended up walking away, but this time leaving behind a child who knew and loved and needed her? Or worse, walked away and took Isla with her? She had been a virtual stranger after all; how could he predict her choices?

But then Madison was also a stranger in many ways and yet the way he felt about Madison, the way he felt he knew her—the core of her—could not be more different. Maybe it was the magic in the week away, but he had talked to her, opened up in a way so new to him. And he felt that he understood her, the fears and loneliness that had shaped her, the sense of betrayal she carried. He wanted to help her fight those fears, conquer that loneliness, teach her to trust.

No, he couldn't regret a path that had led him to meeting Madison. Any fears he had over how she would respond to the most important person in his life had been allayed. Madison was a natural with Isla, completely at ease, laughter pealing out as she and Isla traded stories. She fitted with them. Fitted him.

A tension Luke hadn't been aware he carried eased and slipped away as he watched Madison and Isla together. He'd known he liked Madison—a lot. Knew that he desired her, enjoyed her company, had got comfortable with her surprisingly quickly. He knew that he liked her natural solemnness and how her smiles, less and less rare the more time he spent with her, lit up her face, her determination and courage. But until he knew how she would get on with Isla he'd had to guard himself, guard his heart against anything more.

But that guard was slipping and Luke knew it was time to make a choice. He could hold back, enjoy two more weeks with Madison and then look for the sensible match he'd promised himself, one where emotions and love were muted, where compatibility and family came first. Or he could let his guard down completely and see where that led. It meant risking his heart—worse, it meant risking disappointing Isla, who clearly had a big case of hero worship when it came to Madison. But the pay-off could be so great. For them all.

Luke was used to heading out on court, knowing that loss was just a ball toss away, willing to risk the crushing disappointment for the adrenaline of a win. He could gamble his heart. But could he gamble Isla's?

But looking at the two heads bent over the colouring book and seeing the ease and warmth already springing up between them, another question hit him. How could he not?

# CHAPTER TEN

'So…' JEN GAVE Madison a sly smile. 'Lea tells me you've postponed your flight…' There was a dramatic pause. 'Again.'

On the computer screen, Madison saw her assistant sit back in her chair and fold her arms, fixing her boss with a gotcha grin.

'It makes sense for me to spend another two weeks here,' Madison said, trying to sound calm and not react to Jen's teasing. 'Considering how quickly we pulled together our Pan-Pacific strategy, it's working brilliantly. I have several new clients signed up; there are more applications coming in and scheduled interviews to do. It's a lot easier to handle this flurry of new sign-ups if I am in the same approximate time zone and it means I can do some face-to-face interviews as well—I have two right here in Sydney next week. Plus there's the publicity. I've been interviewed by several upmarket magazines who target exactly the kind of clients we want to attract. It seems silly to rush home when there is still so much more to do here.'

She tried not to glance over at her phone as she

mentioned the magazine interviews, one of which had published an online profile that day. She'd always wondered if her parents had headed over to this part of the world with their purloined money. Would they see her name and be prompted to get in touch? Or, despite her success, did they still have no interest in her now she was grown up and couldn't be manipulated?

The answer seemed very clearly to be the latter. If they were still alive, that was—would she even know if they weren't?

Over the last few weeks the pain not only of their betrayal but of their abandonment had intensified. She barely knew Isla, but already knew she would do anything to protect the child from harm. Yet Madison's own parents had raised her, known her better than anyone else and had walked away without a backwards glance.

That abandonment was something she and Isla shared. Only Isla seemed unscarred by her mother's absence. She was loved and cared for, happy and thriving. But one day she would have questions. Would she feel unlovable like Madison did? Would her mother's actions one day taint her life, her choices, her relationships?

No, because there was one key difference. Luke had chosen his daughter over his career and his lifestyle and he had zero regrets. How could Isla not flourish under such care? But no one had chosen Madison.

Another question from Jen brought Madison's attention back to their conversation. 'And Luke doesn't mind you camping out at his palatial beach house for another couple of weeks?'

'If your eyebrows get any higher, they'll disappear off your head,' Madison told her prying assistant and Jen just chuckled. 'But, for your information, it's fine. I have the beach house to myself during the week, and I've offered to spend weekends elsewhere if he wants time alone with his family. He's been very generous and I don't want to take advantage.'

Luke had laughed her suggestion away before kissing her very thoroughly to prove how welcome she was, but Madison didn't need to share that information with her assistant, who was quite clearly desperate to find out just what was happening between the two of them. Madison had never been the confiding type; her friendships were very one-way in that respect. But, even if she was, she wouldn't be ready to dissect her relationship with Luke. It was too new, too precious, too fragile. Too finite.

'It's very kind of him, especially after the whole Isabella debacle. You must have made quite the impression,' Jen said. 'Just for the record, it's nice to see you so relaxed. I used to worry that you never switched off. Obviously M is your baby, and I know we have to be available twenty-four hours, but the beauty of being small and select means that between us we can manage it all. You don't need to personally work every single hour in the day. You can trust me and trust Lea to do our part. Although now we have so many new prospects in the Pacific area, maybe we need to take someone on permanently in Australia after you come back.'

'That's a good plan.' It was. But Madison didn't want to think about going back. Not yet. 'There's a lot of potential here and I'm only just tapping into it. A permanent office over here would be useful and it would mean we could manage the US and South America from between the two, which would be helpful time difference wise. If all the prospects turn into clients we could absolutely justify it.'

Maybe amongst those prospects there was someone who would be the perfect match for Luke and for Isla. But Madison knew she could no longer lie to herself. She had no professional pride in the thought of matching Luke up with anybody else. Instead, jealousy plunged its claws into her heart at the very thought of it. But she couldn't stay here for ever and he deserved happiness. It would be selfish, unprofessional of her to put her feelings before his future.

She brought her focus back to the matter being discussed. 'Be honest, Jen. Is there a problem if I stay a little longer? Do you need me back in the office?'

'Of course not. Thanks to the joys of the internet, you could be here, Australia or over in Hawaii. Actually, that sounds like a plan. Can we put together a Hawaiian strategy and bagsy me being the one to go and lead it? Of course you should stay longer, whether it's for work or for fun. It's just unlike you to be so impulsive, Madison; it's hard for me to get my head around. But it's good. You seem happy.'

This was Madison's cue to say that of course she was happy because their rapidly put together strategy was working and that as a result their client roster was looking very healthy indeed. But she knew that was just a small part of her new relaxed air, and she suspected Jen did too. 'Good. In that case I'll get Lea to rebook my flights.' Again. Two weeks had turned into four and would now be six. But that had to be the last time. No more giving in to Luke's blandishments, no more excuses. She would conduct the interviews next week, talk to a recruitment firm about hiring someone here in Sydney and return home.

Ending the call with a promise to speak tomorrow, she stood up and stretched. The problem with being the other side of the world was there were limited opportunities when both she and Jen were working, even with the long hours they both put in. Madison would check in at six a.m. when she woke up, and usually started working straight away after those calls, but during the day she found herself doing the hitherto unthinkable and taking long, leisurely lunch breaks: walking on the beach, taking some surfing lessons, and practising her persistently uncontrollable backhand against the practice wall.

Luke had got into the habit of coming up to the beach house for a few hours three or four times a week and he and Isla spent every weekend at the beach. It was good in some ways, this enforced slowdown in their relationship, difficult in others, because although those long weekday lunches often ended up in bed, they were very discreet when Isla was around, the indulgent, constant lovemaking of the first week replaced by snatched moments and afternoon sessions. Sometimes Madison felt stretched tight with desire, ready to explode with every look or casual touch. The only consolation was that Luke evidently felt the same way, his eyes darkening to navy when he looked at her, the heat between them so palpable it was explosive. No wonder she hadn't left yet when they weren't done, when this thing between them was still so all-absorbing, still filled her every sense, every waking thought.

But this undefinable thing wasn't just the sex, or the thinking about sex, or the need to touch him and be touched. It wasn't just the physicality between them. She was, as Jen had noticed, more relaxed than she had ever been before, even on the yacht. She loved Palm Beach with its mix of seaside casual with glitzy glamour, reminding her of Malibu, where she had grown up. But now she was an anonymous part of it, free to walk on the beach, buy her morning coffee from the beach bar, take her surf lessons with no one following or photographing her. She had an early start every day, but there was no car to whisk her to a film lot and keep her there until after sunset. She could step onto the beach at any time, with a surfboard or a book or her laptop.

And she loved the weekends when Isla came rushing to find her, full of that week's small girl drama and gossip. They had fallen into a comfortable routine of heading out for sharing plates on the restaurant terrace before she read Isla a bedtime story, followed by a long leisurely brunch from the beach bar on Sunday mornings before a hike or a swim or a game of tennis, Luke playing the pair of them at once with a patience and calm no one would have expected from the three time Grand Slam winner who nearly lost his career thanks to his temper.

It was like being in heaven.

Madison checked the time, and with a thrill of anticipation closed her laptop. She usually spent Friday evenings alone, Isla's busy schedule of activities keeping Luke in the city until Saturday afternoon, and so Madison had got into the habit of going for a walk after work, stopping for one glass of wine on the terrace of a little restaurant about half a mile up the road. She was more than happy to sit there with her book, the wine and the view and think about how different Friday felt, with the promise of the weekend ahead, so different to her London life, where days and evenings, weeks and weekends all blurred into one.

But tonight Isla and Luke were coming early. Isla's usual Saturday morning football was cancelled and so after that evening's ballet class they planned to hop into the car and drive over to Palm Beach to spend the whole weekend at the ocean. Madison had offered to cook, and ingredients for a simple pasta dish and salad waited in the kitchen for her to assemble. She wanted to impress and had prepared some dough earlier, ready to make homemade garlic bread, and had whisked up a light, creamy chocolate mousse for after, knowing it was Isla's favourite.

Putting some music on, Madison began to prepare the meal, chopping vegetables, washing salad and singing along to her favourite playlist. She was so absorbed, she didn't hear the garage door open and the first she knew of Luke and Isla's arrival was when Isla rushed into the kitchen to envelop her in a hug before hopping onto one of the barstools to regale Madison with a week's worth of gossip and drama. Luke followed, carrying the bags, and although his greeting was a simple hello, the gleam in his eyes and the promise in his smile was enough to warm Madison through.

It didn't take long for dinner to cook and Madison carried the bowl of pasta with roasted vegetables out to the already set terrace table, Isla carefully following with the lightly dressed salad while Luke brought the hot garlic bread fresh from the oven. It all felt so easy, as if this was a well-practised routine. Conversation too was light and easy, as if this was a normal family mealtime, nothing out of the ordinary, but its very normality made the whole meal a novelty to Madison and although she waved off their extravagant compliments on the food with a half embarrassed insistence that it was nothing, she knew she'd remember this evening for a very long time.

She was just wondering whether she could manage seconds when Isla looked up with an excited smile. 'Oh, Madison. Did Daddy tell you? Tomorrow is going to be such a fun day. Aunty Ella is going to come and visit and so are my cousins and my granny and grandpa. And they are bringing Barnacle, who is the best dog in the world. Daddy has said we can have a barbecue on the beach. Won't that be the best? We always play volleyball, and sometimes Daddy puts me on his shoulders, and the cousins always play cricket and football with me and they are so fast...' She finally stopped as she ran out of breath.

Madison tried to smile. 'That does sound like fun...' she hoped her voice and expression didn't give away her alarm to the small girl '...but you know I was thinking I should probably give you guys some privacy. You've been so lovely letting me take up your family beach time, but I've been meaning to explore the coast further, only I'm so comfortable here I've been too lazy to do it. If you have family plans tomorrow then this is the perfect opportunity for me to head out.'

Luke started to speak but, before he could get a word out, Isla had jumped in. 'No!' She shook her head, her red curls bouncing. 'Aunty Ella would be so disappointed. I've told her all about you and she said she can't wait to meet you. Do stay, Madison. I want you to meet my cousins. And Barnacle.'

Madison took a gulp of water, pleading eyes fixed on Luke. It was one thing to play at happy families with Luke and Isla, even though she knew how dangerous this pretend domesticity was, but it was quite another to be introduced to Luke's family. Surely they would suspect she was more than a friend? This visit was a timely reminder, a wake-up call that with every hour, every day, she was getting sucked further and further into this fantasy.

'I was hoping you'd be around,' Luke said easily but his gaze was intent as it rested on Madison. 'Everybody would love to meet you, and they're a nice bunch if I say so myself. Do stay.'

The right thing to do would be to stick to her guns, smile, thank them for wanting to include her but excuse herself from tomorrow's family gathering. But Madison couldn't help thinking about the framed picture in the living room, the tanned, laughing family members, and she yearned so hard to be part of that it physically

162 INDONESIAN DATE WITH THE SINGLE DAD

hurt. Would it really harm her to allow herself just one afternoon? If she made it clear that she and Luke were just friends, that she was just passing through. In fact, wouldn't it look more suspicious if she *wasn't* there? As if she was trying to avoid them? She didn't want to put Luke in an awkward position.

'I really don't want to intrude.'

'You could never intrude.' Luke's smile was understanding, as if he knew her doubts as well as she did.

'Okay, thank you. That would be lovely.'

'Yay! You can be in my volleyball team, Madison. I'll show you the rules; it's very easy.' Isla bounced up and down in her seat and despite her misgivings Madison couldn't help but laugh at the child's enthusiasm.

'That's very kind of you. I'll try not to let you down.' Madison busied herself gathering plates and taking them back into the kitchen. She was aware of Luke close behind with the other dishes and turned to face him, keeping an eye out to make sure Isla wasn't within listening distance.

'I'm still not sure meeting your family is a good idea,' she said, putting the plates down on the side. He did likewise before stepping close to her, taking her hand in his and drawing her to him. Madison leaned in, glad of his quiet strength and support.

'Isla has been talking about you non-stop,' he said. 'It's natural that my family wants to meet you. I didn't mean to spring it on you like this, but Ella only called when we were in the car driving here and it's very hard to say no to my sister. You'll see when you meet her; she's a force of nature.'

'What do they know about me?' Madison asked and Luke squeezed her hand reassuringly.

'That you're a friend who is using the beach house whilst on a reconnaissance business trip and that Isla thinks you're a princess and Mary Poppins rolled into one.'

'They don't know about Indonesia?'

'No, all Ella knows is that my date didn't show up and I'm not sure about my next step. I didn't mention you—and my parents thought it was a business trip anyway.'

'Okay.'

Luke hesitated, then tilted her chin so that she was looking into his eyes. 'Look, Madison. I haven't told them anything about you and me, because I know we haven't quite figured out what we're doing here. But this is more than just a fling and we both know it. One week was one thing, but it's been five weeks now of seeing each other almost every day. We fit, don't you think?'

'I...' Madison didn't know what to say because Luke was right. She did feel as if she fitted here, in his life, with Isla. All she'd ever wanted was to be wanted, to be loved, to fit... But it was early days still. She couldn't drop her protective barriers; she wasn't even sure she knew how to. 'What are you getting at, Luke?'

'That I want you to know that I'd gladly introduce you as my girlfriend to my parents, my sister and Isla. That I want to, if you agree.' He smiled. 'Isla would be thrilled. She's been dropping very unsubtle hints ever since she first met you and they're getting heavier every week.'

Madison's heart hammered, her pulse vibrating through her. If Luke introduced her as his girlfriend, that would make her a part of the family. She'd belong.

'But Isla… Luke, I agree with everything you have said about keeping her safe. It's not fair to ask her to accept me in your life, only for me to leave…'

He looked at her steadily. 'No, it's not. But you don't have to leave, do you? Stay, Madison, give us a real chance, Isla and me. We can carry on like this for a while, living separately, dating, easing ourselves into this relationship. But I want to see where we go, Madison. I want to try a future with you. I'm falling in love with you and I think you feel the same way. What do you say?'

Luke hadn't meant to declare himself, not yet. Every extension of Madison's stay was another victory; every afternoon, every weekend they spent together he felt himself fall more deeply for her. And he was so sure she felt the same way—he just didn't think she knew it. Madison was so scarred by her childhood she didn't know how to recognise love, whether that was giving or receiving it.

And it broke his heart. He'd spent some time reading all he could about her parents but she'd done a good job of covering up for them; none of the *Where are they now?* articles she featured in even hinted at the darkness of her childhood. The media seemed to believe the lies her parents had sold them, painting them as the dedicated, loving people putting their daughter's happiness first they had claimed to be. If she'd continued acting maybe their disappearance would have been commented upon, but as she'd faded from public view so had interest in them. The Morgans had covered their tracks well. The house where they'd lived in Malibu had been rented and he couldn't find any trace of their next address.

He knew he shouldn't meddle. Madison was a wealthy woman. If she really wanted to find her parents she could hire a detective and track them down. But he also knew she was finding it impossible to move on from their betrayal. All she'd ever asked for was their unconditional love. Without it she felt worthless.

Could he show her otherwise? He had no idea, but he had to try.

'What do you say?' he repeated steadily, but his heart wasn't steady. Not at all. This was like the moment before match point, throwing the ball up high and hoping it was true.

Slowly, Madison reached up to cup his cheek, her face unreadable. 'Luke. You and me; we were never about commitment. You're not falling in love with me; you're falling in love with the idea of me, the fun we've had.'

Was that true? Was he taking the sun and the laughter and the attraction that sizzled between them and the stolen moments and the immediate bond that had seemed to spring between Madison and Isla and made it more than the sum of its parts? Was this no more than an extended fling?

'I'm an actress,' she continued, long lashes veiling her eyes. 'I may not earn my living that way any more, but I spent my childhood being someone else. I want you to like me, Luke. So I became likeable. Maybe I succeeded too well.'

She *was* an actress, but she wasn't that good. Luke was beginning to know how to read her, despite her best efforts to hide. She was hiding now, because she couldn't look him in the eye, and her hand still rested on his cheek as she leaned in towards him. For comfort? Support?

'I haven't fallen in love with a character, Madison,' he said, keeping as still as he could so as not to frighten her away. 'Let me tell you who I see when I look at you. I see a woman who has been through something unimaginably soul-destroying but who wasn't destroyed, who got up and rebuilt herself and chose her career. I see a woman who can laugh at herself—a woman who listens, who understands people, a woman who inspires trust. I see a woman who is sexy and desirable, not because of the way she looks, but because of who she is, how she makes me feel. I see a woman I can sit in silence with and be completely comfortable, but a woman I also want to open my soul to. And I also see a woman who really wants a dog but is afraid of even that much commitment, of letting anyone in, and all I want to do is show her that she deserves all the love in the world. That's who I see, that's who I'm falling for. What about you, Madison? What do you see? A teenage tennis player you once watched play, or is there more? Do you see me as I see you? Because if you don't, there's no more to say and I'll never speak of this again.'

There was a long silence. Luke remained still, did

his best not to allow his expression to reflect his emotions. Had he overplayed his hand, spoken too soon? But, before Madison could speak, Isla ran into the kitchen and he and Madison instantly sprang apart, Madison grabbing a cloth and beginning to scrub the scrupulously clean worktop.

The moment had gone, but there would be another one before the weekend finished. He had to know if there was a future for them. It was time for the holiday romance to end—but what came next was in Madison's hands. And relinquishing control had never been something that Luke Taylor did well.

# CHAPTER ELEVEN

BY THE TIME Saturday lunchtime came around Madison's stomach was a twist of knots. She and Luke hadn't had an opportunity to continue last night's unexpectedly intense conversation. Isla had been full of holiday giddiness and it had been late before she settled, after which Luke had crept into Madison's room to make love to her with a tender urgency which felt like both a promise and a farewell. For once she hadn't felt sad when he left to return to his room; instead she had lain awake and replayed his words over and over.

'I see you,' he had said. And he had. And he seemed to want her anyway. It should be a dream come true.

But Madison knew better than most how easily a dream could twist and turn dark. If she left knowing she was loved, even if just for a time, that would surely be enough to sustain her. But if she stayed then every day, every week, every month she'd be waiting for Luke to realise that she wasn't the woman he thought she was, waiting for him to turn away, for the affection to fall from his face, the desire from his eyes. Even if it didn't, even if this was real, the waiting would poison them eventually; she'd always be holding part of her back. How could she live like that? How could she ask him to?

But then again, if she walked out on this chance of happiness, of a family, then that would be it. She was just thirty-four and she would be conceding.

She thought she was doing the right thing keeping herself safe. Not risking getting too close, too deep with anyone. Luke had said she was brave, but she wasn't. She was a coward.

One thing was clear. She loved Luke. She'd fallen for him the first time she'd laid eyes on him and over the last few weeks that crush had strengthened and deepened into something real. Meeting Isla had only reinforced her feelings—and her uncertainty. How could she risk Isla's wellbeing? She couldn't carve a place in Isla's life only to leave months or years down the line. The child had already lost one mother. Luke had been right to prioritise her happiness. Madison needed to do the same.

Thanks to her distraction, the car bringing Luke's family arrived far quicker than Madison had been anticipating. She knew she was no way near mentally ready to face a room full of strangers, but she had little choice as Isla grabbed her hand and towed her down to the garage, where what seemed like an inordinate amount of people were piling out of a large car, accompanied by an overexcited Labrador.

'Aunty Ella, Aunty Ella,' the small girl cried as the group encircled them, 'Jack, Ted, Tom! Look, this is Madison! She's an actress, Aunty, she's in that film that you and I love so much, the matchmaking one. And she was the little girls, both of them. Only now she's grown up.'

Madison found herself exchanging an amused glance with Luke's high-achieving sister, a neat-looking woman a few years older than Madison. Ella's resemblance to her brother was obvious in her kind blue eyes and blonde hair, hers shoulder-length and pulled back in a ponytail. 'It's lovely to meet you at last,' she said, enfolding Madison in a warm hug. 'This is my husband, Ned, and these three urchins are our boys. The biggest is Jack, the smallest Ted—and yes, I know, Ned and Ted, I promise it wasn't on purpose—and the one in the middle is Tom. I've heard so much about you. You are quite Isla's favourite person at the moment.'

Madison wasn't sure exactly what she said in return, but she did know that she was acting the role of family friend with every ounce of her dramatic training, hanging back with just the right amount of diffidence, whilst making sure she didn't seem standoffish.

The three boys clearly knew the beach house well and after a quick if not particularly interested hello to Madison piled upstairs, squabbling amongst themselves over whether they should surf or play cricket first. Finally, Luke's parents extricated themselves from their son and granddaughter and greeted Madison. The pair were older than when she had last seen them but still recognisable from interviews and from the many times the TV cameras had panned to them during a particularly tense moment in a match. Madison found herself hugged yet again and welcomed to

Australia, and if their eyes were curious as they looked
between Luke and Madison, neither parent gave any
hint that they suspected that there was more to her stay
here than a business trip.

Gradually she found herself relaxing. She'd wanted
to know what it would be like to be part of a big, noisy,
affectionate family and here was a chance to find out,
another memory to add to the store she was treasuring
away for the long winter days that lay ahead.

But did she have to live on memories alone? She was
being offered the opportunity for everything she had
ever craved: a family, love, happiness. Maybe this was
her time, her opportunity to put the past behind her, to
finally really move forward. All she had to do was say
yes. Tell Luke that she saw him as he saw her. That she
wasn't just falling in love, she had fallen all the way.

Hope, new and painful and sweet, pulsed through
her. She didn't have to decide right away. But maybe,
just maybe, there was a chance of a happy ending for
her after all.

Luke had been unsure how Madison would find his
family with their non-stop flow of chatter and their
fiercely competitive natures but to his relief she seemed
to fit straight in. She didn't speak much, but when she
did it was with confidence and she threw herself into
the activities, joining in with the cricket, although she
had never played before, and showing herself to be
surprisingly good at volleyball, leading her team to
victory. As afternoon turned into evening she busied
herself making salads to go with the barbecue. They

worked seamlessly together, setting up tables and chairs and picnic blankets on the beach against his garden wall, a perfect team.

Luke could see his sister and parents watching the two of them together and as much as he wanted to slip his arm around Madison, to introduce her to his family as the woman he loved, he trod very carefully. He didn't touch her unless he needed to, tried not to exchange too many intimate glances or secret smiles with her and did his best to treat her with easy affection as if she really were an old friend staying in his house while she was in town on business. Not that he thought they were fooling anyone—it was telling that nobody asked how they'd met. It would usually have been one of the first questions his mother or Ella would ask and its absence hinted at a family pact to stay out of the relationship until Luke and Madison were ready to disclose it. Luke was both relieved and a little suspicious; this kind of tact wasn't usually in the family DNA.

They also hadn't asked Madison about her famous childhood; Luke had warned them before they arrived that she didn't like to talk about it too much and although his sister had at one point admitted to having seen most of her films, the topic was otherwise left alone. Everybody was far more interested in Madison's current role as a matchmaker, begging her to drop hints about famous couples she had set up. But again Luke's suspicions were on high alert when no one suggested that she try and match him up. Obviously his sister had known that he had signed up to M and about his trip to Indonesia—and he suspected that she'd told Ned as well—but he had asked her not to tell their parents. It wasn't that Luke was ashamed about using the service but he hadn't wanted to get their hopes up if his trip didn't work out. He knew how much his parents worried about Isla's solitary childhood—and about him as a single dad—and that they hoped he would fall in love and have more children sooner rather than later.

Luke had set the barbecue going earlier and he judged it hot enough to start cooking the starters, popping on some corn on the cob, lavishly buttered and wrapped in foil, huge fresh prawns marinated in garlic-infused oil and the halloumi skewers that were Isla's favourite, steaks and burgers chilling in a cool box at his feet. He'd propped open the door that led from his backyard onto the beach and he leaned in the archway, half an eye on Isla, who was playing with Barnacle, half an eye on the food, all the time aware of Madison bringing out the last of the salads. She looked up, met his gaze and smiled, her hand going to her pocket as she did so. With an apologetic grimace, she pulled out her phone and half turned away to answer it.

Time seemed to slow down, the air almost treacle-like, sounds too loud and elongated as Luke saw her tense, her hand fly to cover her mouth as she cast one appealing glance towards him then turned away. At the same moment his sister had pulled out her phone and was looking from Luke to Madison, her expression half horrified, half sympathetic, his mother following suit.

His hands seemed to have forgotten how to work as Luke pulled out his own phone, fingers clumsy, worry clenching his chest as he saw notifications lighting up the screen. *What the hell was going on?* Now it seemed as if the entire beach had stilled and turned to look over at his house, at him. The only movement was an oblivious Isla, still whirling across the sand, Barnacle at her side.

Luke had several alerts set up to notify him if he or his business were mentioned online and numbly he pressed on one. Photographs flooded his screen, bright and brash and intrusive. Madison and him, holding hands on the shoreline. Dinner, her holding a fork of food to his mouth, laughing. A kiss, another kiss. Oh, God, a picture of himself and Madison either side of Isla, swinging her in the air, his daughter's face fully visible. A photo of a teenage Madison, posing in a small bikini, himself throwing his racquet down, face contorted with rage.

The accompanying text was short but all too clear.

Madison's playing Love All in the sun!

America's former teen sweetheart, child star and matchmaker to the elite, Madison Morgan, thirty-four, has been engaged in her very own love match with the Aussie Terror, tennis brat and fitness entrepreneur Luke Taylor, thirty-six.

The loved-up couple have been spotted canoodling on Australia's exclusive Palm Beach and enjoying family days out with Luke's daughter Isla. Is this game, set and match for the pair?

'What the hell is going on?' Luke looked around, hardly noticing the smoke rising from the barbecue and the acrid smell as the prawns began to burn, his brother-in-law quickly stepping past him to rescue the food. 'How were those photographers following us? When?' How had he not noticed? How had he exposed his daughter to this kind of media attention, so oblivious, so wrapped up in Madison he hadn't noticed the danger stalking them?

'Me,' Madison said quietly. 'They've been following me. That call was my assistant; she says it's all over the European and US sites. I'm sorry, Luke. I'm usually so careful. But I've given a few interviews over here for the agency, and it must have tempted some tabloid to try and see if they could dig up anything else on me while I'm here. This happens sometimes. I wasn't thinking, wasn't careful enough.' She was pale, still rigid, eyes huge in her face.

'They photographed Isla. They printed her picture.' Cold rage was consuming him, so different from the fiery anger that had characterised his teens, as he tried to make sense of the feeling of violation, his family exposed to a long lens, gossiped and speculated about, intimate moments served up to the world as titillation and speculation.

'I'm sorry,' Madison repeated, and Luke got the sense she was speaking to herself as much as to him. He remembered a conversation, back in Indonesia. *I felt hunted*, she had said. And here she was, hunted once again.

He swallowed back the rage, the temptation to call every editor and vent, to take out injunctions, to build high walls and place his daughter behind them, to storm at everyone watching and gossiping, knowing he needed to tell Madison it was okay, to reassure her. But before he could move Isla came dancing up, Barnacle at her heels, and peered at her aunt's phone.

'Daddy? Why were you a terror?'

Luke tried to think of a reply but, before he could, before his sister could retrieve her phone, Isla looked up, eyes wide with surprise.

'Is that a picture of Madison? Cool! Look, she and Daddy are kissing!' She ran up to Luke and pulled at his arm. 'Are you going to get married? Then I can have a mummy and a dog, and maybe a little sister. Ask Madison to stay, Daddy. Please!'

The party had fallen silent, as if under some kind of wicked spell, and Madison could feel them very determinedly not looking at either her or Luke. She stood frozen on the spot, clutching her phone, dread running through her.

The tabloids' interest in her, low level for the last few years, had been rekindled, her face emblazoned over the internet once again. Worse, Isla's face was emblazoned alongside hers, Luke's teen tantrums once more in the headlines. Luke had told her how important it was for him to raise his daughter away from media intrusion and now here she was, bringing the wolves to his door.

Nausea churned. How long had she been watched? How had her sixth sense not kicked in?

And now Isla had seen the pictures their secret was out, raising hopes in the small girl which Madison didn't know how to fulfil.

She'd been a fool to think there was any chance of a happy ending for her. The only thing to do was to step away, re-erect her barriers, stay safe—and by doing so keep Isla and Luke safe. They had to be her priority. Her own heart didn't matter at all. Of course the small girl wanted a family and siblings; what child wouldn't? Madison understood that yearning more than most. It was cruel of her to have raised Isla's hopes, no matter how inadvertently. To have raised her own hopes. To have allowed hope at all.

She had to put this right, somehow.

After the initial shock, the family pulled together to try and make the barbecue a success, avoiding the subject of the photographs and Isla's reaction. Everyone did their best to put Madison at her ease, discussion revolving around a business deal Luke was putting together and questions about her agency, how she matched people and more attempts to unmask some of her more famous clients.

But, despite the apparently easy flow of conversation, Madison's mind was racing. She appreciated the Taylor family's tact but knew that underneath the small talk they too were wondering about their relationship and what the future held for Luke and his daughter and whether Madison would be part of it.

One thing was for sure; it was time to put a stop to it all. She'd had her fun but now Isla was paying the price. It had to end.

It was late by the time Luke's family said their good-byes, both his mother and sister giving Madison warm hugs and suggesting they get together soon for coffee and a chance to get to know each other better. Madison murmured something noncommittal in reply, wishing she could take them up on their offer and get to know these intelligent, kind women better. She joined Luke and Isla in waving the car off, then Luke carried an exhausted Isla up to bed while Madison cleared up. By the time he returned downstairs she had brought everything in from the beach and was busy loading the dishwasher.

'You didn't need to do that,' he said, leaning against the fridge, blue eyes fixed on her.

'It's the least I can do. After all, you've given me four weeks' bed and board free of charge.' She turned and attempted to smile at him, but her mouth wobbled and she quickly turned away again, busying herself with her chores and trying to ignore the prickle of awareness in her whole body as his gaze assessed her.

'My family liked you.'

'I liked them too.'

'Are you going to take Mum and Ella up on their offer? They meant it, you know.' Luke's tone was casual, but the heat of his gaze was anything but.

'It's very kind of them, but I just don't think I'm going to have time.' She straightened, no longer able to use the dishwasher as an excuse to avoid looking at him. She curled her fingers and summoned all of her strength. 'I've still a lot to do and there's only a couple of weeks left.'

'I see.'

And she knew that he did. He saw everything, heard

everything she wasn't able to say. But she had to say it. She owed him that. 'I've been thinking, Luke,' she said hurriedly. 'Like I said, I've got a lot to do over the next two weeks and I feel as though I've trespassed on your hospitality long enough. And those photos today… There will be more; we both know that. We won't be able to go anywhere, do anything without being followed. It's not fair on Isla.'

His mouth set into a grim line. 'They had no right to do that.'

'But they did, and now they won't stop, you know that, not unless we kill the story at the source. We can't be seen together; it's not safe, not for Isla. We can't risk her being photographed again and…' She swallowed, forcing herself to hold his gaze. 'We can't allow her to get any closer to me. She's a credit to you, Luke. You are an amazing father. She's loved and cared for and safe and secure and that is all any child can ask for. But she wants more and both you and she deserve for you to try to make her dreams come true.'

The grim line deepened. 'We can ride it out. They'll get bored eventually.'

Madison's hands clenched, her fingernails digging into the palms of her hands, but she welcomed the sharp pain; it kept her focused. She didn't know how to do this; she didn't have the arsenal or the armour. She'd never been taught how to deal with emotions even though she spent her days engineering happy ever afters for other people.

'I can't.'

'You mean you won't.'

'No, I mean I can't. I can't do it to myself and I can't do it to Isla. I should never have come here in the first place.'

'Why are you so convinced this isn't worth fighting for?' Luke pushed a frustrated hand through his thick blond hair. 'I told you where I stand, Madison, and Isla made it very clear what she wants. We are here, telling you we love you, telling you that there is a place for you in our family, in our home, in our lives. If you don't want us, tell me. Be honest.'

'I do!' The cry was almost wrung from her, echoing around the spacious kitchen. 'Of course I do. But I just can't.'

Part of her wanted Luke to stride across the kitchen, pull her into his arms and kiss away her fears and doubts, but he stayed leaning against the fridge, arms folded, mouth set firm. 'You can,' he said at last. 'But you won't. What happened to you was a tragedy, Madison; I can't imagine what you went through. What your childhood was like. How it feels to know that the people whose only role is to love you unconditionally and have your best interests at heart stole from you. For your own parents to abandon you. Of course it has left scars; I get that you're scared. Of the tabloids digging deep enough to find the truth, or that you'll be left again. That's normal. But you are allowed to be happy. To want happiness. I can't promise you it will be easy—today proved that—but it would be easier to ride it out together. All you have to do is believe in yourself and believe in me. Can you do that? Will you try?'

How she wanted to say yes. To believe in him. To

believe in herself. But all she could see, all she could hear was the mingled contempt and disgust on her parents' faces when she had returned home in confusion, sure they would have an explanation for the missing money. The twisted amusement when they'd told her that if she wasn't able to support them she was nothing to them. It wasn't just the vindictiveness and hatred that had thrown her, it was the utter shock. She'd not been brought up with displays of tactile affection—at least when there were no cameras around—but she had assumed her parents loved her.

But no. They hadn't and she had been oblivious. How could she ever trust her instincts, her heart again?

'I'm sorry,' she said instead, and as Luke turned away she could swear that she heard her heart break in two.

# CHAPTER TWELVE

THE HOTEL WAS a haven, allowing Madison to work un-interrupted for eighteen hours a day, away from the photographers still looking for a picture or a quote.

If she stepped out onto the balcony she could see the famous harbour, bridge and the tip of the Opera House and looking at them made her a little less lonely; she knew Luke had similar views from his apartment. Maybe he was gazing out at the same view and think-ing of her. But then she would push the dangerous thought from her mind and head back to her desk to distract herself with the welcome stream of emails and tasks and not allow herself to wonder if he was in the next building along, the one opposite or the tall gleam-ing tower she could see rising up into the distance.

The odds of bumping into him on the street—or worse, bumping into Isla—were slim, she knew, but she didn't want to take the risk, nor did she want to risk a photo of her out alone, provoking more speculation on their relationship. So no sightseeing, no walking over the bridge, no attending a performance, no trips to the famous Botanical Gardens.

It was, in some ways, a relief. Madison knew she didn't want to go sightseeing alone. Until the last month she'd been so used to her own company that heading out alone would have been completely normal, but now Luke's absence physically hurt her. The sooner she left Sydney and returned to London and her own life the better. She tried to tell herself it was a relief that her flight was tomorrow and all this would soon be history, but she'd lost the ability to live a lie.

But first today's appointment, her last in Sydney. Her potential client was a world-famous action actor, his love life a source of constant speculation. He'd insisted on a face-to-face meeting, paranoid about his security. This was where Madison's experience came into its own; she knew what it was like to be followed by cameras constantly, for every relationship to be dissected in the press, every outfit scrutinised. Her success rate was high across all her clientele but especially high with celebrities. She knew the right questions to find out what they really wanted. It was ironic that she could be so insightful for others and so blind when it came to her own wants.

No. She knew exactly what—who—she wanted. She just didn't know how.

It had been a huge relief when Luke had taken Isla out for a day's sailing the morning after the barbecue, safely away from the small but determined band of photographers loitering near the house. Madison had told the small girl during breakfast that she had some meetings she couldn't conduct from the beach house and would have to move into a hotel. The hurt and confusion on Isla's face had broken what was left of her heart, and when Isla had begged her to come back to see her again before she flew home, Madison had chickened out of honesty, opting for a 'We'll see...' she knew she wouldn't be able to fulfil. For Isla's sake she and Luke had managed a cordial goodbye, but the disappointment in his eyes had haunted her sleep every night since. What had he seen in her eyes? she wondered. Regret? Sorrow? An appeal for understanding? Love? Those four emotions circled through her constantly; only work could keep them at bay.

She'd done the right thing; she had to keep telling herself that. But if it was right, then why did she feel as if she was sleepwalking through a disaster movie of her life?

Madison took a look in the mirror, straightening her white silk blouse and tweaking her pink skirt into line. Somehow she couldn't quite bring herself to wear the sensible olive and taupe that usually made up her work wardrobe. She pulled her hair back into a loose bun and put on some make-up to try and hide the shadows under her eyes and the hollows in her cheeks. Grabbing her laptop and bag, she left the room and headed down to Reception to meet the driver who was taking her to her meeting.

Shaun Coleridge lived in a mansion by the sea, huge gates and high walls keeping out the paparazzi and fans who milled around outside his home twenty-four hours a day. Madison was glad of the tinted windows in the air-conditioned car as long lenses pointed in her direction, relieved that the last stray paparazzi seemed to have vacated the street outside her hotel, looking for juicier prey.

The car drove her up the long driveway, flanked by immaculate lawns, to deposit her at the front door, where she was greeted by a well-groomed personal assistant who insisted on watching her sign the usual nondisclosure agreement before taking her to meet Shaun.

Whether he was deliberately staging their meeting to show himself in a favourable light Madison wasn't sure, but Shaun had chosen to meet her in his library, a double height room with bookshelves covering three walls, the fourth wall made entirely of glass looking straight out onto the ocean. It was very impressive and not at all what she'd expected from the action hero. But that was what Madison loved about her job, seeing beneath the headlines and the clichés and the posturing to the person beneath, enabling her to find the right person for them.

'Mr Coleridge,' she said as the familiar figure rose to meet her. 'It's a huge pleasure; I've seen all your films.' It wasn't a lie; watching films or reading their books or browsing the websites was part of the extensive research she conducted on every client.

'I can return the compliment. I watched all your films growing up. I wondered what had happened to you, and here you are. Sensible to get out of the fame business while you could; shame that it's not easy to step away entirely. It's not easy to be on the front pages. You have my sympathy.'

The interview went well, a much-needed reminder that she was good at her job at least. Shaun was an engaging interviewee with a dry sense of humour and a self-deprecating streak she appreciated. He was realistic about what life with him entailed and as she went through the usual interview questions Madison was sure she'd match him easily.

'That's all from me, so if you have any more questions now is the time,' she said finally. 'And if not then it's up to you whether you want to continue. I'll be honest; it can be difficult to find genuine matches for people who are as much in the public eye as you are, but it's not impossible and I am sure I can help. There are a couple of women on my books I know would be a good starting point and I am signing new clients all the time. The prospects are good, especially as you're not in a hurry.'

'Thank you,' he said, taking her proffered hand. 'I've heard very good things about your business, Madison. People say you have quite a talent for matchmaking and that sounds good to me. Acting at my level can be a lonely business, as I'm sure you know. If you could find someone willing to take all this craziness on, I'll be in your debt for ever.'

'I'm sure we can help,' Madison said, and he nodded.

'Thank you. I'll be honest. I just want what you have, someone to walk on the beach with, to laugh with. I'm used to the lack of privacy, the lack of spontaneity, but I don't want to give up on companionship. Those photos of you prompted me to finally get in touch. You looked like someone who had found their way. It was a good endorsement.'

Shaun's words echoed round and round Madison's head as she stared at him, speechless. He was right. She *had* found her way, only to lose it again. She'd survived this long by building a fortress around her heart as high as the walls around Shaun Coleridge's estate, but now they were breached she didn't know how to repair them. If she even wanted to repair them. Could she really go back to her lonely, grey life when she knew there was love and sunshine waiting for her if she could just summon up the courage to embrace it? Look at all the people who had the courage to tell her their hopes and dreams, who put their futures and hearts in her hands. How could she ask for that trust if she didn't trust in herself? Didn't take the leap of faith she asked them to take?

She'd been standing on the cliff edge for too long. She needed to jump.

The actor looked at her quizzically and she smiled, forcing an answer somehow. 'Thank you. I'm glad you did get in touch. Let me know if you want to proceed. Thank you so much for seeing me; I look forward to hearing from you.' She took a step towards a door, only to stop as a beautiful golden labradoodle she hadn't spotted before got up and stretched. Madison couldn't resist holding out a hand for the dog to sniff before rubbing it behind its ears. 'Aren't you beautiful?' she crooned.

'This is the most constant love of my life,' Shaun said with the million-watt grin that had won him so many admirers. 'She belongs to my sister but as she's a nurse and works long hours her dogs stay here when she's on shift. When I'm not here my housekeeper spoils them outrageously. It works well, my life is too hectic for me to have pets, but I get all the benefits when I'm home. I hope whoever you find is prepared to share my heart with two shaggy blondes.'

'A dog-lover? Got it. How old is she?'

'Amber here is three. Opal is two but she's confined to the kitchen at the moment. She had puppies eight weeks ago and I'm keeping them there. If I let them into here they'll destroy everything.'

'Puppies?'

'Would you like to meet them?'

Madison hesitated but couldn't resist. 'Absolutely.'

The kitchen was a light-filled, friendly space, clearly the domain of the diminutive housekeeper, who bustled around making coffee and offering Madison biscuits she didn't have the appetite to eat. In fact, she couldn't remember the last time she'd been hungry, maybe not since that pasta dinner two weeks ago. But food was soon forgotten as she was introduced to seven fat, fluffy puppies in shades of gold from buttermilk to a rich tawny.

'This is the last day we'll have them,' Shaun said, picking up the smallest and handing it to Madison, who accepted the warm, wiggly bundle eagerly. 'They all go to their homes this week.'

'Your sister isn't keeping one?'

'She says two is plenty and she's right. They're mostly going to colleagues of hers, all except this one.' Shaun nodded at the puppy nestling in Madison's arms. 'Her home fell through and as she's the runt she's not easy to rehome. She'll need lots of love and attention over the next few weeks.'

Madison looked into the puppy's brown eyes and felt the broken pieces of her heart begin to pulse again. 'She's beautiful, almost red-gold. I know a little girl who would love her. Is she really available?'

Shaun shrugged. 'It's my sister's call and she is very careful who she rehomes to, but I can set up a call tonight if you want.'

Did she? And, if so, what did that mean? A farewell gift? An apology? A peace offering? Or a commitment? Either way, she would have to postpone her flight home again. Would have to meet up with Isla—and Luke. She could hardly just send a dog to them without warning.

The puppy wiggled and then nestled in, its head heavy on her chest, its breathing vibrating through her, its trust absolute. Isla trusted her—or at least she had. Luke had trusted her with the most important thing in his life and she had shattered that trust. She was so busy trying to keep herself safe she'd shown herself to be as selfish as her parents. Luke was right; there were no guarantees and if she went through life needing one then she would be always alone. But if she could learn to trust. To hope. To love and be loved…

Madison dropped a kiss on the small fuzzy head. 'Yes,' she said. 'I'd like that. A call would be good.'

Sunday had gone from being Luke's favourite day of the week to the longest. This week Isla had even suggested they skip their usual trip to the coast and stay in Sydney, but Luke wouldn't allow either of them to wallow. They'd loved Palm Beach before Madison and they would continue to love it.

He scanned the beach but there was no sign of any journalists or long lenses. The beach was its usual laid-back self.

'Isla?'

His daughter looked up from the sandcastle she was building and Luke couldn't help thinking about the last time he'd made sandcastles, the charged competitiveness between Madison and himself, how it had ended in laughter and passion and tenderness, and the sense of wrongness that had dogged him for the last two weeks intensified. His failure to get through to Madison, to get her to trust him, to trust in them, had ramifications far beyond him. It wasn't just Isla's evident sadness; it was knowing that Madison had chosen to go back to a life stripped of colour and vibrancy rather than trust him.

'Yes?' Her smile had only half its usual brilliance.

'What do you think about living here all year round? We could get that dog you're always talking about.'

It was an impulsive offer, but the more he thought about it, the more sense it made. He'd known they needed to make some changes; that was why he'd got in touch with Madison in the first place. Hannah, their nanny, was thinking of going travelling, so if Luke worked from home more, only went into the city a couple of days a week, found someone local to watch Isla after school on the days he wasn't there, then a move here would work. A new start for them both, a more normal existence for Isla. 'You can join the surf school. I know how much you've wanted to. And the sailing school as well.'

'Can I still do dance? And play football?'

'I'm sure you can.'

'And absolutely definitely a dog?'

'Absolutely, definitely.' He couldn't guarantee the mother figure or future siblings; the sensible marriage of shared priorities and mutual respect he'd envisioned seemed absurd now. But a dog? That they could absolutely do.

'Okay.' Isla went back to digging and Luke leaned back and scanned the horizon again, unable to fully relax, the memories of the intrusive photos and their ramifications too raw.

At least he'd made a decision about their future. It felt good, but still hollow. A compromise between the life he wanted and the life he could have. He went over his last conversation with Madison again. Could he have done more? Worked harder to convince her? But no. Convincing her had never been the plan. If they were to have any chance then she had to come to him of her own free will. Her parents had manipulated her enough; he had to give her choice. No matter what the consequences.

'Daddy?'

'Hmm?'

'What time is Madison's flight?'

Luke didn't even need to check, the time imprinted on his heart. 'It's this evening.'

'Can we go see her off?'

Luke's first instinct was to say no but before the word formed he paused. He didn't want Madison to return home thinking the door was closed, that there was no way forward. She had no one in her life; he had to let her know that, no matter her choices, she was wanted and loved. A dramatic rush through the airport to the gates was the stuff of films—and impossible in the security-conscious twenty-first century—but a proper goodbye? Maybe the closure would be good for Isla—and for him.

'I...' He squinted, breaking off the sentence. A woman was walking along the beach, cradling something small in her arms. There was something about her height, the colour of her hair, her bearing that reminded him of Madison. But it couldn't be; she was packing back at the hotel, surely?

Slowly he rose to his feet and took a step, then another, blinking to clear his vision, trying and failing to stop hope swelling in his breast. Isla was not so reticent. She looked over to see what he was looking at and gave a happy cry that tore through him.

'Madison!'

It seemed to take an age, as if he were pushing against the tide, before Luke reached her. Madison looked somehow more relaxed than he'd ever seen her, as if she'd shed a huge burden.

'Hey,' he said and she smiled at him.

'Hi, I was hoping to find you here.'

Luke's gaze dropped to the object she was holding and his eyebrows rose in surprise as he took in the tawny puppy, wrapped in a towel, even as hope hammered through him. He reached out to lay a finger on the small head. 'You've made a new friend.' Was this a farewell gift or a promise? Either way, he could feel all the tension melting.

'I may have been a little impulsive; don't hate me.'

'I could never hate you.'

'I know.'

Their eyes locked and held, the moment all too brief before Isla skidded up, braking just before she threw herself on Madison, her eyes wide in awe and hope. 'You have a puppy?'

'Well...' Madison looked at Luke, her expression a beguiling mixture of mischief, guilt and love that nearly floored him. 'Actually, and only if your dad agrees, *you* have a puppy. I know, I know...' she said hurriedly to Luke. 'It's a huge responsibility and you guys live in an apartment but I thought maybe we could share her, and I could take her for walks and dog-sit her and...'

Luke could resist no longer. Taking care not to squash the squirming animal and heedless of Isla's squeal, he drew Madison close and kissed her.

The kiss was all too brief but it held such love and desire and understanding that Madison could feel it imprinted on her lips throughout the next ten minutes as she took the puppy into the house and settled her on a towel with some water and a toy while Luke helped Isla bring her toys inside.

'What's her name?' Isla asked as she watched the puppy fall asleep.

'That's up to you. But if you're going to keep her then we need to hit the store; she needs a bed and more toys, bowls, a collar, all kinds of things. I have a puppy starter kit with me—' she indicated the back-pack she'd brought with her '—but that will only do for a day or so.'

'Can we keep her, Daddy?' Isla begged and Luke smothered a smile.

'That depends on whether you can show you're ma-ture enough to look after a puppy,' he said. 'Madison and I are going to have a quick chat on the terrace and your job is to watch the puppy, bring her to us if she wakes up, but not to interfere with her sleeping. Can you do that?'

Isla nodded self-importantly and Luke grinned as he towed Madison onto the terrace. 'That should keep her occupied,' he said. 'She'll be desperate to prove she can be trusted.'

'You don't mind?' The certainty that had powered Madison through the last twenty-four hours wavered. 'I know it's a huge commitment.'

'Did you mean what you said out there? About help-ing look after her? It's just I'm wondering how you plan to do that from London.'

This was it. Madison took a deep breath. 'Well. Looks like there's a lot of people in this part of the world looking for the kind of service M provides. I had thought about hiring someone to oversee an Australian office, but Jen, my assistant in London, more than de-serves a promotion, and so does my PA. So I thought maybe Jen could oversee the London office with Lea's help and I could be responsible for over here.' She was going into way too much detail, but there was so much else to say and she didn't know how to broach it. 'It means giving Jen more responsibility to interview and match, and I'm not great at giving up control but recent events have shown me that my life is much fuller when I do. When I trust people.'

'Oh?' The warmth in Luke's eyes, his smile, his voice heated her through. 'Which events?'

'Meeting you, spending time with you…' Her voice dropped to a whisper. 'Loving you.'

Luke didn't reply with words, but he pulled Madison close, his heart pressed against hers, his arms encircling her, dropping a kiss onto her head. She nestled in for one blissful moment, feeling as if she'd come home at last, then pulled back to look up at him.

'You asked me to trust in you, to trust in us, but I couldn't,' she said, her voice shaky but steadied by the love and understanding in his face. 'I felt like I was fated to always look in on other people's lives, not able to experience happiness for myself. That even hoping for more was doomed. When I saw the photos I felt so exposed—and so guilty. That I had brought darkness to your door.'

'I hate to break it to you, but I am quite capable of generating my own headlines,' Luke said. 'I can't deny that I was furious when I saw them. But not with you— *for* you. Furious that something so new had been made public, furious that they had come after Isla. And furious because the moment I saw the pictures I could see you slipping away from me.'

'I had to retreat. But then I looked at my future and it no longer felt safe, just empty, and I realised if I didn't take a chance to live, what was any of it for? You don't owe me anything, Luke. I left you. If you don't want to risk me messing up again, risk me letting down Isla, then that's fine. But I hope we can be friends no matter what.' Friends was such a pale imitation of what she wanted, what she needed, but she'd settle for it if that was all that was on offer.

'Oh, no, you don't get out of puppy training that easily,' Luke said and with those words the last of the tension she'd carried for so many years slid away. 'Isla and I were just discussing giving up the apartment and moving here permanently. The only thing missing from that plan is you. What do you say, Madison? Are you willing to take us on? Like I said, I can't guarantee there won't be bumps ahead. Life is rarely simple; we both know that. But I can guarantee two people who will love you and want you in their lives. Permanently.'

'And I want you in my life. Permanently,' Madison managed. 'Both of you. I want to help you give Isla the kind of childhood I never had and I want you, Luke Taylor. I love every competitive, driven, kind, compassionate part of you.'

'You forgot devilishly handsome and good in bed,' he said, eyes alight with mischief, and she laughed.

'I can see I will need to keep that ego of yours in check.'

'And I will need to help build yours up so that you see what I see. A clever, resilient, brave, beautiful woman who I am proud to stand beside. And a very talented matchmaker as well. After all, you found me my perfect partner.'

And with that Luke kissed her and as Madison melted into him, into the moment, into the promise of a brighter future, she knew she'd found her perfect match too.

* * * * *

# RECLAIMING THE PRINCE'S HEART

## REBECCA WINTERS

MILLS & BOON

To my dear friend Rachel,
who I believe is an angel on earth, giving me her
undying devotion over the years. Her expertise,
her brilliance, her pure heart, her goodness make
her exceptional. How blessed are her three children
and husband. She listened to my ideas, supported my
thoughts and helped with some of the twists and turns
of this novel. Everyone loves her as I do.

# CHAPTER ONE

*San Vitano, an Italian-speaking country bordering eastern Switzerland and northern Italy.*
*June 2. 6 a.m.*

As RINI EASED himself away from his sleeping, delectable wife, she caught him around the shoulders.

"Not so fast, *mi amore*. Tell me again why you have to go today of all days?"

He kissed her mouth hungrily. "This inspection tour can't be put off any longer. I'm implementing some new safety rules with the chief mining engineer, Gustavo, and his assistants."

"I realize it's important, but this will be the first time we've been apart since our wedding. I already miss you so much, I haven't been able to sleep."

"Why do you think I made love to you half the night?" he murmured against her lips. He was so in love with Luna, he could stay in bed with her forever. "Just remember, I'll be home at the end of the day."

"You'd better keep your promise. I have something special planned for our six-month wedding anniversary tonight."

He hugged her lovingly. "I wouldn't miss it. As it happens, I have a surprise for you, too. Now, go back to sleep."

After kissing her breathless, he slid out of bed to shower. Once ready in jeans, a work shirt and boots, he walked out the back of the *palazzo* to his waiting helicopter.

The half-hour trip to the King Midas gold-mining site on the Italian, Austrian and Slovenian border didn't take long. The men were there to greet him in the front office. Together they went down into the mine to get busy. By three in the afternoon, Rini's work was done and the men left.

Alone with Gustavo, they walked through the inclined shaft while they talked. "Is there anything else you want to discuss with me, Your Highness?"

"Gustavo, how many times have we had this conversation in the past? I'm the Crown Prince, not the King. Call me Rini."

He shook his head. "It's impossible to forget. Your new safety rules are going to make a big difference around here."

"I'm glad you approve, and I'm impressed over the excellent job you're doing. Keep me posted on your progress. Now I've got to fly back to Asteria. My wife and I are celebrating our anniversary tonight."

The head mining engineer flashed him a knowing smile. "I don't blame you for being eager. You're still in the honeymoon stage. May it last forever."

Rini chuckled. "Agreed." He couldn't wait to get back home.

They left the winze, which was a connecting shaft at the lower level, and headed for the mine portal above. Suddenly, Rini heard an earsplitting crack that sounded like a runaway train. The earth shook under their feet. It must have gone on for a minute or more. He felt dizzy.

"Earthquake."

"It won't last," Rini muttered. They'd both felt them in this region over the years. The tremors continued. "Let's keep moving until we reach the surface." But the words had barely left his lips when there was another explosive sound like a bomb had gone off and they were both knocked to the ground with force.

Gustavo let out a groan. "This isn't any normal quake, Your Highness."

"You're right. Just keep crawling toward the next shaft. I'm right behind you."

"The ground keeps shifting—I'm terrified!"

"Hang on!" Rini tried to reach him when a wall of rocks came crashing down. Claustrophobic dust filled the interior. Rini could hardly breathe. All had gone completely dark. "Gustavo?" He called to him again. "Gustavo?"

There was no answer. The ground kept shaking and there were boulder-like rocks in front of him, impeding any progress. He kept crying out Gustavo's name. Rini's heart sank to realize the manager had to be partially buried beneath the debris.

"I hope you can hear me, Gustavo. I'm going for help and will be back."

Rini, a top mining engineer graduate from the

school of mines in Colorado in the US, knew the layout of this mine like the back of his hand. It was one of the financial backbones of the Baldasseri royal family of San Vitano dating back three centuries. Rini was in charge.

He knew of another shaft leading out of the winze to an intersecting shaft. From there he could keep going until the opening of the shaft came out on the side of the mountain. Once free, he could get help. It was imperative in order to save Gustavo. Heaven knew how many other miners might have been buried in the horrendous quake.

The tremors continued, creating the rolling swell of the ground. More rocks fell. He kept going on his stomach as he clawed his way up through a winding labyrinth that led to another shaft. A little more progress and the unused shaft would lead to an opening he could see in his mind.

"You've got to keep going," Rini muttered to himself. Gustavo's life depended on it.

Another few feet and large portions of rock started falling on him. One hit his head, sending excruciating pain through his body. "Luna—" he cried her name in desperation before he knew nothing more.

Luna set the dining room table. Rini would be home from the mine soon. She couldn't wait and wanted everything to be just right. After gift wrapping the positive result of her home pregnancy test, she put it at his place. They'd wanted to start a family. Today she'd found out the joyous news. Luna hadn't had time to see her OB, but she'd call him tomorrow. Tonight she and her husband would celebrate!

Delicious smells of a pork roast filled the *palazzo*. She hurried into the kitchen to check on the potatoes in a half shell. Rini would be eating a meal he'd never had before that included roasted asparagus and stuffed apples. Luna had been born and raised in Scuol, Switzerland. She'd prepared some of her late grandmother's recipes. It would be exciting to serve him something she loved in honor of their becoming parents.

While she arranged the apples in a deep dish, their housekeeper, Viola, came into the kitchen. Her normal ruddy complexion had lost color. "Luna—you'd better come in the salon. The King and Queen are here."

Rini's grandparents had come to the *palazzo*? They'd only made an appearance once before at her and Rini's dinner invitation. What on earth would have caused them to do something this unprecedented with no advanced warning?

She rushed through the *palazzo* to the salon and found them both seated on the couch. What could have brought them here? Luna sat down in a chair opposite them. "I know you're here because something is seriously wrong. Tell me."

The look of devastation on their faces caused Luna's heart to plunge to her feet. Leonardo leaned forward. "There was an earthquake. It affected the mine."

Luna started to feel sick. "Were some of the miners injured?"

"I'm afraid eight were killed."

Killed? Aghast, she cried, "Did Rini tell you that?"

He shook his head as Antonia gripped her husband's arm. "It pains us to the core to tell you this, but...he was killed, too."

Rini was dead?

*"No—"* Luna jumped to her feet. "That isn't possible! I don't believe it."

Antonia got up and walked over to put her arm around her. "We don't want to believe it either, but we've had positive confirmation and came over here immediately to tell you."

She turned to her desolate grandmother-in-law. "This couldn't be. Not Rini—" Tears gushed down her cheeks. "He's the love of my life. There's no purpose without him. I can't live without him. Surely, there's been a mistake."

At this point Leonardo walked over and put his arms around both of them. "We know how you feel, darling."

She stared at them both through a blur. "You really believe he was killed?"

"He went down in the mine with the other seven. None of them ever came up again."

"No—no— This is a nightmare. Please tell me this is a nightmare and I'm going to wake up." Her tears had become a river.

"Come and sit down," he murmured, but she couldn't move. She felt numb. The room started to spin.

"Call our doctor and tell him to come here at once," she heard Antonia tell her husband. But the ringing in Luna's ears had grown so loud, everything went black.

In another few minutes she had cognizance of her

surroundings again and found herself lying on the couch. There were voices in the room and the palace doctor, Dr. Norelli, came over to her.

"I'm so sorry, Principessa. Stay still while I examine you." He took her vital signs. "You seem to be all right, but you've just undergone a severe shock. You need rest. I'm going to give you a sedative to help you get through the next few days." He left a bottle of pills on the coffee table.

She struggled to sit up. "Doctor—I'm pregnant even though I haven't seen my OB yet." She heard gasps of surprise come from Rini's grandparents. "I don't want to take anything that would hurt my baby."

"Don't worry. What I've got there will do no harm to you or your child."

By now Viola and her husband, Mateo, had come into the salon. The doctor motioned to him. "Come and help me take her upstairs to the bedroom."

Luna slowly got to her feet. "I'm okay and can make it on my own."

"I'm going to stay the night with you," Antonia murmured.

"We'll both stay," the King added.

"No, Leo," his wife implored. "You go back to the palace in case there's more news. I'll stay in touch with you."

Tears fell down his cheeks. "You're sure?"

"Yes."

"Our hearts are with you." The King pressed a kiss to Luna's cheek and left the room with the doctor.

Antonia reached for the pills and looped her arm

through Luna's. They walked slowly to the staircase in the foyer.

Luna buried her face against the older woman's shoulder. "Thank you for staying with me tonight. If it weren't for Rini's baby I'm carrying, I'd want to die."

"But for my great-grandchild you're carrying, *I'd* want to die, too."

They reached the master suite and Antonia helped Luna get ready for bed. After swallowing two pills, she climbed under the covers and rested her head against the pillows. Antonia sat on the side of the bed and held her hand.

"There are no words, are there?"

"No," Luna whispered, "but your presence means the world to me. I loved Rini the first moment I met him. It was like magic. He's the great love of my life. To think he died in a mine collapse. How terrifying those moments must have been for him! Oh, Tonia... I can't bear that I've lost him."

Luna broke down in heaving sobs. Loving arms reached over to hug her. They stayed that way for a long time. Eventually, she said, "I'll go to the guest room down the hall and we'll talk in the morning. If you need me during the night, call me on my phone. Now, let the sedative help you sleep." She kissed her forehead and left the bedroom.

The next morning Luna awakened in so much pain, she didn't know why she was alive. She turned to reach for her husband, then realized he wouldn't be coming home and was hit with another unbearable wave of grief.

"Luna?"

Antonia had come into the room with a tray. "I've brought us some coffee and rolls. You need to eat something since you didn't eat dinner last night."

She sat up with tears dripping off her face. "I couldn't. Is there any more news?"

"Leo said search parties worked all night, hoping to bring out the bodies, but they couldn't penetrate the blockage. There's no way to recover them."

Luna slid her legs over the side of the bed. "I'm a terrible person, Antonia. I've been thinking of myself without giving thought to you or the families of the miners." She looked up at her. "If Rini were alive, he'd be the first one to visit them and try to bring some comfort. As his wife, that's what I need to do."

"That would be a wonderful tribute to them, but not today. You need to take it easy."

"I can't just lie here, Antonia. I'll get dressed and go back to the palace with you. With Leonardo's help, I can gather the names and addresses of the families involved and make plans to visit them during the week. Rini would want this."

"He'd be so proud of you for thinking of them. But I insist you eat and drink a little to keep up your strength."

"I will, but I'm ashamed that I haven't thought of you and Leo or your needs. I should be waiting on you. Rini's your darling grandson. After losing your two sons and another grandson, I don't know how you're handling this. You're the strongest people I've ever known."

She hurried over to the Queen, who had sat down

next to a table with the tray. Luna threw her arms around her and they both wept again.

"With lots of love and faith, we got through. You will, too."

"I want to do everything I can so Rini will be proud of me."

"He adored you. After he met you, he told me his life was complete."

"He said that?" she cried through the tears. "Oh—I can't believe he's gone. I just can't believe it, but I have to."

They both drank coffee and bit into Viola's wonderful rolls. "I'll hurry to shower and get ready. Leonardo needs us."

Antonia nodded with fresh tears in her eyes.

"He has already called Rini's cousin Vincenzo with the news."

Luna could understand that. "Vincenzo and Rini are best friends."

"Yes. Leo says he's devastated. With Rini gone, Vincenzo is the next in line to be the Crown Prince."

Gone… Her beloved husband was gone. The earthquake had changed all their lives.

Luna hurried to the bathroom in agony. She took two more pills, then got into the shower where she broke down sobbing and didn't come out again for a long time.

*June 12*

Luna had been restless since the call from Rini's secretary at the palace. The acting manager of the mine had phoned to convey a message to Luna. A reminder, really. It seemed that one of the lost miners, Jaka Ravenikar, a Slovenian, had been working for the mine on a visa. His family lived near the mine in the border town of Rezana, Slovenia. It was the only family she hadn't visited throughout the past ten days with flowers and the assurance of financial aid to ease their burden.

Luna wanted to travel to Rezana and pay her respects on the monarchy's behalf. This morning she planned to go to the palace and ask Leonardo for help in visiting this family. She would need assistance, however, since she didn't speak Slovene.

Once that was done, a memorial service for family could be planned for Rini at the palace. But she couldn't accept the fact that she'd lost the love of her life. She never would. A memorial service would mean he was really gone, increasing her pain.

Her own parents had died when she was five in a plane accident. She'd been raised by her wonderful grandparents in Scuol, Switzerland. Her grandfather died first, then her grandmother. The losses had devastated her, but in time she won a scholarship to study business administration at St. Gallen University in Switzerland.

Upon graduation she'd obtained interviews with half a dozen companies. One led her to the Baldasseri Gold Mining Company in Asteria, San Vitano, an Italian-speaking country, where she was offered a position. Luna was bilingual in Italian and Romansh, her native language. Eighty thousand people in the Engadin of Switzerland spoke it. She felt that working there would be a good fit and she liked the staff.

Two weeks after she'd been hired, she met Prince Rinieri, who was the head gold-mining engineer for the mine. He was also the grandson of the King and Queen of San Vitano and was next in line for the throne. It only took meeting him to fall madly in love. They soon married and life couldn't have been more beautiful until tragedy struck. She could still see the article in the newspaper.

> *Crown Prince Rinieri Francesco Baldasseri of San Vitano was killed during an 8.7 earthquake at the King Midas Mine near the Slovenian border.*
>
> *He leaves behind his loving wife of six months, Her Royal Highness, Princess Luna Biancho Baldasseri.*
>
> *World leaders send their condolences to her and Their Royal Highnesses King Leonardo and Queen Antonia Baldasseri.*

For the past week she'd hoped and prayed that by some miracle the bodies would at least be found, but they'd been buried too deeply. As for Luna, in her mind and heart *he was still missing.* A part of her refused to believe he was dead. Maybe it was because of a dream she'd had where Rini appeared to her. It had seemed so real, she couldn't shake it.

Still racked with debilitating grief that attacked her in waves, she stepped into the shower to get ready, then styled her white-blond hair. She wore it neck length from a center part. Before the quake, she'd let it hang down her back the way Rini loved it. But a few days ago, in a surge of pain and disbelief that he was gone, she'd taken the scissors and had started cutting.

When she looked in the mirror, she saw a pale ghost of the woman she'd once been. She'd lost weight due to her anguish and her morning sickness. Her OB had warned her she needed to eat now that she was pregnant. He'd given her medication to help. Luna knew she had to live for herself and for Rini's baby.

Without wasting another moment, she reached for her phone on the bedside table and called the Queen to alert her she was coming. The older woman's love and support had made it possible for Luna to survive these past ten days of sheer agony.

"Luna?"

"*Buongiorno*, Tonia." They'd been on a first-name basis since Rini had introduced his grandmother to her eight months ago. "Forgive me for disturbing you, but this can't wait."

"What is it?"

"I have a favor to ask of Leonardo." She explained what it was she wanted to do to honor the miner. "I didn't know one of the men was a Slovenian. I hadn't realized he'd been working there on a work visa."

"I didn't either, Luna. Of course, Leo will arrange it. Come as soon as you can and we'll both talk to him."

"Thank you so much. Since we've met all the families of the other miners from San Vitano, I'd like to fly there and meet his family, take them flowers."

"I don't see a problem."

Relief filled Luna. "Wonderful. I'll be over within a half hour."

Once she'd hung up, she phoned for her driver to meet her in front of the *palazzo*. Then she rushed to the closet to dress in an aqua-colored, short-sleeved, two-piece summer suit. She matched it with white sandals and grabbed her purse.

"Viola?" she called to the housekeeper when she hurried downstairs to the foyer. "I'm leaving for the palace. I'm not sure when I'll be back, but I'll let you know."

Before long she reached the palace and met Antonia outside Leonardo's private study. The two walked in on him. "Leo?"

He lifted his gray head. Despair was written all over him. "Cara? Luna?"

"Luna has come to ask for a favor."

"Of course. Anything." He held out his arms and Luna ran into them. "How are you doing, darling?"

She wiped her eyes. "The same as you."

"Then that means you're in pain. None of us was ready for losing him."

"No. I never will be. Rini's been the light of my life and yours." Luna sat down on the love seat next to Antonia. "His secretary let me know that one of the miners was Slovenian."

He nodded. "That's right."

"I want to fly there today if possible and pay our respects to the man's family."

"Bless you for thinking of it."

"There's just one thing, Leonardo," Luna added.

"I would need a translator to go with me since I don't speak Slovene."

"You know Carlo. He's my official foreign emissary and fluent in half a dozen languages. I'll send him with you."

"That would be wonderful!" Luna cried. "He's one of Rini's favorites, and mine."

Leonardo nodded. "I'll ask him to arrange your flight to Rezana and pick up the flowers. He can arrange a car and escorts to meet you when you arrive there."

"Oh, thank you. The secretary gave me the address and phone number of Jaka's family."

"Plan to leave from here in two hours."

"You're wonderful." Luna flew off the love seat and ran to throw her arms around him once more. "I love you."

"We love you, too. You and the baby are all we have left of our Rini."

Luna walked out with Antonia, who pulled her aside. "Thank you for remembering this. It makes Leo happy to do something positive."

"I feel the same way. Right now I'll go home to gather a few things, then I'll be back and meet you out at the helipad behind the palace." She hugged her grandmother-in-law again before rushing out of the palace.

Two hours later Luna had been strapped into the royal helicopter with Carlo Bruni. The man had served in the San Vitano Military besides having all the leadership qualities Rini had admired. Luna had always liked him and felt comfortable with him as they flew to Rezana, the town two miles away from the mine.

Rini had called it the Re Mida Mine, named for King Midas. Luna had worked for the mining company business office in Asteria, San Vitano's capital city, but she'd never traveled to the actual mine. Rini had once told her the mountainous terrain there was full of a network of caves. Most of the system was located next to the Slovenian border, with dozens of little settlements clustered on top of the northern rim like a medieval town. Rezana was one of them.

She looked out the window during the descent. Her heart lurched to realize her beloved husband had been caught in the earthquake and lay deep in the rubble that had robbed him and the others of life. Fighting not to break down, she bit her knuckle while they landed.

A driver and government official met them at the small airport, engaging Carlo in conversation. He eventually turned to her. "Since I'm Leonardo's emissary, their government is giving us assistance by escorting us to the Ravenikar home."

"That's very kind of them."

He opened the car door and they got in. The other car followed. Soon, they wound around to a home in the small, picturesque town. They were met out in front by Jaka's father.

"This is Anton Ravenikar," Carlo translated for Luna.

The father of the dead miner looked at the two of them through eyes filled with tears. Luna walked up to him. "My name is Luna Baldasseri. I'm the wife of

Rinieri Baldasseri, who was inspecting the mine when the quake struck. I know you're suffering, Mr. Ravenikar. So am I."

He nodded.

Unable to hold back she asked, "When your country searched for Jaka's body, did they see any other bodies?"

She waited while Carlo translated. Turning to her he said, "No, but he wouldn't know because he couldn't help in the search."

Luna closed her eyes for a second. "Ask him if there's someone who *would* know."

Carlo translated again. Anton muttered something. "What did he say?"

"We should ask Zigo, a policeman at the station. He was Jaka's friend and helped in the search. He could tell you definitively how it went."

It had been a long shot. Of course there was no news. "Thank you so much. Please know how sorry we are for your loss."

He nodded. "Thank you for coming. It means everything."

Carlo translated the man's appreciation that she'd come. Anton invited them inside the house. She learned that Jaka had been married and living with his parents and an older brother and sister. When Luna presented the flowers to Jaka's widow, everyone burst into tears. The family couldn't have been more grateful and thrilled for the visit and the promise of a financial donation.

Once it ended, they went outside to the car. Carlo

murmured, "If you wish, we'll go to police headquarters where you can talk to Zigo before we go home. Do you want to do that?"

"I'm sure he won't be able to tell us anything, but I admit I'd still like to talk to him for a minute." The need to learn anything more was the driving factor for her. *And the dream that had seemed so real.*

"Then let's go."

# CHAPTER TWO

ONCE INSIDE THE BUILDING, Luna and Carlo were shown to the front office of the station. She looked around and smiled at two officers. Carlo asked if they could speak to Zigo.

The younger one came forward. Luna's heart raced as they were all introduced. "Zigo? Do you speak Italian?"

*"Cosi-cosi."*

His answer, "so-so," was better than nothing. She stared into his eyes. *"Did you look for Jaka Ravenikar?"*

*"Sì.* He was friend."

Her pulse picked up speed. "Did you see any bodies?"

"No bodies," he answered without hesitation.

A little moan escaped her lips. "I'm looking for my *marito.*"

At this point Carlo had to translate.

Zigo said, "He died, too?"

Her eyes filled with tears. "My husband didn't come home. Maybe he escaped." Was it possible?

He frowned. "Escaped?"

"Got away." She used her fingers to show him that her husband might have gotten out. Again, Carlo translated.

"Ah," he said. "No. I know nothing."

With her hopes dashed, she asked if she could use the restroom before they got back on the helicopter. Carlo interceded. Zigo nodded and showed Luna where to go.

They walked down a hallway to the rear of the station. She went in to freshen up and say a little prayer to help her get through the rest of this day.

When Luna came out of the restroom, she found Zigo waiting for her near the end of the hall. "*Grazie* for talking to me."

He nodded.

Filled with fresh pain, Luna hurried into the front office. Together she and Carlo left for the car to drive them to the helicopter. As she started to get into the backseat, she heard the cry, "Principessa?" She turned to see who was calling out. To her surprise it was Zigo. He'd run after them.

"Carlo?" she said. "Zigo's Italian is sketchy. Speak to him in Slovene and find out what he's trying to tell me."

A long conversation ensued. She couldn't imagine.

"Luna—when you told the guard you hoped Rini had escaped, it made him think."

She blinked. "What are you saying?"

"A day after the earthquake there was talk of a stranger who was brought into the town by a motorist on the highway. He'd discovered a man wounded and lying at the side of the highway. Our station was called. We responded and took him to the local hospital. So far no one has identified him."

Her heart leaped. "Is he still there?"

More talk ensued. Carlo turned to her. "As far as Zigo knows, he hasn't left, but the man spoke a strange language neither he nor the officer understood."

A strange language? That didn't sound like Rini. Still, this could be something of vital interest for all of them. Maybe it was one of the miners from San Vitano who'd managed to get out. Maybe one of them knew a different language.

"Zigo says they are looking for anyone who might know him. The man had no papers on him, no way to identify him. When you told Zigo you were looking for your husband and hoped he'd escaped the cave-in, it got him thinking, and—"

"And he thinks it might be Rini!" she cried out for joy, interrupting him.

"Zigo didn't say that, especially when the man didn't respond to any languages other officers had tried with him. But he felt your distress. Don't get your hopes up, Luna."

"I can't help it."

"I know," he said in a kind voice.

Luna couldn't imagine the stranger being her Rini. She bit her lip. "I'm thinking it's one of the miners from our country. I can't even imagine how wonderful it would be to find one of them alive. Ask Zigo if we can see him."

After the inquiry, the answer came back that they

could proceed directly to the hospital. She and Carlo got back into the car while Zigo gave instructions to the driver, and said he'd alert the staff. He eyed Luna with compassion before waving them off. A few minutes later they arrived at the hospital.

Thankful for the cooperation, they hurried inside and were met by a woman who showed them to the second floor. They were taken inside an office and told to wait.

After she left, Luna grasped Carlo's arm. "What if it's one of the miners? He could tell us what happened in the mine. He'll be able to tell us about Rini." Her eyes filled with tears. "I'd give anything for the tiniest bit of information about their last moments."

"Let's pray for that much good news, Luna. But remember they said he didn't speak a language they understood."

"I know."

Before long, a man of probably sixty joined them. He spoke to Carlo at some length. Finally, he turned to Luna and spoke to her in Italian.

"It's an honor to meet you, Principessa Baldasseri. I'm Doctor Miakar. I understand your husband has been missing since the earthquake. If this man is the Crown Prince of San Vitano, the government will be anxious to learn what you tell us and cooperate with you any way they can."

"Thank you so much."

"Right now he's under sedation and sleeping. I had to operate on his arm, which is badly infected. He was so agitated, I was forced to give him something to calm him down. He should be awake within ten or fifteen minutes. Come with me so you can see if you recognize him."

With her heart thundering, she and Carlo followed him down the hall to an examination room. He opened the door.

Her eyes flew to the black-haired man in his late twenties lying asleep on the gurney, dressed in hospital greens and socks. His head was turned away. An IV had been hooked up to fight the infection in his arm.

She walked around the bed to see him clearly, then almost fainted.

*"Rini—"*

Carlo grabbed Luna's arm to support her. In a shaken voice he said, "It *is* His Royal Highness. You were inspired to come to Rezana, Luna."

"My beloved Rini." She couldn't believe it. *He was alive! Rini had come to her in her dream!* Joy radiated through her. "He didn't die. God has heard my prayers."

She'd never seen him with ten days' growth of beard and disheveled hair. Nothing could hide the pallor of his gaunt complexion. He'd suffered weight loss. Her gorgeous six-foot-three husband normally weighed two hundred and ten pounds. But none of it mattered because she'd found him and would take perfect care of him until he was well and restored to his former dashing self.

As she leaned over with the intent to kiss him, the doctor cautioned her not to touch him. "He needs the sleep. That will give us time to talk. Come back to my office."

It killed her to leave him when she'd just found him, but she did as the doctor asked. Her heart was thudding too hard to be healthy. The three of them walked back to the doctor's office.

"So your husband *is* the Crown Prince of San Vitano."

"Yes!" she cried, overjoyed to the point the tears were gushing. "Here." She pulled the wallet out of her purse and handed pictures of him to the doctor to prove it.

He studied them and nodded. "I'll inform the staff and the police. They'll inform the prime minister. Now that we know his identity, he'll be released to you. But we must talk fast, Princess Baldasseri. I need your input."

"Of course. Go on."

"Besides the deep gash on his arm, my examination has revealed he suffered a blow to the back of the head. He also lost a great deal of blood and is still recovering. But I am only a general doctor. This village hospital doesn't have the sophisticated equipment to diagnose him. When you get him home, he needs all kinds of care and must see a neurological specialist right away. You will need a medevac helicopter to transport him back to San Vitano."

"I understand and am so thankful you've been here to take care of him. There are no words to tell you how grateful I am." She turned to Carlo. "I'll call the King and Queen to let them know he's alive. Leonardo will send a medical helicopter immediately."

She pulled out her cell and phoned Rini's grandparents, who were speechless with joy when they heard the news. They all wept for a long time.

"I'll explain everything later. Right now Carlo is here with me and we're at the hospital with the doctor treating Rini, who has a deep cut on his arm. It's infected and they're giving him an antibiotic." She heard Antonia cry out in pain. "Can you send a neurosurgeon with the helicopter? We also need to know how soon to expect it."

"It will arrive there within the hour," Leonardo promised. "A miracle happened today, and all because of you. You have no idea the measure of our gratitude for you."

"I love you both. We have our Rini back. It's a glorious day."

"Indeed it is. Come home safely, my dear. We'll have everything ready for you at the hospital."

She hung up and related the news to the doctor. "Can I sit with my husband until he's transferred?"

"I don't see why not but realize he's very nervous and trusts no one. We can't communicate with him. When you get home, he'll need medical help to see to his immediate needs."

"Thank you for taking such wonderful care of him, Doctor Miakar. We'll make sure you and the hospital are recompensed for all you've done."

"It's an honor."

"We're going to be here for a while," Carlo murmured to her. "I'll have the driver take me to the helicopter and tell them to fly home. Then I'll return for you and we'll wait for the other helicopter. It will land here at the hospital."

"You're a treasure, Carlo. I couldn't have done this without you."

After he left the hospital, she turned to the doctor. "Can I see my husband now?"

He indicated she should follow him. Luna was living to see Rini again and just fill her eyes. The wonder of his being alive consumed her.

When she went back to his room and sat down by him, she realized he hadn't moved. It gave her the opportunity to feast her hungry eyes on his face and body. The first time she'd met him, she knew the tall, hunky, black-haired Crown Prince had to be the most attractive man alive.

"Rini—" she sobbed his name quietly, unable to imagine how horrible his life must have been since the earthquake. Why couldn't he speak or understand anything? They said he spoke a strange language. She couldn't get over it.

Luna walked around to see the top of his head. The doctor said he'd received a blow. She couldn't detect anything with all that black hair covering his scalp. Who knew what horrors he'd had to live through?

He was hooked up to an IV, and one of the nursing staff was checking his vital signs. After a while Luna could tell he was coming to because he moved his strong legs and turned his head to the other side of the pillow.

She moved to the other side of his bed to be close

to him. Without thinking, she whispered, *"Jeu carezel tei, Rini,"* in her native language. It meant *I love you.*

Suddenly, he opened those translucent gray eyes she'd thought she'd never see again. They stared at her without recognition. She assumed it was because he was still sedated. *"Ti discurras rumantch?"*

Her heart turned over because he'd heard her outpouring of love and understood. He'd just asked her if she spoke Romansh. *That* was the strange language no one understood?

*"Gea.* Yes, yes, yes."

"How come no one else can communicate? Where am I? I've been going insane that no one understands me. But *you* do. Why? Do you know me?"

His questions were fired one after another. The last question shocked her, but now was not the time to try and understand what was going on.

"I know you very well." Her voice shook. "Your name is Rini and I'm your wife, Luna."

An incredulous expression entered his intelligent eyes. "Impossible! I've never been married."

Help. Something was terribly wrong. *Don't panic, Luna.* "Thank heaven you're alive and that I've found you. You're in a hospital in Rezana, Slovenia. I'm going to take you home. A helicopter is on the way."

At that moment Carlo appeared at the door. He motioned her to come out into the hall. Her gaze shot back to her precious husband, who was so disoriented, she realized he was still under the effects of the anesthetic. "I have to leave you for a few minutes."

"You *can't* go. No one else understands me." He sounded utterly frantic. It wrenched her heart.

"I promise I'll see you in a few minutes. Trust me."

Trust her?

That breathtaking blonde woman, a stranger, had just said she was his wife? How could that possibly be? No man could forget her if he'd been married to her. He realized he must be dreaming. It had to be the anesthetic that had put him to sleep and he'd started to hallucinate.

What was he doing in Slovenia? No words had made sense to him until he heard a voice say that she loved him. Those were the first words he'd understood since waking up in the hospital. Whoever she really was, he would have to trust her all right since she was his lifeline to get out of here.

A nurse came in to check his vital signs again. He kept waiting for the woman named Luna to return. To finally be able to talk to someone, and then she had to leave the room. He'd go out of his mind waiting for her to come back.

What if she didn't?

He broke out in a cold sweat.

The nurse looked worried as she checked his blood pressure. After she'd listened to his heart, she left the room. *Damn.* How long did he have to remain in this limbo?

When he was about ready to pull out the IV and leave the room on his own to find this Luna, a strange man came in wearing a business suit. "Rini?"

According to Luna, Rini was his name.

The man smiled and patted his own chest. "I'm Doctor Romano."

Romano? It meant nothing to him.

The man came around to check Rini's skull. His hands were gentle, but Rini's crown had been tender since he'd awakened in the hospital. The slight probing hurt. What was going on?

He nodded to Rini before leaving the room. Now what? Another endless wait?

Before long two male hospital workers came inside. They removed the IV and wheeled him out of the room and down the hall to an elevator. Once on the main floor, he was taken down another hall and outside where he saw a medevac helicopter standing by.

Where in the hell was Luna? Where was he being taken? He tried to get off the gurney, but they restrained him.

Luna and Carlo stayed in Dr. Miakar's office, waiting to hear what would happen next. Soon, another man came inside. He smiled at Luna.

"Principessa Baldasseri?" He spoke Italian. "I'm Doctor Piero Romano from the Sacred Heart Hospital in San Vitano."

"Oh, thank goodness you're here!" She took in the fiftyish-looking brown-haired man standing there in a business suit. "You must be the neurosurgeon my grandfather-in-law sent. It was marvelous of you to come at a moment's notice when I know how busy you must be. Thank you more than you know."

"I'm honored to have been asked to help your husband. I just wanted to say that San Vitano was devastated over the reported death of the Crown Prince. I don't have to tell you how overjoyed the King and Queen are to learn that he's alive and will be returning. The country will celebrate the moment it hears their favorite son is alive. But I dare say no one is happier than you."

"You're right. No one could know how I'm feeling at this moment." Tears gushed down her cheeks.

"I've already checked your husband."

"You've seen him?"

"I have, and we're going to take good care of him. Before we leave in the helicopter, however, there are things I need to tell you. I spoke briefly with Doctor Miakar and we looked at your husband's record of confinement. I'll know a lot more when I get him scanned, but one thing is clear. He's suffering from amnesia."

"Amnesia…" She stared at him in alarm, unable to comprehend it. *That* was the reason he didn't understand anything?

"I need information. What languages does he speak, Principessa?"

She brushed the moisture off her cheeks. "Please call me Luna."

"If you wish."

"I do. My husband speaks Italian, German, Slovene, English and Romansh."

"Romansh?"

"Yes. It's my native language and Rini learned it living at his second cousin's home in Switzerland. When

I first saw him a little while ago, I told him I loved him in Romansh. He opened his eyes, shocked that I spoke a language he could understand."

"Wonderful. You're going to be the great key to helping him."

"But shouldn't he have recovered his memory since the quake? Surely, it ought to be returning by now."

"Not necessarily."

Paralyzing pain swept through her. Now that he'd explained everything, Luna was starting to understand why Rini had fired all those questions at her. It was incomprehensible to her. All of it.

"Doctor Romano, you don't mean he might never regain it—" she half groaned the words "—that he'll never recognize me or his world?"

"We don't know. I've read of a case history of a man living in Canada who had a blow to the head and forgot who he was. It's called a fugue state, and very rare. Years later he suddenly remembered who he was, but he'd been missing for years."

Years...

"Perhaps when your husband is transferred to familiar surroundings, he'll remember everything. But if he doesn't, then you need to be aware of his condition and prepare yourself that recognition might not happen right away. For now, we'll take it a step at a time."

Another moan escaped her lips. Rini might never recognize her? How could that be? She shuddered.

"As soon as we arrive at the hospital, he'll be taken to the suite reserved for the King where everything will be done for him. The history on him says he's manageable if you give him time to think about it."

"What do you mean by that?"

"He's lost his memory and doesn't know what's happened to him. It has made him paranoid because he hasn't been able to communicate with anyone until now. Doctor Miakar described that condition exactly. Your husband is a tall, strong man, so it's doubly important we try to keep him as calm as possible until we've worked with him. It's no wonder he's skittish."

Rini skittish? That didn't sound like the husband she knew. Out of all the things that could have happened to him, having amnesia would never have been a possibility in her mind. She turned to the doctor. "He must be terrified not to remember anything! I can't imagine it."

He eyed her with compassion. "Exactly."

Her body trembled. "I'm frightened, Doctor Romano."

"Of course you are, but I'm here to help you as well as your husband. With the aid of Doctor Tullia, an outstanding neuropsychologist I've asked to be on this case, you'll be able to deal with a situation new to all of you. If you're ready, we'll go out to the helicopter."

The medevac helicopter team helped the three of them climb in and strapped them in along the side. Her heart pounded hard as Rini was brought out to the helicopter and lifted to the airbed.

"Luna!" he cried when he saw her. "I thought you'd gone."

Oh, Rini, Rini. "I promised I wouldn't leave you," she said in Romansh.

"Where have you been?" His eyes probed hers.

"Talking to the doctors. But you're going home now. Try to relax. It's only a half-hour flight."

Her husband was returning wrapped in hospital green Slovenian swaddling clothes. Where were his own clothes, let alone his wedding ring and watch?

After the helicopter lifted off, Rini held her gaze. "How did we meet?"

"It's a long story. I was born in Scuol, Switzerland, where we speak Italian and Romansh. You have a second cousin Vincenzo, who also lives in Scuol and you learned to speak it.

"I started working for your company. You and I spoke Romansh on the first day we met. When you found out I'd been born in Scuol, it gave us a unique connection. We often spoke it so no one else could understand." It was their private language of love. In truth, it had been love at first sight for them, but he didn't want to hear that now.

"I don't have any family."

Oh, dear. Too much information. "Don't worry about that right now."

Before long they reached the Sacred Heart Hospital in Asteria and landed on the roof, where attendants were waiting.

"We're here, Rini."

"Where?"

"At the hospital in your hometown. You need to be taken care of for a little while longer."

His features hardened. "I don't want to be in another hospital."

"Just for a little while until I know you'll be all right. That infection was a bad one."

"Where will you be?"

"Right here with you. But first you must go with Doctor Romano. I'll join you in a minute."

"You swear it?" The demand broke her heart. He was so paranoid it frightened her.

Oh, Rini. Darling. "I swear."

The doctor got out of the helicopter first to accompany Rini, who was wheeled inside to the top-floor suite of the hospital. With security everywhere, she knew the King and Queen had been waiting on the premises.

She and Carlo followed. When they emerged from the elevator, Antonia cried Luna's name and ran to her. They hugged and cried tears together. "Where's Leonardo?"

"Doctor Romano is talking to him while another doctor is taking care of the gash on Rini's arm and getting him settled. They're already talking over a plan of tests and will call in a nutritionist to get him healthy again. When I glimpsed him, I must admit I hardly recognized my grandson with facial hair and weight loss."

"I know. It's a shock. Before we go in to him, there's something of vital importance you should know first." They hurried toward the door to the suite and walked inside. Dr. Romano saw them and motioned them over to him and the King.

Rini's grandfather wept, but it wasn't for joy. Not this time. Luna turned to Dr. Romano. "Will you tell my grandmother-in-law your diagnosis?"

"Tell me what?" the older woman murmured.

In the next few minutes the doctor explained that Rini had amnesia and how careful they would have to be to hide their alarm. Luna's heart went out to them, but she knew Rini was desperate for her to come to him, and no wonder. He couldn't talk to anyone else! "May I go in to him right now?"

The doctor nodded. "Go ahead. We'll come in soon."

After giving Leonardo a hug, she hurried into the room where Rini lay on the bed. He shot up when he saw her. "Where is this hospital?"

"This is the Sacred Heart Hospital in Asteria, San Vitano."

"San Vitano?"

She moaned. "It's the country on the Italian-Swiss border where you were born and live."

None of it seemed to make an impression. Her beloved husband looked so bewildered she wanted to cry buckets but couldn't. Not in front of him.

"Where's the doctor who operated on my arm?"

"He's at the hospital in Rezana, Slovenia, where you were taken to treat your gash and get antibiotics."

"How long do I have to be in this hospital?"

They were getting into dangerous territory. "If you'll wait a minute, I'll get the doctor, who will answer a lot of your questions."

"Wait—"

"Rini—I promise I'll be right back." She didn't know how much to tell him. This was uncharted territory.

Nervous, yet excited out of her mind that she had

her husband back, she left the room and found the doctor talking with Rini's grandparents. They turned to her and gave her another hug. She knew they were dying to see Rini.

"Doctor Romano? Rini has so many questions. So do I. What I don't understand is, how's it possible that he doesn't remember any of the other languages he knows?"

The doctor shook his head. "I can't explain how amnesia works, but what's happened is miraculous for him and you. Your being able to get through to him speaking Romansh is going to make all the difference in his recovery. It'll mean you need to be around him constantly and serve as his translator."

"I'm his wife and there's nothing I want more." She smiled. "Right now he's so loaded with questions, it worries me. I don't know what I should tell him."

"Understood," the doctor replied. "And it's true we don't want to overload him. I'll go in to talk to him." He turned to Rini's grandparents. "In a few minutes I'll ask the two of you to come in."

Leonardo nodded. "We'll be waiting."

"I won't be long. Now I must see to our patient." His comment relieved Luna. She led the way.

# CHAPTER THREE

RINI WAS STILL sitting up in bed, looking so wonderful despite what had happened to him, she had trouble containing her joy. "I told you I'd be back, Rini. I'll translate for Doctor Romano."

The doctor stood next to him. "I know you have hundreds of questions. I'll try to answer some of them. First of all, you ended up in a hospital in Rezana because ten days ago you were deep inside a mine when an earthquake hit the region near the Italian-Slovenian border. Your head suffered a blow. By some miracle you made it out, but your mind has forgotten a lot of information."

"In other words, I now have amnesia." He spoke with a dry irony that was so reminiscent of her brilliant, super-intelligent husband, she smiled.

The doctor turned to her. "There's nothing wrong with his thought processes." Then he turned back to Rini. "You're twenty-nine years old and answer to the name Rinieri Baldasseri."

"Everyone calls you Rini," Luna interjected.

His penetrating gray orbs played over her. *"Co haveis vus num?"*

She took a deep breath. "Yes, I have a name. It's Luna Biancho Baldasseri." So saying, she pulled out four wallet-size photos of the two of them. After studying them, he handed three of them back and kept the one of them kissing, which he put on the bedside table.

"How old are you?"

"Twenty-six."

"Do we have children?"

"Not yet." She didn't dare say anything about the baby yet. "We were only married six months when you left to inspect the Baldasseri King Midas Gold Mine and got caught in the quake."

"Why was I inspecting a mine?"

"Because you're a gold-mining engineer."

"A what?"

"It's true! You graduated from the Colorado School of Mines in the US and you are the head of the three-hundred-year-old gold mine for your family. It's one of the mainstays of your country. But right now you have grandparents who adore you and are anxiously waiting outside to see you."

He pondered the information. "Where are my parents?"

"They passed away four years ago."

"Do I have siblings?"

"You had a brother, Paolo, who was a year older than you. When you were nine and ten, you both ran out in the road to chase your dog at the beach. A bus came by and accidentally killed him and the dog."

When Rini didn't respond she said, "But you have cousins, including your favorite, Vincenzo, you don't remember. He's a year younger than you and was recently engaged to be married."

She turned to the doctor, afraid maybe she'd said too much. "I told him he has grandparents who'd like to see him. What do you think?"

"Why not ask him how he feels right now? Remember that they'll ask questions. If this is too much, it can wait until tomorrow."

She focused on Rini once more. "Would you rather rest now and see your grandparents another time?"

"No. After staying in that hospital for so long, I can't learn enough fast enough."

That sounded like her dynamic husband.

"I'll tell them to come in."

She hurried over to the door and motioned for them to enter. "He knows you're his grandparents, but not *who* you are if you understand my meaning. I'll translate for you."

They walked toward Rini, their eyes brimming with tears. "We thought you had died," Antonia said, breaking down.

Leonardo cleared his throat. "Thank the Almighty you're alive and back home with us where you belong."

Rini studied the two of them. "There were many days I wondered where I came from, let alone tried to imagine where I belonged."

"We want you to get better and will do whatever we can to help you. The doctor wants you to stay in the hospital until all the tests are done and you're feeling well enough to go home."

The love in Leonardo's voice touched Luna to the core.

*"Engraziel,"* he answered in Romansh, meaning *thank you*. She translated for his grandparents.

It was Rini's handsome face behind the hair on his head and face. It was his tall, magnificent yet under-weight body inside those ghastly mint-green hospital pants and top. It was his deep, thrilling voice that came out of that compelling mouth... But the man they all loved and adored wasn't there.

Her gaze met Dr. Romano's. He'd done his best to warn her about Rini's paranoia. She turned to her husband, who had to be exhausted. "We'll leave so the staff can get your medical regimen going."

"Stay with me." He almost growled the words with an intensity that bespoke his great need.

She wanted to throw herself into his arms and love him into oblivion. "I promise I'll only say goodbye to them. Then I'll be back."

"Luna?" his grandmother said in an aside once they were out in the hall. "We're going to return to the pal-ace and leave you with Rini. What has happened to him is beyond tragic and it's obvious he needs you to communicate. Leo and I will phone the family to let them know everything that has happened. I know Vin-cenzo will want to come and help do some translating."

That might be helpful for Rini. He'd have another person to talk to. Maybe it was possible he'd recognize Vincenzo. She prayed that would happen.

"Keep us posted." Antonia gave her another hug.

"You know I will, and we'll have a long talk." She hugged Leonardo before they both left. The doctor walked them to the elevator.

Free to be alone with Rini at last, Luna hurried to his room. She took a deep breath and pulled up a chair near the side of the bed. She'd rather climb under the covers with him, even if he didn't know her. "You must feel like a baby who's just been born. All these strange people looking down at you in your crib."

She'd hoped he would chuckle, but he didn't. Their happy marriage had been filled with laughter, but no longer.

"Since we had to fly a certain distance by helicopter, how did you know I'd been taken to a hospital there?"

"I didn't." She leaned forward. "After the quake, seven of the miners turned up missing. One of them was Slovenian, who worked for your company on a visa. You're the head of the Baldasseri Gold Mining Company near the Slovenian border. You'd gone there to do an inspection and implement new reforms."

"None of that computes to me."

"I know." She fought not to break down. "To my horror you were caught in the cave-in, too, or so we thought. There were search parties to bring out the bodies, but none were found. I wanted to interview the Slovenian family, who might be able to shed some light on their missing son because I refused to give up on you."

"I take it I didn't beat you often. Otherwise you wouldn't have bothered to try and find me."

He said it without a smile, but there was nothing wrong with the sense of humor she'd always loved. Maybe there was hope for a happy marriage in time.

"In another week we were going to have a family memorial service for you, Rini, but I was dreading it.

I had to be certain you weren't alive somewhere. One night I had a dream that you came to me. It gave me hope."

Rini groaned. "To be frank, I'd hoped never to wake up after they gave me a shot at the other hospital."

That hurt. Her eyes clouded over. "Are you still sorry?"

"I'm trying to process everything."

She looked down, cut to the quick. "There are a lot of people who love you and are thankful you're alive. Your grandparents adore you and can't wait to have a conversation with you, but they realize it will have to be on your timetable."

He didn't respond. "I met a policeman named Zigo, who took you to the hospital. His kindness brought me to you." Her voice caught when she said, "I came close to fainting when I saw you asleep in that hospital room. You've suffered terribly with a gash like that, and the blow to the crown of your head. Are you in horrible pain?"

"No. I was given painkillers."

"Luna?" another voice sounded. She lifted her head. Dr. Romano had come into the room. "Since your husband seems wide awake, I'd like to talk to him for a minute before his dinner is brought in. Would you ask him if it's all right?"

She nodded and turned to Rini. "Are you up for a visit with Doctor Romano? Afterward, they'll bring you a meal."

"If it will get me out of the hospital sooner, why not?" The edgy brittleness of his tone was to be expected, but this part of Rini was unlike the man she'd married.

"He says yes, Doctor."

The older man pulled up a chair on the other side of the bed. "I'm going to record our conversation for my records." Dr. Romano pulled out a tiny recorder. "I'd like you to think back to your first memory."

Rini could hardly concentrate as he looked at the gorgeous woman seated by his side. She'd appeared in his hospital room in Rezana like a vision. Now she'd planted herself next to him in this hospital in Asteria. Her stunning blond beauty and perfection of female form had taken his breath. When she'd told him she loved him, he'd almost gone into cardiac arrest. Until her presence in the Rezana operating room, he'd come close to giving up on life.

In order to concentrate right now, he closed his eyes.

"I remember being in total darkness, completely disoriented. My head hurt like hell. The silence was terrifying because I realized I was alone and the ground beneath me was shaking. I didn't know what I was doing or what was going on. I thought maybe I was dead and in hell."

Luna put a hand to her mouth to silence her sobs, but she had to translate for both of them.

"What did you do at that point, Rini?"

"I don't know exactly, Doctor. My legs were buried under something. It took what seemed like hours for me to remove what felt like rocky debris. Finally,

I could move and made some progress. Then I slept for a long time.

"When I awakened, I realized nothing had changed. It frightened the daylights out of me until I discovered I was breathing fresh air. That had to mean there was some kind of exit out of that hellhole I'd been in."

Dr. Romano cleared his throat. "You now know you'd been in an earthquake inside a mine. After all you've been through, your existence is a miracle."

"It is!" Luna exclaimed. Inside she was dying for him and what he'd lived through.

"Go on if you can. Tell us what happened next."

"I kept crawling until I discovered myself lying on vegetation. I felt thistle-like scratches on my hands. There were more earth tremors. When I looked up, I saw a sky full of stars before I fell asleep again. Obviously, I must have slept all night because sunlight woke me up. I realized I was on a mountain, but I didn't know why or where I was. Nothing looked familiar."

"I can't imagine it." Luna moaned the words.

"Neither could I."

"Continue on if you can," the doctor prodded him.

"The crown and right side of my head had bled like the devil. Blood still dripped down my face. I had cuts all over my hands and arms. My gold watch was broken. I didn't even know I had one or when I'd bought it, let alone where. All I felt was a terrible thirst. When I got up, I could barely walk, but I needed help from someone or to find a stream.

"After a while I came to a highway and followed it until I tripped and fell. The next thing I knew, a car came by and stopped. A man got out to talk to me. He spoke a language I didn't understand. He tried to be kind and helped me into his car. I was in and out of it before being driven to a hospital.

"No one in there could understand me, or me them. I lost track of time over the next few days. I couldn't eat and felt too sick to do anything."

Rini opened his eyes. "That's about it."

The doctor got to his feet. "Thank you for bearing with me. Now it's time for you to freshen up and enjoy your dinner. When you're helped into the shower, try not to get that bandage wet they've put on your arm. Also, be careful of your head when you shampoo your hair so it won't hurt your wound. I'll be back in the morning to order some tests. They will tell me a lot more about your head injury."

After Luna translated, Rini said to her, "*You* can't leave!" His eyes blazed as he stared at her. She saw fear in them and understood she was the only person he could communicate with right now.

"Don't worry. I'll be back soon."

"Tonight?"

"Yes, Rini. Tonight. I promise."

She walked out with the doctor, who told her the agenda for the next day. He'd scheduled a series of scans. "Now that he's home, you can feel comfortable in telling him whatever he wants or needs to know. Don't hold back. We'll see how he gets along."

When they parted, Luna phoned for her driver and went home to the *palazzo* to pack some items for Rini.

That look of fear had her rushing to the hospital

once more. He was the most confident, in-charge man she'd ever known. For Rini to be afraid like that gave her an idea of the depth of his trauma.

An aide helped Rini into the bathroom but stayed outside the door. He clung to the bathroom sink and stared in the mirror. *So I'm Rini Baldasseri, whoever that is.* Rini for short, his alleged wife had interjected. *A mining engineer?* He couldn't fathom any of it.

The only way he could half imagine they'd been married was because she spoke the same language with him when no one else could. Several times he'd studied the photo of them kissing. They'd looked like they were devouring each other. A picture didn't lie about their hunger for each other. Neither did the wedding band and diamond she wore on her ring finger.

She was very, very beautiful. In fact, on a beauty scale of one to ten, his blonde wife with those lagoon-green eyes came out closer to a fifty. They'd been married six months? How was it possible he didn't recognize her or remember her in any way?

The doctor told him he had amnesia. He knew what it meant, but he'd never known anyone who'd had it. Maybe he did, but the amnesia had erased that memory. He simply couldn't believe it was his problem now.

No longer receiving an antibiotic through an IV, he began the task of shaving his beard. The hair on his face itched and drove him crazy. When he'd gotten rid of it, he groaned to see the rest of him. After looking at those pictures, he could tell he'd lost weight.

He wore medical scrubs the other hospital had lent

him. Besides hanging on him, the dull color didn't help his sallow complexion. No shoes. Surgery socks covered his feet.

Well, no more of this!

He stripped down and got into the shower with hot water. Nothing had ever felt so good in his life. But how did he know that? How did he know anything now that twenty-nine years of life had just been wiped from his brain?

Luna would be back in later. She'd promised.

Rini knew he wasn't the same man she'd married, not physically or psychologically. Though she was putting on a good face to be his translator, he couldn't bear the thought that it was possible she pitied him.

He put on the white toweling bathrobe the hospital provided. After reaching for a towel to dry his hair, he walked back into the room. The aide helped him into bed.

The next thing he needed was a haircut. At least he had a picture of his former self. Maybe someone here at the hospital could do the job for him. The sooner he could get back to looking like the man in the photo, the sooner he might recover his memory.

His dinner soon arrived. The smell of hot coffee and lasagna teased his senses, warming his taste buds. He'd never tasted food so wonderful and had finished everything by the time Luna had returned. Though her arms were loaded, he found himself once again noticing her five-foot-seven height and the curves of her womanly figure.

She put two small suitcases on the floor against the

wall and walked closer to inspect him. A smile broke out on her stunning face with its high cheekbones. Her luminescent green eyes played over him.

"Wow! What a difference a shave makes."

He wiped his mouth with a napkin. "Good or bad?"

"Never bad, Rini. The hair made you look like a dashing pirate. But I like what you've done."

Her comment improved his mood, relieving him of some of the anxiety building inside him over his incredible situation. "Do you think there's a barber around here?"

"I don't know, but tomorrow I'll ask Emilio, the one who usually cuts your hair, to come to the hospital. How does that sound?"

"I'd be even more indebted to you."

She glanced at his tray. "You ate everything. Do you want more?"

"Since I'm not used to such a big helping, I'm fine for now."

"I'm glad it tasted good to you." She removed the tray and put it on another table. "Your grandparents chose your menu with all the foods you love."

"That was thoughtful of them."

"They love you. Your *nonna* wants to fatten you up." No one wanted that to happen faster than Rini, who was desperate to get back to the man he'd seen in those little photos. "The fact that you're alive has brought them back to life," Luna told him. "They can't do enough for you."

His gaze darted to the suitcases. "What did you bring with you?"

"In one of them are your own toiletries and some clothes for you, including shoes, for when you're released. I'm afraid until then you'll have to wear a hospital gown."

"Let's hope it isn't green."

A smile came and went. "I don't think so. You've lived through a nightmare, Rini, but you're home now."

Home, as in his own home, meant nothing to him. The realization raised his anxiety level once more. "What's in the other case?"

"A surprise."

"Can I see it now?"

She carried it over and placed it on the end of the bed to open.

"A laptop?"

Her eyes brightened. "It's *your* laptop with all the mining information on it." She pulled it out and set it on his lap. "I'll plug it in." She walked around the bed to find a wall outlet.

Rini's heart pounded. Maybe looking through it would trigger something in his memory. Excited, he turned it on, but there was a prompt to supply the password. He had no idea and his excitement turned to more frustration.

"I'll type it in." As Luna leaned over, a strand of her metallic-blond hair grazed his cheek and he breathed in her fragrance. The delicious smell of strawberries distracted him.

Only then did he notice the icons that had popped up on the screen.

Luna stepped away. "Click anywhere you want, and

you'll see photos, maps, charts, everything you want to know about the King Midas Mine. It's your baby," she added with a wink he found intriguing.

He got started, but after ten minutes of going through material he didn't recognize, he closed the lid.

She got the message. "You're tired. Tomorrow you can go through more of it." After unplugging it, she put the laptop back in the suitcase and moved it over against the wall.

Just then one of the female staff came in to take his vital signs and give him more pills to fight the infection.

"Where are you going?" Rini called to Luna after the nurse left.

"I'm staying right here until you fall asleep." She walked toward him and sat down in the chair next to the bed.

And then what? "I don't want you to leave."

"I wouldn't think of it. I'll be sleeping on the couch in the other room of the suite."

He looked around, realizing this hospital room didn't resemble the one at the hospital in Slovenia. Rini hadn't thought about it until this minute. "This is a suite?"

"Yes, with everything you could want, including the best doctors in the world."

Rini rubbed his chest absently. "Why am I being treated like royalty?"

"Because…you're the Crown Prince of San Vitano. When your grandfather passes away, you'll be King of your beautiful country."

His eyes closed tightly in reaction. "He's the King? You're not teasing me, are you?" She'd overloaded him, but Dr. Romano told her to be natural with him.

She got up from the chair. "While you let that sink in, I'll bring you our family album of photos that will prove your heritage beyond doubt."

In a minute she put a large, heavy album in his hands. He looked at her before opening to the first page that showed the royal family in full dress from years earlier. Rini recognized his grandparents but no other members of the family. Slowly, he leafed through each page, bringing the photos up-to-date.

Luna pointed out the picture of Vincenzo to him. It meant nothing.

Rini studied him for a moment, then kept turning the pages. He stopped when he came to the wedding pictures of him and his dazzling bride, Luna. He felt a quickening of his pulse. Rini might not remember her, but his attraction to her was growing stronger by the minute. In the picture she wore a tiara.

He looked up and stared at her. "This means you have to be Princess Baldasseri."

Luna nodded. "I'm a commoner, married to the prince of my dreams."

A grimace marred his features. "I don't recall anything about my life or yours." This time he shut the cover of the album with more force than he'd done the laptop. How in the name of heaven couldn't he remember her?

"You have to give it time, Rini." On that note she took it from him and put it back in the suitcase. "I'll take your toiletries to the bathroom so you can brush your teeth and get ready for bed." She disappeared. When she returned, she said, "There's a hospital gown in there for you, too. You must be exhausted."

"On the contrary, I'm wide-awake," he claimed. "I'm afraid you're the one who should be in bed after this long day. Ask the staff to bring in a cot. The other room is too far away. I want you to sleep by me in case I wake up in the night and need to talk."

He not only needed her near him, he wanted her near him, too. In truth, he found that he *desired* her. It came as a shock to him.

"Just push the button on the bed, Rini. Someone will come."

Within a minute one of the male staff entered the room. Luna smiled at him. "Could a cot be brought in for me?"

"Of course. I'll see to it housekeeping brings one immediately."

"Thank you."

Rini waited until they were alone. "I'll be right back, Luna." He got out of bed to head for the bathroom. Inside he discovered the things she'd brought. He opened the new toothbrush and got busy, then took off his robe and slipped on the hospital gown. When Rini did emerge, he knew he looked a far cry from the prince of her dreams.

# CHAPTER FOUR

AFTER HOUSEKEEPING ARRIVED and turned down the main lights, Luna went in the other room to change into a pair of pale blue running pants and top. When she was ready, she walked back in his room and climbed under the covers of the cot set up next to Rini's bed.

To think that after ten days of grieving for her beloved, he was alive, and they were together under miraculous circumstances. She said a prayer of gratitude and vowed never to let him out of her sight again. It thrilled her that he wanted her to sleep near him. If he only knew how much she adored him, how much she'd missed their lovemaking.

When she'd finished her prayers, she turned on her side to face him and realized he'd already gotten into his bed and was looking down at her.

"I see tears," he murmured. "Am I so hideous?"

"Oh, Rini—" she cried out in pain, wiping them with the back of her hand. "These are tears of thanksgiving that you didn't die! I'm still trying to absorb the horrendous experience you've endured while we all th-thought—"

"I was dead?" he broke in. "To be honest, I prayed

for oblivion every time I woke up to another day of endless hell, not knowing who I was or where I came from."

She rose up on one elbow. "But you know now, and I'm here to help you for as long as it takes."

His black brows furrowed. "I might never get my memory back," he said in a gravelly tone of voice. "Considering that we're married, have you thought of what that means?"

It was all she'd been thinking about. The possibility that he might never remember anything made her too ill to think about right now. "I'd rather we took this one step at a time. Yesterday morning I woke up to face another day without you. Before the morning was out, I'd flown to Rezana to find out any information I could. Then I found out you were alive!"

"Drugged was more like it," he muttered with irony.

Shades of the old Rini made her smile. "Yet, after you woke up in the hospital, I discovered you could understand and speak Romansh when you hadn't understood any other language.

"Can you have any idea how I felt? I didn't know you could only speak Romansh. My love for you came pouring out, and suddenly you opened your eyes because you understood me. I thought I'd die for joy!"

He moved closer to the edge of his bed. "When I heard your voice say, 'I love you,' I thought an angel was speaking to me. In all that horrific time, those were the only words that I understood. It wouldn't be possible for you to understand how I felt. In that moment there was a connection between us. I didn't remember you, but you became my lodestone to cling to. It was an answer to my anguish I never thought I'd receive."

"From your wife, no less," she quipped. "If two miracles can happen in one day, who knows how many more are in store? What I want to know is why the other hospital didn't send any of your things with you?"

"Things?" He sounded incredulous.

"Your clothes and wallet. Your boots. Where are your watch and wedding ring?"

He actually let out a dry laugh, the first she'd heard come out of him. "You'd have to have been there to understand."

She sat straight up. "Tell me. I want to know everything."

"First things first." His gaze wandered over her. "What are you wearing?"

"Oh—my running pants and top."

"Have you always worn them to bed?"

Heat swamped her cheeks. "No. But I brought these because we're around other people."

"What do you normally wear to bed?"

Honesty was vital between them. "A nightgown, but it never lasts long."

He thought about it. "What do *I* usually wear?"

"Nothing once your robe comes off."

A frown marred his handsome features. "How come I didn't get you pregnant?"

"Oh, Rini." She laughed. "We talked about having a family right away and decided not to use protection. I couldn't wait to have babies with you."

Rini rubbed the side of his smoothly shaven jaw. "Were you worried about it when conception didn't happen?"

It *did* happen, but this was one piece of information her husband wasn't ready for yet. They needed to get closer to each other before she told him he was going to be a father.

"Six months is such a short time to be married, don't you think?"

"You're right. Was I upset about it?"

"No, but we both hoped I'd get pregnant soon."

He rose up and dangled his powerful legs over the side of the bed. "We didn't sleep together before our wedding?"

She smiled. "We only dated six weeks before marrying. You told me you wanted me to be your wife before you made love to me. We were both in a hurry. Your grandparents were shocked that you proposed to me so fast. They'd hoped you would marry a certain princess from Rome."

"So it would have been an arranged marriage?"

"Yes."

"Did I know her well?"

"You avoided the subject of marriage as much as possible."

"So what are you saying about us?"

She flashed him a smile. "The moment we met we knew we were in love. That was it, and you broke off with her. You told me you were never in love with her and I believed you. Otherwise, how could we explain what happened to us?"

He eyed her for a quiet moment. "Were my grandparents upset?"

"If they were, they hid it well and allowed you to marry me, a woman of the people. That's something no other royal has ever done in your bloodline. From what I understood, you often defied convention, but you are your own person and your grandparents' favorite."

At this point he got off the bed and started pacing, then stopped. "What happened to my parents?"

"They died in a boating accident in a ferocious storm four years ago on Lake Diamanti on the outskirts of Asteria. I'm so sorry and wished I could have met them."

He moved closer to her. "What about your parents?"

"They died when I was two in a plane accident, so I don't remember them. I was raised by my grandparents. My grandfather managed a bank. They died separately of pneumonia. I ended up getting my degree in business administration from the University of St. Gallen in Switzerland. I worked later, but didn't find satisfaction, so I applied for jobs elsewhere, even outside the country.

"Being bilingual in Italian as well as Romansh, I was able to interview at the Baldasseri Gold Mining Corporation here in San Vitano. Fabio Machetto, the office manager, offered me a position. I liked the staff and atmosphere and felt I could be happy there.

"Two weeks later you came into the office. I fell so hard for you it was embarrassing."

His hands went to his hips. "Apparently, that worked both ways."

"Yes, thank heaven! My grandparents would have loved you. As for the rest, you and I started to speak Romansh and you took me to lunch. From that time on we were inseparable."

"What about other boyfriends?" he rapped out, as if he couldn't take in the information fast enough.

"I dated some, but meeting you altered my universe. Now, enough about me. I've answered your questions and want you to tell me why you were sent in the helicopter without your belongings."

She heard a sharp intake of breath before Rini got back into his bed, stretching out before turning to her. "As I told Doctor Romano, I tripped and fell on the side of the highway. A kind man drove me to the hospital, but I don't remember what happened. Maybe someone came by before he did and stripped me of everything. When I was dressed in hospital scrubs, they probably threw my clothes away. I don't know. No one in there spoke my language, or I theirs."

Luna groaned. "But the contents of your wallet would have told someone everything."

"Maybe I lost it in the cave-in. Once in that hospital, I figured that one day I wouldn't wake up. I prayed for that eventuality."

"Instead, the policeman, Zigo, helped me find you," she blurted. "If it hadn't been for him, I would never have found you. I plan to do something wonderful for him."

"We'll find a way to do it, Luna. I'll want to reward the doctor, too."

"Of course, we will. Carlo Bruni, the man who came

with me, is your grandfather's foreign emissary. He was responsible for arranging everything. Carlo is one of our favorite people."

For a minute quiet reigned. Luna lay back on the cot, wishing they shared a bed. She ached to hold him in her arms and love them both into oblivion.

"Are you going to sleep on me?" The deep voice she loved sounded close to accusatory.

"No." She smiled. "I thought you had nodded off."

"Anything but. Tell me where we live."

Luna turned to him in the semidarkness. "Our home is a lovely, spacious *palazzo* not far from the royal palace. You were born and raised there. It has fruit trees in the back. When they blossom, it looks like fairyland. We have a housekeeper, Viola, who's also the cook. She's married to the caretaker, Mateo. Both have been with you for close to fifteen years now."

"Do I have friends?"

"You and your second cousin, Vincenzo, are good friends, but with him running the timber business in Scuol, neither of you see each other as often as you'd like."

"That's it?"

"Since you and I met, I'm afraid we haven't socialized that much with other people. I only met him at our wedding. As it is, you have to squeeze in your royal duties with your mining concerns.

"Since the quake, Vincenzo has taken over some of your royal duties. He's your grandfather's grandnephew. He's always had a great relationship with him. Your whole family is very close. Needless to say, you and Vincenzo have been like brothers."

She heard the rustling of his sheets. "Speaking of brothers, if mine hadn't died, *he'd* be the Crown Prince."

"That's true."

Rini let out a frustrated sigh. "How soon can I get out of here?"

He'd grown restless. This was obviously too much information for one day.

"After your tests tomorrow, you'll have your first session with Doctor Tullia. Then the barber will come, and Doctor Romano will make his rounds. You can negotiate with him."

"Am I that impossible?" he asked in a dry tone.

"The hospital record in Rezana indicated you're a tour de force."

"In other words, I'm out of control."

"Not at all. Let's just say you have a convincing way about you."

"That's the definition of a tyrant."

"Hardly, Rini. You're a man who knows what he wants and goes after it."

"Come hell or high water?"

"I'll let you decide. According to Doctor Miakar, you're manageable if you're given time to think about it. I'd say that sums you up very nicely. Now, you need to sleep. I'll see you tomorrow after your first session with Doctor Tullia. *Buna notg*, Rini."

Rini wasn't ready to call it a night, but his wife had other ideas and turned on her side away from him. The clock on the wall said 1:40 a.m. After the day Luna had lived through in order to find him, it shouldn't have surprised him she'd just passed out on him.

Without her, he knew he would have eventually died in Rezana.

To realize that she'd followed her gut instinct to discover if he was still alive had humbled him so deeply, his body shook with sobs. He buried his face in the pillow, needing no convincing that he was married to the most exceptional, courageous wife he could imagine. And exceptionally desirable.

He went over the things she'd told him about their marriage. They'd taken vows within six weeks? Incredible. He'd married a beauty, but it came from her soul, too. Obviously, they'd been so close, they hadn't wanted or needed other people.

But before falling asleep, something had started to disturb him. He planned to bring it up with the therapist Dr. Romano had told him about.

The next day when he was brought back to his room following his tests and had gotten into bed, to his surprise a younger man entered the room with Dr. Tullia. He introduced himself as Chispar, bilingual in Italian and Romansh. "I teach at the college here and have been sent by the head to offer temporary assistance to Doctor Tullia."

Rini didn't like it that Luna hadn't come to this session. For that matter, she'd already left the hospital when he'd awakened. He'd felt abandoned. "Where's my wife?"

Chispar explained there would be other times when the doctor wanted her there, but not for this first session. All Rini could do was accept the situation and they got started.

It was a strange experience because he'd thought Dr. Tullia would ask him a lot of questions. Instead, he said, "Rini? Doctor Romano tells me you've been told you have amnesia and understand the meaning of the word. Do you feel well enough to talk?"

Chispar translated.

Rini had to believe his wife knew about this and decided he'd better cooperate. Otherwise, it would be reported that he was "unmanageable."

After Rini nodded, the two men pulled up chairs by him and sat down. Dr. Tullia appeared relaxed. "Memory loss affects people differently. Everything from frustration to fear. Why don't you tell me what you want to talk about?"

"I feel fine and want to get out of here. How soon can I go home?"

"Do you know where home is?"

"My wife has explained where we live."

"You're comfortable with her?"

"She found me. If she didn't like me, I assume she wouldn't have come looking for me."

"It sounds as if you trust her."

"I don't believe she has lied to me, but—"

"But what?"

"She's been like a saint."

"Explain that word."

"You know. Perfect. In every way."

"And that disturbs you?"

"Hell, yes. How do I know that beneath her facade

she…pities me and really doesn't want me to go home with her?"

He pondered the question. "How do you know she pities you? Has she told you that?"

"No."

"Then maybe you need to discuss that with her privately. It sounds like you are putting your own feelings on to her."

Rini let out an exasperated groan.

Dr. Tullia sat forward. "Rini, from what I've heard about you, you are a powerful, confident man. Even if your memory doesn't return, let's work on getting your confidence back.

"Under the circumstances I'll tell Doctor Romano I feel fine about letting you go home with your wife. Until he sees fit to release you, I'll arrange a session with you every morning here. After you leave I'll want to talk to you twice a week in my office here at the hospital for the next four weeks. You'll always be able to call me at home or the office anytime if an emergency should arise, even in the middle of the night."

Rini felt relieved when both men got up and said goodbye.

No sooner had they left than another man close to Rini's age and tall like him came into his hospital room. He wore sporty clothes, nothing like the hospital staff. He had brilliant blue eyes and dark brown hair in a style worn much like Rini's in the photo of him. For once it was someone he thought he recognized.

The other man studied him for an overly long moment that made him uncomfortable. "You'll never know how good it is to see you," he said in Romansh.

After hearing the familiar language spoken to him, Rini got it. This was his second cousin. "I take it you are Vincenzo."

A broad smile broke out on his handsome face. "Give this man the prize! Was Luna just spoofing me? You haven't really lost your memory, have you, *cus-regna*?"

This surprise visit from his Romansh-speaking royal cousin made him uncomfortable. He couldn't comprehend being royal or the Crown Prince. In fact, he didn't want to think about it. "Afraid so. She showed me a picture of you in our family album."

The smile slowly faded, and Vincenzo sat down by him. "I'm here to be of help in any way that I can."

"I appreciate that, but I have my wife."

Vincenzo leaned forward with his hands clasped between his legs. "I know that. She's the angel who found you. But your grandfather called me last night and explained that you need a translator while you're in the hospital."

"Doctor Tullia brought a man from the college with him who speaks Romansh."

"Understood. But if you need it for other reasons, I'm available."

"Luna told me you've taken over the duties of Crown Prince. I also understand you're engaged to be married. You don't have the time to do anything else."

"I have time for you. She lives in Italy and understands I need to be with you."

His anxiety crept up on him. "Where is Luna?"

"I have no idea. That's why I'm here. To fill in for her and give her some space. My grandfather told me your grandparents are worried about both of you."

Did Luna want space? Had she already told the family that? His fear that she might not want him to go with her grew worse.

"Tell me what you want or need, Rini. I'll do whatever I can."

Rini didn't question the man's sincerity. He saw it in his eyes and heard it in his expression. But he still couldn't handle much more of this. The life of a royal was anathema to him, even if it would offend them if he expressed the sentiment. It was the last job on earth he could imagine wanting. He needed to talk to Dr. Tullia. Right now he didn't want another person from the family involved in his life, no matter how well-meaning. The thought was making him ill.

"Luna says you run a timber business?"

"Yes, but your welfare is much more important to me. When I arrived at the palace, Carlo Bruno was there and told me about your beautiful wife and all she went through to find you. There's a woman who lives by faith. She believed you were alive. How remarkable is that? I swear if my fiancée turns out to be a wife as wonderful as Luna, I'll think I have died and gone to heaven."

"I can tell you mean that, Vincenzo, so I have thought of one important thing you could do for me."

"Name it."

"Luna has explained to me what my princely duties

consisted of before all of this happened to me. From what I've gathered, my grandfather has started to rely on you. Since I can't be the person he used to depend on, I'm glad you're the one he's looking to now."

Vincenzo shook his head. "Your condition isn't permanent, Rini."

"Maybe it is."

"But it couldn't be. Some of my friends who've had ski accidents have suffered memory loss, but it always comes back. Now that you're getting expert medical care, you're going to be back to normal in no time."

"That's where you're wrong, Vincenzo. Doctor Romano says I have a unique case called a fugue state. My amnesia is very different, and I mustn't expect it to ever come back."

His cousin's expression changed to one of shock. "I don't believe it. I bet Luna doesn't believe it, either."

"I'm afraid she's starting to. We're both doing everything we can to accept that our situation is permanent. My grandfather needs to accept it, too. I'm no longer able to fulfill my formal function in the monarchy. Therefore, by royal right, the role of Crown Prince has fallen to you. One day you'll be ruling San Vitano."

Vincenzo shot up from the chair and started pacing. Then he wheeled around to face Rini. "Does your grandfather know how you feel?"

"Not yet. But he will. That's why I'm depending on you. I won't need a translator when I'm released. While I'm here for the next few days, Doctor Tullia has this college teacher to serve as a translator for me. When I'm released, I'll have Luna."

"We all assumed you had temporary amnesia, Rini."

"I hoped the same thing, but it's not going to happen. Luna tells me my grandfather needs a man he can mold to be King. She says the family sings your praises and I take her word for it."

Vincenzo's blue eyes glinted from moisture. "You would have made a great king, Rini. I idolized you and still do for the way you're handling your affliction now."

"I'm trying to handle it, and I'm glad we've talked. I can't be the Crown Prince. I don't have any conception of what that would be like. I'm only glad that you are the designated one now. That's a burden I willingly throw off without knowing anything about it. I wish you the joy of it. Does your fiancée have any idea you're going to be King of San Vitano one day?"

"Yes."

"Tell me about her."

"She's Princess Valentina Di Fiore Visconti of Padua, the daughter of Count Giuseppe Visconti."

"None of that means a thing to me."

"I know. I'm so sorry."

"I've discovered it's life. I was the only survivor of a quake that killed seven other men. For ten days I lay in the hospital, wondering if I would live to see another day."

Vincenzo just stood there and shook his head.

"One thing I *have* learned. My grandparents are good people."

"They're wonderful. You have no idea how much they love and admire you."

"Luna tells me they have great faith in you. It's a worry off my mind if you're helping them because I can't."

"Understood. What will you do?"

Rini lifted his head. "Ask me in a year and maybe I'll be able to tell you."

"Is there anything I can do for you before I go back to the palace?"

"If you see Luna, ask her to come ASAP."

Vincenzo nodded and started to leave.

Rini called to him. "Thank you for coming and being willing to help me. Luna said you and I were best friends. I believe it and wish you well."

The visit from his cousin had relieved him of a burden, but it had also made him antsy. He got up and walked over to the window, wondering what had happened to his wife.

While he was thinking about her, he heard her voice at the door. He swung around as she walked in. She looked stunning in a pale pink matching blouse and skirt. Another strange man had come in with her, carrying a small satchel. "Rini? Good afternoon. This is your barber, Emilio."

"*Buona sera*, Your Highness."

# CHAPTER FIVE

RINI STARED AT his wife, who'd taught his barber how
to say good afternoon in Romansh. "Tell Emilio I'm
impressed." He reached over to the side table. "Will
you hand him this photo and ask him to make me look
like I did here? He may have forgotten."

"I doubt it." Luna grinned and walked over to take
it from him.

He recognized the strawberry scent and was haunted
by her fragrance. She showed the photo to Emilio. The
two of them spoke in Italian. It frustrated Rini that
he couldn't understand them and determined to learn
Italian ASAP.

She lifted her head. Her hair gleamed a golden
white. "He says he finds your disheveled hair an interesting change. Are you sure you don't want to cre-
ate a new style?"

"Positive!"

"Then he wants you to get out of bed. Come and sit
in the chair by the table." She cocked her head. "Can I
watch, or is this a private male thing? I've never gone
to the barber with you."

"Stay with me."

"All right." She pulled the chair out for him while Emilio emptied his bag on the table and picked up the shears and trimmer. Luna sat down in another chair to watch. "How did it go with Vincenzo?"

"I like him. I also fired him from the job of being my translator and asked him to work with my grandfather."

Wow. "Well, that says it all." She smiled at him.

At this point Emilio got busy. "Tell Rini I can see the place on the crown of his head where he was hurt. It's healed but tell him to treat that area gently when he brushes his hair."

Luna translated. "Does it still hurt, Rini?"

"It's a little tender if I press on it. Doctor Romano said it would fade with time."

"Thank goodness."

Before long Emilio used an edger before he declared success. The barber looked at Rini with satisfaction before handing him a small mirror. "Take a look."

She translated while Rini compared the image in the mirror to the picture he held.

Rini nodded and handed back the mirror. His gaze swerved to Luna. "Tell him I can't complain."

"He's paid you a great compliment, Emilio," she said in Italian.

*"Sì?"*

*"Sì.* Rini thinks you did a great job."

A smile broke out on his face. "It's been a pleasure to serve you as usual." He gathered up his things, said goodbye to Luna and left.

Rini watched him go, glad the two of them were

finally alone. He got to his feet. "What does my wife think now?"

Her dreamy green eyes studied him. She walked over and kissed his cheek. "You smell good and look like my old Rini."

"You always smell wonderful," he murmured, wanting to reach out and crush her to him. But he didn't dare. Not yet. First, he'd get in shape and regain the weight he'd lost. He wasn't about to forget she'd fallen in love with his former self.

Luna smiled. "Welcome home eleven days late."

"That's where I want to go. Doctor Tullia said he'd tell Doctor Romano he felt fine about releasing me."

"How wonderful!" Her instant response went a long way to reassure him it was good news to her. He saw no shadow. "The morning you left to inspect the mine was the first time we'd ever been apart." Her throat closed up. "I'd planned a special anniversary dinner for that evening when you got home." She'd apparently planned another surprise, too.

"When your grandparents came to the *palazzo* with the news there'd been an earthquake and men were trapped in the mine, including my beloved husband— I thought I would die."

He heard the pain in her voice. It caught him unawares. As his gaze fused with hers, one of the staff chose that moment to bring in two dinner trays and put them on the table. Luna turned to thank the woman, breaking the trance that held them.

Once they were alone, she invited Rini to sit back down and eat with her. "Um… Your grandmother knows how much you love veal cooked in wine. I love it, too. This *osso bucco* looks tantalizing."

If anything looked tantalizing, it was Luna.

He started eating. "Does our cook make meals like this?"

"Much better, actually. You'll love her *bruschetta*."

Good. He'd gain weight fast and begin to look like the man she'd married.

"Do you cook, Luna?"

"Not well, but *you* do when we eat outside on the back patio."

He put his fork down. "Are you joking with me?"

"Not at all. Your specialty is either grilled swordfish or salmon on a stick with your own signature lemon sauce. I understand you learned the recipes from your mother, who was reported to be a fabulous cook. Three days after we went to lunch, you invited me to the *palazzo*. To my surprise you barbecued our dinner and I knew I was in love."

"How soon did I propose?"

"That night after you drove me back to my pitiful apartment."

"So fast?"

She nodded. "I told you I'd give you my answer after our third date, which was two days later. I wanted to impress you with *my* cooking, which turned out to be a flop because the oven broke down. Raw chicken wasn't what I had in mind. You laughed and said nothing else mattered as long as I would agree to marry you."

He eyed her intently. "How long did you make me wait for your answer?"

"I didn't. I was shameless and told you I'd envisioned you as my husband when we went to lunch. You pulled a ring out of your shirt pocket and put it on my ring finger."

Luna extended her left hand with its engagement ring and wedding band. He gripped her hand and studied the three-carat diamond set in gold. "I can see I had good taste."

"In everything!" she cried. "You told me the gold in both rings came from the Baldasseri gold mine and were fashioned expressly for me. Inside the gold band you'd had words engraved: *Rini and Luna forever.* You'll never know what that night meant to me. At first, I thought I must be dreaming, but from then on we spent every free moment together and I'd never been so happy in my life. But if you want to know the truth, when I found you alive at the hospital in Rezana, *that* was the most thrilling, glorious moment of my life. You weren't lost to me after all." Her voice trembled. "You just can't know what finding you meant to me."

He stirred in the chair. "I know what it meant to hear a feminine voice say I love you. At that moment I knew I wasn't going to die, that I'd been saved."

*"Rini—"*

He rubbed his thumb against her palm the way he used to do as a prelude to making love. Her husband might have lost his memory, but his body reacted the same way it did before the quake. His touch brought her alive.

Luna slowly removed her hand from Rini's and

sat back. The feel of him had sent tingles of longing through her body that wouldn't go away. But maybe she'd revealed too much of herself to him. What had she been thinking? He didn't know her from Adam!

She'd wanted to tell him as much as she could about their married life together. But she'd been an open book about her personal feelings for him. It might be a turn-off if she went too far. She adored him whether he'd lost his memory or not and wanted their marriage to last forever. However, could she say the same thing for him?

In his eyes Luna was a total stranger to him. In revealing her heart, he might be feeling suffocated. Though he'd said he was anxious to go home, he had no idea what that meant. She could understand his wanting to get out of the hospital. It had to be a kind of jail to him. Naturally, he craved his independence. Unfortunately for him, he needed her help to communicate.

She wouldn't blame him if he preferred someone like Chispar to stay at the *palazzo* with them, but that was the last thing she wanted. Under the circumstances it would be better if she didn't go to work at the mining office for a while.

Luna would discuss this with Dr. Tullia. Maybe he would tell her it would be a good idea if someone else was there on weekdays with whom he had no emotional ties. It might make his life much easier while he tried to adapt to a new life. But she didn't want to be apart from him for a minute.

Later, when Dr. Romano came in for his evening rounds accompanied by Chispar, he explained he

wanted to examine his patient. Luna translated for
Rini. "I promise I'll be back after he leaves."

She walked to the sitting room of the suite to phone
Dr. Tullia, who'd given her his card. He didn't answer,
so she left the message for him to call her. Hoping he
would get back to her before bed, she changed into her
running pants and top in the en-suite bathroom. While
she was brushing her teeth, her cell rang.

She wiped her mouth and checked the caller ID before clicking on. "Doctor Tullia? Thank you for calling me back. I'm so grateful."

"I'm here for you and Rini. Tell me what's wrong."

"*I'm* the problem tonight."

"Go on."

She told him about her latest concerns. "I love my
husband and let him know we were madly in love from
the very beginning. But he has no memory of me, and
maybe it has put too much pressure on him. What if he
really doesn't want to go home with me? What if he'd
like some space and Chispar could be home with him
while I'm at work? What do you think?"

"Let me ask you a question. Knowing that he might
never remember you, do you want him to love you the
same as before?"

"Yes!" she cried. "He's my *raison d'être*."

"Then here's my advice. Do exactly what your instincts have been telling you to say and do. Don't hold
back. Continue to be yourself. Ask him if he wants
company when you're at work. In time you'll know if
he feels nonreceptive or smothered."

"That's what worries me. *How* will I know?"

"Is there any doubt in your mind that he'll tell you? Your husband is assertive and doesn't keep his thoughts to himself."

She chuckled. "You're right about that."

"Some things about human nature don't change, do they?"

"I can't thank you enough for your advice, Doctor. You've made me feel better."

"Good. I'm here for you anytime. Good night, Luna."

They hung up and she left the bathroom to find Dr. Romano in the sitting room waiting for her. She hurried over to him. Chispar had left. "How is he tonight?"

"He's coming along well. I'd feared he might have stomach problems getting used to regular meals, but he assured me he's hungry and eating everything. At this rate he'll gain back the weight he lost without problem."

"That's my grandmother-in-law's fault. She's planned all his favorite dishes."

He smiled. "Well, it's showing. I guess you're aware he wants to leave."

"Yes. I can tell he's restless."

"He needs to stay in the hospital two more days while he undergoes more tests and works with the physiotherapist. I'll put in orders to release him on Thursday morning. He's in good shape considering what he's been through. Call me if you have any questions."

"I have one more. Will he be able to drive after he goes home?"

"We don't know, but I'm sure you'll find out. Again, let him be the one to decide."

"Of course. Good night, Doctor. Thank you for everything you've done."

"We're all thankful the Prince survived."

Luna walked him to the entrance before heading straight for Rini's room.

"Hi! I'm back." She wanted to fling herself into his arms.

He eyed her thoroughly. It sent shivers of delight down her spine. "I thought you'd never come." His voice sounded more like a growl. She could believe he'd actually missed her.

"Oh, ye of little faith." She moved the cot away from the wall and laid it out near Rini's bed. "Before I get in, shall I turn on the TV?"

"Is that what we used to do?"

"Sometimes we watched the news or a film. Does a movie interest you? We could pick something easily understandable even if you can't follow the language."

She could feel his penetrating gray eyes appraise her. It made her heart beat so fast she could hardly breathe. "I think I'd rather talk and find out what Doctor Romano had to say to you."

Was he worried? She turned off the overhead light and climbed into her cot to face him. He lay on his side with his head slightly elevated. His eyes never left her face.

"Do you want the good or the bad news first?"

"How am I supposed to answer that?" His hand had gripped the sheet in reaction. She shouldn't have said it. His tension was too severe.

Luna sat up in the cot. "Rini—I was only kidding. It's all good. You can go home on Thursday."

He rubbed his jaw absently. "Not till then?" She heard his disappointment.

"That's only two more days while he runs a few more tests."

"Will I be free to do anything? Like fly?"

Had she heard him right? "You mean like travel on a jet?"

"I want a chopper to fly me to Rezana so I can thank the police officer for listening to you and telling you where to find me."

"So do I. We'll do something for the doctor, too."

She adored her husband, who wanted to repay the people who'd helped him. His humanity was well-known among the mining community, even if he didn't realize it. "Maybe you could talk to your grandfather and find a way to gift Doctor Miakar in a meaningful way."

His gaze narrowed on her. "That's an idea."

Already, he was focusing on others, sounding more and more like her husband. She took a deep breath. "I'd love to go with you."

"I wouldn't go anywhere without you, Luna."

He sounded like he meant it, but was it only because she was his link to communication? "Rini, tomorrow will you ask Doctor Romano if you'll be under any re-strictions about flying in a plane or helicopter?"

"I will." He lowered the head of the bed and rear-ranged his pillow but couldn't get it right. "I also need to learn Italian so I can talk to him myself."

"Agreed." Incredible that Rini had spoken it from birth. It was there in his brain somewhere. "I'll give you your first lesson tonight if you want. Many words in Romansh have a slight similarity to Italian. You'll learn it in no time."

"Try me."

Delighted he wanted a lesson, she said, "Let's go with some simple words. Say *ciao*. It means *hello*."

He answered with perfect inflection.

"*Bene*. That means *good*, or it can mean *well*. Say it."

"*Bene*."

"Now try *buongiorno*. It means *good morning*."

He responded perfectly.

"*Excellente*, Rini. Now two more phrases. *Come va?* It means *how are you*?"

"*Come va?*" he experimented several times.

"*Bravo!*" she cried when he reproduced it correctly.

He rose up. "Are you sure you aren't a school-teacher?"

Luna laughed. "I promise."

"You make a good one. This is fun." That comment thrilled her heart.

"Then let's keep going. When someone asks you that question and you answer it, then you say *E tu?* It means *And you*?"

"*E tu?*"

"*Sì*. That means *yes*. You make a wonderful Italian parrot."

A deep laugh broke from him, the first she'd heard since finding him. This was a magical moment. "All right. Now, let's have conversation number one. Here we go. *Ciao*, Rini Baldasseri."

He sat up. "*Ciao*, Luna Baldasseri."

"*Come va?*"

"*Bene. E tu?*"

"*Bene.*"

She clapped her hands. "That was *perfetto*. You sounded totally Italian and are such a good student, it's scary. Now, let's have conversation number two."

"I'll start it," he offered. His eyes were alive with light.

"Go ahead."

"*Buongiorno*, Luna Baldasseri."

"*Buongiorno*, Rinieri Francesco Baldasseri."

He frowned. "Rinieri? Where did that name come from?"

"That's your full name in honor of King Rinieri Umberto Baldasseri, your great-great-great-grandfather."

"No wonder you call me Rini."

She smiled.

"What's *your* full name?"

"Luna Biancho Baldasseri."

"Biancho... Biancho..." he said several times.

"You sound pure Italian, but I think that's enough lesson for now except to learn the word for good-night. It's *buona notte.*"

"*Buona notte,*" he repeated. "But I don't want to go to sleep yet."

She took that as a compliment. "I think it's one of the most beautiful words in Italian, Rini. Now, I'm sure you're exhausted even if you don't realize it. I know I am."

"*Buona notte*, Luna."

"*Buona notte, tesoro mio.*"

He cocked his head. "What did you just say?"

Uh-oh. Heat flooded her cheeks. She'd married a brilliant man and could hear Dr. Tullia telling her to do what came instinctively. "*Tesoro mio.*"

"Are you going to leave me in suspense?" His voice resonated through her insides.

"It's an expression I often used with you." She lay back and closed her eyes tightly.

"And?" he prodded, not willing to let it go. "What does it mean?"

"My treasure."

"Say it again."

"*Tesoro mio.*"

After a slight pause she heard him say, "*What did I sometimes call you?*"

"*Pulcina mia.*"

He said it several times. "What does it mean?"

"My little chick."

A low chuckle came out of him. "How do I say *thank you*?"

"*Grazie.*"

"*Grazie, pulcina mia. Buon anotte.*"

"You know something, Rini? I think you're a fraud. Listening to you right now, no one would guess you'd lost your ability to speak Italian. Before we were married, your grandfather took me aside and told me you were one of the most intelligent men he'd ever known. When the time came for you to rule, you'd be the greatest of the San Vitano kings."

She heard his covers rustle. "I have no idea what the future holds for me, but I'd rather be dead than be a king."

"How do you know that?"

"I just do."

Ooh. She buried her face in the pillow so he couldn't hear her groan. Where had that thought come from? Had it always been buried in his psyche?

Throughout their marriage he'd never expressed negative feelings about being royal. He'd loved his grandfather and had admired him. With few complaints Rini had managed to balance his princely duties with his career as a mining engineer. He hadn't let them intrude on the glorious time they'd had together as man and wife.

The one time she hadn't wanted him to leave for work and felt it was an intrusion was the day of the earthquake. Her body trembled to remember the horror of learning he'd been buried in the debris.

*Don't think about it*, she lectured herself. *Rini's alive and here in the same room with you. We'll be going home in a couple of days.*

Thursday morning Luna awakened and noticed Rini was still out for the count. That was because on the past two nights he'd awakened and got out of bed, too restless to sleep. She feared he'd had nightmares.

Taking care to be quiet, she got up and left the room to change into her skirt and blouse. Once dressed, she went back in Rini's room and put the suitcase in his bathroom. Today he would be able to wear normal clothes home.

She found her purse. After phoning her driver to come and get her, she left the suite. Out in the hall she told the staff at the nursing station she was leaving. "I'll be back to drive my husband home once he's released."

"Plan on ten o'clock and pull up to the ER entrance."

"I'll be there."

On the way home she phoned Leonardo and Antonia to tell them her plans. "I'll call you after he's settled, and we'll go from there." She'd kept in daily touch with them but couldn't tell them to come over yet. Rini needed to express a desire to see them.

A few minutes later she entered the *palazzo*. "Viola?"

"I'm here." The housekeeper hurried to the foyer.

"Rini will be coming home this morning."

The older woman pressed her hands to her mouth with excitement. "The news is out that he's alive and back in San Vitano. It's a day of celebration! Signor Machetti says the office is flooded with hundreds of calls."

Luna nodded. "I don't doubt it."

A pained expression crossed over her face. "He still doesn't remember anything?"

"No, but I've told him about you and Mateo. Would you ask him to do a favor for me?" She nodded. "Ask him to run to the store and buy a supply of protein shakes. Rini needs calories to put on weight and your cooking will do the rest."

Viola beamed. "I'll tell Mateo now and make sure everything gets done."

"You're an angel. I'm going to shower and change. Then I'll be taking his car to get him."

She dashed up the stairs, so excited to be bringing him home she could hardly stand it.

In a few minutes she left the shower to blow-dry her hair and do her makeup. Last Sunday she'd looked like a pale wraith. This morning the color was back in her cheeks. She wore her favorite lipstick and used some eyeliner.

Next, she drew a short-sleeved outfit from the wardrobe that Rini loved on her. He said the green stripes on the white jacket were the color of her eyes. She matched it with a white skirt and white sandals. The green peridot earrings he'd given her on their one-month anniversary complemented her outfit. He might not remember her, but she planned to do everything she could to make herself attractive to him.

Though it was only nine-thirty, she hurried out the back of the *palazzo* to the parking area for the car. Just knowing she'd be bringing him home had made her eager and breathless. First, however, she stopped at a phone store to buy him a new cell phone and installed an app that would be of great help to him. Luna wanted to surprise Rini tonight before they went to bed.

# CHAPTER SIX

RINI HAD LIVED for Thursday to come, but when he awakened, he discovered his appealing wife had disappeared on him. Where in heaven had she gone on this day of all days?

He had to fight his disappointment. Before falling asleep the night before, he'd worked out a conversation to have with her when he said good morning to her. Now it would have to wait, and it frustrated him no end.

After the staff checked his vital signs and he'd eaten breakfast, he went into the bathroom. To his surprise he found the suitcase and opened the lid. She'd packed a dark blue crewneck shirt and a pair of tan pants. There was also a belt. Like he'd told Dr. Tullia, Luna was part angel. He forgave her for slipping away so early.

Stuck in one of the holders he found a pair of darker tan leather sandals. Real shoes after all this time. These were clothes he'd worn before the mine cave-in. He dressed quickly after a shower and shave, deciding to leave the shirt out.

One of the male staff had come into the room with a wheelchair. Behind him Rini saw Dr. Tullia, an unexpected surprise.

*"Ciao, Dottore."*

The doctor lit up with a smile. *"Ciao,* Rini."

*"Come va?"*

The man looked shocked. *"Molto bene. E tu?"*

*"Bene."* But Rini lifted his shirt to show the doctor he'd had to tighten the belt a bit. Dr. Tullia broke into laughter. It felt good to communicate on his own with a man he'd started to trust.

Luna had taught him well, otherwise the therapist wouldn't have kept smiling as he patted the wheelchair, indicating Rini should sit down. The other man gathered up the suitcase with his things and the three of them left the suite.

*"Buongiorno!"* Rini called out to the cluster of staff at the nursing station. He received several greetings back. They clapped and cheered him with bravos.

*"Grazie."*

The staff nodded in understanding before he was wheeled to the elevator. Before long they arrived on the main floor and he was pushed down the hall. He saw the sign *Ingresso di Emergenza.* More than ever, he needed to learn to speak and write Italian quickly.

He felt his pulse pick up speed as they approached the doors. Where was Luna? All of a sudden, he spotted a sleek black sports car drive up.

In the next instant a drop-dead gorgeous blonde woman got out of the driver's seat and walked toward him in the hot sun.

Luna! His heart raced at the sight of her. He was so hooked on her he couldn't think or talk. Her white skirt swung around her long, elegant legs. She drew closer.

The green jewels of her earrings couldn't match the dazzling color of those eyes he'd loved looking into. Her exquisite features took his breath.

*"Ciao, tesoro mio."*

His mouth went dry. This wife of his was beyond wonderful. No wonder he'd proposed to her in less than a week.

"Rini?" she prodded him. He saw concern in her eyes. *"Come va?"*

He was so overcome with the endearment he couldn't swallow. Finally, he said, *"Bene,* now that you're here. I missed seeing you leave this morning."

"You were sleeping so soundly. I didn't want to waken you."

She smiled at Dr. Tullia and thanked him and the other man. Rini watched her press something on the remote she was holding. She told them to put his small suitcase in the cargo space in back, then she looked down at him. Switching to Romansh she said, "Are you ready to go home?"

"What do you think? I've been living for the two of us to be alone."

"I'm glad you said that because I can't wait, either." She opened the front passenger door for him. He watched her press the tip of the handle, then pull it. He left the wheelchair and climbed into the front. Dr. Tullia shut the door. Luna thanked both men and went around to get behind the steering wheel.

She started the engine and they took off, but he noticed she drove with restraint. "There are several cars following us at close range," he murmured.

"Security. You've been the Crown Prince and were assigned bodyguards. You'll get used to them."

Never.

"How do you like your car?" she asked. "If you want to drive, I'll pull over and change places with you."

"I'm glad you're at the wheel. It gives me a chance to look around." In truth, he loved looking at her.

"Would you like to take a tour of the city? Drive up around the royal palace?"

"I'd rather go home."

"Then that's exactly what we'll do. Viola has made lunch for us. If I know her, she's fixed your favorite pizza and homemade *pasticciotto*. It's a cream-filled pastry to die for."

"That's the goal. To put on weight." He turned to stare at her adorable profile. "*Grazie* for the clothes."

"*Prego*. That means *you're welcome*."

"*Prego...prego...prego...*" He said the word several times. "What am I wearing?"

"A dark blue *camicia* I love, *pantaloni* and *sandali* on your feet."

"Finally, some shoes." He repeated the words several times.

She flashed him another smile. "You're back in your world, Rini, even if you don't recognize it."

"You have no idea how good it feels to be free. But I need to be able to communicate. Can we work on my Italian today?"

"We're doing that right now. For as long as you like."

She'd taken a turn that led them up the lush hillside of the city. On the summit of one hill sat what he considered a small, peach-colored palace. Luna kept driving toward it and turned in to the driveway. They wound around the back next to two other cars. Beyond them he saw a garden of fruit trees. He blinked.

"This is *our palazzo*?"

She turned off the engine and grinned. "You look like I must have looked when you brought me here for the first time. It was built in the eighteenth century."

The fact that this had been his home was surreal to him. "What does it have? Fifty rooms?"

"More like twenty in all. Viola and Mateo have their own apartment on the first floor."

"Where's our bedroom?"

"We have a suite on the second."

"I'd like to see it." He got out of the car and walked around to the rear to wait for her. She joined him and pressed on the remote. The lid opened. He pulled out the suitcase with his unbandaged arm and shut the lid. Suddenly, he heard voices and turned to see a middle-aged man and woman approach. Realizing who they were, he tried out his Italian on them. They teared up and bowed to him.

"Luna? Tell them I like doing things myself and will take my own suitcase upstairs."

She talked to them for a minute, then turned to him. "Let's go in and get settled. Viola will have lunch for us in the dining room whenever we're ready."

He followed her to the rear entrance that opened into an entrance hall. She explained that the kitchen area and laundry were down one hall to the left. He'd find the staff's apartment on the right.

She continued down a hall to the front of the *palazzo* with an ornate salon and sitting room. Paintings adorned the walls, mirrors, frescoed ceilings, chandeliers and parquet floors. But as they ascended the curving staircase, he much preferred looking at the feminine way his wife moved.

At the top of the stairs she turned right and opened the floor-to-ceiling paneled doors to their suite. It was another world, totally modern in decor with white walls, a living room with comfortable couches and a television set, a state-of-the-art business office with a large painting, and a bathroom.

He gravitated to the blue-and-yellow bedroom with a striped spread covering the king-size bed. Sunflowers had been arranged in a vase on the double dresser with some small framed photos. He noticed yellow lamps on the bedside tables. The windows had white shutters that let in the sunshine. How could he not have remembered any of this?

Her green eyes studied him. "What's the verdict?"

Rini liked it. "I can live in this suite." He lowered the suitcase to the tile and looked around, still incredulous that nothing produced a memory.

She broke into a glorious smile. "I'm glad to hear it since we had this part of the upstairs renovated and chose everything together. Whether you know it or not, you picked the blue-and-yellow scheme. I happen to love the combination, too."

Before he knew it, she put the suitcase on a nearby chair and opened it to take his things to the bathroom. Rini took advantage of the moment to remove his sandals and stretch out on the bed. When she emerged, she laughed. "You didn't need to worry. We made certain that oversize bed fit those powerful legs and big feet of yours."

"Join me and let's see how well it accommodates both of us."

Luna walked toward him. "I wanted to join you on the hospital bed in Rezana." After kicking off her sandals, she lay down next to him, turning to rest her head on his extended right arm.

She caressed the side of his jaw and pressed her lips to his. "You have no idea how long I've been waiting for this moment," she whispered in a breathless voice. "I have my husband back and I'm never going to let you out of my sight again."

As her arms went around him, he brushed his lips over her cheeks and eyelids. He relished every part of her, exploring further until he'd covered every centimeter of her beautiful face.

"Rini—" she murmured, chasing his mouth with her own until she caught up to him. The second their mouths met, hers opened to him. He felt himself going under with a hunger that had been building.

Though he knew she was his legal wife, she was a stranger. Anxiety built up inside him. He felt like things were moving too fast with this woman he didn't remember who welcomed him so completely.

Somehow, he couldn't trust that she could be this loving with him when she knew he had no memory of her. Again, he feared that she pitied him and was trying to pretend all was well. Dr. Tullia had told him to discuss it with her. After a slight hesitation, he relinquished her mouth and rolled off the bed.

She sat up looking hurt. "I'm sorry, Rini. Did I do something wrong when I put my arms around you?"

He stood there rubbing the back of his neck in confusion. "You did nothing wrong. I've been wanting to kiss you, but…"

"But what?"

"There's a question I have to ask you."

"Go ahead. Anything."

His body grew taut. "Do you pity me? Because if that's the reason you were so loving with me just now, it's the last thing I want from you."

She moved to the side of the bed and stood up. He could hear her mind working. "I've been dying to crawl into your arms since the moment I saw you drugged at the hospital. You have no idea how much I've missed you since the quake.

"If I was loving with you just now, it's because I'm so wild with joy that you're alive! I never want to leave your arms. But I can see that you have to learn to trust me before we can have an intimate relationship."

"I *do* trust you."

"Outwardly," she came back. "However, it's clear that the closeness we shared as husband and wife is something that will have to come about naturally, over time. Let's let it rest for now. Why don't you freshen up and we'll go downstairs for lunch?"

He'd put his hand in his pocket and made a fist. "I've hurt you, haven't I?"

Her head lifted, causing her gilt hair to swish.

"You're wrong, Rini. You were honest with me, and I'm grateful. If we don't have that, we don't have anything."

Everything she said made sense. "You're right. Luna? Will you do me a favor and ask my grandfather if we can visit him this afternoon?"

"Of course. He and your grandmother will be thrilled. I'll call him now."

Rini *had* hurt her, but he couldn't help it. Luna had gotten on that bed and had climbed into his arms without hesitation. Nothing could have shocked her more when he'd suddenly pulled away from her. Wanting to make love with him, pity had been the last thing on her mind. Dr. Tullia's advice went round in her head.

*Don't hold back. Continue to be yourself. In time you'll know if he feels nonreceptive or smothered.*

*That's what worries me. How will I know?*

*Is there any doubt in your mind that he'll tell you? Your husband is assertive and doesn't keep his thoughts to himself.*

Dr. Tullia had known what he was talking about.

After the bathroom door closed, Luna reached for her purse lying on a chair and phoned the palace. She asked to be put through to Antonia, who wept when she learned Rini wanted to visit. They arranged for three o'clock in their private sitting room.

When Rini joined her, he acted like nothing had happened. They went down to the dining room for lunch. Viola had outdone herself and her efforts paid off. Rini ate everything. At that point they went back out to the car and she drove them to the ochre-colored palace, another larger, eighteenth-century landmark. En route, she taught him a few more Italian words.

After parking in front, they walked inside past staff and went upstairs to the apartment on the second floor. His grandparents were waiting for them. He greeted them with his limited conversation.

"Oh, Rini," Antonia cried for happiness. "*Bravo.* You have no idea how wonderful it is to see you walk into our apartment. I know you don't know me, but can we hug you?"

Luna translated. His gaze darted to her before he said, "*Sì.*"

First, his grandmother threw her arms around him, then Leonardo hugged his grandson. Their eyes filled with tears. They were led into the sitting room. Rini sat on a chair next to Luna. She eyed her grandparents-in-law. "On the drive over here Rini told me he wants to fly to Rezana by helicopter to thank the police officer who helped him and me. Could that be arranged for tomorrow?"

"We'll do anything for him."

Again, she translated his grandfather's response.

"Rini also wants to send a donation to Doctor Miakar at the hospital."

"I'll arrange it today."

She turned to Rini and repeated his grandfather's answer.

Rini tried out the new words he'd learned. "*Grazie mille, nonno mio.*"

Leonardo got up and grasped Rini's hands. "God has brought you back to us."

"How do you feel about meeting the family?" his grandmother asked. "They're all anxious to see you again."

She felt Rini's hesitation. "Could we put that off for a little while?" he murmured to her. Luna translated.

"Of course. I'll suggest we wait on that decision until you've had your checkup with Doctor Romano in a week."

Rini nodded, looking relieved when she explained to them.

"Would you like to walk around the palace and grounds?" Antonia queried.

Luna told him what his grandmother had asked but knew his answer before he responded. "Maybe another time."

"Rini's tired," she explained to his grandparents. "We'll come again in a few days for another visit. In the meantime, let us know when the helicopter will be available." She hugged both of them. Rini had already stood up. He said goodbye and the two of them walked out of the palace.

"If it's all right with you, I'd like to drive."

Aha. "I was hoping you wanted to." Like Dr. Romano said, it was up to Rini. Excitement swept through her that he was ready to take charge. Luna reached into her purse for the remote, which she handed to him. He pressed the icon that unlocked the doors. After helping her in, he walked around and got in the driver's seat. But he had to adjust the seat to accommodate his long legs.

Rini was a quick study. He'd watched her drive and knew what to do. His memory loss didn't hamper his driving. Her husband had always driven fast and today was no exception. He took them on a long drive around the city, probably driving security crazy. She pointed out a few landmarks for him. It shouldn't have surprised her he knew where to go when he'd decided to head to their *palazzo* on the hillside.

After they pulled around the back, he turned off the engine and looked at her. "I've been wondering about the gift I could give Zigo. He's the reason I'm home now."

"Yes, he is. I'll never be able to thank him enough."

"What would you think if we drive this car to the gold mine tomorrow? I'd like to take a look at it. Then we'll head to Rezana and deliver it to him personally."

"You mean give him your car?"

"Why not? I earned it with my own money, right? It won't be a gift from the taxpayers."

"No." Her heart was bursting with love for him. "Little does he realize what his kindness did for you. Oh, Rini. He'll be speechless and won't believe it. I can promise you it'll be the only one in the town."

He nodded. "We could arrange for a helicopter to fly us home from there."

"Your grandfather will arrange it."

His eyes lit up. More and more Rini was acting and sounding like the man she'd fallen fathoms deep in love with.

When they entered the *palazzo*, Viola met them with a bottled protein shake. Luna explained to him what it was. "She thought you might be hungry again. Dinner will be at seven."

He nodded and thanked her. After he'd carried it upstairs, he drank the whole thing while Luna looked on. "That wasn't bad." He put the empty bottle in the wastebasket in their bedroom.

"You'll need the title to the car. It's in your inner sanctum."

He followed her while she pulled an envelope out of a file cabinet. "Thank goodness you've always been so organized. When you give this to Zigo, he'll sign it and that's all there is to it." As she lifted her eyes, the look of desire in his made her go weak.

After a quiet moment, "What would I do without you?"

She couldn't hold back brushing her lips against his. "You'll never have to find out." Then she walked back to their bedroom. He came more slowly. She could tell he was upset about something. "What is it?"

"Luna—I feel so hampered because I can't speak Italian, and I keep bothering you to teach me. It isn't fair to you."

"*Fair* doesn't come into it. I'd be hurt if you wouldn't accept my help, but I can only imagine your frustration. That's why I bought a surprise for you."

She saw him swallow hard. "Can I see it now?"

*My darling husband...* "I don't know." She gave him a sly smile. "Can you wait?"

"No."

Luna laughed. "I knew you couldn't."

"Am I that transparent?"

"In certain ways."

His features sobered. "You have the advantage of me."

She fought to stifle a moan. No matter how much she wanted the barrier between them to go away, it remained. She reached into her purse and handed him his new phone. He lifted his head.

"Come over here. I'll show you an app."

They walked over to the bed and sat down. "The app teaches you how to speak Italian. The woman speaks Romansh and takes you through different conversations. She reads aloud an index. As each subject lights up, you can press it and then repeat what she teaches you in Italian. When you wake up in the middle of the night tonight, you can turn it on and practice."

His dark, handsome head turned to her. "How do you know I wake up?"

"I've been with you from the moment I found you. The last two nights at the hospital you woke up around three and were restless. You'd get up and walk around before going back to bed. I'm sure you'd had bad dreams. I thought this would be a good way to help you."

"Did I call out or say anything?" There was alarm in his voice.

"No."

A bleak look came from his eyes. "I'm sorry. When I asked you to sleep by me, I didn't realize what I was asking."

She moved closer to kiss his jaw. "You don't remember, but three months after we were married, I contracted a strain of flu that put me in the hospital. You stayed with me day and night and nursed me for a week after I got home. After the love you showed me, I could never make that up to you. If you don't believe me, ask your grandparents. You missed a week and a half of work."

"Were you close to dying?"

"Rini—of course not!" She walked over and sat on the side of the bed. "Come on. Push it and let's listen."

He did her bidding. "If I'd had this in Rezana, I would have gotten out of there within a day."

Without thinking, she put her arm around his back. "It kills me to realize what you had to go through."

He put the phone on the side table and pulled her into his arms. "It awes me that you didn't give up on me. If you hadn't talked to the officer and come to the hospital…"

Rini fell back with her and buried his face in her neck. They clung to each other. This time he didn't pull away from her. She felt like they were communicating at last. More than that, they were communing.

His mouth found hers. "Thank you for this gift. I have a feeling it's going to save my life in the dark hours of the night."

"Don't forget I'll be there, too." She pressed her lips to his. They kissed slowly and sumptuously.

"Let's continue this while we're both on top of the bed, *pulcina mia*." Together they got up and lay down so their arms and legs tangled. Luna had wanted this for so long, she was in pain for him.

"Careful you don't hurt your wound."

"It's already healing."

But no sooner were the words out of his mouth than *her* cell phone rang.

"Don't answer it," he whispered against her lips.

"I have no intention." She kissed him hungrily, wanting to forget the world, but the phone rang again.

After a third time, Rini moaned. "Someone is anxious to talk to you."

"You're right. I'd better get it."

He kissed her one more time. "Come right back."

She hated to leave his arms as she eased away from him and rushed to retrieve her phone from her purse on the dresser. Then she hurried back to the bed and checked the caller ID. Rini stared up at her with those intense gray eyes.

"It's your grandfather calling. I'm sure it's about tomorrow's plans." Luna clicked on.

Actually, it was Antonia who conveyed the message that Carlo would fly there in the helicopter and arrange for a car for them. He would be there at two to meet them at the police station. Then the three of them would fly home together.

They hung up and she told Rini what they'd talked about. Then Viola phoned.

Luna thanked her and clicked off. "Our dinner is ready."

"Are you hungry?"

No. She wasn't. But she didn't want to tell him that for fear he would think she wanted to get back on the bed with him. Of course she did, but she didn't want to come across too eager. She'd made herself totally available to him because she loved him and she was his wife. Maybe he was attracted to her, but she was still an unknown to him and his heart wasn't involved yet.

"I'm hungry for anything Viola cooks. Come on. We'll make plans for tomorrow since we'll need to leave early."

She couldn't tell if it was the answer he'd wanted. Dr. Tullia had reminded her that Rini was assertive. If he didn't want to eat dinner, he could tell her he'd rather stay up here with her. As she started for the doorway, he didn't call her back or reach for her. She had her answer for now, but what would happen tonight when they went to bed? It would be their first night strictly alone as man and wife since the quake.

# CHAPTER SEVEN

RINI FOLLOWED LUNA out of the suite and down the stairs. He'd hoped she would have said she wasn't hungry, either. She had no idea how he'd longed for the two of them to spend the next twelve hours enjoying each other in ways he'd been imagining in his dreams.

Though he was convinced she didn't pity him, he'd been lying to himself to believe she was truly ready to make love. He couldn't bear the thought that she was playacting in order to prove her love to the husband who'd lost his memory. Rini might look like the man she'd married, but in his gut he knew he was still a stranger to her.

She was a stranger to him, too. He had to admit he felt somewhat uncomfortable about making love to a woman he didn't know or recognize. Rini might not remember the man he was, but to take her to bed this fast didn't speak well for him as a decent human being. Not with *this* woman. Not with the devoted *wife* who'd saved him from death. She deserved all the respect he could give her while they got to know each other again.

By the time they began eating dinner, he'd made a

decision. For the time being he'd let the intimacy of their marriage grow at its own pace. Instead, he'd concentrate on learning Italian and work out his future. They planned to leave for the mine at six-thirty in the morning and stop on the way for breakfast. Later, they'd drive on to Rezana.

After thanking Viola for a delicious dinner complete with two different desserts he'd apparently loved, he asked Luna to excuse him. He explained that he wanted to spend time on the computer. "I need to familiarize myself with the mine and the maps."

"That's a marvelous idea. And remember that when you come to bed, the app on your phone will help you work on your Italian conversation during the night."

"I haven't forgotten your gift, Luna. It's making all the difference."

Though he wanted to kiss her neck, he resisted the impulse and left the table to go upstairs. Luna had sounded so pleased with his plans; he knew he'd done the right thing.

If pressed, Rini had little doubt she'd do her wifely duty, but he wanted her to desire him the way she'd portrayed in that photo of them. The picture of two people madly in love never left his mind. He prayed that one day he and Luna would get there again.

Two hours later he crept into the bathroom for a shower and shave. Luna lay on her side asleep. He could tell she wore a nightgown. It pleased him that she hadn't put on her running clothes.

To his surprise he didn't wake up until he heard her in the shower. Rini took advantage of the time to get dressed in casual trousers and a polo shirt. He'd found a valise in his study to pack some maps and graphs he'd run off the printer. It also held the title to the car. He was set.

When she walked into the bedroom, she looked a vision in a short-sleeved print blouse and white pants. Luna's figure did wonders for anything she wore, and she smelled divine. The woman took his breath. *"Buongiorno, sposa mia. Sei bellissima."*

Her luscious mouth curved into a smile. *"E tu, Rini. Molto, molto bello."*

He knew what it meant. *"Grazie."*

"I'm serious. You look wonderful, and already so different from the man Carlo and I flew home to San Vitano. I can tell you've been studying your Italian. *Bravo, sposami.* I'm speechless over the way you're picking it up so fast. If you can speak this well already, the men at the mine won't believe you have amnesia. Neither will Zigo."

A chuckle escaped his lips. "I've memorized a few paragraphs here and there. We'll see their reaction. Are you ready? My things are packed, but I don't have any money."

"Don't worry. I've got plenty. Day after tomorrow we'll go shopping for everything that was taken from you and go to the bank." She looked out the window. "It's going to be another hot, lovely day. You usually wear sunglasses. If you want them, your favorite pair is in the top right drawer of the dresser."

"I didn't notice them."

"They're probably under one of your casual shirts."

Rini walked over and found them where she'd predicted. He put them on and turned to her.

She studied him in a way that said she liked what she saw. "In the sensational car you plan to give away, you'll look like the most dashing race car driver on earth. When you pull up to the police station wearing them, they won't believe you're the same man who was fading away in the hospital just a few days ago."

"All the credit goes to you, Luna. *Mi hai cambiato la vita.*"

"That goes both ways, Rini. Just so you know, from the moment we met, you changed *my* life, too." The throb in her voice touched his heart. He couldn't doubt her memories of him. That was something to treasure.

"Let's go."

They left the *palazzo* through the rear entrance. Rini helped her into the passenger side of the car before putting the valise in the cargo space. After he got in and started the engine she said, "Last evening I asked Mateo to take the car to the service station for gas and a quick inspection. He assures me all is well."

Rini should have known his wife would be on top of everything. "I was going to suggest we do that before leaving the city. You're amazing."

She shook her head. "Thank you. I'll remember that when I start doing things that displease you."

One black brow lifted. "Is that possible?"

"Oh, yes. Just give it time. We're still in the honeymoon phase." She'd said it with a twinkle in her eye.

"Is that what you're calling it?"

*The honeymoon phase with no honeymoon.* That needed to end soon.

He drove around the *palazzo* to the street.

"Rini? Before we reach the autostrada entrance, would you mind heading for the palace?" It sat on a hillside, visible from the highway. "The Baldasseri Gold Mining office is in a building at the rear of the estate. I haven't been in touch with Fabio, who must wonder if I'm even alive. He's always there by seven."

Rini had been so concentrated on himself and their world, he'd forgotten she'd been living another life without him for close to two weeks. "How long have you been out of the office?"

"Since the day before you left for the mine. I'll only pop in for a moment. You don't need to go in with me."

His hands tightened on the steering wheel. "Would you rather I didn't?"

Her head jerked toward him, swishing her silky hair against her cheeks. "Rini—why in heaven would I care? I only said that because I know you're anxious to get to the mine and I don't want to hold you up. You and Fabio are friends. Once he sees you, he'll want to talk. Please forget I asked. I'll call him tomorrow. It isn't important."

Her reasonable response made him feel like an inconsiderate heel. She'd sacrificed every minute for him since she'd discovered him in the hospital in Rezana. "Of course it is. Otherwise, you wouldn't have asked."

He sped up to reach the palace and she guided him around to the neoclassic building located beyond the greenhouses. Rini's grandmother had wanted to take him on a tour of the estate. However, on that day he hadn't been in a frame of mind to appreciate much of anything except being with Luna. He felt that way about her more than ever.

Last night Rini had decided to let the intimate side of their marriage grow at its own pace. But looking at her now, the last thing he wanted was to wait. Everything about her stirred his senses. The desire for her was more real than ever.

Before he'd turned off the engine in the parking area dotted with a dozen cars, Luna opened the door and was ready to jump out. "I promise I'll only be a minute."

"Luna—take all the time you need." He needed to calm down. "We're in no hurry."

"As long as you're sure."

"I am."

She closed the door and hurried up the walkway to the main doors of the Baldasseri Gold Mining Company. Unable to sit there, Rini got out to work off his restlessness. He looked around, incredulous that all this had been his world until his head had been injured in the earthquake. This estate, the palace, the office building—none of it meant anything to him.

Anxiety started to build inside him, but the sight of Luna coming out the doors of the office brought him relief. She filled his eyes. His wife was incredibly beautiful. Then he saw a brown-haired man who cupped her elbow as they walked toward the car where Rini lounged.

They were both laughing, and the way the thirtyish,

good-looking guy acted proprietorial with her caused Rini's muscles to clench. He straightened as Luna ran toward him. "Rini? This is your friend and manager, Fabio Machetto."

"*Buongiorno*, Fabio," he responded. *"Come va?"*

Fabio answered something back Rini couldn't understand and it frustrated the hell out of him. Luna rushed to translate. "Fabio said he's so thrilled to see you. He feels like he's dreaming."

In the next instant the guy hugged him before stepping back and talking to Luna again. Their conversation didn't last long, and she got in the car before Rini could come around to help her. Fabio shut her door and walked back to the office.

Rini climbed behind the wheel. He couldn't take off fast enough for the autostrada leading to the border. The GPS guided him without problem.

"I'm sorry Fabio came outside with me, Rini. I asked him not to, but he didn't listen." The tension inside the car could be cut with a knife. "I know he made you uncomfortable hugging you like that, but he didn't mean to."

"The hugging didn't bother me."

"Then what's wrong?"

He took a quick breath. "I realize he's the one who hired you. Did he ever date you?"

She didn't answer right away. Finally, "He asked me to go to dinner with him a week after I was hired, but I turned him down because I wasn't attracted to him. We've been friends, nothing more."

"I think it's possible he hasn't gotten the message yet."

Luna looked over at him. "What makes you say that?"

"Because I just watched a man come out the door who's in love with you."

"No, Rini. He's my boss, nothing more."

"You're not a man and didn't see what I saw. The poor devil. I realize it's nothing you can help."

"Rini, you're the only man in my life who ever made my heart come close to jumping out of my body. I'm so in love with you it's ridiculous!" She laughed, sounding too happy for words. "I can quit working. If you want to know the truth, I'd much rather stay home with you full-time and be your wife and Italian tutor. After almost losing you, I want to spend every living moment with you from now on. Say the word and I'll send in my resignation in the morning."

Rini shouldn't be so excited over her reaction. "You mean it?"

"Yes. When we were married, I didn't want to become a clingy wife, so I told you I preferred to keep working. But I didn't plan on doing it once we started a family."

"You won't miss going to your job every day?"

"There's a different kind of work being home with a husband who's having to learn a new language. I plan to be there every step of the way while you put your new world together piece by piece."

"Let's think it over, Luna. I don't want you to make

a decision you'll regret." He'd talk to Dr. Tullia about it at his next session.

Luna rolled her enticing green eyes at him. "If anyone will regret it, it will be you, having to put up with a wife around the clock."

If she only knew...

Luna squeezed her eyelids shut for a moment. Had Rini been jealous? If it was true, it meant he was starting to care for her on an emotional level. She'd leave her job in a second knowing it was what he wanted.

But once again, he hadn't asked her to quit. Was that because *he* had to think it over? She'd promised herself she wouldn't push him. What would Dr. Tullia have to say about it? Maybe she'd call him and get his opinion.

Halfway to the mine they came to a village and enjoyed an al-fresco breakfast of *caffe al vetro* and large croissants that melted in your mouth. Rini ate four of them piled high with butter and plum preserves. At one point he reached out to flick some preserves at the corner of her luscious mouth into his. Little by little he was clearly finding it difficult to keep his hands off her.

Before they left the *trattoria*, Rini bought a half dozen more croissants to take to Zigo. The tension between them had vanished and she was in heaven.

They drove on toward the border, passing lush greenery and forests. Rini looked at her as they neared the signs for the mine located at a higher elevation. "You've lost your smile. Are you all right?"

"Yes and no," she answered. "My emotions are bittersweet knowing that I got my husband back while seven of your former miners are buried here."

"I have no memory of them. But after waking up to find myself covered in debris, I'm as horrified as you are."

"Oh, Rini—" she cried out and gripped his arm. "I shouldn't have reminded you."

"I'm glad you did." He rubbed her hand before she let go. "I'll be meeting whoever is at the head of the mine in a minute. Everyone working there has lost a friend or coworker."

How she loved her husband! "They realize you were in the mine when the quake struck and will be overjoyed to see you alive and well."

"Stay with me when we go inside. I'm going to need you."

"Maybe now you know how I feel about you. I was barely alive after your grandparents came over with the news."

Rini slowed down as they turned down the road leading to the above-surface portion of the mine. "I brought some maps with me. This appears to be the entrance."

She undid the seat belt and leaned forward. "I've never been here. You promised me that one day you'd bring me."

Their gazes locked. "Who would have thought it would be under these circumstances?" After putting the sunglasses in his pant pocket, he got out of the car and walked around to help her. Once he'd retrieved his valise, they entered the modern-looking building.

Luna never stopped praying that he'd see something that would bring back a memory.

Once inside she heard a man call out Rini's name. Suddenly, five people came running out of the office and engulfed him in bear hugs. He'd already had his christening with Fabio. She'd known he was loved and revered by people, but this show of affection had to warm his heart as it did hers.

One of the men turned to her. "Princess Baldasseri, I'm the acting head of the mine, Pesco Bonetti." He introduced the other men in turn. They all shook hands with her. "This is a great day." Their eyes had filled with tears. "Thank you for what you did for the miners' families. We won't forget."

"I did it for Rini," she said, wiping her own tears away. "I'm sure you've all heard my husband has lost his memory. He's working on his Italian, but for now I'll translate for him. We've come unannounced. If you don't mind, he'd like to meet with you for a few minutes."

"Come this way."

Luna looped her arm around Rini's and they followed the men into the office. Some chairs were pulled around and they met in a circle.

Rini opened his valise and pulled out the papers he'd brought. "Luna—ask Pesco to provide detailed information on the areas that I've checked and ask him to fax them back to me."

She handed the papers to the other man and explained what Rini wanted.

"I'd also like him to send me a review of the state

of the mine since the quake. Everything he can think of to fill me in."

Luna continued to translate.

"Does this mean he's still in charge like before?" Pesco asked Luna in an aside.

"I don't know yet. We haven't discussed his future, but he feels a terrible responsibility even if he doesn't remember."

Pesco nodded. "Understood. I'll prepare everything and have it faxed to His Highness."

Rini turned to her. "One last thing. Thank him and all the men here at the mine for carrying on. I'd like him to send me any issues that haven't been resolved yet. The men of this mine have been the mainstay of the country and the monarchy. I'm here for them."

Struggling not to break down, she translated what Rini had said. After she'd finished, heads lowered and she heard sniffing. Pesco got to his feet and eyed her husband. "Tell him we're behind him all the way and welcome him back. This visit has renewed our faith."

Luna relayed this last message to him before they walked out of the mine to the car. Rini remained quiet. When she couldn't stand the silence any longer, she said, "You may not remember your past, but what you said and did today has won the hearts of those hard-working men.

"They'll never forget that the Crown Prince is a man just like they are. They know he's fair-minded and kind, that he's watching out for them and their families. You couldn't have sent a more important message. I'm so proud of you, I could burst."

"Please don't." His teasing voice brought laughter and tears. "What was it Pesco said to you at the beginning?"

"He thanked me for honoring the families of the miners who were killed."

"What did you do?"

"I met each family with flowers, and had the palace send them financial compensation for their loss."

His dark eyes pierced hers. "I'm the proud one that you would do that."

"I learned from you."

He reached for her hand and squeezed it. "You did exactly the right thing for them. Do you know you're the perfect wife?" In an unexpected move he leaned over to press an urgent kiss to her mouth. She never wanted him to stop.

In a minute he pulled away and put on his sunglasses. They were off, but she reflected on what he'd said. Luna didn't like being described as perfect, but knew it was meant as a compliment.

Before long the cluster of villages Rini had once described to her came into view on the horizon. Rezana was the first town located over the border, the one she'd seen from the air before the helicopter landed. By some miracle Rini had made his way out of the mine and had walked this far, looking for help.

What a shock it must have been to have fallen on the highway, let alone be taken to a hospital. He hadn't been able to communicate. The thought of it knotted her stomach.

They drove into the small town. She looked at the

buildings until she saw police headquarters and the word *policija.* "There it is, Rini."

"I see it. Reminds me of *polizia* in Romansh."

"It's the same in Italian."

"I've got a lot to learn, don't I?"

"You've made remarkable progress already."

He pulled up in front.

"Does the front look familiar?"

"No. Neither did the mine. I had prepared a speech to say to the miners, but when the men ran over to hug me, I forgot everything."

"That was a sight I'll never forget."

Rini reached for her hand one more time and kissed it. "Thank you for being my savior." Again, she understood what he was trying to say, but she'd rather be thought of simply as his wife. "Shall we go in and hope to find Zigo?"

She got out before he could help her. Rini opened the cargo space to pull out his valise and the sack of croissants. Together they entered the police station. Luna rejoiced to see Zigo in the front office. He was alone. This was going to be fun!

"*Ciao,* Zigo," Rini called out to him, setting his valise on the floor.

The man looked up and got to his feet. His gaze swerved to Luna. "It's *you!*"

She nodded. "My *marito* has come to thank you for saving him."

Rini took off his sunglasses and approached Zigo, whose eyes almost popped out to see the change in him. *"Impossibile!"*

Her husband smiled and put the sack of croissants on the desk. *"Per te."*

"For you, Zigo," she said. "You were his salvation. He has another present for you out in front. Come with us."

Zigo appeared to be in a daze as he followed them out the front doors. Already a group of teenagers stood nearby, rhapsodizing over the car. In the distance she could hear the sound of rotors. Carlo would be landing any minute.

Luna smiled. "This is your car now."

Rini handed him the remote with the key. *"Grazie mille."*

"I don't understand."

"You helped my *marito*. He wants to thank you."

Zigo shook his head. "You give me this car?"

*"Sì."* Rini nodded.

*"Aie-yai-yai!"* Zigo's reaction was priceless. He held up his hands with his palms facing Rini. It was his way of saying he couldn't believe what was happening.

Thank goodness the helicopter landed at the side of the station and Carlo emerged to join them. "I'm so glad you're here, Carlo. Rini is giving this car to Zigo for his help, but he doesn't think this is real. Will you explain to him in Slovene?"

She walked over to her husband while they waited for Carlo to talk to Zigo. In a minute the light dawned, and the officer hurried over to Rini. Carlo translated as the words came pouring out of Zigo.

"I never had anything given to me so wonderful. I don't deserve it."

Rini nodded. "Tell him when he helped my wife, he gave me my life back. I want to repay him with something I hope he will love. It's easy to drive and there's a booklet in the car."

Luna translated so Carlo could convey the message. Zigo's eyes filled with tears before he gave Rini a huge hug and broke down. She watched her husband hug him back.

"Carlo," Luna murmured. "Rini has the title and will sign it over to him with you as witness. We'll do it inside."

After the officer had recovered, the four of them entered the office. Rini pulled the title out of the valise and signed it over to Zigo, who also signed and dated it. Then Carlo explained about the sack.

Zigo kept staring at Rini with tears in his eyes. Her husband's dramatic transformation had shocked him. Bit by bit her husband was acting more himself even though he remembered nothing.

But what if he never did recover his memory? She'd tried not to think about it, but that eventuality had to be faced.

Before they left, Luna had a last message for Zigo that Carlo translated. "You helped me when I thought all hope was gone. Bless you for your goodness."

Zigo smiled at her and told Carlo, who said, "Your eyes spoke to my soul when you talked about your husband. I wanted to help."

Luna reached out to hug Zigo. Rini followed with a strong handshake and picked up his valise. The three of them walked outside to the helicopter. Zigo accompanied them. While Rini helped her on board, Carlo chatted with Zigo for a few minutes, then came on board.

Luna could tell by the gleam in those gray eyes that her husband was pleased. She knew the second part of today's mission had now been accomplished.

For the short flight back to San Vitano, Rini kept his fingers tangled with hers, never letting go. There was only one problem. She wanted to feel more than his hand holding hers. Luna experienced pain that she couldn't appease her hunger for him.

She craved the physical closeness they'd once shared. She wanted to tell him about the baby, but that raised another disturbing question. Would he want to start a family now? So much had to be going on inside him. It was another point she needed to discuss with Dr. Tullia.

Today's visit to the mine where Rini had been caught in the quake had to have filled him with terrifying memories, yet he hadn't indicated he was disturbed. The visit with Zigo seemed to have made him happy.

Luna stared out the window at the velvety green landscape below. If only she could get inside his brain to know what was really going on.

His wife was being particularly quiet. Once again, Luna had asked nothing for herself and did whatever he wanted with a smile. His needs had reduced her to a caregiver who waited on him around the clock, and his guilt hung heavy. This evening he wanted to do something to thank her but would wait to talk to her about it until they returned to San Vitano.

The helicopter landed at the rear of the palace. After parting company with Carlo, a limo drove him and Luna to the *palazzo*. He noticed their bodyguards following them. It was something he would have to get used to.

Their driver wove around to the rear. Rini helped her out, relishing the excuse to hold her arm. Anything to be close to her. When they reached the *palazzo* back entrance, he paused.

"What do you think if we go in and get dressed up?" He'd seen a summer suit in his closet that would do. "I'd like to take you to dinner where we can eat and dance. I'm sure you know such a place, so I'll leave the choice up to you. Would you like to do that, or are you too tired?"

Her expression lit up. "You've been reading my mind."

*"Bene,"* he murmured with satisfaction. On impulse he lowered his head to kiss that enticing mouth. The second they connected, she slid her hands up his chest and around his neck. Her action brought her body close to him and he deepened their kiss. "I've been wanting to do this all day."

*"Amore mio..."* she murmured, kissing him again with an ardor that set him on fire. At least this time he understood the words she spoke. That was progress.

*"Oh!"* a cry resounded. Viola had opened the doors. *"Scusa!"*

Luna broke away from him with a flushed face and said something to the housekeeper who nodded, then scurried off. In the next breath Luna turned to Rini. "I told her we're going out for dinner."

Much as he'd rather stay here and make love to her until morning, he'd promised her an evening out. "Let's go upstairs and get ready."

"While you shower, I'll phone to reserve a special table at Gilberto's."

He got the message and followed her up the stairs to their suite. "How special?"

"The one you arranged for us the night before we were married."

"Why is it so unique?"

"You'll find out." She flashed him an impish smile before heading into his study.

Rini rushed to shower and shave, excited at the thought of holding her in his arms while they danced. He pulled the pale blue suit from his closet and chose a darker blue shirt. As he was fastening it, Luna came into the bedroom.

"The bathroom is free, *mi biscottina*."

She chuckled. "So now you're calling me a cookie?"

"Didn't I before?"

"No. Your Italian vocabulary has increased. *Bravo*."

"Are we set for tonight?"

"We are."

He spun around. "Do I need a tie?"

"Not if you don't want to wear one."

"I don't."

"You look perfect to me." She disappeared into the bathroom.

# CHAPTER EIGHT

LUNA'S COMPLIMENT CAME so easily, but did she say that to him when in reality he probably should wear one? Because Rini was royal, was there a different standard of dress for him? Every time when things seemed to be going so well, he found himself second-guessing her responses. He needed Dr. Tullia's help. Tomorrow he'd ask Luna to phone the hospital and get Rini in to see him before the day was out.

He went into the study to put his valise away and work on his Italian to give her privacy. Before long he'd be able to call Dr. Tullia on his own and talk. That day couldn't come soon enough for him.

"Rini?"

He looked up and almost fell out of the chair. Tonight she wore a stunning black dress with spaghetti straps. The black high heels made her taller. She'd put on small diamond earrings that sparkled through her gilt hair.

*"Incantevole—"* He blurted another new word.

Her smile filled his universe. "What do you mean you don't speak Italian? For my husband to call me ravishing has made my day. I'm ready to go."

"We will in a minute. I can see I'm going to need a tie after all." He raced past her to get a silver striped tie out of the drawer and put it on. She waited for him at the top of the stairs. "Have you called for a limo?"

"No. We'll take our other car. It's the dark green sedan you saw parked in back next to Mateo's car. Here are the keys." She handed them to him, and they went down to the foyer.

Viola wished them good-night and they went out the back entrance to the car. Rini helped her into the car, loving the strawberry fragrance he now associated with her. Her skin looked like porcelain in the night light. It felt like velvet as he ran his hand down her arm before letting go, unable to stop himself.

Once ensconced in the elegant interior, Rini turned on the GPS to guide them to Gilberto's. Once they reached the street, he opened up and they took off.

She put a hand on his arm. "Just remember your bodyguards aren't race car drivers like you. Give them a little slack."

"Was I such a terror?"

"Yes."

"Finally, an honest answer!"

A delicate frown marred her brow. "What do you mean?"

Too late Rini realized his slip. "Forget what I said."

"I can't."

He took a deep breath. "Luna—you're always so wonderful to me and make me feel so good, I—"

"But you don't think I'm telling you the truth?" she broke in on him.

His wife sounded hurt. He groaned. "Yes, I do, but I know I couldn't have been a paragon to live with. Just now your comment seemed—"

"Real?" she cried out. "Does that mean you believe I've been lying to you from the beginning?"

"No. Of course not. It's just that I've had a hard time understanding how I married such a fantastic woman I couldn't possibly be worthy of."

"Worthy— Don't you think I have those same worries about you? At the hospital you woke up to find out you were married to a woman who means literally nothing to you. I've been shocked you wanted to come home with me. You could have asked Chispar to help you settle somewhere else."

"You're the only person I want to be with," he insisted.

"I'm thankful for that because I love you so much. But if the time comes and you want to move on and figure out your life without me, all you have to do is say so. I would never blame you if you wanted a divorce. You'd be free to do whatever you wanted."

He pulled onto a side street. Her words kept pouring out, crushing him.

"Rini? I've tried to imagine how ghastly it would be to wake up with amnesia and discover I was trapped in a marriage I didn't remember, with a stranger no less. Today you proved you can handle everything on your own."

He found a parking space and hit the brakes. "Except I need *you*, Luna!" A soft gasp escaped her lips. She stared at him with eyes full of tears. "I may have lost my memory, but I'm a man. Even before you told me you were my wife, I knew I needed the beautiful woman helping me with every fiber of my being."

She broke down sobbing quietly.

"Now is the time for total honesty, Luna. Do *you* want a divorce? Tell me the truth. We've got to have that, or we don't have anything."

Luna smoothed the hair out of her eyes. She cleared her throat. "Here's *my* truth. I want my life back with you, and I'm willing to do whatever it takes."

Rini reached out to squeeze her shoulder. "You took the words out of my mouth. I'm going to work on our marriage, and I have an idea. Let's pretend that we just met and want to get to know each other. On the flight home from Rezana earlier, I thought about how you've been waiting on me. I wanted to do something for you tonight to show you what you mean to me."

"Oh, Rini." She leaned over to kiss his jaw. "I love it. A new beginning for both of us."

"Amen." He'd married an angel.

After kissing her mouth, Rini sat back and started the engine. He made a U-turn to get back on the autostrada and they took off until they came to Lago Diamanti. In the distance he saw a castle on the shoreline.

"You'll love this place," Luna murmured. "Part of the dining room extends out over the water."

His eyes took in the pines studding the landscape. "You're right. It looks like something right out of a storybook."

Incredible that he remembered none of this. Tonight he got the sick feeling that he'd never recover his memory. The blow to his head had wiped out that part of his brain. It appeared he'd spend the rest of his life working on a new life.

As for being a royal, he might have been born to royalty, but he wanted no part of it. Tonight he didn't want to think about it. Not when his exciting wife filled his vision.

"When you brought us here, I almost died it was so enchanting, Rini. The ripples on the water catch the light the way a diamond does. Long ago someone called it Diamond Lake and it stuck. The diamonds I'm wearing tonight are the ones you gave me that night for a wedding present."

"I'm starting to like myself better and better."

Her giggle made him smile.

A number of luxury cars filled the parking area. Rini found a space and shut off the engine. In the distance he heard dance music. The castle had been lit up like a Christmas tree. He helped Luna from the car, keeping his arm around her waist as they entered what looked like a thirteenth-century castle.

"Your Highness!" The host came running and greeted them, beaming from ear to ear. "It's an honor." He put his hand over his heart. "Come right this way."

Luna translated before following the man through a corridor to doors leading out to the patio. Couples were dancing to the music of the terrific band. Trees decorated with twinkling white lights gave the individual tables privacy. The host led them to the other end of the patio. Their table overlooked the water.

Once seated, he gave them menus, and a waiter took over. He poured them wine.

She looked at Rini across the small, candlelit table. Her eyes shimmered like green diamonds. "Do you trust me to order for you?"

"Why don't we eat the same meal we had when I brought you here before."

Luna gave the waiter the order before he left them alone.

"What are we having besides ham?" He drank some of the wine and liked it very much.

"You *knew* that word! As for the *pappardelle funghi*, it's a pasta with mushrooms."

He said the words, committing them to memory. Then he looked at her, needing to get her in his arms. "Signora Baldasseri, *ballerai con me*?" Rini had been practicing that phrase.

*"Mi piacerebbe."* She got out of her chair before he came around. That action told him what she'd said. Another word to put to memory. He caught her curvaceous body to his. She melted against him. "I can't believe I'm dancing with you again." Her voice caught. "It's a miracle that you're alive."

His lips roved over her soft cheek. *"You're* the miracle."

She nestled closer, clinging to him. "I'm in heaven, Signor Baldasseri."

He couldn't help running his hands up and down her back. "Luna—I want to make love to you when we get home. Is that asking too much of you? Don't be afraid to tell me the truth. If it's too soon…"

"Too soon?" She hugged him harder. "I'd hoped it would happen the first day I got you home from the hospital. But you held back because you thought I pitied you."

"I know that's not true now, but I need an answer to one more question. How badly do you want a baby knowing I've got amnesia? Does that change the idea for you?"

"Not at all. We're married and have decided to move forward. I want your child. Nothing would ever change that."

"So if I get you pregnant—"

"I'll shout from the rafters!" She stopped dancing and cupped his face in her hands. "Besides marrying you, Rini darling, I've wanted your baby more than anything else in this world. We've said we want to begin again, so the answer to both your questions is *yes!* I want to sleep with you in every sense of the word, and I can't wait for children. Whatever the future holds, we'll deal with it."

Rini let out the breath he'd been holding. "You've made me the happiest man on earth. I don't know if I can eat dinner."

"You *have* to, remember?" she teased. "Come on. Let's sit down so the waiter will serve us."

The next half hour passed in a blur. The food was sensational, but he couldn't take his eyes off Luna. "Do you want dessert?"

"I couldn't. What about you?"

Rini reached for her hand across the table. "I think you know the answer to that."

"I do." She put money from her purse on the table. "Let's go home." The pleading in her eyes was almost his undoing. He rushed around to help her, and they left the castle with indecent speed. On the drive back to the *palazzo*, he managed to elude a police car and his bodyguards.

She laughed as they pulled around the back. "All you have to do is present yourself as a race car driver and you can make your fortune in a whole new, exciting way."

"Well, there is this about it. At least if I crash during another earthquake, it will be above ground. Maybe I won't be able to speak Romansh anymore."

"Rini—you mustn't kid about things like that!"

He put a hand on her arm. "I agree that wasn't funny. Forgive me."

They got out of the car and went inside. She disappeared into the bathroom of their suite. He got ready for bed and threw on a robe while he waited for her. She emerged a few minutes later wearing a cream-colored nightgown.

"Rini? I should never have gotten so upset. The horror of believing I had lost you still lives inside me."

He shook his head. "I can't relate to your pain. What I do know is that if I lost you now, I wouldn't want to live."

The throb of Rini's deep voice resonated through Luna's body. She sucked in her breath. "You haven't lost me, and you never will." She flew into his arms.

*"Adorata."* Rini buried his face in her hair, then picked her up and carried her over to the bed. His eyes

burned with desire as he lowered her to the mattress. "*Ti amo.* Do you hear me?"

Yes, she heard his avowal of love, but he didn't give her a chance to answer because his mouth had covered hers. This was the Rini she'd married over seven months ago, devouring her with the kind of hunger that aroused her deepest passion. He was alive and whole. She couldn't get enough of this beloved man who was her husband and had been returned to her.

With the robe and nightgown discarded, they lay there entangled while they tried over and over again throughout the night to assuage their need for each other. No man could be a better lover than Rini. She never wanted this rapture to end.

Toward morning she got her wish when he rolled her on top of him and made love to her all over again. Several hours later she cried, "I love you." She kissed every masculine feature of his handsome face. "I love you so much you can't possibly imagine. You've been so brave and courageous through all of this. I want to take away your every fear."

"You already do that by loving me."

"I want to do more. How can I help you?"

He propped some pillows and turned her in his arms. "I did a lot of thinking while we were at the mine. Obviously, it has been one of the mainstays of the family for three hundred years. Though I don't remember it, I believe it's still my responsibility.

"Since I have to do something with my life, I could choose anything. But it will mean I have to learn whatever it is from the bottom up and keep working on my

Italian. So why not get involved in the administration aspect of the mine?"

She sat straight up. "That's a brilliant idea, darling."

"I could take a business class at the college along with a beginning Italian class. I'll discuss it with Doctor Tullia."

"Good. I have another idea."

"Of course, because you're my amazing wife." He gave her another kiss that swept her away.

"You could intern at the Baldasseri Gold Mining office several afternoons a week to get on top of the accounting. I could help you there, too. In no time you'll be in charge of the whole business you ran so beautifully for the country. I have no doubt of it."

The moment she said the words, Rini covered her mouth with his and once again he swept her away with unbridled passion. Her husband might have lost his memory, but he knew how to make her feel immortal.

Two hours later he lay on his side, drinking in her beauty. Because he didn't know she was pregnant and didn't remember what she'd looked like before, he didn't realize her body had changed. But in another month, he'd figure it out.

Right now she didn't want to worry about it and would have stayed here with him all day if her cell phone hadn't kept ringing until they couldn't ignore it.

Rini handed it to her from the bedside table. She answered, but because she was lying against him, she was in no state for a conversation with anyone. Dr.

Tullia's secretary was calling to remind Rini of his appointment at eleven.

"He'll be there," she promised and hung up before kissing Rini. "You're due at the hospital at eleven for a session with Doctor Tullia. You're going to have to hurry to make it on time. Why don't you shower first while I ask Viola to get our breakfast ready?"

A sigh escaped his throat before he reluctantly moved away from her and reached for his robe. "Being in your arms has made me forget everything, *cara*."

He wasn't the only one with that problem. While he hurried to get ready, she called downstairs before phoning Antonia. "I know you're dying to see Rini again. I promise he'll talk to you before the day is out. I love you."

She passed Rini on her way to take a shower. He looped his arm around her shoulders to give her another kiss before releasing her.

Within a half hour they'd eaten and had hurried out to the car. Rini drove them to the hospital. Being independent made him more like the husband he'd been before the quake. She encouraged him to do as much as he could by himself.

After he turned off the engine, she put a hand on his arm. "I'm sure Chispar will be there, so I'll wait for you here."

"One day soon I won't need a translator. After I'm through, let's go to lunch and then stop by the office. You can orient me." Another quick kiss and he got out of the car. He'd worn a tan summer suit and white shirt with no tie. No man on earth looked as handsome as he did. Already she could tell he was putting on weight even though it hadn't been that long since his rescue.

She phoned Fabio and told him she was bringing Rini into the office later so he could familiarize himself with the accounts. Luna didn't have to get permission. Rini was in charge of everything and always had been. But she didn't want to surprise Fabio.

"How will he do that when he can't understand?"

"He's working on his Italian constantly. You'd be surprised how well he's progressing. See you later."

A half hour later Rini returned to the car, looking relieved. She flashed him a smile. "I can tell that session went well."

He started the engine. "I had a short conversation with him in Italian. It surprised him. When I told him of my plans, he said taking an English class online was fine, but no college yet. He says I need more time to work on my marriage to you. A trip to the business office might not hurt, but don't get overwhelmed."

"That's excellent advice. I'm sure he can't believe you're in such good spirits."

Rini drove out to the street. "I gave you all the credit for my rehabilitation. But my guess is he already figured that out the first time he met you. Besides being a stunning beauty, there's no woman to measure up to you."

"You spoil me with compliments like that." After a night of being loved by him, there was nothing wrong in her world. *Until* she remembered this was a new relationship to him. Maybe he was falling for her. But how long would that infatuation last? Could it survive while he tried to rebuild his life?

Luna was getting ahead of herself and needed to slow down. Take one step at a time and be thankful.

"That's quite a conversation you're having with yourself, *sposa mia*."

Warmth crept up her neck into her cheeks. "I've been thinking about the great strides you've made since a week ago. You're so courageous, I'm in awe."

"There you go again. Building me up so I feel I could accomplish anything."

She studied his chiseled profile. "You already have by staying alive until you were found. A lesser man would never have made it. You walked to the highway after crawling out of the mine. I don't know how you did it."

Luna's words found their way deep into his soul. Last night she'd taught him what it was like to be married to the most wonderful, giving, passionate woman on earth. Rini didn't deserve her. Not yet. But he'd do whatever it took to win her love again.

After leaving the hospital, they drove to the office. He parked in a reserved space near the entrance. Luna had told him there were eighty staff members who filled the two-story building. They dealt with the various departments. The accounting department contained three offices including hers on the main floor. Fabio had his own private office nearby.

Rini helped Luna out of the car and kept his arm around her waist as they entered the building. They passed a glassed-in office where an attractive young woman waved to them.

Luna waved back. "That's Suzanne. She and I have become good friends."

Within seconds they were ensconced in Luna's office. She put another chair next to hers in front of her desk so they could sit together. He looked around, noticing she had a wedding picture of the two of them on one wall. They'd just come out of the cathedral where she'd said they'd been married.

"That was the happiest day of my life," she murmured after noticing where his gaze had settled. "The only happier day was when I walked into that hospital room and saw you lying on the gurney."

He gave her a piercing glance. "As I told you before, I heard an angel's voice speaking to me. I couldn't believe it and opened my eyes to see this exquisite woman at my side. She'd just told me she loved me in a language I understood. I'll never forget that moment. I thought I was hallucinating when you said you were my wife. It didn't seem possible I could be married to you."

*"Rini..."*

Unable to suppress his desire for her, he reached over to cup her face. Hungry for his wife, he started kissing her.

*"Mi scusi."*

A male voice broke in on them. Rini slowly relinquished her lips and turned. The manager stood in the doorway.

Rini got to his feet. *"No c'e problema. Ciao, Fabio. Come va?"*

His expression registered utter disbelief that Rini was speaking Italian. *"Bene, Rini. E tu?"*

*"Molto, molto bene."* He darted Luna a smile. *"Sto lavorando con mi bella moglie."* Rini said the words to make it clear to Fabio that he was back from the dead. Not only was he working with his wife, he was also more in love with her than ever.

Fabio's eyes swerved to Luna, staring at her. After a minute he left and shut the door behind him. Rini sat down again and hugged his wife. "How did I do?"

She leaned into him. "You already know the answer to that. Your transformation surprised the daylights out of Fabio."

"Did you tell him I would be coming to the office with you?"

"Yes. I phoned him while you were in session with Doctor Tullia. You'll always be in charge of this office and the mine, but I wanted to give him the courtesy of a heads-up this one time."

There was nothing about Luna he didn't admire. "You're a wonder."

"I hope you feel the same way after we've spent a few hours together on the books."

"I love being with you no matter what we do."

Her eyes gave off green sparks. "That sounds perfect. Are you ready to plunge in?"

"Ready and eager. Let's see what kind of a teacher you make."

"Oh, dear. I wish you hadn't said that."

He chuckled as she pulled up a file and they got started. Since numbers didn't have to be translated, Rini was able to grasp quite a bit for a first round. He hadn't lost his math capabilities. Luna made it easy by compiling a list of headings in Romansh. In another day or two he'd have the terms memorized into Italian.

An hour later they left the building to eat lunch. "What are you in the mood for, Rini?"

"I think fish."

"Then I know a perfect spot." They got into the car and she showed him where to drive to a port on the lake. "It's the place we love after we've been out swimming and fishing."

"On what?"

"You have a cabin cruiser."

"I do?"

"We've spent many a night on it."

Soon, they reached the port and she pointed out his sleek blue-and-white cruiser moored at the pier alongside half a dozen others.

"I've got an idea, Luna. We could move to the cruiser."

She laughed. "You used to say that to me whenever we'd been out on it. You loved being on the water."

"I'd like to see it. Why don't we pick up some lunch and eat it on board?"

"Let's do it, but I don't have the key for us to take a drive."

"I don't care about that."

It didn't take long for them to buy crab and pasta to go. The delightful news that they had a cruiser had excited him. She waved to the security guard at the dock, who recognized them. Rini helped her get on board and they went below deck out of the hot sun to eat. They sat together on the couch while they ate.

"Let's come out here tonight."

"I'd love it, but maybe we should wait until tomorrow."

"Why?"

"First of all, we need to go shopping so you'll feel like you've joined the world. You need a watch and wallet. And I think a few new casual shirts, too. And then this evening your grandparents are hoping to hear from you. We could run by the palace."

"I'd rather not."

"Then we'll set up a video conversation with them at the *palazzo*."

"I'm not ready to spend time with my grandparents yet."

"Why is that?"

He let out a sigh. "I had a long conversation with Vincenzo and ran it by Doctor Tullia. Vincenzo is being groomed to take over the monarchy when the time comes. I refuse to interfere with that. The earthquake changed everything. I have no desire to take on former duties I know nothing about. I don't want to do them, but I hate disappointing my grandparents.

"I realize they have expectations of me I can't fulfill. That's why it's hard to be around them. Can you understand that when it's clear my amnesia is here to stay?"

"Yes. I *can* understand. But you need to tell your grandparents the truth of your feelings."

"Doctor Tullia said the same thing. So tonight we'll call them and I'll explain what's going on with me. That's the best I can do."

"That's all anyone could ask."

"While we're on the subject, I've been thinking I could video call with the general manager at the mine."

"You used to do it with the various managers when you had to be away from the mine on your princely duties," she informed him.

"Good. With your help I can discuss the fax he sent."

"After a couple of months, you'll be able to handle everything on your own."

"As long as I'm with you. I need you in my life, Luna. You'll never know how much," he whispered, covering her lovely face with kisses. His appetite for her had become insatiable.

"Right now all I want to do is get you in my arms. He stood up and pulled her to him. Within seconds they reached the cabin and fell on the bed, feverish for each other. They ended up getting home in time to call his grandparents, but the shopping had to be put off for another day.

# CHAPTER NINE

"Rini?"

They'd just gotten off their online meeting with his grandparents. It had been a painful experience.

He shut down his laptop and shot to his feet. "I've done it now."

"You had to do it, *tesoro mio*."

"I may not know them, but I felt their pain."

Luna had felt it, too. She got up from the chair and threw her arms around him. She rested her head against his shoulder. "They're doing their best to understand. Give them time. Don't forget. Vincenzo is already there, ready to take over when the time comes."

He threw his head back. "I'm a monster, aren't I?"

"No, *amore*. You came out of that mine a different person. It's been in God's hands and they know it. Come to bed."

That night they held each other and clung. Her beloved husband had been carrying a terrible burden. Thankful he'd made the necessary phone call, now maybe he'd finally get some peace.

The next morning she found him in his study on a call with the manager at the mine. The two managed to communicate with Rini's very modest grasp of Italian. Her pride in him was off the charts.

When the call ended, he turned and saw her. "You're awake. I didn't realize. During the night I got the idea to go down into the belly of the mine where the cave-in occurred. I know they've tried to remove debris, but I want to try it again to see if we can find some bodies. I despise feeling helpless. Maybe it's a fool's errand, but I have to try."

"No, Rini. I don't want you to go down inside."

"I'll be fine, but knowing how you feel, you won't be coming with me."

"You can't go!" she cried. "I won't let you."

He grinned. "I can see we're having our first fight."

"This isn't funny."

She heard him draw in a deep breath. "I knew you wouldn't like it, but it's something I *have* to do."

"Why?"

"I may have given up the idea of being Crown Prince, but a Baldasseri has been in charge of the mine for three hundred years. Now it's my turn. I'm responsible for the entire operation. The men look to me for direction. What kind of a leader would I be if I let my problems defeat me? I need to do everything possible."

She struggled to keep back the tears. "But all of that has been done."

He stared hard at her. "Did you give up on me?"

Rini had made his point. "I understand, but I have a horrible feeling about it."

"That's your fear taking over."

Yes. She *was* afraid. For him, for them, for their

baby. If there was another quake or a cave-in, their son or daughter would never know him.

"Luna—I *must* do this." She heard his determination. His vibrant voice resonated to her insides.

She could tell him the truth now, that they were expecting a child. The knowledge would probably force him to accede to her wishes. But that would be a cruel thing to do to him when he'd just made his first big, courageous decision to stand at the helm.

"I know you do," she said at last, defeated by his excitement and that feeling inside him. "I'm sorry I had such a strong reaction."

"Forgive me for upsetting you, Luna, but nothing's going to happen to me. I'll be home by the end of the day."

Those were the very words he'd said to her before he'd left their bed to inspect the mine. To go through that horrifying experience again would be the end of her, but she couldn't think that way.

"Of course you will, and I'll be waiting."

She wanted her husband whole and healthy in mind and body. He'd been born with this drive. Rini needed to act on it in order to thrive.

He may have lost his memory, but he hadn't changed in the most fundamental way. Few men were natural-born leaders. His name had been preordained to be on a very short list. From an early age, he'd been revered. Now he was loved and respected by his country. This was his destiny.

Another quake could hit in the same region at the same intensity. But she couldn't live in fear of that or she'd never get through life. To hold him back for her own selfish reasons would be wrong and unworthy of her.

"We'll have today and tonight on the cruiser," Rini reminded her.

"I can't wait."

They got busy and left for the port, taking food with them from the *palazzo*. After they arrived, Rini started up the engine and they took off for a fantastic day of fishing and sunbathing. By that evening they'd stuffed themselves with food and went to bed.

Rini rolled her on top of him. "We'll make the most of this night. Tomorrow morning we'll drive to the palace and I'll take off for the mine in the helicopter. I promise I'll be home by six for dinner." Once again, they began the age-old ritual that brought both of them rapture. No woman ever had a husband as wonderful as Rini.

The next afternoon, as Rini walked through the claustrophobic labyrinths of the mine, the full realization of what had happened to him during the quake hit him. For the next few hours he and Pesco and the staff explored the area where the miners had been buried. It was an incredible sight to see all those boulders that filled the chutes. He lost total track of time because he was so deep in thought.

The massive damage was testament to the power of that quake. How he'd escaped death was absolutely astounding to him.

He'd studied the maps and found the shaft that led to the exit where he'd crawled out. Rini followed it and looked up at the sky. Maybe if he stood here long enough, a miracle would happen, and another quake would restore him to his former self.

He waited, but by eight o'clock he felt no tremors or rumblings. The ground remained solid beneath his feet.

"Rini?" Pesco murmured. "The men have gone home. Shall we go, too?"

He nodded and followed Pesco up to the surface of the mine. Of course the men had left after such a disastrous meeting! Rini could never blame them. He wasn't the person he'd been pretending to be, and they knew it.

It would take him a lifetime to relearn what had taken him twenty-nine years to accomplish. There was no point in prolonging this nightmare. Not only couldn't he speak fluent Italian, he also didn't know what in the hell to communicate to the men. He knew nothing about running the mining world.

The only reason the men had treated him with the greatest deference was because they saw him as the Crown Prince, whatever that was. But Rini had seen the sadness in their eyes while he'd struggled to find words and come up with ideas that meant nothing!

They'd sent each other nonverbal messages when they'd thought he wasn't looking. But Rini had known what they were thinking. What was this shell of a man doing in their mine when it was the last place he was wanted or needed? He thought he could just walk in like nothing had changed because he was the grandson of the King? Who did he imagine he was kidding?

After thanking Pesco, he walked to the helicopter and told the pilot to head back to Asteria. His wife would be waiting for him.

Luna looked up and closed the book she'd been reading. "That's a morose expression on your face, *mi amante*. I have to admit I was disappointed to receive your text late in the afternoon. Thank heaven you're home safely. I worried something might have happened to you."

"Something *did* happen," he muttered. "Before I say anything else, I need a shower."

*"Rini—"*

The terror in Luna's voice didn't stop him. Rini tore off his clothes and got under the water. Ever since he'd been flown back to Asteria, he'd wished he could wash away this creature he'd become. Last night in talking to his grandparents, he'd felt depression descend because he couldn't remember anything about his former life.

Now he had to face the woman who'd been responsible for keeping him alive body and soul. He couldn't comprehend that a feat of that magnitude had even been possible.

He stayed under the spray until the hot water turned tepid. It wasn't until he realized nothing but cold water poured down that Rini shut off the taps and reached for his robe. Forget shaving. That could wait for another time. The talk with his wife couldn't.

Close to midnight, he entered the bedroom. Luna sat on the side of the bed in her robe, waiting for him. Her gilt-blond beauty with those beguiling green eyes never failed to stun him. She smiled. "The hot water must have run out long ago. If you hadn't made an appearance in another minute, I planned to come in after you."

Rini moved closer, needing to steel himself for what

had to be said. "It was insensitive of me to stay in there so long. To compound my sins, not only was I late getting home and that frightened you, I also left you with unanswered questions. You would never do that to me."

She shook her head. "Rini—what's going on inside you? You're being positively mysterious."

He cocked his head. "Maybe that's because I *am* a man of mystery."

"An exciting one." The chuckle he loved escaped her lips, making this moment that much harder for him. Before long she wouldn't be chuckling.

Over the past few days, he'd tried to adopt Dr. Tullia's rule after being in a few sessions with him.

*Don't impose on her what you believe are her assumptions about you. Be honest with her. Let her tell you her honesty.*

But he couldn't follow the doctor's advice to be patient any longer. It was time to express his feelings that were ready to burst.

His heart thudded. "There's only one way for me to say this. I want a divorce."

She didn't move a muscle. Only shock could have caused the color to drain out of her complexion. But he'd started this, and now he had to go on even though it was killing him.

"There was a moment in the mine when I wished there'd been another quake." A small gasp escaped her throat. "If miracles were being handed out, I would get hit in the head again and awaken the same man I'd once been."

"Don't even think it!" she cried.

"You're not in my skin, Luna."

Another muffled sound came from her. A shudder shook her beautiful body. "I don't know how you dared venture inside."

"You know why."

"Darling," she whispered.

"I didn't belong down there, Luna, and have no wish to put those men through that agony again. Or *you*."

She clasped her hands. "You think I'm in agony?"

"I *know* you are," he bit out. "You think I didn't understand what went through your mind when you learned I'd completely lost my memory? We were both strangers to each other. I'll never live up to your expectation of who I used to be. I don't want to try. I'm exhausted trying to reinvent myself. It's not working."

Spots of color stained her cheeks. "You don't know what you're saying."

"Oh, yes, I do. Like I told Doctor Tullia, you're an angel. Too perfect. You never make a misstep. When we vowed to love each other for better or worse, we didn't know I would turn into the amnesiac I've become. You deserve to start over again with someone who will fall in love with you."

"Because you're *not* in love with me?" she fired at him.

"I'm not worthy of you, Luna. You need to be free. Since the moment I woke up in the hospital in Rezana, I've clung to you. My total selfishness has made your life a living hell."

"Stop, Rini! Don't you know how thrilled I've been that you've wanted me with you every second? After all, I'm a stranger to you."

"But you can't leave a room without my questioning it. Every second I'm awake, I need you. When I'm asleep, I need you right by me. No move has been made without my devoted caregiver right there at my side."

"There's no other place I want to be."

"Spoken like a dutiful wife."

"Not dutiful. I love you. If I didn't, I would have told you I wanted a separation before we ever left the hospital."

"Because of your selflessness, you've brought me through the worst of my reincarnation. But from now on I'll be able to survive on my own. The whole point is that you must be released from the bondage of our marriage to be the person you were meant to be. I've become too possessive of you. It's not right. You're only twenty-six with a lifetime ahead of you. To be chained to me would rob you of your destiny."

She got to her feet. "Where has all this come from? What have you been holding back I know nothing about? Tell me!"

"Vincenzo mentioned that he'd come to the rescue because you needed space and my grandparents were worried about you having to be there twenty-four-seven."

Luna shook her head. "You mean to tell me that what Vincenzo said has caused all this doubt and fear in you?"

"Can you deny you feel chained to me?"

"I deny it a million percent!"

"No, you don't, but you're too committed to me to say anything else. This isn't the life either of us signed up for. I can't live with the guilt of depriving you of your expectations. You say we met and fell madly in love. I accept that we did. But I came out of that mine a different man.

"You should be able to meet another man and fall in love with the knowledge that he'll always be that same man. The two of you can build a life together and realize your dreams."

She clasped her arms to her waist. "What about yours?"

"I don't have any, Luna. I'm still trying to survive. My grandparents are waiting for some transformation that isn't going to happen. As for my position at the Baldasseri Mine, I'm giving it up."

"How will you live?"

"I do have the savings in my account that I've earned. It's enough money to get me started in a new direction. More important, I'll make certain that you will always be taken care of and retain your title. This *palazzo* and everything in it is yours for your lifetime. You will want for nothing."

"Except for the man I love." The tremor in her voice could have been his undoing if his mind wasn't already made up.

"Face it, Luna. He died in the quake."

"Have you talked to Doctor Tullia about this?" She sounded frantic.

"I don't need to. He can't change me into the man I once was. No power on earth is capable of that."

She stood in front of him, her eyes burning like green fire. "So there's nothing I can say?"

"No. For better or worse doesn't apply to us. I'm not the man who made that vow to you. I could never live up to the person you married. I'm not the man you chose to be your husband. It isn't possible."

Luna put a hand on his arm. "I want the man I'm looking at right now, flaws and all."

Rini stepped away. "But I don't want you, not under these circumstances."

Moisture glistened on her eyelids. "Can't you pretend we've just met and start all over again, like we decided at the lake?"

He shook his head. "We'd be living a lie for the rest of our lives. It's not going to work for either of us."

Tears ran down her cheeks. "So you're going to end everything, just like that? Rini—" She staggered to the nearest chair and sat down.

He couldn't take much more of this and headed for the door of their suite. "On the flight home from the mine I worked out a plan. Tonight I'll sleep in the guest room down the hall. Tomorrow I'll go to a hotel."

"And then what?"

"In the morning I plan to buy a car. By afternoon I'll meet with an attorney to expedite the divorce. Don't worry about anything. My grandparents are kind people who've given me the breathing room I've needed. I couldn't ask for better. They love you and will supply you with the best counsel available."

He opened the door. "With that said, I'll say goodnight. As of now, you're free to embrace the life you were meant to live. In case you didn't know it before, I'll tell you now. You *are* the best."

\* \* \*

Through blurry eyes Luna watched her husband leave. He'd delivered his ultimatum. She'd known no power under heaven would cause him to change his mind. If she'd told him they were going to have a baby, that would have hastened his exit from the room. His guilt over divorcing her would increase. The last thing she wanted to do was overwhelm him. The revelation they were expecting would have to come later when she could think.

An hour passed while she toyed with the one what-if idea she'd been entertaining in her mind. He'd thrown down the gauntlet, but unlike the knights of old, he didn't expect her to pick it up.

Luna had news for him.

Considering she had nothing to lose, she got to her feet and started for the entrance, determined like she'd never before been in her life.

"Rini?" She knocked on the guest bedroom door.

"Come in," sounded his deep voice.

Surprised it was that easy to gain access to his new inner sanctum, Luna entered the room. He'd propped himself on top of the bed with his laptop. Those long, powerful legs were visible below the hem of his robe. "If you're here to argue with me, it would be useless." She noticed his gaze never left the screen. He'd gone into battle mode.

"I know that. I came for a different reason."

"What would that be?"

She sat down on the end of the bed, close enough to touch him, but she resisted the temptation. "Before you put your plans into motion tomorrow, I'd like to ask a favor of you."

That request captured his attention. His dark head lifted, and their eyes met. Rini's male beauty had never been more evident. "Go on."

"Since you've been home from Slovenia, it dawned on me we haven't taken a trip or been anywhere together. There's been no time for us to relax and just have fun. Between everything, we haven't had the opportunity to simply enjoy ourselves."

He closed his laptop. "I wasn't aware you wanted to get away. Why didn't you say something sooner?"

"We've been so busy I haven't even thought about taking a break from routine. But since you've decided you want a divorce I'm hoping you'll take me on a vacation before we go our separate ways."

"You can leave anytime."

"I wouldn't want to travel alone. That wouldn't be any fun at all."

One black brow lifted. "You never mentioned wanting to go on a trip."

"Where would I go? Why would I want to do anything without you?"

"You could have asked your friend Suzanne at the office."

"No, Rini. I was too grief stricken to make any plans. But all that changed after Zigo helped me find you and bring you home. Since we've built a friendship over the time you've been here, I think we could have a terrific time together. Why not celebrate your freedom? We'll speak Romansh to our heart's content and forget Italian. When we get back to San Vitano, you can visit with your grandparents and tell them your future plans."

She could hear his mind working. It was a good sign he hadn't shut her down yet. Her heart leaped when he said, "If I were to agree, do you have a destination in mind?"

"Yes! I'd love it if we took a driving trip down through Bolzano and Venice. We could visit some wonderful little out-of-the-way spots and walk around without worrying about a schedule. I was thinking a week maybe. Does any of that appeal to you?" They'd gone to Venice on their honeymoon. This was a last-chance effort to see if anything triggered his memory.

Though he said nothing, at least he hadn't given her an outright no yet.

"Why don't you think about it, Rini? Tell me in the morning at breakfast. Remember it's only an idea. I promise I won't fall apart if the answer is no."

Not wanting to overstay her tenuous welcome, she got off the bed and headed for the door. It delighted her that silence followed her into the hall and back down to their suite.

Dr. Tullia had told Rini he could call him anytime, even the middle of the night. After being unable to sleep, he took him at his word and phoned him at home at six in the morning. Somehow, he'd try to make himself understood despite his difficulty with Italian.

"Rini—what a surprise!"

"Sorry, but I need help."

"Talk to me."

"I divorce Luna. She wants vacation first. I don't."

"Why not?"

Frustrated by the question, Rini jumped out of bed and began pacing. "I want divorce now."

"She found you?"

He blinked. *"Sì."*

"She made you happy?"

*"Sì."*

"Then no problem. Your turn to make her happy now. *Correto?"*

Rini heard the words loud and clear. *"Correto."* Good old Dr. Tullia knew what he was doing all right. The woman hadn't asked anything of him until now.

Bowing to the older man's wisdom, Rini said, *"Grazie, Dottore."*

"You're welcome. Call me anytime."

He hung up, standing there in a daze. As Rini thought over the time they'd been together since the quake, and all that Luna had done for him, shame consumed him. After breaking his promise to her yesterday, he'd come home late from the mine last night. With no lead up at all, he'd blurted that he wanted a divorce. To make certain she understood, he'd announced he'd be sleeping in the guest bedroom until he moved to a hotel.

But he *would* agree to take her on a trip.

With his mind made up, he went down the hall to their bedroom. He could hear the shower running. Now would be the best time to get dressed in casual clothes and meet her in the dining room.

Once he was ready, he grabbed his wallet and hurried downstairs. Viola greeted him with a cheery voice. She poured hot coffee for him and Luna and put a plate of freshly baked rolls on the table.

Rini enjoyed the homemade plum jam he'd learned came from their fruit trees out in back. He piled it on with butter. When Luna entered the dining room looking ravishing in a yellow print sundress, he'd eaten three rolls.

Her green eyes widened in surprise to see him. "*Buongiorno*, Rini."

He got up and pulled out a chair for her. As usual her flowery fragrance assailed him. "I thought we were going to speak Romansh from now on."

She lifted her head. "Does that mean what I think it means?" The happiness in her voice told him all he needed to know.

"I'm ready to leave on that trip whenever you are."

Viola appeared with plates of eggs and ham. Rini dug in. Luna barely touched her food. He'd put her lack of appetite down to shock that he'd capitulated. She told the housekeeper they were leaving on vacation and would be gone a week.

"I'm so happy for you." Viola beamed.

"So am I. All we have done is work, work, work. It's time to play."

She put her hands on her ample hips. "That's exactly what you should do! Mateo will get the car ready for you."

"Thank you, but we won't be taking the car, Viola."

"You're going to fly?"

"No." Luna looked at Rini. "We're going to buy another car."

"Ah. To replace the car you gave away." With that response, Viola left them alone.

"Why would we want a different car?" She'd aroused Rini's curiosity.

"We're going to travel incognito. Everyone stares at us when we're out in public. 'There's the Crown Prince!' people cry out. I want us to be unrecognizable, like a typical couple enjoying the day. We can pick up the car I have in mind on our way out of Asteria. It's commensurate with our income."

He grinned, loving her creative mind. "How much do I make?"

"We work in a laundry and barely bring in enough to afford a seven-day trip, let alone a vehicle to get us where we want to go. I'll call your grandparents and tell them we're leaving. I'll also let Fabio know I won't be in for another week. Finish your breakfast while I hurry upstairs to change and pack. We'll only need one medium-size suitcase."

Again, she'd piqued his interest. "How come?"

"The car we're buying will only hold one. All we'll need are shorts, T-shirts, sandals and hats. We'll throw in a swimsuit. That's it!" On that note she disappeared from the room.

# CHAPTER TEN

RINI WAS STARTING to get excited.

Once he'd finished eating, he hurried upstairs. *"Ehi!"* he burst out after opening the door.

At first, he thought another woman had invaded their bedroom. His attention was caught by the blue tie-up sandals on a pair of gorgeous legs. It took a moment to realize Luna had changed into pale blue shorts and the craziest T-shirt he'd ever seen of a fat marshmallow whose hair was on fire.

Most amazing of all, she'd swept her blond hair on top of her head. It was hidden by a baseball cap she wore backward. Green sunglasses completed the picture of a wacky woman with the most sensational figure he'd ever seen on a woman.

"Think I look like Princess Baldasseri now?"

He shook his head. "Your transformation has left me speechless."

She laughed. "Good. I've put your stuff on the bed. Go ahead and shock me."

His gaze took in the purple T-shirt with a T-Rex riding a motorcycle. He whipped off his clothes. After putting on a pair of tan shorts, he pulled the T-shirt over his head. Next came the baseball cap he also wore backward and reached for the purple sunglasses.

She clapped her hands. "You look perfect! If my grandmother were alive, she would faint if I brought you home and told her you're the man I want to marry."

Her words had sobered him. He wanted to do something meaningful for her. "Even if she isn't, why don't we drive to Switzerland first? You can show me where you used to live. Afterward, we'll drive to Venice and visit Bolzano on our way home."

His suggestion brought new light to her eyes. "I'd love it! There's a bed-and-breakfast a few blocks away from the house. We can stay there. You and I were always going to take that trip but didn't get around to it."

That was probably his fault for not fitting in time for her wishes.

"Why don't you finish packing whatever you want to bring, Rini? I've left half the suitcase for you. Then we can take off and buy our car. I'm going to pay for it with my own money."

Rini found he was eager to get on the road and do whatever they wanted. It felt like he was being let out of prison. Not that his world with Luna hadn't been wonderful. But the suggestion of a trip where they could throw off all the conventions had given him an unexpected breath of life. For the next seven days he'd live it to the fullest and not think about the empty years ahead.

A half hour later they drove to a dealership under a hot sun to pick up the car his wife had chosen. The owner told them to drive around the back and park. In a minute their purchase arrived.

Rini laughed at her choice, a tiny classic car that looked like a toy. He reached for their suitcase and locked up the sedan.

Luna did the paperwork, then handed him the keys. "Our chariot awaits us. Our bodyguards won't have any trouble keeping an eye on us."

It wasn't just the bodyguards. The owner and the guy who'd brought the car around hadn't been able to take their eyes off Luna. Talk about a sight to behold!

He put their suitcase in the small backseat and got in behind the steering wheel. "Let's pray it gets us as far as the border." Rini started the engine and drove them out to the street. "So far, so good."

She pushed a playful hand against his arm. "When we reach Switzerland, let's stop at the nearest train station. They sell the most fabulous meat pies in the world. I'll run inside to get some. I'm already salivating for one."

"That doesn't surprise me since you didn't eat your breakfast."

"I know. To be going on a trip made me too giddy to eat."

No. The truth was, Rini had been the cause of her lack of appetite. He suffered that he'd burst in last night asking for a divorce.

The car didn't have a guidance system. Trust his wife to have brought some maps in her purse. She played navigator as they left San Vitano and entered Switzerland in the little car. Every vehicle on the road passed them, but he didn't care. He was having the time of his life, as if they were playing hooky. The radio worked and they listened to music on the way to Scuol.

"See that railway station over there, Rini? Pull up in the parking and I'll get us some lunch."

He did her bidding. While he watched her run inside on those beautifully shaped legs, he realized he could read all the signs printed in Romansh *and* Italian. Elation shot through him he could understand both languages. Back in Rezana, he hadn't been able to make sense of anything.

*You've come a long way, Rini, and all because of Luna.*

"Here we go!" She ran back to the car with a sack in hand. Every male head turned in her direction. Once inside the car they began to eat.

"I have to admit these are the best pies I ever tasted."

"Didn't I tell you?" She'd finished hers. There was nothing wrong with her appetite now. "I bought four in case you get hungry later. Here's some Grapillon, too." She pulled out the fruit drink for him. "It's non-alcoholic and one of my favorites. I have another treat, but it's for later."

He couldn't wait. His wife had to be the most delightful companion on earth, not to mention the most entrancing. Being next to her without touching her was becoming more and more intolerable. Once again, they were on the move. "I can see mountains ahead."

She nodded. "They're spectacular. We'll be coming to Scuol soon. I used to love to ski."

"I don't remember doing it."

Luna flashed him a smile. "You were an excellent skier, like you are at all sports."

Everything she said touched his heart.

In time they arrived in the village of Scuol. "Take the boulevard to the right. You'll come to the church that was once a monastery and turn right. My grandparents' house will be at the end of the street."

"Who lives there now?"

"A professor and his wife."

Rini followed her directions until they came to the two-story chalet with flowers filling the window boxes. "What a charming home."

"I loved it." She pointed. "That was my room on the second floor."

Too bad they couldn't go inside and spend the rest of the day in bed.

"Do you want to stop and pay a visit?"

She shook her head. "No. It won't be the same without my family there."

He heard pain in her voice. "But I'm so glad you suggested we drive here. Would you like to run by your cousin's home and say hello?"

"I don't think so. This trip is for the two of us. Let's keep it that way."

"It means a lot to me that you wanted to bring me here. As long as we've come, there's one thing I would like to see if you're willing. It will give us a chance to stretch our legs. Afterward, we can have dinner at a restaurant close by."

"Sounds good to me. That is, *if* we can manage to climb out of this contraption."

Her full-bodied laughter warmed him clear through. "Maybe we'd better stop and reserve a room first. The bed-and-breakfast is around the corner beyond the park."

Every house and building exuded a quaint, alpine flavor Rini liked very much. His wife had grown up here. He marveled that after marrying him she'd adapted to a new life in San Vitano. If she'd ever expressed that she'd been homesick, he didn't know. There was a lot about her he didn't know.

Luna took the lead and registered them before they left for the castle on the hill. "Schloss Tarasp dates from the eleventh century," she explained. "It's the glory of the lower Engadin. If we hurry, we might be able to hear a piece on the organ. When I was little, my grandmother told me it had two thousand five hundred pipes. I spent hours trying to count all of them."

Rini chuckled. He was so crazy about her, he didn't know how long he could hold out before wanting to make love to her.

Unfortunately, they were too late for a concert, but he enjoyed seeing the knight's halls and ballrooms. Mostly, he enjoyed listening to Luna's anecdotes about her youth.

Later, they stopped for cheese fondue on their way back to the B&B. For dessert she handed him the treat she'd bought. A Frigor chocolate bar, one of her favorites. All in all, it had been a great day. He felt totally relaxed.

Soon, they dismantled their disguises and got ready

for bed. Once under the covers, he turned away from her, hugging his pillow for dear life. "What do you feel like doing tomorrow?"

Luna stayed on her side of the bed without looking at Rini. Last night they hadn't slept in the same room. Tonight it was agony being this close to him without rolling into his arms. "To be honest, I want to drive straight to Venice. I went there once but didn't have time to explore. On this trip I'd love to see everything we can. It's the most gorgeous city on earth."

Luna held a prayer in her heart that when they arrived, something might trigger a memory inside him.

"Then that's what we'll do."

"You're sure?" He was just being nice to her, of course. In fact, he'd been marvelous about this vacation when she knew he'd wanted to hibernate in a hotel away from her until the divorce. More than ever, she wondered what had caused him to agree to travel with her when he'd been so adamant about an immediate separation.

"This trip is for you, Luna, but I admit I'm enjoying every moment of it. Get a good sleep."

"You, too." She couldn't imagine it when her beloved husband was lying inches away from her. Somehow, she had to get through the night without breaking down and begging him to love her one more time.

She lay awake for several hours and finally lost consciousness. When she came to, she realized Rini had already gotten up. She could tell he'd showered and shaved. He smelled wonderful and was wearing another pair of shorts and another hilarious T-shirt.

She'd bought their shirts and caps after they were married to wear once in a while for the fun of it. Those items had been hidden away to come out at the right moment. Never did she dream it would be for such an important journey as this.

He darted her a glance, noticing how disheveled she must look. "While you get showered and dressed, I'll zip out and bring our breakfast back. Then we'll leave for Venice."

"Terrific." But it took all her self-control not to get up and throw her arms around his neck to prevent him from going anywhere.

In his absence she phoned the Villa Marvege off San Marco Square in Venice where they'd stayed on their honeymoon. On behalf of the Crown Prince of San Vitano, she asked for their old room with the canal view. Otherwise, she wouldn't be able to get a room when so many tourists flooded Venice.

The concierge assured her it would be ready, and they could check in at one o'clock. Though Luna had wanted to travel incognito, she knew she needed to reserve that exact room. It was her prayer that Rini might see something that would spark his memory.

Their honeymoon had been a week of utter enchantment. They'd been so crazy in love it was pathetic. They'd talked and made love for days on end. She'd experienced real pain when the time came for them to drive home.

By the time Rini returned with croissants filled with melted cheese and ham, she was ready and had arranged her hair on top of her head. He approached her as she was putting the baseball cap in place. "It's a shame to cover up your crowning glory."

"Is that what it is?" she teased.

"Not even gossamer compares."

The tone in his voice sounded like the old Rini, causing her to tremble. "You don't look so bad yourself. Do you realize you've gained back the weight you lost? I don't know another man who's as fit and handsome as you. The women tourists at the castle should have been examining the knights' armor. Instead, they couldn't take their eyes off you."

He flashed her a compelling smile. "I didn't notice. I was too busy imagining you as a little girl who grew into a sinfully beautiful woman."

"Sinfully?" she mocked with a smile. "I'm surprised you weren't snapped up before we met."

Her breathing grew shallow. "If you want to know the truth, I'm surprised you didn't end up marrying an American while you were in Colorado getting your mining degree."

"None of it matters because we found each other," he muttered before sending her a penetrating glance. "I'm only sorry to say that our meeting resulted in your ultimate detriment."

"Can we not talk about that?" Luna turned away, not wanting to be reminded that he planned to divorce her at the end of their trip.

"I'm sorry, Luna."

She reached for a croissant. "Shall we eat and get going?"

Once on the road again with their disguises in place,

they headed for Italy. She turned on the radio to a music station playing soft rock. Luna put her head back and closed her eyes. Alarm filled her heart that she would have to tell Rini about the baby before they returned to Asteria. He was determined to leave her. But the news would upset him in ways she didn't want to think about.

Down in the mine he'd come face-to-face with his feelings of inadequacy. Now to hear he was going to be a father would add the crushing blow that would tear him apart. He would want to be all things to his son or daughter yet believed he could never fill that need.

She dozed on and off until they reached Venice. The sight of the city on water brought back so many memories of the two of them wildly in love, she could hardly bear it. But as she turned to look at him, she could see nothing had changed. Being back in Venice hadn't brought back one memory for him.

Luna had been a fool to think another miracle could happen like the one when she'd found him alive in Rezana. To expect two miracles had been beyond the realm of credulity.

"What happened when we were in Scuol, Rini? You're acting different."

"When we drove past your grandparents' home, it reminded me that you have no family to rely on once we're divorced."

"But I do. Your grandparents have become my family. I adore them."

"Forgive me for bringing it up."

"I do."

Tomorrow after a walk around San Marco Square,

she'd suggest they go back home. This trip had turned out to be a painful, torturous idea. On the drive to San Vitano, she'd break the news about the baby.

Luna had already worked out ideas for visitation. Rini would always be welcome at the *palazzo* when he came. She would stay at the palace, so he'd have free rein to be with his son or daughter for as long as he wanted.

They parked their car and walked to the villa, fighting the crowds. After being shown to their room with a view of the Grand Canal, they left to visit the city. Rini didn't show the slightest indication that he'd ever been here before.

For the rest of the day, they visited the Doge's Palace and saw the sights of the Rialto Bridge on a gondola. Later, they went to San Marco Square. Rini bought them pizza at one of the many pizza shops. They sat at one of the tables to watch the world pass by.

While Luna was eating, she felt something drop on her head. She reached up and discovered that a pigeon had left its droppings on her baseball cap. "Oh no!" Her eyes met Rini's and they both burst into laughter.

"A souvenir for you to remember," he murmured.

But it would be the last of any souvenirs once they returned home and Rini moved out.

Luna left the cap on. Twilight fell before they finally ended up going back to their room. She was exhausted after losing so much sleep the night before. After washing her cap with hot water and soap, she hung it up to dry. When she came out of the bathroom, she noticed Rini at the window, watching the traffic on the canal.

"There's no sight like it in the world, is there, Rini?"

At the sound of her voice, he turned to her. He'd removed his cap and sunglasses. "It's a delightful city. I'm glad you wanted to come here. Have you noticed how hard the gondoliers have to work? They don't have an air traffic controller to help them navigate. They do it by instinct. It's fascinating they don't have more accidents."

"I've never thought about it, but you're right." She took a deep breath. "What do you want to do tonight?"

"That's up to you, Luna."

"In that case, I'd like to stay in. The pizza filled me up and I have to admit I'm tired."

"Then that's what we'll do. Why don't you get ready for bed while I watch the tour of Venice on TV?"

"Good idea."

Relieved he didn't want to go anywhere, she showered and changed into her nightgown. At last, she was able to climb under the covers. Rini turned on the TV and lay on top of the bedspread still dressed. She'd felt he'd been having a good time, too, but she couldn't allow this to go on.

Luna gripped the sheet to keep from reaching out to him. No doubt about it. Tomorrow she'd tell him she wanted to go home and explain she was pregnant. For now, she was truly exhausted and in emotional agony. "Good night, Rini."

"Get a good sleep, Luna."

The video bored Rini. All he could think of was his breathtaking wife lying asleep next to him. Her gilt hair lighted by the TV drew him like a beacon. He wanted to plunge his hands into the silky strands and kiss the daylights out of her.

He'd promised himself that during this trip he wouldn't let anything break down his resolve to keep his distance from the woman he adored. But he knew he couldn't keep that promise much longer. Tomorrow they'd have to go home. He couldn't take being with her like this without making love to her. That would be beyond cruel when he'd determined to divorce her.

Frustrated beyond endurance, he shut off the TV and turned on the radio. He could only make out the news in bits and pieces. After changing it to music, he lay back on his side away from her, still dressed in his shorts and T-shirt.

Yesterday Rini had been excited to come on this trip. She was so clever and creative. Her plan had worked, jerking him out of his depression for a little while. But at this point the novelty had worn off. He needed to get away from Luna where he could come up with a plan to live life on his own. As the minutes wore on, he grew more depressed and shut his eyes, praying to lose consciousness.

The loudest noise Luna had ever heard in her life reverberated in the darkness, bringing her wide-awake. It sounded like a train barreling right through the walls.

"Gustavo!" Rini yelled and shot up in bed.

*Gustavo?* Luna was mystified. He was calling for the mining engineer who'd died in the cave-in.

Rapid gunfire resounded, then another crashing boom followed that lit up the entire hotel room.

"Rini?" She grasped his arm. The muscles stood out in his neck.

"Follow me, Gustavo. I'll get us out of here." He spoke in fluent Italian. She couldn't understand what was going on.

"Darling— It's me. Luna. Wake up, my love. You're dreaming." The loud noises continued, and she suddenly realized it was fireworks.

"We're in an earthquake." Again, his Italian was perfect. He leaped off the bed and got down on the floor on his hands and knees. "Follow me. I know a way out of here. There's a little chute that leads to the side of the mountain."

From the trance-like look on his face, she realized Rini was reliving his horrific experience in the mine. *Her husband was speaking Italian.* But he couldn't hear her and was like a sleepwalker you couldn't wake up.

He crawled over to the open window and got to his feet. One look outside and she realized it was definitely fireworks going off with sizzles and whooshes. Venice put on their Redentore fireworks show once a year, but she'd forgotten it took place this month, let alone that it would be tonight.

She put her arms around him and hugged him tightly. "It's all right, darling. There's no earthquake. Come back to bed."

His arms and body were like steel. He wouldn't move. "Gustavo? I hope you can hear me. I'm going for help and will be back."

When he started to climb out the window, it terrified her. She grabbed his right leg so he couldn't lift it. "Turn around, Rini!" she screamed at him. "Look at me!"

He stared down at her, not seeing her. "I swear I'll get all of you out."

She held on to him tighter so he couldn't move away. "Wake up, Rini! Wake up!"

"I need to get help for the men."

Luna reached for his arm, never letting go of him, and stood up. "They're all right. So are *you*. Listen to me."

"But the earthquake—"

"There was no earthquake. Venice is having a fire-works show."

His eyes showed confusion. In the next breath his black brows knit together. "Fireworks?"

"Yes. Come back to bed. They're still going on. We'll enjoy them together."

He started to come out of his trance, looking out the window, then staring at her so strangely. "Luna?" he murmured as if he wasn't sure she was real. "It *is* you. You're here."

She ran fingers through his hair. "Yes, my love. You're not at the mine. You're in Venice with me."

Rini rubbed his hands up and down her arms. Before the earthquake, he used to do that as his desire to make love.

"Luna—" It was as if he were seeing her for the first time.

Her old husband was back.

*He* was back!

The miracle *had* happened. Her joy was so great she

came close to fainting as he picked her up in his arms like a bride and carried her to the bed.

The old Rini had come alive. So had the new one. It was like two men were making love to her at once. His mouth engulfed hers.

He followed Luna down onto the mattress, burrowing his face in her neck.

Rini knew the exact spot to kiss her and drive her absolutely mad with desire. Their clothes went flying and they melded together while fireworks lit up the Venetian night.

Hours later he cradled her head in his hands. "Please tell me I'm not dreaming, Luna. Please tell me I'm the man I used to be," he whispered against her succulent lips, unable to get enough of her. Their legs were entangled, trying desperately to get closer.

She kissed every inch of his face including the cleft in his firm chin. "You're all that and more, *mi amante.* Can't you tell you're thinking and speaking fluent Italian?"

"I am!" he cried out, jubilant. His yelp of excitement rivaled the fireworks outside. "I can remember everything. This hotel room. We stayed here on our honeymoon."

"Yes!" She flung her arms around his neck. "The other day I asked if you would bring me to Venice. Deep inside lurked this hope that you might see something that would trigger your memory. But I never imagined that fireworks would produce the needed magic to free you from your prison."

He shook his head. "I swear I thought I was in the

earthquake again. The sounds of the fireworks sounded exactly like the sounds of the earthquake. It triggered something in my brain."

"Thank heaven. I heard you call out for Gustavo. You were worried about the miners and determined to get them out. It broke my heart to realize what you lived through, the terror you experienced. When I first heard the fireworks, I thought a train was coming for us."

"That's exactly what the quake sounded like in the mine."

"Thank heaven it's all in the past." She clung to his body, kissing him with urgency. "Your doctors will go into shock when they hear the fireworks brought your memory back. You'll make history in the medical journals. Your grandparents will go into shock again to realize their grandson is back in every sense of the word."

He nestled her closer to him. "I know I said a lot of things the other night after I got home from the mine. I wasn't in my right mind when I declared I wanted a divorce. It was the last thing I wanted because I couldn't see another way out. But now all that has changed. My grandfather is depending on me to take over one day. It's my duty. More important, can you ever forgive me for hurting you like that?"

"Of course I forgive you." Happiness exploded inside her. "Rini? Why don't we go home today and surprise your grandparents?"

He rose up on one elbow. "That can wait. This trip is for you." He traced her lips with his finger. "We're going to enjoy it for as long as you want."

"But I'd like to get back to the *palazzo*. There's a lot we need to talk about."

Rini smiled before giving her another sumptuous kiss. "What's going on in that beautiful head of yours?"

"It's more a case of what's going on somewhere else in my body."

"Hmm." He started squeezing her here and there. She giggled. "Tell me when to stop."

"Right there," she said when his hand reached her belly.

He went quiet, then slowly smoothed his hand over her skin. His gaze fused with hers. She felt him tremble.

"Yes, *amore mio*. A new little prince or princess is on its way to being born. You can do the math about the month of delivery. I found out I was pregnant the day you were in the earthquake. I still have a present to give you about it after we get home. Speaking of home, some changes will have to be made at the *palazzo*. Viola and Mateo will be over the moon. They never could have children and will rejoice in ours."

Tears filled his eyes. He clasped her hand. "I'm not sure I can handle all this happiness. But what if I hadn't recovered my memory, and—"

"There are no more buts, remember? Our child will be so blessed because he or she will have the greatest father in the entire world."

"Luna—" He said her name under his breath before lowering his head to kiss her stomach. From there he pulled her next to him and kissed her with such tenderness, it made her cry. "Our son or daughter will have the most marvelous mother alive. I can testify to that."

"Rini..." She couldn't talk.

"I may be a man, but you found me in Rezana and took me in as a little lost child. You taught me how to live enough to function. You brought me to Venice and found me again as I am now. There's no woman sweeter or more wonderful on this earth. I worship you, Luna. Right now I want to make love to you all over again, for as long as we can."

"For as long as we can is right," she teased. "Soon, I'm going to blossom. You'll have to use that engineering brain of yours to figure out the logistics if we're to continue loving each other into oblivion."

His low, exciting laughter set off her desire for him in a brand-new way. Who cared if they ever left the room? Luna knew she didn't as she welcomed her husband into her very heart and soul.

# EPILOGUE

RINI KISSED HIS very pregnant, sleepy wife good morning and slid out of bed.

Luna moaned. "Do you have to go to the mine?"

"This will be the last time until after our baby is here and you've recovered." They hadn't wanted to know the sex of their child. All they hoped for was that it would be healthy.

He felt all right about leaving. She wasn't due for another month. "I promise that today I'll be home for dinner at five." According to Pesco, there might be great news for the monarchy about more veins of gold appearing. He wanted to be on site to witness it.

"Stay safe, *tesoro mio*."

"You, too, *pulcina mia*."

"I look like a stuffed one at this point."

"But never more beautiful." He leaned over and kissed her lips one more time before leaving for the palace to fly to the mine.

An hour later he joined the mining staff. They went down deep to see a new series of labyrinths unblocked by boulders. Pesco was waiting for him with a grin that took up his whole face. "It's gold, Your Highness. A lot of it if you follow the veins."

Rini walked with him as they examined everything. This mine had been producing for three hundred years. Today's discovery ensured the mine could go on helping fund the monarchy for years to come.

Pesco looked at him. "If you hadn't come up with a new idea to remove some of the debris, we would never have found it."

"But no bodies."

"No, but this means more work for all of us."

"You're right, and I'm grateful."

"We're grateful you have your memory back." All the men clapped. How different this experience from months ago when he'd come close to walking away from his soul mate and everything else. Right now he couldn't wait to rush home to the wife he adored. Between this find and the baby they were expecting, he could barely contain his jubilation.

They went up on top and he left for Asteria in the helicopter. The second it touched down, he hurried to the car, eager to be with Luna and tell her the news.

But when he drove around the back of the *palazzo* to park, Viola came running out to him, a little out of breath. "It's good you're home, Rini. Did Luna call you?"

He frowned. "No. What's wrong?"

"Your wife just left for the hospital. The doctor says she's in labor."

His hands froze on the steering wheel. "She isn't due for a month!"

"Well, this baby wants to come now."

Excitement filled his whole being. Rini started the engine and drove out to the street. On the way to the hospital his phone rang. Luna!

He clicked on. *"Amore mio?"*

"It's Antonia. I'm calling for her. The baby is coming. She was in labor all day."

"Why didn't someone tell me?"

"She didn't want to bother you at the mine until she knew this was the real thing. When the pains got worse, Mateo drove her to the hospital."

"I should have been there," he bit out.

"No one could have foreseen this, Rini. Where are you?"

"I'm almost to the hospital now."

"Thank heaven. She needs you."

"I need her more than life itself."

This time it was Luna in the royal suite at the hospital. The King and Queen stayed in the other part of it while they waited. With a new royal heir about to make an appearance, she had all the help she could ever need. The pediatrician and staff had all gathered to get things ready. But there was only one person she needed to see.

As her tall, gorgeous husband came walking into the room masked and gowned, she was hit by another pain. He rushed over to her. All she could do was greet him with a moan.

One of the staff brought a chair over by her head so he could sit down. "Luna—*mi amante.*"

She gripped the hand he'd extended. "You're home.

Thank hea—" That was all she could get out before another pain hit hard. By now the gowned OB had come into the room and had placed himself at the end of the bed. "After being in labor all day, you're more than ready. Shall we do this, Luna?"

The pain was so bad, all she could answer was, "Please, yes."

"On your next pain, bear down as hard as you can."

Being in labor was a revelation. How women who'd had six, eight, a dozen children did it was beyond her comprehension.

"One more time, Luna. Give it all you've got."

"You can do it," Rini urged her on.

If this didn't get over soon, she felt certain she would die. Suddenly, it was like a whoosh and she heard a baby's gurgle.

"You and Rini do good work, Luna," the doctor exclaimed. "You have a fine boy here. He's got your black hair, Rini, and all the important parts."

Both she and Rini laughed for joy.

He placed the baby on her stomach. He cried that amazing cry she'd been waiting for.

She looked into Rini's tear-filled eyes. "Can you believe we have a son?"

"He's beautiful, just like his mother." Rini kissed her lips.

"Do you have a name picked out?" the doctor asked.

"Yes," she answered. "Andreas Giulio Leonardo Vincenzo Umberto Baldasseri. Andreas was my father's name. We'll call him Andre."

"If you'll let him go, we'll get him cleaned up, weighed and measured. I'd say he's a good six pounds and breathing well. Very good for coming a month early. Right now I know the King and Queen are waiting anxiously to greet the newest addition to the Baldasseri royal family."

Two hours later, after all the excitement, Rini had been left alone with his wife. Andre had been taken to the nursery, but he'd be back soon. The nurse had made Luna comfortable, but Rini knew she was exhausted.

He kissed her warmly on the mouth. "I almost had a heart attack when Viola met me at the car and told me you'd gone to the hospital. I wanted to be here for you."

"You got here in time, Rini. That was all that mattered. How did it go at the mine?"

"A new vein of gold has been discovered."

She studied his features. "Another miracle. We've had so many."

He nodded. "Our new son is the prize. He's perfect."

"That's because you're his father."

"With an angel mother. You are angelic. *Ti amo, mi bellissima moglie.*"

\* \* \* \* \*

# COMING SOON!

We really hope you enjoyed reading this book.
If you're looking for more romance, be sure to
head to the shops when new books are
available on

## Thursday 14<sup>th</sup> October

**To see which titles are coming soon, please visit**
**millsandboon.co.uk/nextmonth**

# MILLS & BOON

## THE HEART OF ROMANCE

---

## A ROMANCE FOR EVERY READER

---

### MODERN

Prepare to be swept off your feet by sophisticated, sexy and seductive heroes, in some of the world's most glamourous and romantic locations, where power and passion collide.

### HISTORICAL

Escape with historical heroes from time gone by. Whether your passion is for wicked Regency Rakes, muscled Vikings or rugged Highlanders, avel the romance of the past.

### MEDICAL

Set your pulse racing with dedicated, delectable doctors in the high-pressure world of medicine, where emotions run high and passion, comfort love are the best medicine.

### *True Love*

Celebrate true love with tender stories of heartfelt romance, from the rush of falling in love to the joy a new baby can bring, and a focus on emotional heart of a relationship.

### *Desire*

Indulge in secrets and scandal, intense drama and plenty of sizzling he action with powerful and passionate heroes who have it all: wealth, sta good looks…everything but the right woman.

### HEROES

Experience all the excitement of a gripping thriller, with an intense romance at its heart. Resourceful, true-to-life women and strong, fearless face danger and desire - a killer combination!

---

To see which titles are coming soon, please visit

### millsandboon.co.uk/nextmonth

# MILLS & BOON

## Coming next month

### THE WEDDING PLANNER'S CHRISTMAS WISH
Cara Colter

Alexandra firmly held out her hand. "Come on, we have to find your nan."

The tiny minx actually looked like she was considering darting the other way, but then, with a sigh of surrender, she took the proffered hand.

There was that feeling again, as Alexandra's hand closed around the warmth and sturdiness of the little girl's smaller one. She felt almost dizzy with longing.

This was ridiculous! She spent all kinds of time with her nieces and nephews and didn't feel as if she was being freshly immersed in grief, as she did now.

The child obviously knew her way around this tiny wood very well. She led Alexandra straight out and to the path.

A man's deep voice, edged in desperation, penetrated the silence of the woods. "Genevieve!"

The child giggled.

"That's you, isn't it?" Alexandra asked.

She nodded.

"It's not nice to frighten people," Alexandra said firmly. "It's quite naughty." They stepped out of the shade of the trees and onto the cobblestones.

A man was standing just outside the double oak doors at the top of the sweeping staircase that led into Parker and Parker, his gaze anxiously scanning the grounds. Even from a distance, and even though he was obviously agitated, it was apparent he was an attractive man.

A very attractive man.

He looked to be about midthirties and was dressed with the casual and utter sophistication that those comfortable with wealth were able to pull off: a dark gray sweater over a crisp white shirt and narrow-legged dark denims over boots.

He was tall, probably an inch or two over six feet, and beautifully proportioned, with wide shoulders, a broad chest and the flat stomach of the very fit. His legs, encased in those denims, were long and powerful-looking.

"Who is that?" Alexandra said on a breath. Obviously not nan!

"That's my daddy."

*Continue reading*
**THE WEDDING PLANNER'S CHRISTMAS WISH**
Cara Colter

*Available next month*
www.millsandboon.co.uk